Fortune's Child

Lee Austin

Registered with the IP Rights Office
Copyright Registration Service
Ref: 242796151

This paperback first edition 2010

ISBN 978-1-4452-6168-3

Printed in Great Britain
by Lulu.com

Cover photograph by Guillaume Piolle

To Naomi.
This work wouldn't exist without you.

Contents

Part Two

Prologue

11 Years Ago…

Plumes of water sprayed high into the air as the man at the wheel struggled to control the car on the slippery road. The rear wheels lost traction for a moment, threatening to spin the car, but with a grunt the man wrestled it straight again.

"Careful, Warren!" the woman next to him cried. She clutched the blanket-wrapped bundle closer to her chest.

The man spared her a glance. "Yes, dear," he muttered. "How about you hold the baby and I'll do the driving, okay?"

"How can you be so calm?" she shot back. She glanced back over her shoulder, saw headlights rounding a corner in the road some way behind them. "Oh, god…" she moaned. "They're here."

The man glanced in his mirror, cursed and jammed his foot to the floor, causing the car to shake and protest again as it struggled to find purchase on the rainy road.

"We're almost there." He peered intently at the dark country road in front of him, searching for the signpost he hoped was near.

"It's not going to do us much good if we find the place while we're being followed," the woman said, uncertainty in her voice. "They'll know where he is, and they'll take him, you know they will."

The man glanced at the blanket-wrapped bundle that was his son, fear and concern warring for control of his face. "I know."

"Can't we take him with us, Warren?" the woman pleaded again, voice breaking, tears trembling at the edges of her eyes. "I've changed my mind!"

"You know we can't, Lydia," Warren replied. They both knew how much the decision hurt. It was all they'd thought about for the past few days. "We've looked at this from every angle. This is the only thing we can do now to keep him safe." He shook his head with slow resolution. "If there were some other way…"

"I'll stay with him," Lydia declared, glaring at Warren, challenging him to defy her.

He kept his eyes on the road. "We can't let them get you," he stated, "or the baby." He paused. "You of all people know what they'll do with him."

Lydia was silent. Warren knew her so well, understood how and why she had to fight until the very end, even when there were no other options left. He could feel her turmoil, felt it as much as his own.

She was well trained and disciplined, however, just as he was.

She drew a ragged breath. "Okay. How will we get him to the Home now without being seen? They're right behind us."

Warren glanced at her now. "Have you got him?"

"What? Of course I have!"

"Good." He abruptly skewed the car to the left, killing the lights as he did so. The car bumped over a lump at the side of the road and dipped as gravity grabbed it and pulled it down a short slope.

"Warren!" Lydia shrieked. The baby bundled against her chest began to cry in harmony, a thin, reedy sound that pulled at both their hearts. Warren gritted his teeth and concentrated on guiding the car down the narrow rutted track he had spotted at the last moment. Huge trees loomed on either side, branches lashing at the car's roof and doors. Mud sprayed high and coated the windscreen and passenger side window, momentarily obscuring their view. With grim determination he fought the car to a juddering halt. Quickly he peered behind him through the rear window.

The hammering rain and the small cries of the baby were the only sounds to be heard. Soothingly, Warren reached out to place a gentle hand on his son's head. "Shh, it's okay." Instantly the baby stopped crying, eyes drooping closed in contented sleep. A small smile pulled at the corners of his lips.

Lydia immediately calmed too. They'd both been through worse situations than this. She turned to look behind them. "Did it work? Did they see us?"

As if in answer, up on the road a car trundled slowly past, an ancient wooden-sided jalopy with steamed-up windows. The interior lights were on, throwing into relief the similarly ancient silhouette of an old man hunched over the steering wheel, peering myopically at the road in front of him. In the passenger seat a wild-haired old lady screamed at him, brandishing a crumpled map in one hand and a tartan thermos flask in the other. Definitely not the kind of vehicle the people who were really after them would use...

Warren and Lydia watched the old couple move slowly out of sight and then turned to each other wordlessly, relief etched on their faces. "Okay, false alarm," Lydia spoke for both of them after a moment or two. She looked pale, giddy with spent adrenaline, yet her eyes blazed with purpose. She visibly asserted her training again, gathering her thoughts. "So what now?" All around them was a slick wall of green. Rain gushed down through the branches to clatter on the roof of the car. She cracked open the door, noting the wheels of the car up to their axles in mud. "I don't know how we're going to get out of here."

"We don't have to," Warren said, hope surging. He gestured ahead down the track. "Look."

Lydia squinted. Was that – a light?

Warren switched on the wipers and the headlights at the same time, illuminating a small, overgrown sign just ahead that declared:

PEREGRINE HOUSE
PRIVATE HOME FOR CHILDREN.
TRADES AND DELIVERY ENTRANCE.
ALL ENQUIRIES TO MAIN GATE.

Lydia shook her head with slow apprehension. "Warren, I don't know about this."

"Come on," Warren said and climbed out of the car.

*

Lydia waited uncomfortably out of sight at the edge of the wide driveway fronting the vast building. From her vantage point behind a massive oak tree, she surveyed the imposing structure with a critical eye. The house was obviously very old, a monolith in local red stone and granite, complete with ornamental turrets and narrow windows of leaded glass. There had been little time to do much research, and the help they had received had been obtained at great risk, both to themselves and to their source. She couldn't begrudge the results, not really, not when so much was at stake. In fact she considered it lucky a place had been found at all. Time was desperately short, and the net was closing in. She and Warren had been left with no choice but to take this terrible course of action.

She couldn't afford to be seen, even though she'd been assured of Peregrine House's discretion. It was a risk that Warren especially had been unwilling to take. If their pursuers ever traced them here, they would have little trouble obtaining any information they wanted from the staff and residents. No, it was best to be as nondescript as possible, despite the highly unusual circumstances. The less Peregrine House knew, the better. And anyway, it would only be for a few weeks, perhaps a month at most – then they could come back, quietly, discretely, and hopefully undetected, to retrieve their beloved son.

No one knew what Warren looked like, and coupled with his peculiar ability to appear ordinary and unremarkable, the two of them had agreed to let him be the one to deliver their son into the care of Peregrine House. Later, if the situation ever arose, the staff would be unlikely to give a clear description of him. Lydia, on the other hand, was a different matter. She was well known to their pursuers. So now she waited, fretting, gazing anxiously at the shiny black double front-door through which her husband had entered what seemed like hours ago, but which was likely only minutes. The door her only child had been taken through...

The tears on her cheeks were invisible, blending with the cold rain, but she could feel them there nonetheless.

*

Warren re-emerged a short time later, his face a mask, expressionless. He didn't approach Lydia's position directly; he didn't know who could be watching. Instead he strode purposefully for the front gates, trusting his wife to make her way to him unseen. She would join him on the road outside.

We planned this, he repeated to himself, over and over, like a mantra. *We planned this. There's no other way.*

He tried to ignore his misgivings. *There's no other way.* Was that really true? Were they really doing the right thing? His feet wanted to stop, to turn him around and run back to his son, but he forced himself to continue. It didn't matter how many times he questioned the decision, or how many times he and Lydia argued about it. There was no real choice. Grimly he continued on, not looking back.

That man – the skinny man with the nasal voice who looked like he'd never seen the sun. Warren had handed the basket containing his son to him with great trepidation. The man's face had been creased and lined with years of constant frowning; a stern fellow indeed, perhaps just the sort to help run a children's home, but forbidding and disapproving all the same. Warren had taken an instant dislike to him. Then there was the woman, Mrs Fisher...

Warren sighed as he passed through the gates. He could find fault all he liked, but it was done now. His son had been handed over as they had planned and arranged. *See you real soon, my boy.*

There's no other way.

Lydia joined him and together, in resolute silence, they turned and disappeared into the rainy night.

*

The basket was taken through the dark, gloomy house into a similarly gloomy study. Bookshelves lined the walls, and a small fire crackled in the fireplace.

"Put it up there," Mrs Fisher ordered, indicating a battered desk in front of the curtained window. She was a large, florid woman with meaty limbs, hair carefully pinned in rollers beneath a flowery hair net. Despite the lateness of the hour, the short notice and the highly unusual circumstances, there was absolutely no way she would give any impression she was not in command.

"Mr Pring, fetch a light over here," she said, fussing over the basket. Her assistant, a thin man dressed in shabby black clothes reminiscent of a school-master from a bygone age, immediately turned to a wide-eyed young boy lurking behind him. "Bring that lamp," he ordered, pointing to a heavy standard-lamp in the corner. "Quickly!"

The boy hastened to drag the lamp over to the desk, struggling under its weight, and receiving a hefty clip around the ear for his troubles as he passed Mr Pring.

"Now, then, let's see what we have here," Mrs Fisher murmured. But she ignored the tiny bundle in the basket, instead concentrating solely on the heavy envelope the strange man had given her. She tore it open and a wad of money fell out onto the desk, fifty-pound notes tied up with a rubber band. In a flash she had pocketed the money within her voluminous robe, and extracted a folded piece of paper from the envelope. She read it through quickly, expressionless, then turned to the eager Mr Pring. Clearing her throat, she read:

"Mrs Fisher and staff;

Please take care of our son. His name is Lucas Warren Fortune, he will be 1 year old on May 5th, and his mother and I love him very much, but we can't look after him properly right now. We're deeply sorry we had to leave him with you in this manner. In addition to the money you have already received, please find enclosed with this letter a little extra to help cover the costs of his care, your inconvenience and, not to put too fine a point on it, your discretion.

We will send more money as soon as we can, and hopefully very soon we will be able to come and collect him.

Please take care of our precious boy, we beg you.

Thank You."

Mrs Fisher and Mr Pring exchanged glances, calculation glittering in their eyes. It was then that Mrs Fisher noticed the small boy cowering meekly behind Mr Pring.

"Get that child out of here!" she shrieked, pointing a chubby finger at the trembling boy. Mr Pring rounded on him, hand already raised, but the boy ducked and ran for it, skittering out of the door before the blow could fall.

Mr Pring made to follow, but Mrs Fisher called him back. "Leave him," she snapped. "Deal with him later." She raised the letter up and read it through again, then turned to stare down into the basket. Mr Pring sidled over to join her.

An unpleasant smile formed around the corners of her lips. "Oh, yes, little boy, we'll take *good* care of you," she cooed, gazing down at the tiny child. "Yes, we will."

Lucas Fortune smiled sleepily up at them.

Part One

Chapter One – The Balloon Incident

11 years later…

Early summer sun shone down from a flawless sky as Lucas Fortune crawled on his belly through the bushes down by the brook. He was a lean, wiry boy, with a shock of unruly dark-brown hair that never behaved. People who saw him for the first time often did a double take, and not always politely, because his left eye was brown, while the right was green. No one had ever tried to explain to him why this was.

Now, he stopped for a second, listening intently. He carefully levered himself forward on his elbows to peer out through the branches, absently blowing a strand of hair that kept flopping down over his eyes.

To his left, about three metres away and similarly concealed, his best friend Aaron Osborn grinned as he readied the water-bomb. Almost permanently grubby, Aaron had a curly afro and wide, curious brown eyes with a sometimes faraway look in them. In front of them both now, on the bank of the brook, lay their targets: the five girls that constituted the 'Girls Only Club' – a select group of girls that seemed to have made it their mission to make the boys' lives a misery whenever they could. Now, after yesterday's events – it was payback time.

The leader of the G.O.C. was Sabrina Celestine, a tall, willowy, blonde girl of thirteen years, who nursed within her a deep hatred of boys and all their dirty little ways. Lucas had never been able to figure out why this was. He himself generally tried to be nice and treat everyone fairly, yet Sabrina, it seemed, maintained a special dislike for him. She would go out of her way to make snide remarks and hurtful comments whenever she could, and she loved playing up to an audience. The other members of the G.O.C. looked up to her with unthinking awe.

She stood with her back to Lucas, the other members of her gang seated on the grass at her feet, listening intently.

"Lois, you and Sammi will do my hair," she was saying, hands on hips. "I want a French plait, with a yellow...no, red ribbon. Dana, you get me a ribbon from Fishy's repair cupboard."

"But, Sabrina…" an older girl protested, looking scared at the prospect. "I can't go into Fishy's cupboard, she'll kill me…"

"Just do it, Dana," Sabrina snapped, tossing her head imperiously. "It's got to be perfect."

"But, Sabrina, what if Fishy or Pring see you with one of her ribbons in your hair?" one of the other girls asked reasonably. This was a dark, pretty girl with freckles, called Tamsen. Lucas quickly glanced over at his friend, who he knew fancied Tamsen quite a bit. Sure enough, Aaron had forgotten what he was supposed to be doing, inching forward to get a closer look, the water balloon clutched dangerously tight in his grubby hand. Lucas waved frantically, but Aaron took no notice.

Sabrina looked momentarily uncertain. She glared at Tamsen. "They *won't* see me," she declared after a moment's thought. "You'll have to get Marshall to come to the bower, away from the house. Yeah, that's it."

Sabrina didn't see it, but Lucas clearly saw Tamsen make a face. He smiled to himself. It seemed not all of Sabrina's cronies were completely under her spell. However, he'd just heard some interesting news – Marshall would be going to the bower later, possibly alone…his mischievous mind began to race.

Aaron was still inching forward. Lucas turned and saw what was about to happen with a feeling of resignation, thoughts of Marshall instantly fading. He shook his head with a sigh.

A thin twig poked Aaron in the eye and he yelped, pulling back, getting himself further entangled in the foliage.

The G.O.C, as one, gave out a girly squeal and jumped up in alarm. Sabrina rounded angrily on this new intrusion. "Who's that?" she demanded, striding forward and peering into the bushes. "Who is it?"

With much muttering and breaking of twigs, Aaron lurched to his feet, leaves and mud sticking to him. The G.O.C. squealed again, all except for Sabrina, who had a dangerous look in her eye. She stood a good ten centimetres taller than Aaron, and she loomed over him now. "What the *heck* are you doing lurking in the bushes, you *filthy* little *boy*?" she exclaimed, fists bunching dangerously.

Aaron, for his part, didn't show any fear. He stared up at her resentfully. "Nothin'", he muttered. "Catching bugs."

"Eeew!" the G.O.C. chorused.

"Really?" Sabrina replied. "Trying to find your family, are you, frogspawn?" She looked round at her cronies, who laughed dutifully.

Aaron puffed up angrily, bringing his hands up. Of course, he was clutching a water balloon, a little too tightly…

It burst, spraying water all over the front of Aaron's trousers. The girls laughed uproariously, and Aaron reddened like a post-box as he saw Tamsen laughing too. Awkwardly, he fought his way out of the bushes and made to dash off, back to the house – and ran smack into the bony legs of Mr Pring.

The old man grabbed him roughly by the collar, nearly yanking him off his feet. Aaron gave a strangled yelp.

"What the devil is going on here?" Mr Pring demanded, his grating voice cutting through the air like a police siren. Instantly all the hilarity ceased, the girls transforming at a stroke into meek, respectful young ladies.

"Please, Mr Pring," Sabrina piped up, "Osborn was hiding in the bushes, spying on us." A calculating look passed quickly across her face. "And, look," she added nastily, "he's wet himself too."

"Well," Mr Pring said, peering down at the unfortunate boy like he'd just found something unpleasant on the sole of his shoe, "has he now? Still can't control your bladder, eh? Well, we all know what happens to little fellows who can't control their bladders, don't we?"

Aaron struggled like a fish on a hook. "But I didn't…" he protested.

"Maybe he should be in nappies," Sabrina suggested.

"Thank you, Miss Celestine," Mr Pring said. "I'll handle this. Come on, sonny, let's go and see what Mrs Fisher has to say about this, shall we?"

This was too much for Lucas. He jumped up, startling the girls and Mr Pring, who let go of Aaron's collar. Aaron fell to the ground with a grunt.

"It's my fault, Mr Pring," Lucas said, glaring daggers at Sabrina, who gazed back at him innocently, fluttering her eyelashes. "It was a water bomb, and I told him to throw it at the girls, but it burst."

Mr Pring looked as though he might explode. His face was dangerously purple, and his hands clenched spasmodically at his sides. "A water bomb? And just *where* did you get a water bomb, boy?"

Lucas paused, but he knew he had to admit it. "I took a balloon from Mrs Fisher's Christmas Box," he said tonelessly.

There was a collective, disbelieving groan from the G.O.C. Worryingly, though, Mr Pring actually smiled.

"Oh, did you?" he said, almost pleasantly. "Did you, indeed?" In a lightning quick movement, he reached out and yanked Lucas bodily from the bush where he had been hiding. He tried to pull Lucas up, but Lucas was both bigger and heavier than Aaron. Pring was unable to lift him in the same way. Instead the man leaned down, bringing his greasy face unpleasantly close to Lucas's. "I knew I'd catch you one day, Fortune," he whispered, fishy breath gusting through his horrible yellow teeth into Lucas's face. Lucas blinked, trying not to cough. "You're a born trouble-maker, sonny, but you won't get off this one lightly, I guarantee it. *Stealing!*

"And as for you, pant-wetter," Pring continued delightedly, scooping Aaron up with his other hand, "we'll have to send you to the Special Room, won't we, until you've learned more self-control!"

"I didn't..." Aaron protested again, but Mr Pring was already dragging them away, back up to the house. As they went, Lucas caught a glimpse of the girl's faces. Sabrina looked ecstatic, doubling over with laughter, and most of the others were grinning at each other; however, Tamsen was not one of them. Instead she frowned at the ground, chewing her lip.

With a resigned sigh, Lucas readied himself to face Fishy's wrath yet again.

*

Mrs Fisher glared at the two boys from where she sat behind her heavy desk, listening intently to Mr Pring's voice as he listed their crimes.

"This one," Mr Pring spat, poking his bony finger sharply into Aaron's shoulder, "was hiding in the bushes, spying on *girls!*"

Mrs Fisher fixed her beady eyes on Aaron, who fidgeted uncomfortably. His grubby, muddy clothes were quite clear evidence of his guilt, and the twigs and leaves protruding messily from his hair didn't help much either. He stared angrily at the ground.

"And..." Mr Pring continued, voice trembling, "...he has – *wet* himself!"

"Dear me, Osborn," Mrs Fisher said, voice like ice. "You really don't seem to be making much progress with your 'little problem', do you? Whatever shall we do with you?" She looked up at the old man. "Mr Pring?"

"The *Room*, Mrs Fisher," Pring said instantly, placing a heavy hand on Aaron's shoulder, ready to drag him off right away, but Mrs Fisher held up a hand.

"All in good time." She turned her gaze onto Lucas, who looked back at her calmly. "And what of our little foundling here?" she mused. Lucas knew better than to rise to the bait. He kept his face expressionless.

"I'm sorry, Mrs Fisher," he intoned before Mr Pring could condemn him. "I took a balloon from your Christmas Box without permission." Behind him Mr Pring gave a startled snort, surprised and no doubt disappointed that he himself hadn't been the one to deliver the devastating news. Lucas knew, however, through long experience, that it was pointless trying to argue or deny any accusations levelled against him, so the best policy was just to get it over with as quickly as possible. He watched as a strange expression, almost one of triumph, passed briefly across Fishy's doughy face.

"That's a real pity," she said, all mock sympathy. "Really, it is. You see, Fortune, I had a letter from some very special people just yesterday, hoping to arrange a visit with you next week, but after this...I'm afraid I'm going to have to decline them. Again." She stood up and came around the desk, to loom over Lucas threateningly. "I don't know how many times I'll have to turn them down before they give up on you, young man."

Lucas looked down at the floor, keeping his body perfectly still, so as not to give Fishy the pleasure of seeing him react. She'd been promising to let him meet his parents for over a year now, and when he'd first heard the news, directly from old Fishy herself, he'd been so happy that he'd nearly burst.

For a while, at least.

It hadn't taken long for Fishy to start finding all kinds of reasons to delay that meeting, ranging from cold dismissals to cruel taunts and angry punishments. It was true enough that he often found himself in trouble, having been caught performing some form of minor mischief or another, but mostly the punishments that were dealt him seemed out of all proportion to his crimes. He wasn't a bad boy by any means; he knew enough about himself and his motivations that most of his schemes stemmed from little more than boredom, not malice.

If he'd ever had any kind of positive feelings towards Fishy, they'd long since been well and truly crushed. Now, all he felt when he looked at her was a kind of distant, empty resentment.

"Yes, Mrs Fisher," he muttered.

"And as for you, Osborn," Fishy said, "perhaps we should go along with Mr Pring's suggestion, let you stay in the Room for a while; give you a chance to, ah, master your little problem. Hmmm?"

"But, Mrs Fisher, I didn't do it," Aaron protested, hot faced. "It was an accident…"

"And that's precisely the problem!" Fishy shouted, perhaps deliberately misunderstanding Aaron's protest. He was cowed into silence. "A boy of eleven years, unable to control himself! It's bad enough wetting the bed, but to do it in broad daylight…!"

Lucas couldn't stand it any longer. "He didn't wet himself!"

Fishy turned to him silently, eyebrows raised, as though waiting for him to dig himself in even further. Lucas ploughed on heedlessly, on the basis that he was going to be punished anyway. "It was a water balloon that *I* gave him, and it burst by accident! That's all!"

Lucas couldn't recall the last time he'd seen Fishy look so pleased, but found he was past the point of caring. Let her do whatever she wanted to him. It didn't matter.

She smiled. "Mr Pring," she said, eyes boring through Lucas like two watery drills, "take Osborn to the Room. He shall remain there until school time on Monday morning."

"And this one?" Mr Pring asked, pointing a trembling, veiny finger in Lucas's direction.

"I'll deal with him myself. Go."

Mr Pring dragged Aaron from the room, but not before Lucas caught his friend's eye. They exchanged a momentary look of resignation. *Don't worry*, Aaron's expression seemed to say, and then he was gone.

Fishy took a second or two to compose herself, then stomped back around the desk to lower her bulk onto the protesting springs of her long-suffering chair.

She stared at him for long moments, eyes narrowed. Lucas seethed inside, over the unjust punishment of his best friend, the horrible way he was always treated, and yet another missed opportunity to finally meet his parents. It was all so unfair!

The only outward sign he gave of all these thoughts was a slight clenching of his fists. He stood silently, passively, waiting for Fishy's sentence.

She stared at him for a long time. "What can I do to make sure you don't forget your crimes today, hmmm?" she said in a conversational tone, looking around the room as if for inspiration. "What will get through to you?" She drummed her pudgy fingers on the edge of the desk, thinking.

She appeared to reach a decision. "I'm not sure if there's anything more we can do for you here at Peregrine House, young man," she said. "Clearly, my regime of basic rules, strict policies and fair treatment for all is not enough for the likes of you. Perhaps you would benefit from a different approach. Perhaps my friend Mr Kwame could find a way to make you show some respect."

This time Lucas was unable to hide his reaction. His expression fell. Fishy was watching for it. She pounced on his discomfiture, another smile creasing her pudgy face. "That's right, Fortune. Perhaps a spell at the Mill will turn you around. Yes indeed."

Lucas's heart sank. Everyone had heard of the Mill, the children's home in the next town, where really naughty children were sometimes sent and never seen again…

Fishy's eyes were bright, fixed on him like a hawk's on a dormouse. So Lucas did the only thing he could think of – he smiled back at her. She blinked, and Lucas felt a small glow of satisfaction at this tiny victory. If he was going to be sent away, if he was going to once again be denied the chance to meet his parents, it was good to know that he could still surprise this horrible old woman. That was something at least. "Yes, Mrs Fisher," was all he said, however.

"Funny, is it?" Fishy retorted, thumping her desk. "We'll see how much you laugh after a spell at the Mill, won't we? I'll have you out of this home by the end of the week, young man, you see if I don't! In the meantime, you are restricted to the boys' wing, no, *to your room* and, believe me, you'd better not try anything else!" She stood again, pointing dramatically to the door. "Now, get out! Straight to your dormitory! Move!"

Lucas turned and ran from the room, struggling now to hold back the tears, and as he ascended the stairs to the boys' dormitory wing they finally came, coursing down his cheeks like a dam had burst, and he wished everything could be different.

Soon enough, he would get his wish.

*

"That boy," Mrs Fisher sighed later. Mr Pring was seated opposite, nursing a hot cup of tea. He nodded sagely.

"Trouble from the first time I laid eyes on him," he said. "Always get trouble with foundlings." They always referred to the Fortune boy that way, though it was not strictly true, of course; he hadn't been abandoned on their doorstep, after all. Still, it was a useful term, full of unpleasant connotations.

Unexpectedly, Mrs Fisher said, "You were a foundling yourself, weren't you, Mr Pring?" She sipped delicately from a wide glass of brandy, watching him.

Mr Pring was surprised. She knew that already. "Yes, Deirdre," he replied, setting his cup down, "but *I* turned out fine, as you know. Nothing wrong with a harsh upbringing, puts steel in the spine, I always say. But that Fortune boy…"

"Hmmm, a strange one, to be sure." She raised her glass to the lamp light, watching the rays twist through the amber liquid. "Handy to have around, though."

"Oh?" He considered. "You mean the parents?"

"Yes, of course I mean the parents!" she snapped, causing Mr Pring to rattle his cup in its saucer. "Do try to keep up, Tarquin!"

"Of course, Deirdre," he said soothingly. He looked around Mrs Fisher's study, at the fine furniture, the expensive silver ornaments and the oil paintings on the walls. "Generous people."

"Stupid, more like," she snorted. "I mean, what kind of parents dump their children with complete strangers and never make contact again, except to send a couriered envelope every month with two thousand pounds in cash, hmmm?"

"Stupid people, indeed," Mr Pring agreed, wishing some of that stupidity would come his way once in a while. It had turned out those people had also left their car the night Fortune had come to them. It had been discovered the next morning, abandoned in the lane outside the rear gate, keys in the ignition. All very odd.

"And best of all," Mrs Fisher continued, beginning to sound just a little bit tipsy, "their brat knows nothing about it! We can feed him whatever stories we like to keep him in line!"

"Yes, well," Mr Pring muttered into his cup, "that doesn't appear to be working too well, does it?"

Mrs Fisher wasn't listening. "Who knows if the parents will ever come back?" she was saying, waving her glass around, "But they surely wouldn't object to their *brat* of a child being taught some much-needed lessons in respect and discipline! No, sir!"

"Ah, the Mill," Mr Pring said, managing to suppress a shudder. He'd spent some time there as a child himself, many years ago, though he rarely allowed himself to think about it these days. Of course, that had been before Jacob Kwame's reign, but still, things hadn't been that much different way back then…

For the briefest of seconds, he felt almost sorry for the Fortune boy, but he shrugged it off. "Do him the world of good," he muttered. Outside, cool rain began to patter against the window.

Chapter Two – The Best Laid Plans…

Early on Monday morning Aaron was led back to the boys' dorm, grey- faced and miserable-looking. The older boy accompanying him, a tall, spotty youth named Rowan Cole, led Aaron to his bed next to Lucas's, shook his head reproachfully at them both and padded out without a word.

Lucas sat up as Aaron flopped onto his bed. "Okay, mate?" he whispered, trying not to wake the other boys in the room. There were five other beds here, two of them currently occupied. Snores and wheezes rent the air.

"I'm starving," Aaron groaned, rubbing at his bleary eyes.

"I know. I saved you this." He produced a small piece of film-wrapped carrot cake and tossed it over. "Better than nothing."

Aaron sat up, grabbing the food eagerly. "Thanks, Lucas." He ripped off the film and stuffed the stale cake into his mouth. "You're a mate!"

"Some mate." Lucas lay back and stared at the yellowing ceiling. "Got you chucked in the Room, didn't I?"

"Yeah, so? All they do is starve you. Anyway, we almost got those snotty girls that time!"

"Almost," Lucas agreed.

"Next time, yeah?"

Lucas didn't say anything.

*

At breakfast the usual crowd joined them at their table, all eager to hear of Aaron's latest jail term.

"What's it like?" Dion Raven asked, wide-eyed. He was a tiny boy, all messy blond hair and snotty nose, looking far younger than his eleven years. He was blessed with boundless enthusiasm and energy, along with an almost unfailingly sunny nature. He was sometimes affectionately referred to as 'brainbox' or 'spaceboy' because of his interest in science.

"Ah, it's nothing," Aaron said, waving his hand in a dismissive gesture. "Just a white room, painted-out window, lumpy bed, no food. No problem."

"Wow," Dion breathed, dribbling cereal from his spoon. "And how many times have you been in it?"

"*Loads*," Aaron said, rolling his eyes.

"And we all know why that is, don't we, bed-wetter?" a new voice chimed in from behind them. Lucas and Aaron spun round.

"Can't hold his water, that's what I hear," said Marshall Graves with a sneer. He stood holding his breakfast tray, a group of his cronies arrayed around him like some sort of honour guard.

Graves seemed to dislike Lucas and his friends with an almost religious passion. He went out of his way to taunt and tease them whenever he could. He was very tall, the tallest boy at Peregrine House by a clear three or four centimetres, with carefully combed auburn hair and an aristocratic bearing. He made much of the fact that he was here by choice, or at least the choice of his parents, who had apparently decided he needed the kind of education that could only be found under Mrs Fisher's tutelage, and what's more were prepared to pay for it.

"Shut your face, Gravy," Aaron shot back. "What do you know, anyway?"

"More than you ever will, frogspawn," Graves retorted. "I hear you need to wear special pants at night. Is that right?"

Lucas stood up. "Get lost," he said flatly, and for a moment, oddly, it looked like Graves might actually do it. He frowned minutely then blinked, looking round at his friends for support.

"Oh, it speaks," he said with exaggerated emphasis. Beside him Graves's main cronies, Billy Elsdon and Myles Lovell, guffawed dutifully.

They looked like clones of each other, big beefy boys with shaven heads, ruddy cheeks and dull eyes.

Lucas was about to speak, but a loud voice cut across the room. "You boys!" Mr Pring called from where he was lurking down by the food line. "Sit down and eat your breakfast this minute!"

Graves pointed a finger threateningly at Lucas. "We'll speak later, basket-boy," he promised, but turned and went to another table at the far side of the room. Billy Elsdon and Myles Lovell trailed along behind him like two misshapen puppies.

"What is his problem?" Aaron muttered, hunching over his plate of soggy scrambled eggs. "Git."

"Forget about him," Lucas said. "Spoiled rich kid." He toyed with his own food. "I think we should probably keep out of trouble for a while."

"Good idea," said Timothy Koray from where he sat opposite them. Timothy was a large, serious boy, quiet and thoughtful, with jet black eyes and hair. He'd only recently arrived at the home, but had immediately fitted in with Lucas and his friends, who had welcomed him eagerly. It was nice to have someone new on their side.

"You think?" Dion retorted. "What, just let Gravy get away with that?"

"They're just words," Timothy said. "Doesn't matter."

"...mumble mumble *special pants* mumble..." Aaron muttered into his breakfast. "Haven't wet the bed in over a *year*."

"I know that, and you know that," Lucas consoled him, "so it doesn't really matter what Gravy says, does it? Tim's right, it's just words."

"Yeah, well, Gravy wasn't saying them to you, was he?" Aaron stabbed a greyish lump of egg with his fork. "How would you like it?"

"I wouldn't, probably, but there's not much we can do about it, is there?" He wanted to tell them about the Mill, how he was going to be taken away and might not ever see them again, but didn't know how to say it. He felt foolish and helpless, but even worse would be to have his friends feel sorry for him. He decided to change the subject.

"Hey, Dion, did you know they've taken the word 'gullible' out of the dictionary?"

"Did they? When?"

*

School that day was boring as usual, double maths in the morning and history after lunch. It was only redeemed by a fun game of football in last period P.E, even though Lucas received a painful boot in the thigh from

Myles Lovell in the second half. Lucas limped off and watched his team win two-one from the touchline. Thoughts of the Mill and his other troubles were never far from his mind, though, troubling his mood.

At Peregrine House, during the last hour before lights-out, the children were allowed some social time, provided it was used 'productively', whatever that meant. That evening Lucas, Aaron, Dion and Timothy were sitting on Dion's bunk, looking through some football stickers that his previous foster parents had sent him.

The door thumped open and Graves sauntered in, followed closely by his little band. He immediately focused on the group sitting peacefully on the bed. "Looking for your family there, basket-boy?" he quipped, prompting obedient laughter from his buddies. "Reckon your old man's actually a famous footballer, do you?"

Aaron and Dion rose quickly to their feet, ready for a fight, but Lucas remained where he was, coolly looking through the stickers, ignoring the taunts.

"Nothing to say, little orphan?" Graves mocked him. He spoke over his shoulder to Myles Lovell. "Must be some sort of genetic defect," he said in a stage whisper. "Boy can't talk. No wonder his folks dumped him here."

"You lanky git!" Aaron cried, instantly leaping to Lucas's defence. It seemed his time in the Room had not been all plain sailing. He wasn't normally quite so quick to anger. "Shut your fat face!"

Graves was about to reply when a small voice from out in the corridor interrupted him. He turned his back on them with a snarl. Some quiet words were exchanged which Lucas couldn't hear, though he made out the name 'Sabrina'. Graves seemed annoyed. "Alright, alright," he snapped. He said something to his cronies, who moved out into the corridor.

"This isn't over, losers!" he promised Lucas and his friends. He stomped away down the hall.

"You okay, Aaron?" Dion asked solicitously.

Aaron made a visible effort to calm down, closing his eyes and breathing slowly. He sighed and sat on the bed. "I'm just peachy," he said. "Don't know why I let him get to me."

"Thanks for sticking up for me, mate," Lucas said. Aaron looked surprised.

"Eh? Of course. That's what we do, isn't it? There's no one else, so we look out for each other. Way it is."

Now it was Lucas's turn to sigh. "Yeah. About that." It seemed the right time to finally tell his friends about what had happened on Saturday in Fishy's office with Juvenile Services, Kwame and the Mill. After he'd finished there was silence as they all looked at each other dejectedly.

"S' not fair," Aaron sniffed. Dion was crestfallen, whilst Timothy...well, it was sometimes hard to know what Timothy was thinking.

"I've got 'til the end of the week, I think," Lucas said, "and in the meantime...I've got an idea. One last little plan. Listen."

"I thought we were going to stay out trouble," Timothy reminded them, for which he received a pillow in the face. Laughing, he threw it back at Aaron.

They talked until lights out.

*

Tuesday and Wednesday came and went without much incident, which was just fine as far as Lucas and his friends were concerned, as it gave them a lot of uninterrupted time in which to plot and scheme. They kept their heads down, doing nothing to incur the wrath of Fishy, Pring or the other boys, quietly meeting up whenever they could. It was to be Lucas's final act as a resident of Peregrine House, so it needed to be a good one.

On Thursday morning Lucas was gazing out of the classroom window, trying to tune out the droning voice of Mr White, the geography teacher, when he saw a posh looking black car pull up the driveway and stop outside the front entrance. From it emerged a very fat man, skin the darkest shade of brown he had ever seen, dressed in a plain grey suit. He carried a briefcase as he entered the house, the door opening before him as he approached.

This must be Mr Kwame from the Mill! Lucas had not seen him before, but somehow knew he was right. Had the man come to get him already?

He worried about it all day, but the expected call from Fishy never came. His concentration, never absolute at the best of times, was ruined. Every footstep in the corridor outside his classroom, every distant voice or banging door had him almost leaping from his seat. A few times he had to apologise to his teachers for disrupting their lessons. He wondered how much more he could take, but when he had a chance to look out of the front window later, he saw that the posh car had gone. He felt almost giddy with relief.

Maybe they'd changed their minds?

*

Lucas and his friends were lucky enough to have the big dormitory to themselves at the present time, the four of them sharing the long seven bed room. The three spare beds lay empty at the far end of the room, near the door. This ought to have meant that they had relative privacy, but in practice this was not the case. Mr Pring would stop by regularly to sneer at them, and often older boys would come in uninvited and lounge around on the spare beds, playing cards or scuffling with each other. There wasn't much the rightful occupants could do about it, so they tended to keep their heads down and talk quietly amongst themselves.

Soon, regular school term would be ending for the summer, a time which was ordinarily looked forward to by the permanent residents of Peregrine House, as it meant that many of the term timers, the boarding kids, would be going home, leaving the place quite empty and relatively peaceful for a couple of months.

That evening, it was time to put the plan into effect. Lucas kept an eye on the corridor outside their room, watching for other children or for Mr Pring on one of his patrols. They'd watched Graves and his gang going past earlier, probably on their way over to the girls' wing (which was strictly forbidden, but somehow Graves always seemed to get away with it). Making sure no one was around, Lucas signalled to Aaron, who was lurking around the other end of the hall, near to the older boys' dorm. Aaron nodded and peered around the door into the room shared by Marshall Graves and his mates.

"Okay, it's empty," Aaron called back, then looked guiltily around in case anyone had heard him. "Sorry," he mouthed.

"Alright, your turn," Lucas said to Dion and Timothy, who grinned and moved past him into the hall, heading towards the older boys' dorm. They sauntered casually up to the door where Aaron waited, then all three ducked inside.

Lucas was left to wait anxiously. He wished, for the hundredth time, that it could be him taking the risk on this one, but he knew he couldn't leave his room. Somehow, Mr Pring always seemed to know when mischief was occurring, and would appear as if by magic to catch out the perpetrator.

In fact, someone was coming up the stairs now. A misshapen shadow climbed the wall ahead of the unseen figure, a familiar shape Lucas knew all too well.

He ducked back into his room, worriedly scanning the makeshift lumps in his friends' beds that were supposed to look convincingly like sleeping children. Suddenly they didn't look so realistic at all...

The door banged open and Mr Pring poked his birdlike head into the room, eyes darting everywhere, looking for trouble. His gaze settled on Lucas, who was sitting innocently on his bed, school books spread out before him. Mr Pring's lip began to curl back, but Lucas boldly ssshh'd him, indicating the slumbering shapes of his friends around him. He tried to radiate a feeling of innocence.

Something very odd happened then. Lucas saw it clearly. Mr Pring's eyes seemed to slide unseeingly away from the makeshift dummies. He blinked several times, rapidly, jaw hanging slack, before refocusing his eyes on Lucas for a long moment. Confusion clear, he then backed uncertainly from the room, a slow frown creasing his forehead. The door shut softly.

Lucas was amazed. Somehow, it had worked! Old man Pring had been fooled! Lucas listened intently for a second, heard Mr Pring moving away down the hall back towards the stairs, and breathed out a huge sigh of relief, some of the tension draining from his body. He jumped up and ran over to the door, cracked it open and peeked out.

Mr Pring was moving slowly away, scratching his head. He stopped for a second, shook his head, then moved on, disappearing down the stairs.

At that moment Aaron, Dion and Timothy burst forth from the other room, giggling, spilling into the corridor. Lucas made frantic ssshh'ing gestures. They sobered immediately, tiptoeing back to their room.

"Everything okay?" Lucas asked his friends in relief as they piled through the door.

"Perfect!" Aaron chortled. Dion and Timothy went to high-five, but missed. "You?"

Lucas looked around bemusedly at the unconvincing decoys. "I...guess."

At the foot of the stairs, Mr Pring came to a slow stop in the hall. He blinked several times, trying to recall what had just happened. It was sort of fuzzy in his head, like an image seen through frosted glass...

His head snapped up. Some deep sense was telling him that mischief was afoot, and that the Fortune boy was right in the middle of it. He didn't know what it was, but his instincts rarely served him wrong.

With a snarl he turned on his heel and pounded back up the stairs.

Lucas was back on his bed when Mr Pring crashed into the room again, purple-faced and sweating. He filled the door frame and gazed wildly around the room, searching for anything out of place. With a triumphant grunt he spotted the unconvincing lumps in the beds and strode towards the nearest of them. He raised a skinny fist high, ready to bring it down…

…and Dion Raven turned over, appearing from under the sheets. He saw the sweaty apparition looming above him and let out a piercing shriek, eyes popping. Mr Pring froze, the grin sliding from his face like butter dripping off a hot crumpet.

"M – Mr Pring?" Lucas said in the following silence. "Um…"

There were shouts from elsewhere in the house and the sound of running feet. Slowly, Mr Pring lowered his arm, looking about him in confusion. "Oh, dear."

Mr Pring was led away by Miss Spencer the school nurse, staring around him numbly. When he had gone, the friends looked at each other for a second. They burst out laughing.

"Brilliant!" Aaron chortled, banging his fist on his bed. He peeled back his covers, still fully dressed, and jumped up happily. They'd only just managed to get back under the covers, seconds before old man Pring had burst in. It had been a close thing. "Great scream!" he congratulated Dion, who gave him a sickly thumbs-up.

"Thanks," Dion managed.

Lucas asked, "So did you manage to set everything up?"

"Yep, just like we said," Aaron confirmed. "Old Gravy's going to get a surprise tonight!"

Some time later, the sound of Graves's voice coming down the hall alerted the boys to his return. They exchanged mixed glances. Aaron and Dion looked like kids on Christmas morning, grinning madly. Timothy, as ever, wore a neutral expression; it seemed to say that whatever would be, would be. Lucas, for his part, now found himself entertaining one or two doubts about the whole thing, which wasn't like him at all. Normally it wasn't in his nature to second-guess his little schemes. Was he losing his touch, or just his desire to cause trouble? Maybe he was growing up – starting to worry about consequences.

He dismissed that thought with a small shake of his head.

Soon enough lights-out was called and the boys lay in their beds, listening tensely in the dark. Sure enough, after only a few minutes, there was a commotion from down the hall, voices complaining loudly, and one or two yelps of surprise. Aaron began to snigger from under his covers.

Feet pounded up the hall, doors were opened and voices were raised. An adult voice shouted something, and more people came, presumably other carers or teachers. Lucas couldn't quite make out what was being said, but they sounded quite annoyed...

Suddenly Lucas's door crashed open and the light was flicked on. Mr Pring stood there, wild-eyed, veins standing out on his skinny neck like strands of spaghetti. The boys sat up, squinting.

"I don't know how you did it," Pring hissed, advancing into the room like a wading bird, "but it seems that, *somehow*," he emphasised the word, "all of the hot water bottles in young Mr Graves's room appear to have broken at the same time. More, they *somehow* managed to end up under the sheets, filled with warm water, and all of the beds are now *soaking wet!*"

The boys kept their expressions carefully blank. "We don't know anything about it, Mr Pring," Aaron said, all innocence. "We've been in here all evening. We even went to bed early!"

Mr Pring spluttered but couldn't contradict that, not after what had happened earlier. "I know it was you lot," he said. Then an idea seemed to occur to him. He looked around slowly at the empty beds, a calculating expression on his face. He gave a short laugh, like a bark; turning on his heel, he disappeared back up the hall in the direction of the ongoing commotion. Lucas began to get a sinking feeling and sure enough, minutes later, Pring returned grinning triumphantly. "I'm sure you won't mind," he said, "good boys like you, helping out your fellows in their time of need." He called back over his shoulder, "Come in, lads," and stood aside.

Marshall Graves stood there, an unholy light in his eyes. Behind him loomed the lumpy shapes of his henchmen, Lovell and Elsdon. They were dressed in their pyjamas, each clutching a bundle of pillows and sheets. "Well, isn't this cosy?" Graves said. He sauntered in and dumped his burden on the nearest bed, which happened to be right next to Aaron's.

Aaron groaned, slumping back.

"Sleep tight, chaps," Mr Pring said happily. "We'll get everyone, and I mean *everyone*," he looked significantly at Lucas, "sorted out in the morning. Until then, everyone on their best behaviour, understood?"

There was a chorus of half-hearted affirmatives.

"And, Mr Graves," Pring finished, addressing the boy directly, "as the eldest here, perhaps you would be so kind as to keep a particular eye on these younger ones. You know how they get frightened sometimes, eh?"

Graves grinned nastily. "My pleasure, sir," he replied. "They'll get my *special* attention."

It was going to be a long night...but not at all in the way any of them expected.

*

After lights-out (for the second time that night), it was a long time before things settled down in the dormitory. There was much arguing in the dark, and a fair amount of scuffling and hair pulling, but no-one received any major injuries. Soon enough a resentful silence fell, and all the boys, one by one, fell into a troubled sleep.

And they dreamed.

Chapter Three – Things That Go Bump

Lucas awoke with a start some time before dawn, sweating, shaking violently, breath coming in great gasps. He stared around him in the gloom, unseeing, clawing at his sheets. He'd been running, there had been shouts, people shoving…but already the memory was starting to slip away, as such things do.

Around him, his roommates began to stir also. A low moaning came from the direction of Timothy's bed. At the other end of the room it sounded as if someone was trying unsuccessfully to stifle small sobs.

Lucas shook himself, the dim room coming into better focus. He sat up, trying to calm his racing heart. Unexpectedly his right leg gave a sudden sharp twinge. He gasped, the pain coming suddenly like someone had flipped a switch. He must have been thrashing about in the throes of his dream.

"Lucas?" a small, frightened voice called out from the next bed. Aaron.

"Sorry," Lucas whispered, "I think I had a bad dream. Didn't mean to wake you."

There was a small pause. "You had a bad dream?" Aaron sounded hesitant, about as confused as Lucas was feeling right now.

"Yeah, I think so. Guess I must have been shouting, or something."

There was another pause. "Okay." There was something in Aaron's voice. Lucas strained to see him in the pre-dawn half-light.

"Are you alright, mate?" he asked. An idea occurred. "Did you – you know…"

"What? No, I didn't! I'm dry as a bone, although…I'm busting to go, actually."

Lucas felt an uncomfortable feeling in his own belly. "Yeah, so am I. Come on, let's get to the bathroom."

"Can I come with you?" another voice called out. "It's me, Dion. I gotta go too."

"But we're not allowed," Aaron hissed. "And…it's awful dark…"

"Just stay with me," Lucas reassured them. "No-one's around at this time of night anyway, not even Pring." He paused. "I hope." He heaved his aching legs out of bed.

"Alright, alright," Aaron conceded. The three of them threaded their way gingerly through the room, trying not to cause any more disturbance.

A dim, wall-mounted night lamp was all that illuminated the hall outside, putting out just enough sallow light to throw the whole corridor into sinister shadow. Aaron whimpered. Lucas grabbed him and pulled him through the door. The entrance to the bathroom on this floor was off along the hall, near the top of the stairs. The three boys crept along on silent, fearful feet, listening hard for anyone approaching. It was a strict rule of Fishy's that no child was allowed out of their room after lights-out unless they had special permission.

"Wish it was lighter," Aaron said, while Lucas peered ahead in the gloom. He could just about make out the white door of the bathroom ahead; in fact, as he watched it appeared to grow clearer…

He stopped dead in the middle of the hall, Dion bumping into him. "What is it?" his friend whispered fiercely.

"I can see," Lucas murmured, staring at the bathroom door, which was now clearly visible.

"Yeah? Me too." Dion sounded confused. "Come on, we can't stand around here like this!" He pushed past Lucas and scurried over to the bathroom. Aaron scuttled along right behind him.

It was definitely getting lighter in the hall. Lucas stared about him as the light increased. He could now see his own shadow stretching out ahead of him. The source was behind him…

He spun about, squinting as the now brightly glowing night-light hurt his eyes. A few seconds ago it had been a dull orange colour, yet now it was burning so brightly he could barely look at it!

"Come on, Lucas!" Dion called, clearly more concerned about his pressing business. He and Aaron shoved open the door and disappeared into the bathroom. Immediately the light began to fade, which was finally enough to send Lucas running, his bladder bursting. By the time he'd covered the short distance to the bathroom it was almost as dark as when they'd first left the dorm. He piled inside hurriedly.

"Where's the light switch?" he puffed, feeling along the wall next to the door. It was pitch black in here, the venetian blinds that covered the windows blocking out even the feeble light afforded by the stars. His fingers scrabbled, growing more desperate. He couldn't hold himself much longer –

Abruptly the lights flicked on, the fluorescent tube on the ceiling buzzing for a second then catching, bathing the sparse room in a very welcome, if weak bluish glow. Aaron and Dion rushed over to the urinals, faces slick with desperation. Lucas scrambled to join them.

"Nice one, mate," Aaron congratulated him as they stood side by side. The relief in the room was palpable. "Couldn't have held it for a second longer."

"Uh-huh," was all Lucas could bring himself to say. He didn't know how to mention the fact that he hadn't actually found the light switch at all…

There was a minute or two of blissful, companionable silence. Eventually, both emotionally and literally drained, the children made to head back to the dorm. As they cracked open the bathroom door, they heard distinct voices from elsewhere in the house. At this time of night, when all was relatively quiet, sound travelled a long way in the old building, echoing and reflecting at odd angles, down corridors and up staircases. The boys paused for a moment, listening.

An indignant, high-pitched voice was saying something angrily. A door banged. Shrill female voices shrieked in response, and a few words became clearer. "*..you girls, you know you're not allowed out of your dorm after lights-out…*" something unintelligible, then, "*…don't care if you were desperate for the toilet! No-one leaves their room…*"

"Come on," Lucas shrugged, thinking only about getting back to his bed. Too many weird things had happened recently. He reached out his hand and, very deliberately, switched off the bathroom light.

They made it back to their room without further incident; that is, apart from being nearly bowled over by the rushing shapes of Billy Elsdon and Myles Lovell, who barged past them in desperate silence on their way to the bathroom. Lucas watched them go, bemused, then continued tiptoeing fearfully along the once-again dim hallway. He didn't look up at the softly glowing amber night-light as they passed beneath it.

The dorm room had a very peculiar odour about it as they entered, not pleasant, like sweat but sharper, mixed with something else - like the smell in the air before a thunderstorm…

"That mings!" Aaron commented, a little too loudly. The huddled shapes of their remaining roommates began to stir. Lucas realised he could hear no sounds of sleeping, of heavy breathing. It was completely quiet in the room, yet there was a definite atmosphere, heavy with expectation, or perhaps something else – like fear…

Was *everyone* awake?

"What – what are you doing, Fortune?" an unfamiliar, strangled voice called from the darkness. It sounded a little like Graves, but something wasn't right. It took a second for Lucas to identify the wrongness. Ordinarily the older boy said everything with a habitual sneer of superiority in his voice. Now, that was gone. What Lucas could hear sounded much more like the terror of a small boy in the night. Graves must have been huddled, awake, in his blankets for ages, too afraid to move until now.

Lucas didn't know how he knew this, but it just seemed, somehow – correct. "None of your business," he retorted, but found he didn't have the heart to taunt the boy further. He really was changing! "Are you – alright?"

"I'm telling Mr Pring of you," Graves whispered savagely by way of reply. The momentary pity Lucas had felt for the older boy evaporated like a puff of smoke.

"Whatever." He flopped onto his bed. He didn't expect to sleep, but the very next thing he knew it was morning. The seven a.m. alarm bell was ringing to wake them all for school.

Groggily he stood, shaking off vague memories of dark corridors and distant voices. He shook Aaron's foot, who hadn't yet stirred. Around him his roommates were groaning, limbs sticking out from under blankets like random branches on a tree. Bright, clean sunlight poured through a gap in the curtains. Outside, birds sang joyfully.

For some reason he felt unaccountably happy, despite the strange events of the night and the knowledge of his impending deportation to the Mill. The subdued melancholy of the last few days appeared to be gone. In its place he had the oddest feeling that something important was going to happen – or maybe, was already happening…

He glanced down, and recoiled at the sight of his right leg. Disbelieving, he peered closer at his ripped pyjama leg, at the dark bruise on the side of his calf. In the centre of the bruise sat a purple scar, a short crescent of raised flesh like a half-moon. He had no idea how it had happened, but stranger still, it looked to be at least a few days old. How was that possible? No wonder his leg hurt!

There was no time to think about it now though. The room was waking up, and a long school day beckoned – maybe the last one he would spend with his friends.

He hoped it would be a good one.

Scrambling about for the bits of his school uniform that lived on the floor around his bed, he noticed there was very little movement from the direction of Graves's bed. He stole a covert glance. Next to Graves Billy Elsdon was sat up, rubbing his eyes grumpily, while Myles Lovell leant half out of his bed, rooting around on the floor for something. Graves himself was still huddled under his covers, unmoving. Lucas considered going over there, but thought better of it. Let Graves sleep in if he wanted. He'd only get himself into trouble.

Timothy and Dion rolled themselves out of bed, dark circles around their eyes. They looked like they hadn't slept for a week. Lucas frowned. Surely his bad dream couldn't have affected the whole room like this? Had he been shouting in his sleep, or something?

"Sorry about last night," he mumbled to his friends, embarrassed. They looked at him blearily.

"Sorry for what?" Timothy said thickly. "I just had a nightmare or something, that's all. I get them sometimes."

Lucas paused. "You had a bad dream too?"

"I think. Can't remember much about it now." He screwed up his face. "Oo, I think I'm gonna bust." He hurriedly pulled on some socks and disappeared off to the bathroom.

So Timothy had dreamt too. Well, that was not so unusual, Lucas supposed. Perversely, it also made him feel a little better. It seemed he hadn't been solely responsible for everyone's poor sleep.

Dion was getting dressed. He kept stealing little worried glances in Lucas's direction, until finally he spoke. "I had a weird dream too," he confessed in a small voice.

Lucas looked back at him, not sure what to say. He settled on, "Did you? Oh."

Aaron watched them apprehensively. "You all had bad dreams?"

"Seems like." Lucas sat on his bed, chewing his lip. Okay, so three people in the same room had had odd dreams in the same night. So what? After the events he'd witnessed last night after waking, bad dreams didn't seem all that peculiar.

"Did you dream about dark corridors, and a voice, and, and – stars?" Aaron asked then, hesitantly. Lucas stared at him.

"Yeah... I did," he said, bemused, some of the dream coming back to him now. "How did you –?"

"And a big room with a glass ceiling, and some weird things with shiny eyes?" Dion put in. They all looked at each other in wondering silence. Had they all dreamed the same things?

Billy Elsdon came towards them, his customarily belligerent expression replaced for the moment with something else. Elsdon was a large boy, not exactly fat but with the build of someone who might one day be. He kept his dark blond hair trimmed thuggishly short. Lucas looked up at him apprehensively. Elsdon's mean little eyes regarded them all for a moment.

"How – how do you all know what I dreamed?" he demanded. Lucas realised this was the first time he'd actually really heard Elsdon's voice, at least doing anything other than grunting or making unimaginative threats. That voice was shaking a little, he noted.

"We didn't," Lucas said slowly. "Why? Did you dream those things too?"

Elsdon opened his mouth to reply.

"Billy!" Graves called out. Elsdon's mouth shut with a snap. Instantly his face reshaped itself into its customary facade of angry menace. He glared at the boys for a second, his expression promising great retribution if this conversation was ever mentioned again, then turned away.

How many of them had dreamed last night? Had everyone in the room experienced the same dream? What was going on here?

Worriedly, the boys finished getting dressed and went about their morning routine. As they left for the bathroom they heard Graves, who was still in bed clutching the blankets up to his pale, clammy face, whispering urgently to his two friends. He stared at Lucas as they went past.

Outside in the hall Aaron started chuckling, a low sound that grew progressively louder, bubbling forth from his lips. He leant against the wall, shoulders shaking in mirth.

"What's so funny?" Lucas quizzed him.

"Gravy," he giggled. "He wet the bed!"

"Yeah? How do you know?"

"Oh, I know the signs. You wait 'til I see him later! Brilliant!"

*

Predictably, Lucas found it pretty hard to concentrate on his school work that day. He couldn't stop thinking about all the spooky things that had happened last night. As his brain churned everything around, though, he began to see some connections – if not an actual pattern, then at least some linking factors.

Somehow, they'd all dreamed the same thing, possibly at the same time. He didn't know if Graves had too, but it seemed likely it had happened to everyone in the dorm. Did this kind of thing ever happen to people? He didn't know. For all he knew it occurred all the time, but somehow...that explanation didn't feel right. On some deep level he was certain something significant had gone on last night, something important. But what? Added to the dreaming itself, there had been the glowing night-light, just when they'd needed it, and the bathroom light coming on – also just when it was needed.

On a lesser note it was also kind of strange, he thought as he sat through yet another dull English lesson, that there had been such a pressing need for the bathroom, just after they'd all woken up. Normally in Peregrine House the rules didn't allow anyone to leave their rooms after lights-out, not even for the toilet, so the children were all used to visiting the bathroom just before bed and not needing to go again until morning. Almost everyone had woken up bursting last night though, even leading to Graves apparently wetting his bed (and it would be a long time before Aaron would let the bully forget that). At breakfast this morning even the girls from the other wing had looked tired and fearful. Lucas remembered he'd heard them being told off in the night for leaving their rooms too. Had the whole house been affected?

So what could it all mean? So distracted was he that he didn't even notice Mr Pring entering the classroom until the man was standing right by Lucas's desk, looming over him. Lucas gave a start.

Mr Pring smiled nastily. "Mrs Fisher will see you in her office, boy," he said. "Now. Come along with me, leave your things. Someone else will deal with them."

All eyes were on Lucas as he stood, suddenly fearful. All his worries about the Mill, temporarily forgotten in the mysteries that had been occupying his mind, came crashing back in on him. He looked around at his friends, catching the eye of Aaron at the next table, and beyond him Timothy and Dion, who all returned worried glances. Would this be the last time he'd ever see them?

With a heavy heart he trudged from the classroom, Mr Pring hovering over him like a large and scruffy crow.

Peregrine House, for all its failings and silly rules, was his home. It was the only home he'd ever known. Every memory he had was of this place, and as for his friends…

He didn't want to leave. He couldn't. As he approached the heavy wooden door of Fishy's office and an uncertain future, a seething, dark knot of anger began to form deep inside him.

Chapter Four – Smoke And Mirrors

The first thing Lucas noticed as he was ushered into Fishy's office was the heavy, cloying smell of cigarette smoke. It hung in the air like a pall, flat sheets of bluish smoke drifting lazily, illuminated here and there as it caught the odd stray mote of light. The room was dark, curtains pulled shut, lit only by a couple of lamps. Then, through the haze and gloom, he realised there were several people already in the room. He stopped uncertainly, until Mr Pring prodded him hard in the back and he stumbled forward into the centre of the carpet.

"Why, there you are, young Lucas!" Fishy greeted him loudly. Lucas was instantly wary. She never called him by his first name!

She was seated behind her desk, dressed in some kind of hideous flowery outfit, beaming at him hugely. As his vision adjusted to the gloom, he made out the shape of someone else standing to her right, face hidden in shadow.

"Everyone here has been so desperate to meet you!" Fishy continued brightly. Lucas began to see better, a circle of faces looming out of the darkness around him. He wasn't sure if he was supposed to feel intimidated, but he wasn't. The little hot core of anger in his belly warmed him, lending him strength. He stood up straight, looking Fishy directly in the eye, waiting.

The figure to Fishy's side laughed then, softly, suddenly, and Lucas realised it was a woman. She leaned forward into the pool of light cast by the desk lamp, long hair falling loosely about her shoulders, and Lucas saw her face. For a second he forgot how to breathe.

She was beautiful, in a way that Lucas found difficult to articulate, hair of the lightest blonde casually long and loose, skin pale and smooth. Her lips were painted sensuously red; fluttering black lashes shadowed eyes of the clearest, iciest blue. She smiled directly at him. His heart gave an odd lurch in his chest. He swallowed.

"What a handsome young man," she purred, still looking straight into his eyes. "And how are you feeling today, Lucas?"

"F – fine," he stammered, not entirely truthfully, but for some reason he couldn't think of anything else to say.

"I'm very glad to hear that," she said. Who was this woman? Lucas had never seen her at Peregrine House before. Fishy was acting funny too, the way she did when rich parents visited, all fawning attention and false, brittle laughter. This person must be someone quite important, he thought.

Then a new voice spoke up from somewhere behind him, breaking the spell, a rumbling bass voice that seemed to come at Lucas through the soles of his shoes.

"This is the boy, Deirdre?" the voice said. It came from a man sitting in a comfy chair on the other side of the room, a fat man with black skin, piercing eyes staring at Lucas like he was some kind of mildly interesting bug. Lucas knew straight away that this was Mr Kwame, here to take him away to the Mill at last. His heart began to sink, some of his protective shell of anger beginning to fall away.

"Yes, Jacob," Fishy said with a sidelong glance at the woman next to her. "That's him."

The blonde-haired lady laughed again, an easy tinkling sound. "Mrs Fisher, I realise that you weren't expecting a visit from Juvenile Services today, but you really have nothing to fear from me. It's policy for us to review every application of transfer between care facilities."

Fishy looked annoyed. "Is it?" she replied, some of her customary waspishness creeping back in. "This is the first I've heard of it."

"It's new," the lady said airily, waving her hand in a gesture of dismissal. "And perhaps now is not the best time to be having this discussion." She nodded significantly in Lucas's direction.

"Of course," Fishy agreed quickly. "You're right, Miss Fox. I appreciate any input you may have."

The lady smiled again. "Just go about your business, Mrs Fisher. My colleague and I are merely here to observe and record." She glanced at Lucas then and suddenly, shockingly, she winked. His heart thudded again.

"The paperwork is not yet finished, Deirdre," Mr Kwame said then, shuffling some documents that lay on a low coffee table in front of him. "But that shouldn't delay things unduly. We can make the transfer as soon as the boy has collected his things. If," he glanced significantly at Miss Fox, "that is okay with Juvenile Services?"

"As I said, Mr Kwame," Miss Fox replied smoothly, moving around the desk to stand near to Lucas. Her scent filled his nostrils, a delicate yet sweet aroma that caused his knees to tremble slightly. "I'm not here to disrupt the normal running of your businesses. I'm aware there is a fair amount of traffic between your two facilities. That fact would lead me to assume that you both know what you're doing by now."

There was an uncomfortable silence. Fishy fidgeted in her seat, whilst Mr Kwame stared fixedly at Miss Fox who, for her part, merely returned his look with a calm half-smile. Lucas gazed up at her wonderingly.

"Very well," Mr Kwame said gruffly, breaking the tension. He turned his burning gaze on Lucas then, sizing him up. "Fetch your things from your room, boy, one suitcase worth, and be back down here in fifteen minutes." He dismissed Lucas with a casual wave of his hand, turning back to his paperwork.

The little ball of anger in Lucas's belly suddenly flared up again. He began to clench his fists. So this was how it was to be decided, how he would be torn from everything he knew? He'd known this was coming all week of course, had tried to mentally prepare himself for it, but now he was presented with the stark reality of the situation it was suddenly very different. He felt hot tears stinging his cheeks.

Mr Kwame looked up, surprise registering on his face. He saw that Lucas hadn't moved, and the surprise instantly hardened. "I told you to fetch your belongings," he rumbled dangerously, eyes boring once again into Lucas. "Why aren't you moving?"

"I don't want to go," Lucas whispered through gritted teeth, glaring back at the man with an intensity he'd never known. He stared directly into Kwame's black eyes, the anger boiling up inside him.

Mr Kwame blinked then, an expression of consternation crossing his face for a second. His eyes seemed to glaze over, almost like he'd forgotten what he was supposed to be doing. He looked from Lucas to

Miss Fox and back again, licking his suddenly dry lips. He shifted his attention to Fishy, who was looking at him in some surprise.

"It seems there has been some kind of mix-up, Deirdre," he said, looking slightly puzzled at the words coming from his own mouth. He shuffled his papers self-consciously, clearing his throat. "I'm afraid the Mill doesn't have the space at the moment to accommodate this young man. We'll have to look over our arrangements again at some time in the future."

"Jacob?" Fishy said, bewildered. "Are you alright?"

"I'm fine, Deirdre," he snapped, stuffing the papers into his briefcase. He stood quickly, clearly anxious to be away from this place. "Apologies, Miss Fox," he said gruffly to the lady from Juvenile Services. "You've had a wasted day, it seems."

"Not at all, Mr Kwame," Miss Fox purred, placing a light hand on Lucas's shoulder. "I got to visit this wonderful home, and I had the chance to meet this pleasant young fellow here." She squeezed his shoulder, hard, and Lucas winced.

Mr Kwame glanced at Lucas uncomfortably for a moment, then nodded curtly and hurried from the room.

Miss Fox chuckled, very softly.

"I'm – I'm very sorry, Miss Fox," Fishy stammered, flustered, rising from behind her desk like a whale surfacing from beneath the ocean. "I had previously discussed with Mr Kwame the transfer of Fortune to the Mill, and he had assured me that everything was in order. I – I don't know what's changed."

"Mistakes happen, I'm sure," Miss Fox said graciously, managing at the same time to convey the impression that they rarely happened with her. "Mr Withers and I are not at all put out."

It was then that Lucas became aware of the last person in the room, and the source of all the cigarette smoke. Sitting right on the far side of the room, swathed in smoke and darkness, a man sat on a hard chair, motionless, his eyes glowing in the occasional light from the tip of his cigarette. He had not moved or spoken up to this point, but now he unfolded himself like an umbrella, rising ponderously to his feet, impossibly tall. He surveyed the room from his high vantage, head very nearly brushing the ceiling, calmly watching. Blue smoke poured from his nostrils as he exhaled slowly. "We go where we are required," he said, his voice fluting, oddly accented.

"Quite," Fishy said faintly, staring up at him.

For some reason Lucas had a strong feeling of unease as he looked at this man Mr Withers. There was something very odd about him, something Lucas couldn't quite define. He was tremendously tall, but that in itself wasn't so unusual. No, there was something else, like – he didn't quite fit, like his shape was somehow wrong...

Lucas felt the hairs on the back of his neck rising, sending a quick shiver down his spine.

Mr Withers stared back at him calmly, slowly pulling on his cigarette, eyes giving nothing away.

"And as for you, young man," Miss Fox said to Lucas, moving in front of him and crouching so that they were at eye level, "It seems you'll be staying right here at Peregrine House for a while longer. Isn't that right, Mrs Fisher?"

Fishy harrumphed self-importantly. "Why yes, Miss Fox, of course." She sniffed. "That seems to be the case."

"Good." Miss Fox kept her eyes locked intently with Lucas's for a second longer, her gaze disconcertingly piercing. He stared back bemusedly, the emotions of the last few minutes threatening to overwhelm him. He felt light-headed, but he still managed to catch an odd look in her eye, of something like surprise, and even a little…fear?

She stood then, quickly and gracefully, ending the moment. "Come along, Mr Withers," she commanded, "we have a lot more to do today. Please have the car ready, I'll be out in a moment."

Without a word Mr Withers crossed the room with a few long strides, trailing smoke like a car exhaust. He pulled a pair of dark sunglasses from his pocket and put them on before opening the door. Bright light poured in suddenly from the hallway outside, causing Lucas to squint. Then the creepy man was gone.

"Mr Pring, if you would," Fishy said stiffly, indicating the draped windows. Her subordinate hurried to open them, bright daylight and fresh clean air flooding into the smoky room.

"I apologise for my assistant's habits," Miss Fox said, not sounding sorry at all. "He has a certain intolerance to bright light, unfortunately, and as for the smoking, well…" She gave Mrs Fisher a sly, knowing look, "…everyone has their vices."

Fishy paled slightly, eyes flicking involuntarily, guiltily around the expensively decorated room. She forced a smile. "Don't let me detain you, Miss Fox."

"I won't. We'll be in touch, and in the meantime," she gave Lucas a shrewd look, "we wish to be informed of any new or otherwise pertinent information concerning the children under your care as soon as it becomes available. Policy, you understand."

"Yes, of course," Fishy agreed. Her face was the colour of ashes.

Miss Fox nodded. "Good day, then." She swept from the room without a backward glance.

Fishy stared into space for a moment, swaying slightly on her feet. Mr Pring crossed solicitously to her side, but she quickly came out of her reverie. "I'm fine!" She turned her gaze on Lucas, several different emotions competing for control of her face. She pointed a stiff finger at him. "Mr Pring, get this *child*," she spat the word, "back to his class immediately!" She was back in charge and furious.

"Yes, Mrs Fisher," Mr Pring said in a subdued voice. He took Lucas's arm in a rough grip and propelled him from the room.

"Don't think you've won anything here today, boy," Mr Pring said as he pushed Lucas along the corridors back to his classroom, but Lucas couldn't help smiling a little.

He felt like he really had won something important, only…he wasn't sure what.

Or how.

*

His friends were overjoyed at the news that Lucas would not be leaving after all. Poor Aaron even had a tear in his eye that evening, though he claimed gruffly that he'd accidentally poked himself in the eye with a pencil. To make matters even better, it was the weekend; time to relax and talk things over.

They were all itching to find out exactly what had happened in Fishy's office, so he went over it again and again, trying to recall as much detail as possible. They were especially interested in what Mr Kwame had said, and how he'd seemed to change his mind at the last moment. They'd never even seen the man before, only heard dark stories and rumours from some of the older boys. They were amazed at how Lucas had faced him down. Kwame had been like the bogeyman. Now, after this, he didn't seem quite so frightening anymore.

They were all sitting in the downstairs common room. This was a large, airy space with tall windows that was scattered with chairs and small tables. It was the only place that boys and girls were allowed to mix together outside of school hours, though the separate groups tended not to mingle as a rule. Instead they sat in tight single-sex clusters, eyeing each other warily. Several children sat alone, quietly reading or catching up with homework, whilst in the background the constant presence of Mr Pring hovered, watching them all like a sentinel for any evidence of rule-bending. No action had apparently been taken over his behaviour of the night before, though he glared at Lucas with a special intensity whenever their eyes met. The single TV set was switched off as usual; it was rarely used.

Lucas and his friends looked up as a gaggle of girls noisily entered the room. It was the G.O.C., led by the snooty Sabrina Celestine. She scanned the room for a moment, spotting Lucas's crowd. She bustled over to them, an arch look on her pale features.

"I've got a message for you," she said curtly. She paused. "From Marshall." If she expected them to be impressed, she was disappointed.

"Ah, yes, how is old leaky?" Aaron replied, provoking much merriment from Dion, who giggled loudly and punched Aaron on the arm. "Haven't seen him about much today. Hanging around the toilets, is he?"

Sabrina's face went white. "How dare you talk about Marshall that way, frogspawn!" she squealed, attracting Mr Pring's attention. He began to move in their direction, eyes narrowed in suspicion. Sabrina saw him and leaned closer to the boys. "You'd better not tell anyone about last night," she hissed in a much lower voice. "Else, you'll be sorry!"

"Oo, were we not supposed to mention that? Whoops!"

Sabrina bared her teeth at Aaron, but she was prevented from saying anything further by the arrival of Mr Pring, who sent the girls on their way with a few curt words. He reserved a special glower for Lucas, before returning to his post by the opposite wall.

The G.O.C. moved off some distance and sat, muttering darkly amongst themselves, while the boys continued their conversation, Lucas retelling the whole story again to his avid audience.

After a while Lucas became aware of eyes watching him, and he looked up curiously. One of the G.O.C. was looking over. He couldn't tell who it was. She ducked back down too quickly into her huddle. He shrugged and told his friends the bit about Mr Withers again, who by now in the retelling had grown to monstrous proportions; the man had to bend down to avoid banging his enormous misshapen head on the ceiling.

There it was again, someone looking at him, and this time he saw who it was: Sammi River, a tiny, elfin girl with thick ginger hair and large brown eyes. They stared at each other for a second before she ducked down again. She looked a little scared, he thought.

After a while the G.O.C. must have grown bored. They got up as one, surveyed the room haughtily and stalked out. A minute or two later Lucas was dimly aware one of someone coming back in and moving hesitantly up to his side. He didn't really pay this person any attention until they self-consciously cleared their throat. All talking stopped, the boys turning to stare at the newcomer suspiciously. It was Sammi River again, looking very nervous indeed.

"What do you want now?" Aaron said gruffly, sitting back and glaring at her.

"I heard..." the girl began in a tiny voice, then stopped, swallowing. "I mean, I wanted to ask…did you have bad dreams last night?"

Lucas sat up straight. "Why?" The other boys were staring now.

Sammi licked her dry lips. "I heard Sabrina talking to Marshall earlier," she confessed. "He said something about everyone having bad dreams in your dorm last night." She gave them a wild-eyed look. "I didn't know who else to tell…" she whispered, close to tears.

"You too, huh?" Lucas said shrewdly. She looked at him with something like gratitude.

"Not just me," she said, "all of us."

"What, every single girl?" Aaron demanded.

She paused uncertainly. "No, just the ones in our dorm. The G.O.C."

Lucas thought about it for a second. "So why are you telling us? Why not talk about it with your own friends?"

"It's Sabrina, she…she said we're not to mention it again. She was real scared, I think."

Lucas looked at his friends in turn, who returned looks of bemusement. He made a decision. "Sammi," he said, turning to face her directly, "tell me; in your dream did you hear strange voices, see glowing eyes?" He thought about his own dream. "Running down dark corridors? Stuff like that?"

Her eyes widened. "Yeah, I did! And some giant rocks floating in space, and...some sort of fight, I think! How did you know?"

Lucas saw the look of recognition on his friend's faces, felt it in himself. He remembered that part too! "Because we all dreamed it," he breathed as realisation came. "All of us, all at the same time."

Sammi stared at him, not questioning it. She must know he was right. They all did. It seemed, though, that they each had slightly different memories, or at least were remembering different parts of the same experience.

"You know," Timothy said thoughtfully, "I reckon if we all tell each other what we remember we might be able to piece it together a bit more. Sort of like building a jigsaw, or something."

"Yeah," Aaron breathed. "Let's do that."

Sammi was shaking her head. "I can't stay," she said fearfully, "I only told Sabrina I was going to the loo." She started to back away.

Lucas thought quickly. "Okay, how about tomorrow, then? We could meet up, maybe…"

Sammi shrugged, turning to go. "I don't know," she said over her shoulder, then ran from the room without another backward glance.

The high spirits of a moment ago began to fade fast. The boys all looked a little sheepish, trying to avoid each other's eyes. Lucas knew it was really fear. So far, they'd all carefully avoided talking to each other about last night's events in any detail. The unspoken consensus seemed to be that if they ignored it, then maybe it hadn't really happened. The whole thing was just too…weird. Things like this didn't happen in the real world. If they were to speak of it now, wouldn't that make it, somehow – true?

But maybe that was exactly what was needed. No one spoke, but a buzz seemed to go around the group. As one they looked up and met each other's eyes. It was time.

It was Aaron who began. "It was – big," he said slowly, eyes half-closed in thought. "I mean, the whole dream was long, there was lots happening, but also, something else – a big place, like a house, rooms and stuff, but all bent and twisty."

"Odd corridors, all rounded, with, like, lights on the walls, glowing yellow," Timothy added.

Lucas listened passively, letting the images fall into place in his own mind. The vision wanted to slip away, as dreams often do if you try too hard to grasp them, but he was being very careful. "I wasn't alone," he contributed, seeing the vague shapes of other people in his head. "There were – others. Lots of us. We were all together."

"I was cold at first," Dion said, "but it soon got a lot warmer. We were all in a big room, kind of circular, with no ceiling. I could see stars twinkling above."

They sat quietly, deep in thought, now not looking at each other. An uncomfortable chill ran down Lucas's spine. He had a momentary flash, for some reason, of Marshall Graves's face all twisted up in anger, yelling furiously. Then it was gone. "Did any of you see Graves in your dream?" he asked, but they just shrugged helplessly. It seemed they could remember no more. Whatever it was that had momentarily connected them was already fading.

Suddenly tired and drained, the energy and high emotions that had carried them through the day were now ebbing fast. There was a good half-hour to go before curfew, but the boys elected to return to their room early, each hoping they would sleep properly tonight.

Lucas wondered if he would dream again. In a strange kind of way, he almost hoped he would.

*

It was an ordinary house in a quiet part of Exeter, only a few kilometres from Peregrine House. Well maintained and neat, the residents of the street were reasonably content with their new neighbours, who had only moved in a week before.

They did keep odd hours though...

A plain black car came slowly up the street, gliding to a stop in front of the house. Curtains twitched here and there within the nearby properties. Who was this now, visiting so late? It was nearly eleven o'clock!

Two dark figures emerged from the car, indistinct in the moonless gloom. They hurried along the short driveway up to the house. The front door opened immediately, allowing a flash of light to briefly illuminate a flowing curtain of blonde hair, before the house swallowed the visitors up.

"Is it him?" the man asked bluntly. He regarded Miss Fox with dark, expressionless eyes.

"I'm not sure," she replied, making no attempt to hide her annoyance. "It was hard to tell."

"Was it?" the man snapped. "Tell me, Danielle, what exactly do we pay you for?"

Miss Fox bit back an angry reply. "I'm sorry, Mr Stanford," she said. "I didn't have enough time with the boy to get a clear sense of him. However," she held up a hand to forestall his protests, "I think it's safe to say there is something going on at Peregrine House."

"Something," Mr Stanford repeated. "Really." He rose from behind his desk, pacing up and down in a short arc.

Miss Fox watched him nervously. "If nothing else, it's a good place to focus our attentions," she said into the silence. "There are lots of children there of the right age. With our cover as representatives of Juvenile Services, Ptolemy and I can visit and make extensive checks as often as we like."

Mr Stanford stopped his pacing. "Ah, yes, where is your partner?"

"He's outside in the back garden. You know how he likes to smoke."

Mr Stanford made a face. "Filthy habit," he muttered. He thought for a moment. "Very well, Danielle, I want you to continue checking up on Peregrine House. We know Agent Smith was seen in this area of the country before she disappeared, so it's as good a place to start as any."

He looked her directly in the eye. "Questions are being asked, Agent. People are watching this case very carefully. The lack of firm leads or any kind of concrete results up to now are becoming a cause for concern. I shouldn't need to explain to you exactly how important this matter is to the organisation."

Despite herself, Miss Fox bridled. "That's right sir, you don't." She couldn't keep the bitterness from her voice. "I know my duty."

"Glad to hear it." He sat back down. "But I trust my point is clear. One of our own people *defected,*" he said the word with distaste, "and consorted with the enemy. Who knows what secrets she's given the other side?"

Miss Fox chose her words carefully. "Yes sir. I am aware of the details of Agent Smith's... indiscretion. She and I worked together, many years ago. She was..." She paused. "A friend."

"Indeed." He eyed her again. "Indeed."

What was that supposed to mean? "Sir –"

"No more talk, Danielle. I want results. Make your investigation, do what you have to do, but my patience is wearing thin. This could make your career, Agent – or break it. Am I making myself clear?"

Fuming inside, she nonetheless clamped down hard on her emotions. "As crystal."

"Good. Find Agent Smith, Danielle, track her down, but remember your number one priority:

Bring me her child. Nothing is more important than that."

Chapter Five - Changes

Sleep, deep and dreamless, came easily that night and every night for the next week, which was the final week of the school term. The boys talked no more about their shared experience. After a while it began to seem as though the whole thing was some crazy story they'd heard from someone else. Aside from the rapidly fading bruise on Lucas's calf, there was little to remind them anything had happened at all. For that week, at least, life seemed to return almost to normal.

Almost. They saw very little of Mr Pring, which was unusual in itself, and even less of Marshall Graves, which was unheard of. Altercations of varying kinds had long since become an almost daily occurrence from one or the other of those two. In fact it appeared as if Lucas and his friends were being avoided generally. No one in the house said anything outright but there was a palpable sense of unease in the air, which apparently bothered Dion the most. It seemed to affect him almost like a physical pain, subduing his normally high spirits.

It was the first Saturday of the school holiday. Dion was moping on a big armchair in the common room, legs pulled up to his chest, staring into space.

"There you are," Lucas said as he came into the room. "We've been looking for you."

Dion looked at him oddly. "I know."

"Well, come on, they're waiting in the garden."

Dion licked his dry lips. "Can't you feel that, Lucas?" he said plaintively. "It's everywhere."

Lucas sat in the chair opposite him. "I'm not sure what you mean," he said slowly, diplomatically, though in truth he was aware of the sense of disquiet. He'd been feeling it for a few days now. He hadn't said anything, hadn't really been able to put a name to it, but there was definitely something...

Dion struggled for words. "It's like – like, hearing someone talking in the next room, just a noise, I can almost hear words, and…" he trailed off, eyeing Lucas strangely. "You've felt it too, haven't you?"

Lucas was surprised. *How had Dion known that?*

"Doesn't matter." Dion shook his head. "I just do." He stared at Lucas, eyes widening. "You didn't...say that out loud just then, did you."

Lucas didn't know what to say. What had just happened? He'd been thinking something in his head. Had Dion somehow...read his mind? Was this what he meant?

"Yeah, kinda," Dion said slowly, eyes screwed up in concentration. "Except, with you, it's much clearer. Like I'm hearing your actual voice." He stared at Lucas in consternation. "What's happening to me?"

Lucas opened his mouth, but found he had no reply. He snapped it shut again, searching his feelings. Why wasn't he shocked? Sure, he felt surprise, even a little fear, but overlaying it all was something else, like he'd just been told something he'd known all along but had forgotten. These things, happening now, seemed – right, somehow.

It was almost as if he'd been expecting this.

He shook his head slowly, gravely, mind beginning to race. "I think – it's okay," he said carefully, wondering how much of this Dion could sense.

"What do you mean?" Dion squeaked, sitting up and leaning forward urgently. "What's going on?"

"I think it may have something to do with the dream," Lucas explained as his mind began to assemble the pieces. "Things have been a bit – strange around here since then, don't you think?"

Dion couldn't deny that. Lucas could see it in his eyes.

"So, what? What do I do now?"

"That's something we need to find out," Lucas said with more confidence than he felt. "We can't keep acting like nothing happened." There were others they could speak to...

Dion picked that up, nodding slowly. "The girls." He looked around the room, but none of the G.O.C. were in sight. He screwed up his eyes for a moment. "They're in the bower." He gave Lucas an embarrassed look. "I just know, alright?"

"Fair enough."

Aaron and Timothy were in the garden, a large, neat area of ground next to the house which was laid out to lawn, with sculpted hedges and wooden benches dotted about. There were quite a lot of people in it today, as parents arrived to collect the children who'd been boarding at Peregrine House all term. The weather was fair. Fishy had laid out some tables with drinks and nibbles on the lawn, 'to keep the rich parents sweet,' as Aaron neatly put it.

He and Timothy were hanging around one of the tables, trying to swipe vol-au-vents and sausage rolls from under the beady eye of Mr Pring, when Lucas found them. Dion mooched along behind him, looking preoccupied.

"Alright, D," Aaron greeted him happily. "It's the summer, mate! Cheer up!"

Dion gave him a wan smile. "I'm alright. Feeling a bit off, that's all."

Lucas led them away from the table to a quieter area, much to Aaron's dismay. "I had my eye on those little sausages," he muttered.

Lucas explained what had happened in the common room, while Dion looked a little sheepish, scuffing his shoes in the grass.

"Cool!" Aaron exclaimed when Lucas had finished. Dion looked at him quizzically.

"What d'you mean, 'cool'?"

"I mean, mate, it's cool, very cool! What d'you think I mean?"

"You believe me, then?"

Aaron looked confused. "Why wouldn't I?"

"I dunno, it's just so...you know, weird. Isn't it?"

Aaron thought about that. "I guess," he admitted as though that hadn't occurred to him. It probably hadn't, Lucas observed wryly. Aaron just wasn't made that way. He was a very accepting person, taking things at face value until he had cause to think otherwise. "Weird – but cool!"

"So how long have you been able to do this?" Timothy chimed in. He didn't look concerned at all, but he rarely let on what he was thinking.

Dion considered. "I'm not even sure what 'this' is," he said. "I've been hearing all kinds of strange things for a few days now. Like," he tried to find the right words, "like..."

"Far-off voices?" Timothy suggested.

Dion stared at him. "What, you too?"

Timothy licked his lips before replying. "Not exactly, but it does sort of remind me of that night we had the Dream. Remember, distant voices, sort of in our heads..." he trailed off, looking sheepish at their sudden attention. "Or something like that."

The boys gazed at each other silently, minds racing. Was there really some connection between the Dream and the strange events since then? With people's odd behaviour in Lucas's presence, and Dion's ability to pick up other's thoughts?

There was a moment of electric silence...

Aaron, predictably, broke the mood. "Well, you've always wanted to be different, haven't you, spaceboy?" His face lit up. "Hey, mate, what am I thinking now?"

Dion shook himself. He gave Aaron a withering look. "You're thinking how you'll look with a bleeding nose," he said with mock menace, and jumped on him. They rolled around on the grass scuffling and laughing, until Lucas and Timothy got dragged in too. It was a great way to relieve the tension; just like old times.

After a while, grass stained and ruffled, they began to talk about what they were going to do next.

For his part, and not for the first time, Lucas considered he was very lucky to have such good friends around him.

Sabrina Celestine was not happy. She'd not really slept well at all since – well, since last weekend. Her schoolwork had suffered. She'd actually got a C in Home Economics! Also, she had rather unattractive dark circles under her eyes, and her hair simply wouldn't do what it was told. Sometimes she almost despaired.

She sat moodily on one of the benches in the bower, which was in reality an old potting shed on the edge of the house's small private woodland. It had been lazily converted at some point into a little meeting place for the children, a few benches here and there, and it was also the official headquarters of the Girls Only Club. She'd had some of the other girls decorate it a bit, so the place was festooned with glittery paper chains and out-of-date pop-star posters (which were generally frowned upon by Fishy, but she never came out here anyway).

The other girls seemed to be fairing a little better, not that Sabrina took much notice of them. They were sat around her now, idly chattering, plaiting each other's hair and giggling occasionally.

Marshall had been acting awfully funny for the last few days. In fact, it was almost as if he was avoiding her. She wished he would be more open with her. Sometimes it seemed like he didn't really like her at all. She knew he'd had a weird dream too, which for some reason had affected him very badly. She could help him, if only he'd let her! She sighed theatrically.

"What is it, Sabrina?" Dana Jackson asked her, concerned. She was a wiry girl with coffee-coloured skin and hazel eyes, and a mane of thick, curly hair that formed natural ringlets. Of all the G.O.C., she was the one Sabrina most considered a friend. They had both been here at Peregrine House for nearly five years, had grown up together really, and she was the only one that Sabrina confided in. Not today, though.

"Nothing," she snapped. Dana shrugged. She was used to Sabrina's moods. She was about to say something, when she froze, mouth half open.

Sabrina stared at her. "What?"

Dana looked puzzled. "There are…people coming." She screwed up her eyes. "Boys."

Sabrina jumped to her feet with an unladylike snarl, peering through the window. Outside was a small grassed area, hemmed in by some wild-looking rhododendron bushes that, in the summer as now, provided great concealment from the main house. A narrow path threaded its way through the tangle, but there was no one on it.

She rounded on Dana angrily. "What boys?" she demanded. "There's no one there!"

Dana looked wretched. "It's that Fortune and his gang," she insisted. "They're coming here!"

Sabrina took another look through the window. "I don't see…" she began, but trailed off in confusion as she heard voices outside; then a procession of boys appeared on the path, wending their way carefully through the rhododendrons.

Sabrina was incensed. Boys, here? Everyone knew the bower was for Girls Only! (Well, except for Marshall, of course). She hissed as she saw the Fortune boy, leading his pathetic troupe of grubby little urchins. He was actually approaching *her* bower, her private domain! How *dare* he!

She glared at Dana, who was still sat on the floor in bemused silence. "We'll talk about this later," Sabrina said darkly. She drew herself up and went to meet the intruders.

As Lucas and his friends approached, Sabrina Celestine came storming out of her shed to confront them. Eyes blazing, she took up a hostile stance, folding her arms dramatically.

Seeing her now, Lucas began to entertain serious doubts about the wisdom of coming here. Of course, he'd known they would receive a less than friendly reaction, and ordinarily it would have taken a fairly determined team of wild horses to get him to come; and as for Sabrina herself –

"She's mental," Aaron muttered, eyeing her.

"I don't know *what* you think you're doing coming here, but you'll regret it!" Sabrina raged. Behind her, her little gang formed up silently.

Trying to ignore his misgivings, Lucas held up his hands. "We, uh, just wanted to talk about something," he said in his calmest voice. "That's all, okay?" Despite his unease, he nevertheless put forth a special effort to appear friendly. There was just too much weirdness going on around here to lose his nerve now.

Sabrina stopped, mouth open. Her eyes glazed over, as though she'd completely lost her train of thought. Beside her, Dana Jackson looked at her worriedly. "Sabbie, what is it?" she whispered. "Are you okay?"

With a start, Lucas realised he recognised this reaction. He'd seen it before, on the faces of both Old Man Pring and Mr Kwame, just when he'd wanted them both to believe him. He'd been trying to radiate calm this time...

Distracted, he let his concentration slip for just a moment. Sabrina opened and shut her mouth, blinked, then spotted Lucas again. "I don't care what you want!" she rallied. "Get away, all of you!"

Lucas didn't reply immediately. Could he do it again? More to the point, should he? Was it right to do that to people? Possibly not, but now was hardly the time to be asking himself this kind of question. With an effort he forced himself to focus. "It's about the dream," he blurted.

There was an immediate silence, the two groups staring at each other. Once again it appeared Sabrina was at a loss for words, only this time from good old-fashioned surprise. She glared at Lucas hatefully.

"They know," Dion said in a quiet voice, scanning the girls' faces. "Lucas, they know. They just – pretend not to."

Sabrina regathered her wits. "There was no dream!" she declared in a shrill voice, eyes wild.

"She's scared," Dion continued.

"Shut *up!*"

"And the others…they're scared of her."

Sabrina flew at Dion then, arms outstretched. Moving impossibly fast, she crossed the short distance to Dion before anyone could so much as blink. She slammed bodily into him.

Lucas watched in stunned silence as Dion was catapulted backwards, tumbling head over heels to land in the rhododendron bush. He gasped as the air was knocked out of him.

Sabrina stopped, appalled. She looked down at her hands in astonishment, then up to where Dion struggled in the tangles. "I told you...to shut up," she said in a shaky voice.

"Alright, alright, we're going," Lucas said, backing off quickly. He didn't know what had just happened, but the whole situation was already getting out of hand. It certainly hadn't taken long.

Timothy scooped Dion out of the bush, keeping a wary eye on the girls. Dion clutched at his chest, wheezing mightily, eyes streaming as he struggled for breath. As the boys left, Lucas turned back one last time. He saw Sammi and Tamsen exchange an obscure glance, then turn to face him directly, their expressions unreadable. The other two girls, Dana Jackson and Lois Christie, smirked nastily.

Sabrina was still standing there, breathing heavily and staring at her hands, as the boys went back through the bush.

"I'm alright," Dion puffed on the other side of the rhododendron. He winced, winding his shoulder gingerly. "Pretty much."

"What was that?" Aaron demanded. "Lucas, she punched Dion!" He paused. "I think. We can't just walk away! She'll tell everyone!"

Lucas shook his head. "Doesn't matter. Let her. We got what we came for. Right, Dion?"

Dion nodded painfully, wiping his eyes. "Yeah. Come on, I need to sit down for a minute. I'll tell you all about it."

Aaron grumped but went along with them.

Dana went up to Sabrina, touched her on the arm. "Don't think we'll be seeing that lot again," she said happily. Sabrina gave her a slow look.

"No," she murmured. She raised her head to survey the rest of the G.O.C. Tamsen gazed back at her coolly, almost challengingly, while Sammi looked slightly tearful and more than a little guilty, though Sabrina couldn't imagine about what. Could it be they doubted her actions? Sabrina resolved coldly to have a little chat with the two of them later about that. It wouldn't do to have anyone questioning her decisions.

She hadn't meant to hit the boy so hard, but it had felt good! She'd shown the little tyke not to come around here blabbing about things which didn't concern him.

Feeling slightly better, she flicked her hair haughtily and led her troupe back into the bower.

"They don't know much," Dion reported as they sat on a picnic bench in the garden. "Or, at least, I couldn't tell much." He smiled sorely. "I'm not so good at this yet."

"What did you – hear?" Lucas asked. "Is that the right word?"

"Good enough. That Sabrina girl definitely knows something, but she refuses to talk about it. Even to think about it. She keeps it pressed down hard, in her head." He tapped his temple. "That's the only way I can describe it."

"And the others?"

"It's…I'm not certain, but Sammi wants to talk, and I think Tamsen Nicoletta does too. It'll be better if they tell us themselves. Clearer, I mean." He frowned.

"What?"

He made a face. "That Dana Jackson. There's something weird about her. It was almost like – like she could see into my head too."

Timothy chewed his lip. "So, what does it mean? We all had a weird dream, it seems like, but what about all these other things?" He looked around carefully, making sure no one was watching. "Look," he said quietly, and laid his bare arm on the table.

The others peered at it. "What are we looking at?" Aaron asked, puzzled.

"Keep watching," Timothy said, concentrating. As they watched, the skin on his arm began to darken, fading slowly, until it was the same colour as the table top. It blended in perfectly. Timothy looked up at them with a small grin.

"Pretty cool, huh?"

Aaron let out his breath in a whoosh. "That's awesome! How do you do it?"

"I dunno. I just noticed it happening yesterday, but I felt a bit…silly, so I didn't say anything."

"Does it hurt?" Lucas asked him incredulously.

"Can you do it whenever you want?" Aaron said at the same time.

Timothy answered seriously, "No, and yes." He looked around at their amazed faces. "Something big's happening, isn't it?"

Lucas nodded slowly. "Yeah. And we need to find out what it is."

Aaron made a disgusted sound. The others looked at him quizzically.

"'S not fair," he sniffed. "You all get really cool powers. Even that Sabrina's like Supergirl. What about me?"

Lucas sat back and thought about that while his friends joked. Aaron had a good point there. Could there be some reason that only some of those who'd experienced the Dream were developing these abilities? Was the Dream actually the cause, and not just a linking factor? Aaron had not shown any changes yet, while many others already had: Timothy, Dion, Sabrina, maybe even Dana Jackson. Who knew what else they could expect?

Come to think of it, what exactly had Lucas himself been doing? After all, he still didn't really know what had caused Mr Kwame to change his mind that time in Fishy's office, just when Lucas had been wishing for it. And Sabrina, just now? He was coming to recognise that glazed look. If each of them were developing different abilities, for whatever reason, could Lucas's be the particular talent to influence people's minds?

He felt like he was making some progress, if only of the stumbling, flailing-in-the-dark variety.

However, there was the small matter of the glowing light bulb, and the bathroom light-switch on the night of the Dream. Were they in some way also connected to him?

His head was beginning to hurt with all these questions. Where could he go? To whom could he talk to get some answers? He felt like he should know. If only he could remember!

Inside the house, up on the first floor of the boy's wing, Marshall Graves kicked open the door to his room savagely. He'd had Billy and Myles stay downstairs. He didn't want them to see him like this.

He'd known all week about his parent's intentions, of course, but seeing all those other adults coming to collect their brats had really hammered it home. He was being abandoned!

So his folks were taking their yacht to the Mediterranean; big deal! He could look after himself at home while they were away, he had Smiggs the butler and the housekeeping staff – but no, apparently they'd all been given the next month off!

Now he was stuck here all through the summer, stuck with those cretinous younger boys and that annoying Celestine girl who seemed to think he was her boyfriend or something. How was that fair?

He focused his furious gaze on a metal wastepaper basket next to the desk. Concentrating, he poured all his anger into it. It twisted and deformed, screeching as the metal bent, scraps of paper flying as if caught in a breeze. He squashed it flat to the floor, until it resembled a grey metal pancake.

It was the best one he'd managed so far, but it did little to please him. How *dare* they! Still fuming, he thought about all the ways he could make people's lives a misery this summer, most especially Fortune and his little gang.

Chapter Six – Summertime Blues

Peregrine House was a lot quieter after the term-time residents had left. They made up about two thirds of the normal population, so it made quite a difference to the atmosphere of the place. For Lucas especially, it was a time he very much looked forward to each year. He'd spent his entire life at the House. He felt like it was his, in a way, and that all the term-timers were somehow intruders in his territory. He knew it was silly to think that way, yet it made an obscure sort of sense to him.

This was doubly true for Marshall Graves. For Lucas, the holidays felt like the only time he could properly relax, knowing the snooty bully was miles away in his big mansion somewhere. His buddies, Lovell and Elsdon, were permanent residents, but without Graves's direct input they became harmless and sort of pathetic, drifting around the place like rudderless boats, keeping mostly to themselves.

Lucas was not aware until that evening that the situation this year was to be somewhat different. A heavy hand landed on his shoulder, spinning him round as he was heading alone for the common room to meet his friends. Marshall Graves glared at him, pale blue eyes full of loathing. To his sides bulked Lovell and Elsdon, spiteful grins on their faces. No one else was around. The corridor was deserted.

"Guess what, basket-boy?" Graves spat. His fingers dug painfully into Lucas's shoulder.

Lucas stared back at him, masking his dismay. "Thought you'd gone home," he replied, shakily. He twisted from Graves's grip, backing off a step or two, until his shoulder blades met with the wall.

The older boys surrounded him. Lucas looked around desperately, but there was still no one else in sight. Where was Pring when you needed him?

"Thought wrong, didn't you?" Graves said triumphantly. "I'm staying here all summer. Won't that be nice?"

"Triffic," Lucas muttered.

"What did you say?" Graves demanded. "Myles, I think Fortune is having some trouble with his manners. Shocking, eh?"

Myles Lovell grinned. He reached out and grabbed Lucas's arm with a fist like a bunch of sausages. Lucas cried out as sudden pain flowed through his body, coursing through every limb. It felt like he was on fire!

Lovell let go with a grunt. The fluorescent tubes that lit the hallway were flickering, but Lucas barely noticed. He fell to his knees, shuddering and gasping as the pain switched off. He felt like he'd been punched all over.

Graves nodded in satisfaction. "Nice one, Myles," he congratulated his crony. Lovell looked smug.

Graves bent over Lucas. "You'd better stay out of my way, mucus," he hissed in Lucas's face. "This dump is mine now. Got it?"

Lucas grunted noncommittally, but this seemed to satisfy Graves, who gave him a spiteful shove and stalked away, followers in tow, laughing as they went.

Lucas struggled to his feet, checking himself over for injuries. His movements felt sluggish, like he couldn't control his limbs properly.

What was that?! What had Lovell done to him? It felt like that time he'd touched a frayed wire coming from a bedside lamp. The electricity had pulsed painfully through his fingers until he'd pulled away with a startled yelp.

He found no damage. Already the pain had faded to a tingle, like pins and needles.

The common room door burst open farther down the hall, disgorging the flapping shape of Mr Pring, closely followed by Lucas's friends.

"What's going on out here?" Mr Pring demanded. "Who's shouting?" His beady eyes zeroed in on Lucas. "Fortune? I might have known!"

Graves was already out of sight, leaving Lucas standing shuddering in the corridor, alone and guilty-looking. He thought quickly. "Sorry, Mr Pring," he said, his voice cracked. "I tripped and banged my knee."

Mr Pring stared at him, searching for any sign of wrong-doing. With a disgusted grunt he dismissed Lucas, turning to go back into the common room, where goodness knows what mischief may have occurred in his absence.

"Out of my way," he grumbled at the cluster of boys in the doorway, shoving them brusquely aside.

Aaron rushed up to Lucas, Dion and Timothy close behind. "We knew," Aaron said, concern in his eyes. "Dion could tell what was happening, but we couldn't get past Pring in time. Are you hurt?"

Lucas rubbed at the spot on his arm where Lovell had grabbed him, which was still throbbing. "Not really," he said thickly. "I'm alright, but it looks like Graves is staying on this year."

They looked at each other miserably.

Timothy asked, "What did he do to you?"

"I'm not sure," Lucas admitted. "But it looks like everyone who had the dream is changing. Lovell had some kind of – electricity in his fingers, or something." He thought about it. "And Graves knew." The idea of Graves commanding that kind of power was unsettling, to say the least.

"What do we do now?" Aaron wondered.

"I should have tried to talk him out of it," Lucas muttered. He hadn't thought about it at the time, but now he wished he'd attempted it. If he truly could persuade people to do what he wanted, this would have been a great time to put that theory to the test.

Aaron made a face as if to say 'why bother?', but Dion got it right away. His face lit up. "So that's it," he said. "Mental powers. We sort of wondered what yours would be. Didn't we?"

Lucas looked at them quizzically for a moment, then smiled.

The others grinned back at him.

*

After lights-out that night, the boys lay tensely in the dark, each of their minds racing, churning over all the strange things that had happened in the last week; the shared dream, Timothy's arm, Lovell's painful grip, Sabrina's strength, Dion's mind-reading, Lucas's persuasive ability and all the rest of it.

Why now? Lucas thought to himself as sleep began to relax his mind. He felt like he was swimming, or being sucked down in a whirlpool, spinning out of control. What was the reason for it all? What would happen to them?

He fell down into darkness, still spinning, fear beginning to creep in now. He flailed blindly, crying out, until abruptly the gloom cleared, flowing away like smoke. He found himself standing on a cold, hard surface. His feet were bare, the ground beneath them ridged like rough concrete.

He was in a large open space, a circular room with no windows, the smell of damp and disuse hanging in the chilly air. All around him shapes hunkered, like furniture covered with sheets, a thick layer of dust laying over everything. He didn't recognize where he was, had never been here before. So why did it feel so familiar?

"H – hello?" he called out fearfully. The silence seemed to grab his voice and pull it away, like he was speaking through cloth.

He sensed someone behind him. He spun on the spot, eyes bulging in fright, but there was no one there. The cold of the floor was climbing his legs, penetrating his flesh. He started to shiver. How could he get out of here?

A dim, sourceless light began to glow, yellow and sickly looking, illuminating the surrounding walls. He saw the walls were panelled, or covered in some kind of mesh or grid, irregular lines criss-crossing the surface. He began to hear a kind of throbbing, a deep booming reverberating through the very floor as though some vast machinery was coming to life far away.

Come back to me, a voice whispered in Lucas's ear, causing him to jump in fright. He spun around again, but still there was no one else there. His heart was pounding, a fast counterpoint to the distant booming. "Where are you?" he called out plaintively.

Near, the voice said. Lucas couldn't tell where it was coming from. **You do not remember me. I am sorry for that. It was…unavoidable.**

"I don't understand," Lucas cried, tears coming. He wasn't sure if it was fear or frustration.

There is much you have lost, the voice said cryptically. **But you are strong. Your father would be proud of you.**

That got his attention. "How do you know about my father?" he demanded. "Why can't I see you?"

You will, when the time is right, the voice answered distantly. It was fading, getting weaker, along with the yellow light and the distant booming. **Find this place. It will be yours. Our enemies seek you. They will not find you here.**

"Who are you?" Lucas shouted into the gathering darkness.

Rith, came the faint reply, and then Lucas was alone. He sank onto the soft floor, his head pressing into the warm pillow, mind swirling. He heard soft snores, the familiar sounds of the boys' wing, and he realised he was back in his bed, awake. The voice echoed in his head.

"Rith," Lucas whispered, tasting the unfamiliar word. He sat up, eyes wide in the gloom. He could still see the dusty circular room in his mind, feel the sensation of cold concrete beneath his feet. He'd be safe there? From whom? And how was he supposed to get there, anyway? He was just a kid!

"Rith," he muttered again, eyes already closing, and sleep claimed him once more, this time deep and untroubled.

A distant scream woke them later in the night. It sounded like it had come from elsewhere in the house, possibly the girl's wing.

The boys all sat up, looking around unseeingly in the dark.

"Wazzat?" Aaron mumbled thickly.

"Someone's dreaming," Dion murmured. "It's – Dana Jackson." His voice sounded pained. "Ooo."

"What?" Lucas asked him, concerned. His own dream was still very clear in his mind. Was it happening to them all again?

"She was…running," Dion said slowly. "Down weird corridors, all covered in gridlines, yellowy light everywhere. Something was chasing her." He shuddered visibly. "She's pretty shook up."

"Serves her right," Aaron muttered uncharitably. "Cow." He slumped back down on his pillow.

"Anything else?" Lucas demanded. Gridlines and yellow light?

"You dreamed it too," Dion commented. "Didn't you?"

"Sort of. What happened in Dana's dream?"

Dion paused. "Can't see it too well…" he murmured. "Uh, there was something there, a metal thing, all oily and dirty, it was following her – it had eyes, glowing. It wasn't friendly." He paused again. "That's when she woke up."

"Did you hear – a name?" Lucas said hesitantly.

"...No," Dion replied. "Should I have?"

Lucas didn't reply straight away. Dana's dream had clearly been different from his, though some of the elements had been similar. It sounded like the same place he had seen. But the voice he'd heard had not been threatening – in fact now that he thought about it, the whole dream hadn't really been frightening at all, just weird. The voice had claimed it wanted to help him. "Not sure," he said in answer to Dion's question. "Maybe."

"Hey Lucas, what name?" Timothy's voice joined in.

"It sounded like –" he trailed off, cudgelling his brain. What was it again? "Drift, or…fifth…"

"Rith?" Timothy said.

"Yeah, that's it! Did you dream it too?" Lucas was excited now. It felt like, somehow, the answers were getting closer.

"Yeah, I think so, but not tonight. It was last week, when we all dreamed the first time."

Interesting. The dreams were definitely connected, then. But just who was this Rith person? Was he responsible for all the changes that had befallen them? Out loud, he said, "Alright, that's something. I had a new dream tonight, and this Rith, whoever he is, said that I wasn't safe. I don't know what that means, though."

"Not safe from who?" Timothy wondered.

"*Whom*," Aaron corrected him from within his pillow. Timothy blew a raspberry.

"Tim, in your dream, did you get the feeling that this Rith was...you know...okay?" Lucas asked.

"I think so," Timothy said slowly. "There was a voice, but I couldn't see who was speaking. It was telling me things. I didn't feel afraid."

"So the thing in Dana's dream – that could be something else, then," Lucas mused. "Not Rith."

Aaron sat up. "D'you reckon this Rith could help us, then?" he asked. "If we could find him, I mean?"

"Yeah," Lucas breathed, remembering something else. "He said to 'come back to him'. He wants us to find him!" He didn't mention the bit about his father. That was too much to think about right now.

"Great," Aaron said cheerily. There was a long pause. "So, where do we look, then?"

"We should ask the girls," Dion said.

"Are you joking, mate?" Aaron argued. "After last time? That Sabrina nearly took your head off!"

"They know something. We'll have to try again."

"If we could get Sammi River on her own, she might tell us," Timothy suggested. "Maybe."

"Well, I'm not going near them," Aaron declared. "And anyway, we don't even know if this Rith bloke is going to help us! What if he wants to kill us, or something?"

Lucas was certain this wasn't so, and he said as much. They argued back and forth for a while, until the approach of Mr Pring on one of his nightly patrols silenced them. They drifted back to sleep, troubled and undecided.

*

As it happened, Sammi River actually came to them the next day. The boys were out in the woods, keeping out of sight of Graves and Mr Pring on the basis that if they couldn't be found, they couldn't get into trouble. There had always been clashes and skirmishes between the two gangs in the past, and even once or twice outright fighting, but things had taken an altogether more sinister turn since the Dream (with a capital 'D', as they now thought of it). Graves and his crew could do some real damage now. It seemed they had the upper hand for the moment.

Aaron was subdued that day. He was growing more annoyed that he didn't seem to be manifesting any new abilities. It was causing him to be a bit snappy with his friends.

They were skulking around near the brook, idly tossing stones into the water. Swarms of mayflies traced erratic paths over the stream, circling endlessly. A heaviness hung in the still, humid air.

"Someone's coming," Dion announced. They all raised their heads.

"Who?" Timothy asked. They didn't need or want any clashes today.

"Girls." They all jumped to their feet, memories of yesterday's events at the bower still fresh in their minds. They spread out silently, tense and alert.

There were only two girls, as it turned out, though that did little to ease the boys' nerves. Sammi River came first, peering over her shoulder nervously as she approached. A little way behind her, Tamsen Nicoletta followed with a guarded expression. They stopped warily as they spotted the boys.

Aaron stepped forward. "What do you want?"

Sammi and Tamsen glanced at each other. "We…we were wondering," Sammi began, "if you could – maybe help us?"

Aaron looked annoyed, but Lucas cut him off quickly. This could be a good thing.

"To do what?" He kept his voice level.

This time it was Tamsen who spoke. "Strange things are going on," she said, understating the situation somewhat. Her voice was quiet, throaty and dignified. She moved forward, coming to stand bravely in front of Lucas. He felt Aaron forming up protectively beside him.

Tamsen looked at them both for a moment, one eyebrow raised. She continued, "And we heard," she licked her lips nervously, "that you were involved. You boys, I mean."

Lucas said nothing, unsure what she was getting at. Aaron fidgeted beside him.

"Why don't you talk to your 'Girls Only Club' about it?" he demanded.

Tamsen snorted. "What, those idiots? Fat lot of good that would do."

The boys exchanged surprised looks. What was this, dissent in the ranks of their enemies?

Tamsen watched them shrewdly. "Oh, don't be surprised," she said. "That whole 'girls only' thing never really appealed to me. I just went along with it because it was quite funny at first. And Sabrina – she's a bit of a..." she searched for an appropriate word.

"Nutter?" Aaron supplied, and she beamed at him. He blushed deeply.

"I was going to say 'tyrant', but that works too," she agreed.

"So now you come to us," Lucas said, intrigued. "But, why? What can we do for you?"

"And what about her?" Timothy put in, gesturing to Sammi. She gazed back at him with frightened eyes. Tamsen raised her eyebrows at her, prompting her.

"Sabrina frightens me," Sammi said in a little voice. "More and more. Yesterday, she – she hurt me…" she broke off, holding up her arm. A dark bruise encircled her wrist and forearm. There were distinct finger marks in it.

She looked at Lucas. "The other day, you said you wanted to talk," she said. "About the dreams. We think they're important, too."

Lucas wondered if he could trust them. He glanced at Dion for confirmation, who raised his eyebrows back at him noncommittally. "Okay," Lucas decided. "Why don't you tell us what you know?"

Sabrina Celestine stomped down the corridor and flung open the door of her dormitory. It was empty. "Lois!" she called out. Her friend trotted obediently up to her side.

"Yes, Sabrina?" Lois said placidly. Lois Christie was a skinny girl with dark blond hair, cut almost boyishly short. She sported unflattering thick glasses, and tended to squint. Sabrina enjoyed her company because she was so easy to boss around.

"Go find Dana, tell her to meet me in the common room straight away," she ordered. She glared at the empty room almost as though it had insulted her. She'd been sure she would find Sammi and Tamsen skulking in there. Where could they be? They hadn't said anything to her about going off on their own!

"Okay," Lois said amiably and scampered off down the hall.

Sabrina felt she was losing control these days. No one had any respect for her authority anymore! With a put-upon sigh, she wheeled around and went to find Marshall. His cold charm was usually just the thing to calm her down.

"In my dream, there were big rocks, floating around everywhere," Sammi said with a trace of embarrassment. She cast her eyes down. "Sounds stupid, doesn't it?"

"This whole thing is pretty mad," Timothy demurred. Dion waggled his eyebrows at him, which he ignored. "We all had weird dreams that night."

Sammi flashed him a look of gratitude. "Sabrina always told me to shut up about it."

"Yeah, well that's why you came to us."

"Do you remember anything else?" Lucas asked her. He'd been thinking hard, but he couldn't remember anything about flying rocks.

"Something about a big room, and stars glittering. There might have been…some kind of voice, or something."

"The voice," Timothy said to Lucas, who nodded.

Tamsen was watching them intently. She did that a lot, Lucas noticed. She listened very carefully to everything around her, only giving her opinion when she was fully ready.

"Well, I dreamt about a big room too," Dion said, "sort of circular and low, with no ceiling." He thought for a second. "Or maybe it was a glass ceiling. Also, something with big, glowing eyes. Hey, a bit like in Dana Jackson's dream, now I think about it."

Tamsen looked puzzled. "How do you know what Dana dreamt?"

"I can sort of…hear other people's thoughts. Sometimes, and only when I concentrate."

"Oh, come on," she scoffed, but Dion just smiled at her. "I'm not actually 'reading' you now," he said, "but I can tell that you believe me. Sort of. You've experienced something similar, haven't you? Something you can't explain, I mean."

She didn't say anything, just looked back at him, troubled.

"What about your dream, Tamsen?" Lucas said to break the awkward silence.

She sucked her lip. "Pretty much like yours, the round room, the yellow lights, the twisty corridors, the voice. I wasn't frightened. I felt – like I was doing something important. But there's something else."

Lucas felt a sudden tightness in his chest. "What?"

"It's the reason I knew I could come to you about this." She looked him coolly in the eye. "I saw you there.

"All of you."

Chapter Seven – Taking Sides

Growing angrier with every step, Sabrina stormed along the corridors of Peregrine House, scattering smaller children unheedingly as she passed. Marshall Graves was nowhere to be found. Was everyone hiding from her?

She shoved open the door to the common room with unthinking force. It flew back in a blur, handle crushing the plastered wall into powder where it hit. She didn't care.

"Dana," she called, spotting her friend waiting for her. Lois Christie sat meekly next to her. Apart from them, the room was empty.

Dana looked at her in concern. "Sabrina, calm down. Whatever's the matter?"

Sabrina plumped into a chair, a thunderous expression on her face. "Where is everyone?" she complained, realising she sounded slightly silly and petulant. She was getting so angry over nothing! She took a deep breath, imposing calm on herself.

"Tamsen and Sammi said they were going flower picking down by the stream," Dana explained. "Who else are you looking for? Marshall?"

Sabrina gave her a sullen look. "Of course not," she lied, feeling foolish. If Marshall wanted to hide from her, it was his loss.

"I'll check," Dana said, closing her eyes in concentration. She'd been practicing, ever since the dream last weekend and her discovery of this new ability. Sabrina didn't approve, of course, but sometimes it was handy having someone like Dana around, especially when she wanted someone found. Dana thought the whole thing was wonderful, and didn't hide it.

She didn't look too happy now, though. "That's odd," she muttered. "I can't hear Marshall. I've found his horrible friends, but not Marshall." She opened her eyes. "He's nowhere."

"Don't be silly," Sabrina chided her. "He's probably just sulking somewhere."

"No, I'm serious," Dana said earnestly. "I can find where people are by following the sound of their thoughts, like a trail they leave behind. I know the sound of Marshall's mind, it's quite distinct, and I'm telling you, he's not here."

That was impossible. No child was allowed off the premises, especially not during the summer holidays. "Well, that must mean there's something wrong with *you*, then," Sabrina said nastily. "*If* you can manage it, tell me where Tamsen and Sammi are. They've been gone for ages!"

Dana scowled, but did as she was told. After a second she nodded slowly. "Yes, they're in the woods," she confirmed. She frowned. "There's someone there with them. Boys!"

Sabrina jumped up as though electrified. "Some horrid boys have got them? Are they okay?"

Dana looked puzzled. "Yeah, they're fine. They're just…sitting around, talking."

Sabrina's anger level began to rise again. "Who?" she said through gritted teeth, though she already suspected the answer.

Dana winced. "It's Lucas Fortune," she admitted, "and his little pals."

"Is that right!? Come on!"

"You dreamt about us?" Aaron repeated incredulously. A sly look crossed his face. "Was I there?"

"I told you, it was all of us," Tamsen confirmed with a roll of her eyes. "We were all together."

"I remember a group of people," Lucas said, "but I couldn't see their faces."

"Me too," Timothy added. "The voice was speaking to us, telling us things. I don't know what."

An unpleasant tingling sensation crept down Lucas's back. "Do you know what I think?" he said slowly, assembling the thought as he spoke it. "We weren't just all dreaming at the same time. We were sharing the *same* dream."

Aaron frowned. "I don't get it," he confessed.

"He means," Dion clarified, "it's like the dream was happening somewhere else, and we were all watching it like a TV show, except – we were actually in it. Right, Lucas?"

Lucas tilted his head. "I'm not sure if that's right," he said, "but it's close enough for now."

"So where did the dream come from, then?" Aaron said quizzically. "Maybe it was that Rith, whoever he is."

Sammi started. "Rith?" she repeated. "Yeah, that was the name. He spoke to me."

Aaron made a disgusted noise. "Here's another question: why us, huh? What's so special about us?"

Once again, Lucas wanted to mention his father, but instead he kept his mouth shut. Of all the weirdness that was happening, his unknown father's possible involvement in it all was troubling him the most. He wasn't ready to speak about it yet. Worst of all, though, was he thought he knew the answer to Aaron's question. Could it be all to do with Lucas? Had his friends been dragged into something huge and scary because of him?

"Nothing's special about you!" a furious voice cut in. They spun round to see Sabrina Celestine advancing on them, Dana Jackson and Lois Christie in tow. Sammi gave a frightened peep and backed off hurriedly.

"You!" Sabrina cried, pointing a claw-like finger at Sammi. "What's going on here?"

"I'm sorry, Sabrina," Sammi mumbled. "We weren't doing anything wrong."

"You were talking to these filthy boys!" Sabrina corrected her. "What were you talking about? Tell me!"

Tamsen stepped directly in front of Sabrina, face calm. "Why don't you shut up for once, you horrible cow?" she said quite pleasantly.

It was like a bucket of cold water had been thrown over Sabrina. She gasped, face going white as a sheet, blinking rapidly. Her mouth opened and closed soundlessly, like a fish in the bottom of a boat.

"Ooo," Aaron muttered appreciatively. The other boys exchanged glances of surprise and amusement. No one had ever stood up to Sabrina before!

Dana and Lois stepped up to flank their stunned leader. "What did you say, Tamsen?" Dana said incredulously.

Tamsen gave her a look of regret. "Sorry, Dana, but someone had to say it."

Lucas was watching Sabrina, and he clearly saw what happened next. Colour rose into her cheeks, her eyes closing to slits. She raised a clenched fist and swung it all in one smooth motion at Tamsen's head. Lucas had no time to act or even cry out. The fist connected with the side of Tamsen's face…

…and carried on going straight through in a blurring arc, throwing Sabrina off balance. Tamsen stood unmoved as Sabrina twisted and cried out, toppling to the side, the momentum of her swing pulling her over. She fell onto Lois Christie and they both crashed to the ground.

There was a stunned silence. Tamsen put her hands on her hips, looking at Dana challengingly, who backed off immediately, bending to help her fallen friends.

"Why don't you just go away, Sabrina?" Tamsen suggested. "I don't like fighting. Just leave us alone, okay?"

Sabrina stared at her mutely, dried mud and leaves clinging to her white dress. She clambered to her feet, shaking off Dana's hand on her arm.

"Come on, Sabrina," Lucas put in reasonably. "No fighting, eh? Why don't you come and talk to us? Maybe we can help each other." He sent a friendly impression to her. Perhaps his own ability could help here.

Aaron made a strangled noise in his throat, shaking his head vigorously.

Sabrina transferred her silent gaze to Lucas, and for a moment he was taken aback at the sheer ferocity of loathing in her eyes. He knew then that she would never talk to them, never share her piece of the puzzle, not in a million years. Maybe not even he could placate someone with that much enmity…

"Sammi?" Sabrina croaked instead, burning eyes moving onto the tiny girl standing fearfully to one side. "Come along. Now."

Sammi went to follow, but Timothy stepped in front of her. "No," he said flatly. "She's staying with us."

Sabrina looked at him like he was mad. "You said what?"

"You're a bully, Sabrina," Timothy stated. "I don't like bullies. It's time you went."

"Is that so?" she said, beginning to regain some of her former poise. She brushed herself off, pointedly ignoring Tamsen now. Her anger had gone, transformed into something else, a kind of lunatic calm that made her eyes shine like little stars. She grinned. "What if I don't want to go?"

There was another silence. Tension hung in the air.

"Sabrina, this is pointless," Tamsen tried to placate her. "We're all in this together, can't you see that? You, me, these boys, even Marshall."

"Don't say his name," Sabrina hissed with knife-edge menace, still not looking at her. "Ever. Understand?"

"You can't hurt me, Sabrina," Tamsen informed her. "Not anymore."

Sabrina finally turned her megawatt gaze on Tamsen, grinning again. Tamsen, despite herself, swallowed and took a half step back. "Maybe not," Sabrina said. "But *she* can. Lois?"

Lois Christie smiled vacantly and pointed a finger at Tamsen. The air between her and Tamsen shimmered like a heat haze. Something struck Tamsen in the chest, knocking her off her feet with great force. She tumbled backwards with a whoosh as the air was forced from her lungs, landing in an untidy heap some distance away. She lay gasping, staring at the sky in shock and pain.

Aaron started forward, and immediately Lois's finger swung round to point at him. She was still smiling in a frighteningly empty way. Aaron stopped dead. It must have been like looking down the barrel of a gun, wielded by a vacant child.

"Anyone else?" Sabrina challenged. No one moved. "Didn't think so. Sammi? I told you to come away."

Reluctantly, Sammi went to join the girls. This time no one stopped her.

"You're out of the Club, Tamsen," Sabrina pronounced as though this were the worst punishment imaginable. "We don't ever want to see you again. You're welcome to these boys. Who else would want them?" She laughed at her own joke, Dana and Lois joining in. Lois lowered her hand, while Sammi stared blankly at the ground.

"Let's leave these losers to…whatever it is losers do. Come on." She swept away, taking her followers with her.

Aaron rushed over to Tamsen, squatting next to her. She looked up at him dazedly, wheezing and clutching her chest. His lip trembled slightly. He looked like he wanted to reach out and help her, but he just sat there uncertainly. Boys didn't touch girls!

Tamsen didn't seem to know that rule. She grasped his arm shakily and pulled herself into a sitting position, grimacing. "That went well," she groaned. Aaron guided her carefully to her feet. "Thanks," she said to him with a weak smile. "I'm alright, just a bit shook up. That hurt."

"Okay," Aaron said dumbly, staring at Tamsen's hand still on his arm.

Lucas looked around at his friend's shocked faces, sharing their dismay at what had just happened. "This is bad," he said. Four pairs of eyes turned to him mutely. "Sabrina, Lois, Dana, even Myles Lovell," he continued, "all the people who don't like us, all with the power to really hurt us if they want to." He paused. "My ability didn't seem to have much effect on Sabrina just now, though. Maybe I need to practice more."

"This is wrong," Timothy said unhappily. "I don't like it at all."

"It's not as if we're completely powerless, though, is it?" Dion interjected. "I mean, some of us can do – stuff too. Did you see what Tamsen did?" He looked at her quizzically. "Yeah, Tamsen, what did you do?"

And just like that, Tamsen was now one of them.

She sat uncomfortably on an old tree stump. Aaron hovered nearby. "I found out about it a few days after the dream," she replied. She looked slightly sick. "I can sort of make myself – thin, like smoke." She made a face. "It feels weird."

"We're all different," Lucas articulated the thought as it occurred. It was like climbing a ladder; each new piece of information was a new rung, allowing him to climb higher towards – whatever was at the top. "But I don't get it. Why has this happened to us? And what are we supposed to do now?"

Timothy said impatiently, "Look, this getting us nowhere. We're just going round in circles."

"How do you mean?"

"I'm not sure we'll get any answers by talking amongst ourselves. We just don't know enough. Maybe the only one who does is this Rith."

"But we don't know anything about Rith," Dion protested. "Who he is, even where he is! We can't ask him anything if we can't find him! Where do we look?"

Lucas turned to look through the trees. "That way," he said, pointing.

"Huh? How do you know that?"

Lucas shrugged. "Not sure. I just have a feeling." In his head he saw the cold stone room from his dream again. Would it hold any answers? He didn't know, but something was telling him to go there…

"But there's nothing through there, just the outside wall," Aaron argued.

"No, it's much farther than that. Kilometres, I think."

The others looked at each other in dismay. "But – we can't leave the House," Dion said. "And even if we could, there's no way we could go kilometres. Is there?"

Lucas shook his head doubtfully. "We'll have to think of a way."

*

Sabrina slouched in her seat in the bower, staring pensively into space. For some reason she wasn't angry, or at least not spitting mad. Instead, she felt a cold, hard core of something deep down inside, like a ball of iron in her belly, a magnet pulling her thoughts inward.

Tamsen had betrayed her, gone over to the enemy. Worse, she'd made Sabrina look foolish in front of that Fortune boy and his buddies. It was something Sabrina had never experienced before. Usually people just did what she wanted, especially if she shouted loud enough. In her experience people needed someone strong to show them what to do.

The remaining members of the G.O.C. sat in thoughtful silence around her. Lois was absently brushing Dana's hair, eyes distant. The skinny blonde girl had never been much of a one for conversation, and recently she'd been speaking even less. Sabrina approved of that, in a distant sort of way. Lois never questioned Sabrina's orders or argued with her, just did as she was told. A useful trait.

Dana Jackson, on the other hand, could sometimes be a bit of a pain. She was pretty smart, though obviously not as smart as Sabrina, and sometimes showed open disapproval of Sabrina's ideas. Having said that, though, she did generally go along with those ideas anyway. Sabrina possessed just enough self-awareness to be able to appreciate that not all different viewpoints were necessarily wrong.

Just most of them.

That left Sammi River, little Sammi the mouse, who was usually so quiet she seemed to fade into the background. Sabrina had never quite been able to figure the girl out, not that she'd spent much time trying. Sammi didn't do much for the Club and she cried on an almost daily basis, it seemed. Sabrina had very little time for such weakness. On any other day she might even have been inclined to let Sammi stay with Tamsen and that Fortune boy, and good riddance to her, but now…

No, it was a matter of principle. People had to know that Sabrina was not someone to mess with, especially weaklings like little Sammi the mouse. And with Sabrina's newly discovered abilities –

She clamped down on that thought hurriedly. She was supposed to be a young lady, not some super-strong freak! The other girls were changing too, but that was okay, as long as they knew who was in charge. Sabrina could use them. But herself? No, she just preferred not to think about it.

Sammi needed to be taught another lesson, that much was clear. It seemed their little talk the other day had not been enough. Sabrina turned the problem over idly in her mind, until there came a heavy knock at the door.

"Hello?" a dull, male voice called. Had that Fortune boy come back to gloat? Sabrina jumped up in eager anticipation, but Dana shook her head.

"It's only Billy Elsdon," she said. "He's got a message for you."

"It's me, Billy," the voice called. "I've got a message for Sabrina." There was a pause. "Uh, from Marshall."

Sabrina sneered. So, now Marshall wanted to come crawling back, did he?

She wrenched the door open.

"Do tell," she said sweetly.

The Elsdon boy stood there nervously. "Marshall says he wants to see you," he mumbled, scarlet cheeked, not meeting her eyes. Sabrina couldn't help but smirk. At least this buffoon showed her the appropriate respect.

"Oh, really?"

Elsdon fidgeted. "Um, yeah. He said to meet him by the Well. It's important."

Sabrina looked down her nose at him. "I'm busy."

"He said you might say that, and to tell you it's about Fortune. Marshall knows something."

Sabrina perked up a little at that. "What about Fortune?" she demanded.

Apparently unable to improvise, Elsdon stuck to repeating what he'd been told. "Marshall says to meet him by the Well, in half an hour." He backed off, then lumbered hurriedly away.

Sabrina watched him go, a frown creasing her forehead. What was that all about?

Dana came to stand beside her. "You should go."

"Oh, should I? Who asked you?"

"I think it's important," Dana continued resolutely. "Elsdon didn't know, and I still can't hear Marshall, but it's something big."

Sabrina thought about it. "Okay," she decided. "I'll go. But you're all coming with me."

Inside the bower, Sammi began to cry.

Chapter Eight – More Questions Than Answers

Marshall Graves was seated calmly on the ground when Sabrina found him. She had meant to keep her stony expression in place, to show him that he was not really all that interesting to her, but the moment she saw him her heart gave a lurch in her chest.

Dana looked at her sidelong, the corners of her mouth twitching.

Behind them came Lois Christie, humming merrily to herself whilst dragging a sniffling Sammi River by the wrist. They all stopped and regarded the scene.

"Hello, Sabrina," Marshall greeted her pleasantly. He surveyed them critically. "You brought your friends, I see. That's good, this concerns them too." He rose smoothly to his feet, and once again Sabrina was impressed by his height. He was filling out to be a pretty husky young man. They made a good match, she'd always thought.

"Where have you been, Marshall?" Sabrina heard herself saying. Darn! She hadn't wanted to show him her concern.

He smiled thinly. "Nowhere," he replied. Billy Elsdon and Myles Lovell loomed up behind him. They were pretty big too, Sabrina noted nervously.

Marshall cocked his head. "Aren't you one short? I thought there were five of you in your little...'club'."

Sabrina frowned at his mildly mocking tone. "Tamsen, she – she decided not to come."

Marshall shrugged, already losing interest. "Whatever." He beckoned them closer. Next to him was the overgrown shape of the Well, the old manor house's original water source, now long disused and covered with a heavy duty metal grid. Ivy climbed over it, and flowers grew from cracks between its crumbling bricks. Set in a small walled-off garden some distance from the house, it had always been a popular meeting place for the children, but not so much recently; Marshall had taken to coming here often, and the other kids knew better then intrude on his chosen domain. Noisy rooks also frequented the place, screaming their harsh cries from the surrounding pine trees.

The children gathered around Marshall in an uncomfortable, loose huddle. He watched them all with an aloof expression, especially Dana, who wore a look of perplexity on her face as she stared at him. Sabrina gave her a little shove, and she looked down at her feet quickly.

"What's happening, Marshall?" Sabrina said warily. She had a strange creeping feeling, a shiver down her back. For some reason, she found she didn't want to get much closer to him. There was something wrong with his eyes, she realised. There'd never been much warmth in them at the best of times, but now they looked dead, like the eyes of a shark, flat and soulless.

"That's the question, isn't it?" he said. "What, and why?"

The others waited, puzzled.

"The 'what' - well, I know about as much as you, I'm afraid. Some of us seem to be...*changing*." He spat the word, almost like it offended him. A dark frown contorted his fine features, and once again Sabrina felt a small shudder. Energy seemed to radiate from him in throbbing waves.

"I don't know about the rest of you," he went on after a moment or two, "but I find it bothers me a bit."

Sabrina had the impression he was understating his feelings considerably. Something warred behind his flat expression, something dangerous, something he was struggling to keep under control.

"I don't know what you mean," Sabrina said out loud. This was skirting perilously close to her own issues, which she had no wish to air right now.

Marshall gave her a withering look. "Your self-denial makes me tired, Sabrina," he snarled. "You're stupid if you think you can pretend nothing is happening."

Ordinarily she would have bridled at that, rising up to answer the challenge head on, but this time some tiny shred of common sense held her back, like survival instinct. Arguing with Marshall right now felt like a very bad idea…

Instead she looked back at him in sullen silence.

He went on, "I've heard that some of you have been…" he licked his lips, "…*enjoying* your changes. Like they're a *good* thing. Like you're better off."

Lois Christie chose this unfortunate moment to finally speak. "But, Marshall, they are a good thing," she said brightly. "Have you seen what I can do? Look." She held up a hand and pointed at a rook that was circling above them. The air between her fingertip and the unsuspecting bird shimmered, like heat radiating from a hot road. The rook gave a startled cry and spun off to one side, shedding feathers from its wing. It began spiralling, calling out in desperation, spinning lower and lower until it plummeted behind the tops of the trees with a crash. It didn't come out again.

There was a frozen moment. Marshall stared at Lois with a puzzled expression, as if she'd suddenly gone green or grown an extra nose. Sabrina moved carefully away from her.

Marshall surprised them then by suddenly bursting into laughter. He slapped his leg, pointing his other hand like an imaginary gun at Lois. He mimed pulling the trigger, which only made him laugh even harder. A nervous ripple of laughter passed around the group in accompaniment.

It ended as quickly as it had begun, the amusement fading from Marshall's face like a snowflake melting on a windowsill. Lois carried on tittering unheedingly.

With a snarl Marshall raised his arm and crooked his fingers in a grabbing motion at Lois, who was standing some distance away. Several metres separated them, yet she yelped in alarm as she was jerked into the air as though on invisible wires, struggling, her arms pinned immobile to her sides.

"You see?" Marshall grated, closing his fingers slowly. Lois's cries became breathless squeals, her feet kicking frantically in thin air. "This is exactly the kind of thing I'm talking about."

Sabrina looked about her in alarm. How was Marshall doing this? The stupid girl had brought it on herself, it was true, but Lois was a member of the G.O.C., one of Sabrina's gang. It was Sabrina's job to look out for them, wasn't it? How would it look if she just let Lois suffer like this?

Then she glanced at Marshall, at his twisted expression, his waxen skin. What could she do?

Paralysed by indecision, she watched numbly as Dana Jackson pushed past her, running straight at Marshall. Immediately Billy Elsdon stepped forward into Dana's path, blocking her. Dana dropped her shoulder to barge him out of the way.

Billy was considerably larger than her, but Dana was also quite strong and agile herself. She played netball and tennis, and was a keen swimmer. She should have been at least able to move Elsdon. Instead she bounced off him like she had run into a brick wall. Elsdon didn't move a centimetre, just smiled cruelly as Dana spun to the side with a surprised grunt. She clutched at her shoulder, grimacing in pain as she fell.

Sammi was rooted to the spot, eyes round and horrified. Lois continued to kick and shriek as she hung impossibly in the air, drawing great racking breaths into her constricted lungs, eyes bulging. That left Sabrina. She turned fearfully to face Marshall, wondering what she was going to do…

Marshall opened his hand suddenly, allowing Lois to crumple to the ground. She drew a great gasping breath, feet still kicking as though her legs were trying to run away. With a shocked expression she propped herself up on her elbows, shaking her head to clear her vision.

"This is what happens," Marshall said in an almost apologetic tone, abruptly perfectly calm. He gave a slow head-shake in apparent sorrow. "It makes us fight amongst ourselves. We should be working together."

Dana struggled to her feet, glaring daggers at Elsdon, who smirked at her. She went across and helped Lois to her feet, favouring her bad shoulder.

Sabrina watched all this in silence. She found her voice. "Working together? Doing what, Marshall?"

"I said I didn't know *what* was happening to us, but I think I may know why," he replied with a knowing expression. All eyes turned to him, which he acknowledged with a nod. "You remember the dream, the one we all had?"

Heads nodded.

"Well, Billy and Myles here have told me what they dreamt, and some of it matches up with what I remember. I expect you girls had similar experiences. But I dreamt something else, too." He paused for effect, making sure everyone was listening intently.

"I think this was done to us by chance," he declared. "We just happened to be near when it came for him."

"Who?" Sabrina asked, not sure where this was going.

"Who do you *think?* The voice in my dream was talking to him, like it knew him, like he was special. It needed him, but not as he was, so it *improved* him. We were just taken along for the ride."

"Marsh, I don't –" she began, but he cut her off with an impatient gesture.

"Lucas Fortune," he hissed, real venom behind his words. "This is all his fault. He's the reason this has happened to us." He turned his black gaze directly upon her then.

"And one more thing, Sabrina," he said flatly, "don't call me Marsh. Ever."

*

The subdued atmosphere still pervaded Peregrine House that evening, a heaviness that pressed down on everyone like a physical weight. Conversation was stilted, heads bowed in quiet contemplation. On a normal Saturday night the common room was a place of laughter and bright chatter, but tonight the children sat around in sullen groups, staring out of windows or half-heartedly playing board-games in glum silence. Summer activity weeks were coming up soon, but even the thought of these did little to lighten the general mood.

Lucas felt it too. Sitting alone, it felt as though the whole place was waiting for something, some event like a thunderstorm to release the tension. What with everything that was happening around here, it was not hard to believe that it would involve him somehow…

He sighed. After the events in the woods that afternoon, it now seemed even more pressing to him that he find some answers for his friends. There was no suggestion they resented him in any way, yet he couldn't help feeling responsible all the same. Both Dion and Tamsen had already suffered directly at the hands of Sabrina's little gang. Who knew what would happen next?

As if in response to his thoughts, a distant rumble of thunder sounded from the west, from the direction of Dartmoor. A warm breeze stirred through the open windows, setting the curtains undulating. The children shifted uneasily. It was not yet fully dark outside, the clear sky the colour of a plum where the sun had set, shading to purple and navy blue overhead. The first stars were coming out. The chorus of rooks that lived by the Well had fallen silent, earlier than usual tonight.

At least his friends were with him, Lucas's thoughts continued, even if they weren't physically in the room right now. He didn't know how he would cope without their support. If only he knew what to do! He felt an urge to move, to get away, to take his friends with him to a place of safety. The comfortable environs of Peregrine House no longer felt like the (relatively) safe haven they'd once been.

"Lucas Fortune?" a voice said, startling him out of his reverie. He craned around to see.

It was Rowan Cole, an older boy who could often be seen running errands for Fishy or Mr Pring. Some said he was the House's longest serving resident. Indeed, Lucas couldn't remember a time when the skinny, ungainly youth couldn't be found mooching around the place.

"Yes?" Lucas said politely. He had no memory of the boy ever speaking directly to him before. What could he want?

Rowan looked around furtively. Mr Pring was currently on the other side of the room, berating a young lad who'd dropped a set of chess pieces on the floor. "Not here," Rowan murmured. "I've got something to tell you. Meet me outside by the bin shed in ten minutes."

"We're not allowed outside after dark," Lucas reminded him, suspicious.

"Exactly," Rowan replied, rolling his eyes. "No one will look for us there."

Lucas raised his eyebrows. "Forget it."

"Look, I know you don't know me, but I reckon you'll want to hear this. You'll have to trust me."

Lucas gave him a steady look. "If it's so important, why not just tell me now?"

Rowan looked around again. Mr Pring had spotted them, was looking over at the two of them oddly. "I can't, okay? Just do as I say." He paused, aware he was not convincing Lucas. "It's about the night you came here," he hissed. He turned on his heel and strode away, keeping one of his hands behind his back out of sight of Mr Pring. Something dropped from his palm and hit the carpeted floor with a muted thump.

Lucas watched the older boy go in a sudden daze. The night he'd come here? He knew nothing about that time, save the meagre information Fishy had been willing to give out in the past; how he'd been given over to the care of Peregrine House, how Fishy had taken him in out of the goodness of her heart with no thought of reward, and how his parents had recently been back in contact, wanting to see him again. How could Rowan Cole know anything about that?

The boy had been right about one thing, however; Lucas did want to hear what he had to say. He looked down at the object Rowan had dropped. It was a key, the attached label reading 'KITCHEN: REAR.' He leaned down and scooped it up in one quick motion.

Rowan had already gone, Mr Pring frowning after him. The old man turned his attention to Lucas now, glaring at him as though daring him to commit an act of mischief. Lucas looked away, thinking quickly. How could he get out from under Mr Pring's suspicious gaze? If he tried to leave so soon after his odd conversation with Rowan Cole, Pring would surely know something was up.

His eyes settled on a possible solution. It might work, but how to do it from here? Maybe he could…

He concentrated on what he wanted, not at all sure if anything would happen. Did it only work on people? Nothing happened. Lucas began to relax, feeling slightly foolish. Then –

From across the room the TV set suddenly switched itself on, raucous music blaring. A group of young children who were clustered idly near it jumped up with a cry of alarm. Mr Pring's reaction was equally electric. He seemed to rise up on the balls of his feet, swelling in indignation like a shabby hot-air balloon.

"What do you think you're doing?" he screamed at the children, instantly forgetting about Lucas. He rushed towards the group of cowering children, intent on punishment for this dreadful transgression.

Behind him, Lucas slipped quietly from the room.

Lucas felt a little bad for leaving those young children to deal with Mr Pring, but he suspected they wouldn't be in serious trouble. There was no way to switch on the TV directly anyway. The set was in a cabinet, the drop-down control panel glued shut, the remote kept in a locked drawer elsewhere in the House. Mr Pring would realise this, once he calmed down, and think it must have been some sort of weird electrical accident.

But aside from that, Lucas was pretty pleased that he'd managed to use his abilities so effectively. His suppositions had turned out to be correct, as far as they went. As well as persuading people, it seemed he could also coax inanimate objects into doing his bidding. He stopped dead in the corridor as a flash of comprehension suddenly hit him. He finally realised what had actually happened after he'd woken from the Dream, when he'd been scrabbling about in the dark for the bathroom light switch. His own abilities must have flicked the switch for him, because he'd been thinking so hard about it! That meant his changes had actually manifested much sooner than he'd thought, immediately after waking from the Dream itself.

But what about the glowing light bulb in the corridor? He was pretty sure that hadn't been him. In fact, now he thought about it, hadn't it been Aaron who'd been complaining about the darkness then? Interesting. Lucas resolved to think some more about that later.

He let himself cautiously into the dining room, which was deserted at this time of night. Steel shutters were down over the serving hatches from the kitchen. Near to these shutters was another door marked 'Staff Only'. Lucas gave it a hopeful shove. It resisted for a second, then gave with an audible click. He was learning to use his new...powers, for want of a better word. For a brief moment he felt like some sort of spy or secret agent, on a mission that only he could accomplish.

He smiled tightly as he padded across the darkened kitchen, peering around him. No child was allowed in here. If he was caught, he would be in serious trouble, maybe even sent to the Room. He'd been to the Room a few times in the past for various reasons, and it was no joke. It meant several days of isolation and, sometimes, no food at all. He was not anxious to go back. But that was what made things like this fun; the danger of getting caught!

The rear door to the outside world was illuminated from above by a green exit sign. To one side hung a row of white coats, matching white shoes arranged neatly beneath them. The only other illumination in the echoing kitchen came from an ultraviolet bug light on the far wall. Lucas fumbled the key into the lock. Sometimes the old ways were still useful.

A warm gust of damp, humid air blew past him as the heavy door swung outwards. It was almost fully dark now, and Lucas's heart began to speed up even more. He'd only ever been outside at night once before, and that little episode had earned him a three day spell in the Room a year previously. He shook off the memory and stepped cautiously into the dark.

"Over here, Fortune," Rowan called in a loud whisper from the direction of the bin shed. A tall silhouette appeared briefly, beckoning. With one last glance around, Lucas scurried over to join him.

Rowan's face was a grim oval in the gloom. "Feels pretty good to be out, eh?" he said, teeth flashing in the dark.

Lucas nodded nervously. "Yeah, kind of. So, why did you get me to come out here?"

"Ah, straight to business. Okay, that's cool." Rowan paused to gather his thoughts. "Well, it's like this: I'm going to tell you something I probably shouldn't. Something I'm not supposed to know, and something you were probably never supposed to find out. That a good enough reason?"

"I guess," Lucas said, intrigued. "You said something about my parents?"

Rowan cocked his head. "No, I didn't. I said something about the night you came here. I never saw your parents."

"Oh." Lucas was crestfallen. "What, then?"

Rowan licked his lips. "Okay, I'm telling you this because – well, you remind me of myself when I was your age. We're in a similar situation, you and I; we've both spent pretty much our entire lives here. Everything I know is here." He turned and spat into the dark. "And now they're making me leave. Know why?"

Lucas shook his head dumbly.

"Because I turn eighteen next week. That makes me an adult, and 'no longer entitled to the care of Peregrine House'. After all I've done for this place, for them!"

Lucas said nothing.

"I know things," Rowan went on darkly, "things that have happened around here, the sort of things old Fishy wouldn't want Juvenile Services to hear about. She thinks I'm just a dumb kid, but I remember a lot." He tapped his head. "It's all up here."

"I'm sorry," Lucas said quietly. After his near deportation to the Mill last week, he had a pretty good idea what Rowan must be going through. "But, why are you telling me this?"

"I told you, we're the same. This may happen to you some day, so pay attention to what goes on around here. You may be able to use it." He paused. "Anyway, I might as well tell you what I know about your situation. I've got no reason not to, now."

"Okay. Go on then."

"I was there, the night you arrived. Old Man Pring had me swiping food from the kitchen for him and Fishy, so I happened to be in Fishy's office when you were brought in. It was late wintertime, cold and rainy. I remember that because you were all wet in your basket from the rain. They left you on the doorstep, you see."

Lucas had a horrible sinking sensation. "Who did?" he said faintly.

"Your parents, I presume. I never saw them. Old man Pring must have found you, brought you in. They did leave this, though." He handed a folded piece of paper to Lucas, who took it with trembling hands. Surely it couldn't be true? His parents had abandoned him? He knew he was a foundling, it was no secret around the House, but he'd never known exactly how it had happened. Left outside in the rain? Fishy had never mentioned that! He unfolded the paper, squinting at it. He had to angle it into the faint light afforded by the emerging stars to see it at all. He read the words written all those years ago, tears blurring his vision.

"Mrs Fisher and staff;

Please take care of our son. His name is Lucas Warren Fortune, he will be 1 year old on May 5th, and his mother and I love him very much, but we can't look after him properly right now. We're deeply sorry we had to leave him with you in this manner. In addition to the money you have already received, please find enclosed with this letter a little extra to help cover the costs of his care, your inconvenience and, not to put too fine a point on it, your discretion.

We will send more money as soon as we can, and hopefully very soon we will be able to come and collect him.

Please take care of our precious boy, we beg you.

Thank You."

"Pring told me to destroy it," Rowan said softly, "but I decided to hang onto it, just in case."

"But, why?" Lucas whispered. "Why did they do it?"

"Your parents? That I can't answer. But I do know something else. Want to hear it?"

Lucas nodded numbly.

"Fishy's been promising you can meet your parents, hasn't she? Saying they've been in touch, wanting to see you?"

Lucas nodded again. He'd been clinging onto that hope for more than a year now.

Rowan shook his head fiercely. "Never happened. There's been no other contact from them since the day you arrived. Well, except for the money."

Lucas found his voice. "Money?" he croaked.

"Yes, old Fishy's done pretty well out of you over the years, Fortune. Have you checked out her office recently? All that fancy stuff in there doesn't just appear under the tree every Christmas. Whether or not your folks are really out there somewhere, and whatever their real reasons were for leaving you at Peregrine House, someone has been paying for you to stay here this whole time."

This was too much. Was everything he believed a lie? Had Fishy really been spinning him tales all his life, whilst skimming off the money that had been sent for him?

"And they never came back," he whispered to himself. He crumpled the note into a tight ball.

It was hard not to think badly of his parents right then. Why had they never come back? Why say they were going to come back in the note, and then not do it? It didn't make sense. Maybe…maybe something had happened to them. Maybe they hadn't been able to come back. Lucas desperately wanted to believe that, unpleasant as that thought was. It was better than the alternative...

Rowan was watching him silently. "Sorry you had to find out like this," he said. "But that's how it goes, Fortune. There are no happy endings, no parents suddenly turning up out of the blue to sweep you up and take you away. Better learn to toughen up, sunshine." He sounded bitter.

There was a noise from around the corner of the house, a door opening somewhere. Distant footsteps crunched on gravel, coming closer. Rowan pulled something from his pocket. Light flared, and Lucas realised he'd lit a cigarette.

"You'd better go, before Pring catches you," Rowan whispered around a mouthful of smoke. He waved the cigarette around. "Better he catches me with this than you out here. He can't do anything to me anyway. I'm out of here next week. Go on, go." He shoved Lucas roughly away.

Blindly, Lucas stumbled back to the kitchen door, just managing to pull it closed before a voice outside began berating Rowan for his filthy habits.

Lucas had no memory of how he did it, but somehow he made it back to his room just in time for lights-out.

Chapter Nine – Hiding The Truth

Lucas half-heartedly toyed with his cereal at breakfast next morning, mind far away. He hadn't slept well, only in fits, and was sandy eyed and listless. Aaron and Timothy were munching their way happily through their plates of toast and poached eggs, while Dion was doing his best not to intrude on Lucas's bleak mood, though he was clearly aware of it. Lucas appreciated his friend's discretion.

Everything seemed grey today, from the walls of the dining room to the faces of the other children, even the sky outside. It had rained in the night, but the distant thunderstorm had come no closer. The atmosphere was still heavy and damp with humidity.

There was to be a program of activities in the coming weeks, as there was every summer for the permanent residents, designed to keep the children occupied and out of mischief. Normally Lucas looked forward to this time with great anticipation as a welcome break from the normal routine. A group of enthusiastic twenty-somethings from the outside would descend on Peregrine House, taking it over for a brief time with their loud voices and trendy haircuts, whisking the kids off to Dartmoor for Tor climbing, or to the reservoir for swimming, or down to Exmouth for days at the beach. Fishy always kept a beady and unhappy eye on these proceedings. It was no secret that she disapproved of them whole-heartedly, but had to go along with them because they were organised directly by Juvenile Services.

Lucas couldn't summon much enthusiasm for the whole thing this year, though. The lists would be published later that day, usually a time of intense excitement as the children vied for places on the best trips, but Lucas didn't really care. He pushed the spoon around in his bowl idly.

At first he'd been bewildered at Rowan Cole's revelations, then tearfully upset, and finally angry with his parents for their inexplicable behaviour. He'd spent the night turning it over in his mind, the main theme being 'why?' What was the reason? He'd remembered something from the second dream at some point as he lay there in the dark; the voice of Rith had said that his father would have been proud of him. For what, he'd asked himself? And if the guy was so proud, why hadn't he come back? And so his thoughts had churned around uselessly until dawn.

During the process, though, he'd found his fury slowly redirecting towards another source. If, he reasoned, he couldn't get any answers from his actual parents, then there was someone here at Peregrine House who apparently knew more about the situation than they'd ever let on, at least to him. He thought about her now, and his fist clenched tightly around the spoon he was holding.

Deirdre Fisher.

Perhaps it was time they had a little chat.

The activity lists were published that afternoon, Mr Pring having to shove his way through the knot of eager children who'd gathered around the notice board outside the common room. He pinned up the list with a glower. Happy children were uncontrollable children, in his well-known opinion.

Lucas left his friends there and slipped away unnoticed, seizing the opportunity. With Pring occupied for a while it would be easier to get into Fishy's office. He hurried through the mostly empty corridors, passing the occasional child heading the other way. They gave him curious looks as he passed. His expression was bleak and preoccupied.

He paused outside Fishy's door, lifelong conditioning telling him to knock politely. He didn't feel very polite right now though, and the faint sound of Fishy's grating voice emanating from the other side only served to lower his brow even further. He grasped the handle and pushed the door open deliberately.

Fishy was sitting curled up on a green leather sofa to one side of the room, a telephone cradled to her ear. Soft piano music drifted from hidden speakers. A silver tea set rested on the oak coffee table in front of her, tea pot gently steaming.

She looked up in shock, mouth dropping open. Lucas came in and shut the door firmly behind him. He turned to face her silently, folding his arms. The sight of her sat there, all pale flesh and piggy little eyes in this comfortable little nest she'd built, seemed to solidify in Lucas's mind like a lead weight. He hadn't been entirely sure how and what he was going to say until now.

Fishy spoke first, though. "*What* –" she spluttered, incensed. She jumped to her feet. "Fortune!? How *dare* you come in here!"

Lucas stood unmoved. Once, he been frightened of her, as were most of the children under her 'care'. She was large and intimidating, and knew how to use that fact. Children would tremble under her glare, or run crying after one of her scoldings. Now, Lucas felt nothing but cold fury.

"Sit down," he suggested, prodding her with his mind. She froze where she stood, looking like an unpleasant sculpture. The telephone she still clutched in her hand gave a squawk. Very slowly, she sank back down onto the sofa.

"Tell them you'll call back, then hang up," Lucas continued.

Tremblingly, Fishy obeyed. "Jacob, I'll call you back later," she whispered into the mouthpiece. "What? Oh, nothing, just…something's come up. That's right. Bye." She pushed the end-call button.

She stared at Lucas uncomprehendingly, her mouth working.

"Yes?" Lucas said coolly. "Something bothering you? Say it, then."

She found her voice, or part of it. "I don't – I don't…"

"What? Understand? No, probably not, but that doesn't matter." He took a good look around the room, seeing it properly now he had leisure to do so. Rowan Cole had been right. It was packed full of expensive looking things, lead-crystal decanters, heavy ornaments, silk rugs hanging on the walls, and other things Lucas couldn't readily identify. He had little experience of such things outside of what he'd seen in books, but he suspected the stuff must have cost a pretty packet.

"You've done alright for yourself, haven't you, Deirdre?" he said.

She looked like she was going to explode.

"Calm," Lucas told her, and she immediately subsided like a bubble in a tar-pit, looking dazed.

"Luckily, I don't really care what you do with your money," Lucas went on. "Or should that be, my parents' money?" He moved over to the sofa, so that he was standing over her. She looked up at him blankly.

"That's right, isn't it?" Lucas pressed. "My parents' money? I mean, you've spoken to them, haven't you? How do they feel about how you've been spending their money?" He leaned closer. "Tell the truth."

She blinked rapidly. "They don't know," she said in a faraway voice. "I've never met them. But..."

"Yes?"

"There was – a man. He brought you here."

That made Lucas pause. "What man? Who was he?" This wasn't what Rowan Cole had told him...

"Don't know. The arrangements were made over the phone. Money was transferred before you ever got here. No names were given. I don't know anything about your parents."

"Oh, really? But, Deirdre, didn't you say they wanted to meet me?"

"Yes."

"Why would you say that?"

"To give you hope, to control you."

Lucas paused, feeling cold. "How?"

"You would behave better if you thought they were coming, if you thought I would stop that from happening if you misbehaved."

Lucas stared at her. "Is that right?" he said softly. "So that's why you let everyone believe I was a foundling, is it? No one else saw the man who brought me here, so you could say whatever you wanted, right? Even that I'd been abandoned on the doorstep?"

She visibly tried to pull herself together, some of the light returning to her eyes. "You wait 'til Mr Pring hears about this…" she managed.

"Sshh," Lucas said. She subsided again. Despite himself, his heart was racing faster. He'd sort-of known what to expect, but hearing the cold facts of his existence spilling directly from Fishy's thin lips sent a chill down his spine.

"Okay," he said. "So, what about the money, then?"

Fishy didn't answer, and he realised he hadn't been specific enough. "Where does the money come from?" He had only a sketchy notion of how the banking system worked.

"It arrives by courier post every month."

"Delivered straight here? No bank accounts or anything?"

Fishy shook her head.

"Who's sending it?"

"I don't know. Your parents, I presume."

"What do you mean, you don't know?"

"It comes in a plain envelope, cash, always the same amount, two thousand pounds in brand new fifty pound notes."

The amount meant nothing to Lucas. "If it's in a plain envelope, then how do you know it's got anything to do with me?"

"When you were first brought here I was given a note and some cash, exactly the same as the monthly deliveries since, all in new fifty pound notes."

This didn't make sense. In the letter, it had said that his parents would come back for him as soon as they could. Clearly, that had not happened. Instead, they'd apparently been sending regular, anonymous payments to Fishy for his upkeep. He didn't care that Fishy had squandered the money on herself, only that it represented a tangible link with his mysterious family. Were they still out there somewhere?

He turned his cold gaze on Fishy now. She shrank back fearfully in her seat. "Mrs Fisher," he said evenly, "I don't think you're really a bad person, just mean, selfish, small-minded and vindictive. Do you agree?"

"I'm mean, selfish, small-minded and vindictive," she repeated hollowly.

"That's right. Now, I think you should feel pretty bad about what you've done, don't you?"

"I'm sorry," she whispered, eyes glistening. Lucas relented. He took no pleasure in seeing her like this. It just wasn't in him to be so callous. He sighed, letting some of the anger drain from his body.

"Okay, Mrs Fisher. Now here's what we're going to do. I'm going to leave your office now and go back to my friends. You will wait five minutes, then carry on like nothing has happened. You won't remember this conversation. Understood?"

She nodded quickly. "Yes."

"You will, however, decide to be a bit nicer to the children from now on. In fact," he looked around the office again, "I think it would be nice if you spent some of your money on the children themselves. Okay?"

Fishy appeared to struggle with that one, so Lucas prodded her again. "Y-yes," she gasped. "Of course."

"Good." He went across to the door. "Bye, Fishy," he said impudently, and left.

Surprisingly, Lucas found himself feeling ambiguous about what had happened as he headed back to the common room. He didn't feel so angry now, but neither did he feel satisfied at having finally had it out with Fishy. She was a horrible person, it was true, but even so what Lucas had done in there didn't sit very easily with his conscience. When you looked at it from a different angle, it was little better than a bully twisting someone's arm up their back for their pocket money. If anyone deserved that kind of treatment it was Fishy, but still…

Well, it was done now, and at least he'd learnt something else useful. Thinking it over as he went, he hurried back to tell his friends about it, passing Mr Pring along the way. The old man stopped and gave Lucas a quizzical stare, but Lucas just kept his head down and carried on.

Mrs Fisher hummed to herself as she poured her tea. *That's funny*, she thought, *it's almost cold*. She'd only made it a minute ago. And she'd been talking on the phone too, hadn't she? She paused, trying to remember, but it all seemed a bit hazy.

There was a rapid series of knocks on the door, a pattern she knew well. "Come in, Tarquin," she called.

Mr Pring stalked into the room, face even more pinched than usual. He lowered himself carefully onto a stuffed chair with a grateful sigh.

Mrs Fisher regarded him. "Your back, again?"

"Hip, this time," he replied grimly. "Those damn kids don't make it any easier, making me rush around after them all the time."

"Oh, they're not all that bad," Mrs Fisher heard herself say. She paused, a small frown creasing her forehead. Mr Pring was looking at her oddly. "Anyway, those Service helpers will be here tomorrow," she blustered on self-consciously. "They'll take some of the little blighters off our hands."

"Yes, of course," Mr Pring agreed doubtfully. "I just saw that Fortune boy, skulking around the corridors. Up to no good, I expect."

Mrs Fisher said nothing. Lucas Fortune? Wasn't there something…?

"Are you alright, Deirdre?" Mr Pring asked her, worried. "You look a little pale."

"I…" she faltered, "I…I'm fine, thank you, Tarquin." Her office looked strange to her, like she no longer knew it properly. Some of the ornaments in it were quite ugly, she noticed. What had she been thinking when she'd bought them? "I think this place needs a bit of redecoration," she murmured.

Mr Pring leaned forward in his chair, perplexed. "Redecoration?" he repeated. "Deirdre, are you sure you're alright?"

"I told you, I'm fine!" she snapped. That seemed to satisfy Mr Pring, who was used to her imperious nature. He shrugged and reached out for the tea set.

Behind him, carefully concealed in amongst the topmost fronds of a tall rubber plant in the corner, the tell-tale red light of a security camera glowed steadily, watching and recording everything in the room with a dispassionate eye.

*

Anyone else would probably not have believed Lucas's story, but his friends accepted it without reservation, even with admiration.

"I don't know if it'll really work," Lucas finished his tale as they walked along the corridor, "I mean the bit about Fishy being nicer to everyone, but at least I got something useful out of her for once."

"Fantastic!" Aaron crowed, pounding him on the back.

Timothy smiled grimly. "You'd just better hope your memory trick holds," he said with his customary caution. "She'd go bats if she ever remembered."

"Hey, don't ruin this for us!" Aaron admonished him.

Dion cast his mind wide, eyes going blank for a moment while he concentrated. "She's feeling a little confused right now," he reported. "But she doesn't remember a thing. I think it'll be alright."

Tamsen made a face. "What, are you the expert on mind powers now?"

Dion turned a stony expression on her. "Around here, yes, I am," he intoned. Tamsen snorted, then turned to Lucas.

"I'm glad you know more about your family now, Lucas, but that doesn't really help us with our other problem," she said. "We still haven't figured out a way to find this Rith person. How are we going to get out of the House?"

Lucas was about to reply when he spotted something out of the corner of his eye. He stopped dead in the corridor where they were walking, an idea hitting him like a thunderbolt. Aaron walked into him with a grunt. Lucas turned to the notice board, upon which hung the lists of this year's summer activities.

"The same way we do every year," he answered with a slow grin.

*

Tarquin Pring found it very difficult to rest that evening. Something had been bothering him all afternoon, and it wasn't just his aching joints. Mischief had occurred somewhere in the House that day, he was certain of it.

He didn't know why he had such a finely-tuned ability to sense trouble, only that it had often come in very useful over the years. He put it down to his own misspent youth, filled with hell-raising and troublemaking of the worst kind, now thankfully long behind him. Having been on the wrong end of a birch cane on several occasions as a youngster tended to give one a heightened sense of the rightness and wrongness of things.

In any case, he felt it now, a little tingling across the back of his neck, and knew he'd been outfoxed. He also knew, with a cold, clammy certainty, that the Fortune boy was involved.

The lad had been acting suspiciously when he'd passed him in the corridor earlier that day, scurrying along like he was trying not to be noticed; the actions of someone with a guilty conscience, if Tarquin Pring was any judge. Yes, that boy was nothing but trouble. It seemed to follow him around like a cloud, and his little friends were no better.

How could he find out more about what Fortune had been up to? Perhaps someone had seen the boy, one of the few children who hadn't been crowding around the notice board like cattle around a feeding trough. Or perhaps one of the carers, or a cleaner?

With a dissatisfied snort Mr Pring shifted uncomfortably on his narrow bunk, jammed up under the window of his tiny attic room. *Tomorrow*, he thought acidly. *Then we'll find out what you were really up to, Lucas Fortune.*

Chapter Ten – The Plot Thickens

At nine a.m. on Tuesday morning three buses from Out & About arrived at Peregrine House. This was the company Juvenile Services employed to organise the activity weeks for the children. Staffed mainly by over-eager university students on voluntary placements, they had been coming to the House every summer for the last four years. Faces changed year by year as the volunteers moved on and new ones replaced them, but there was always one constant: Colin Herbert, the organiser of the group, an incredibly earnest fellow in his early thirties with watery grey eyes and an unkempt blond beard. He favoured shorts in all weathers, and prided himself on never getting angry.

He stepped from the lead bus and inhaled the country air, his hiking boots crunching on the gravelled driveway. He liked coming here every year. It was one of his favourite jobs. The children at Peregrine House were so polite, meek even. He couldn't say the same about that Mrs Fisher though, or her creepy deputy Mr Pring. They both looked like they'd never smiled in their whole lives. Funny how people of their sort often ended up running care institutions, he mused. There must be some part of them that cared, even if it was not that obvious…

Anyway, he wasn't here for them, but for the poor orphaned and abandoned kids, who must so look forward to his annual visits to bring some fun into their sad little lives. Secretly, he liked to think of himself as a sort of younger version of Santa Claus, bringing happiness and joy wherever he went.

With a contented little sigh he turned back to his small group of eager helpers and began to unload the buses.

"It's that Herbert bloke again," Aaron called from the window of the common room.

There was a small groan from the children within earshot, which included Lucas and his other friends. They'd just finished breakfast a few minutes earlier.

"He's weird," Dion said. He mimicked the man's customary chin-stroking pose, provoking much laughter from those around him. "Wonder what he'll be like this year?"

Colin Herbert was well-known for his often odd pronouncements and idiotic behaviour. He would stand and make grand speeches, heartfelt tears sometimes running down his cheeks, oblivious to the mocking giggles of his young audience as they made faces at him. One year he had slipped and fallen from a stepping stone in the river Dart, and then proceeded to give a lengthy talk on the correct procedure to be used when crossing water, while still standing knee-deep, weeds in his hair, caked in mud, water cascading from his shorts. The children had laughed about that for days.

He was well-meaning though, and relatively harmless. The children regarded him as a sort of bumbling, hairy clown.

According to the list on the notice board, the pick of this year's activities was to be a three day camping/hiking expedition to Dartmoor, complete with campfires, tents and marshmallow roasting (and probably earnest guitar-led singing if previous expeditions were anything to go by). Lucas and his friends had all signed up immediately, before all the places went. It was to be a special treat for over-twelves only this year. Younger groups were going day-tripping down to the waterpark at Quay West or to Woodlands Adventure Park near Totnes.

The Dartmoor trip was scheduled to depart that afternoon at one o'clock. As well as the five of them, there were six other children joining Lucas and his friends, every place taken. Excitement was high, the melancholy of the previous few days banished like morning mist in the first rays of the sun. Children ran about the place in frantic preparation, chattering and calling to each other, all under the ferociously disapproving glower of Mr Pring.

It promised to be an exciting summer.

*

"You okay, Tamsen?" Aaron asked with studied casualness a bit later. She'd seemed just as excited as everyone else at first, but now she was distant, preoccupied. There were still three hours to go until the expedition was due to set off.

"I'm fine. It's not me I'm worried about."

"Oh." Aaron thought for a moment. He still found it awkward trying to talk to her. "Um…"

"It's Sammi," she admitted. "She's still with Sabrina. We – I mean, I... left her there."

They were all waiting impatiently in the gardens next to the house, their packed bags already piled next to the front door ready to be loaded into the buses. There was nothing to do now but wait.

"She chose to go with Sabrina all by herself," Aaron reminded her. "We asked her to stay with us."

Tamsen made an indelicate noise in her throat. "She didn't *choose*, Aaron. She was too frightened of Sabrina to say no. Weren't you there?"

"Yeah, I was," Aaron said, bridling. "but there wasn't much we could have done, was there? I mean, think about it; what with Sabrina and Lois Christie going all super-powered on us, we couldn't do anything to stop them."

"Well maybe we should have tried! We're not powerless ourselves, are we?"

Lucas said: "But what would have happened if we'd ended up fighting with them, Tamsen? It could have got really bad. We could have been seriously hurt."

"Isn't that what you do for your friends?" she shot back. "What, you'd just let them get hurt because you're too afraid for yourself?"

Lucas was stung. He shared shamefaced looks with his friends, who all realised that Tamsen had a valid point. Would any of them have stood by if it had been one of them getting pushed around?

"No," Lucas muttered. "We wouldn't." He gave Tamsen an appraising look. She glared back at him.

"For what it's worth," Dion contributed, "at the moment Sammi is okay, at least physically. She's pretty afraid though." He frowned.

"There's something about Marshall Graves. I can't see it too well...damn, I wish I was better at this!"

Tamsen sat upright. "What about Graves?"

"Not sure. It's not very clear, but I think Sammi saw or heard something that really scared her. She doesn't want to be there."

"Where is she?"

"With Sabrina and those other two girls, up at their little meeting place."

Tamsen chewed her lip thoughtfully. "We should go get her."

"'Get her'?" Aaron echoed. "What is she, your pet cat? You want us to just walk into Sabrina Celestine's camp and, what? Say 'hey Sabrina, please don't hit us or anything, but we're taking Sammi River, have a nice day'?"

She looked at him coolly. "You're an idiot, Osborn."

"At least I'm not suicidal!"

"Afraid of a bunch of girls?"

"These girls, yes I am!"

They glared at each other.

"Maybe there's another way," Lucas said diplomatically. "I've got an idea."

*

Colin Herbert came out of Mrs Fisher's office with a weary expression on his face. She'd spent the last half hour informing him of her expectations for the children, their behaviour, Colin's role in maintaining it, and the general standard to be upheld should the children meet anyone whilst away from Peregrine House on this 'little excursion', as she called it. He had nodded and shaken his head agreeably at the appropriate times, even suggesting evenly at one point that she herself might like to come along, but she'd just looked down her nose at him like he was speaking gibberish.

It was the same every year, he reflected. Mrs Fisher made it very clear that she thought him an incompetent idiot, and that he was only here at the behest of Juvenile Services, and that she resented his very existence. But, he reminded himself, he didn't do this for people like her, or for the pay (which was pretty good, as it happened), he did it to see the children's little faces light up with happiness.

He put Mrs Fisher deliberately out of his mind. He knew what he was doing, for heaven's sake, he had a college diploma and everything. Right now he had only to concentrate on the camping trip ahead of him. Just the thought of it filled him with a happy glow, and he knew the children would love it too. In fact, there was one of them now, hovering around the notice board. He dredged through his memory of previous years, trying to match a name to the face.

"Luke?" he hazarded. "Luke Fountain? How are you, young chap?"

"It's Lucas, sir," the boy replied levelly. "Lucas Fortune."

"Right, right. Lucas. Sorry." He remembered now, the boy with the weird eyes, one brown and one green. "Looking forward to today, then? What adventure will you be embarking upon, hmmm?"

"I'm on the camping trip, sir," Lucas answered him politely. Colin hid a smile. The children were all so *nice* here! Some of the other Homes he visited – well, you wouldn't want to walk around alone there, that was for sure.

"Brilliant, excellent!" he enthused. "That means you're with me then, dude. It's gonna be great this year, I just know it! And by the way, you don't need to call me sir, I'm not a teacher. Colin will do, or Col, or Herbie, whatever you want as long as it isn't rude!"

Lucas's face twitched. "Okay."

"You and your friends, is it?" Colin continued, peering at the lists on the notice board. "Ah, a good crowd this year!"

"Actually, s...Colin, I wanted to talk to you about that," the lad said bashfully.

"Oh really? What can I do you for?"

Lucas looked embarrassed. "Well, I know there aren't any places left on the camping trip, but I was wondering – see, there's this girl who I want to come, and…" he faltered, cheeks reddening.

Once again Colin suppressed a knowing smile. Young love, eh? It all seemed so complicated at that age! "So," he guessed, "you'd like to know if we could pack one more little passenger into our minibus, would you?"

Lucas nodded sheepishly.

Colin pulled a face, shaking his head sadly. "I'd love to, sport, but I can't, you see. It's first come, first served, you know that. Sorry bud."

"I reckon you could," the boy said with quiet conviction.

Colin frowned, opening his mouth to deny it once again, but a sudden thought struck him. It wouldn't be so difficult, he reasoned. They could probably squeeze one more in, in fact it would be easy. What had he been thinking?

"Yeah, actually you're right," he said dreamily. "No problem."

"Great! There's just one other thing. She doesn't know I want her to come, so I can't tell her myself. Could you go ask her for me?"

Even though that sounded faintly ridiculous, Colin found himself nodding agreeably. "Ah, you crazy kids, all secrets and whispers with you, isn't it? So, who is the young lady, then?"

"She's called Sammi River. She's out in the grounds right now. If you could go have a word with her, that'd be great. Get her to come back with you, and don't take no for an answer, okay Col?"

"Yeah, yeah, alright, I'll go and do it now. Be back soon." He turned and trotted away, a tiny urgent voice in his head trying frantically to tell him something. He ignored it, whistling a merry tune. Anything to make the kids happy! He stopped and turned back for a second. "Uh, where is she?"

"At the bower, it's a little shed just past the bushes with the pink flowers. She's waiting!"

"Cool! See you later, crocodile!"

Lucas watched the man go with a bemused expression. Some people were easier to convince than others, apparently. That had been ridiculously easy. Or maybe he was just getting better…

Mr Pring lurked moodily around the entrance hall, trying to think what to do next. None of the carers he'd asked had seen anything of the Fortune boy the day before, and it bothered him increasingly. Had there really been no one around at that time? It seemed suspiciously provident that the lad had chosen the exact time when most of the House were otherwise engaged with that whole outing-list business to sneak off somewhere. The boy was smart, that much was obvious. But old Tarquin Pring was smarter!

Usually.

If no one had physically witnessed what had happened, then was there some other way he could see…?

He froze in shock and consternation, berating himself for not realising the obvious much sooner. Of course there was another way! He looked up at the CCTV camera mounted above the door, its sleek modern lines clashing uncomfortably with the fine old moulded woodwork of the House. The camera pointed away along the hall, taking in a wide field of view that included the short passage leading up to Deirdre's office and the bottom of the main staircase.

The boy isn't that smart, Mr Pring thought with relish. *Maybe he was foolish enough to have been caught on camera!* The only problem was that the CCTV monitor station, complete with VCRs, was kept in a locked cupboard in Deirdre's office, and he didn't have a key.

No matter, he snorted. Deirdre would let him have access once he told her of his suspicions. She respected his judgement in such matters. With a gleeful little skip (and a slight wince as his hip gave a twinge), he hurried towards the office.

Mrs Fisher gruffly ushered Mr Pring into her office at the sound of his urgent knock. She was busy with some Juvenile Services paperwork, a pile of forms and reports that had suddenly appeared on her desk with the arrival of those dreadful Out & About people. Honestly, she fumed, the JS staffers were so inefficient. This paperwork should have been sent to her weeks ago, and now she had to get it all done in the next few days. At times like this she wished she employed a secretary.

"What is it now, Tarquin?" she said crossly, leafing through the stack of paper. "I'm really rather busy –"

"Yes, sorry Deirdre," he puffed, and she looked at him fully. He was red-faced and agitated.

"Whatever is the matter?" she scolded him. Honestly, sometimes the poor man could wind himself up so tightly!

"I need…" He paused, catching his breath. "…to see the CCTV footage from yesterday."

Mrs Fisher was taken aback, momentarily forgetting her paperwork. "Why, has something happened?"

Mr Pring looked slightly sheepish. "I…think so," he admitted. "I need to see the tapes to prove it, you see."

"No, I don't see, Tarquin," she said sternly. "You know only representatives of Juvenile Services can have access to those recordings, for legal reasons. What do you think happened, for goodness sake?"

Mr Pring clenched his fist in frustration. "I think something was going on yesterday, Deirdre," he said cagily. "One of the children, up to no good."

"Did anyone see it?"

"No, they didn't."

"Well, did you see it?"

"Not as such, no."

There was a pause. Mrs Fisher drummed her fingers on her desk. "Tarquin…" she began threateningly.

"Deirdre, just humour me!" Mr Pring pleaded. "I know something's up, I can't explain how, but you've trusted me in the past over things like this!" His expression became sly. "It's to do with Lucas Fortune."

If he was expecting a reaction from her, he didn't get one. At the sound of Lucas's name, a peculiar change came over her. She sat back in her chair, feeling slightly giddy. "Lucas Fortune?" she repeated slowly. She shook herself and gave Mr Pring a piercing look. "What is it with you and young Mr Fortune, Tarquin?" she demanded. "That poor child."

Mr Pring's jaw flapped like it had come unhinged. He swayed back on his feet, threatening to topple over at any moment. "I'm sorry?" he whispered, dumbfounded. "Poor...child?"

"I think this vendetta of yours has gone on for quite long enough, Tarquin," she declared. "Why don't you just leave Lucas alone, hmmm?"

Mr Pring stared at her mutely. He made a visible effort to pull himself together. "Whatever you say, Deirdre," he croaked. "Excuse me, won't you?" He turned and stumbled from the office, bumping blindly into the doorframe as he left.

With a sad shake of her head, Mrs Fisher returned to her paperwork.

Mr Pring found himself in the entrance hall again. He was dumbstruck at what he had just witnessed. It had been like someone else had been speaking through Mrs Fisher's lips. In all the time Lucas Fortune had been at Peregrine House, in all those eleven long years, Mr Pring had never once heard Deirdre say a kind word about the boy, a sentiment he himself heartily shared. The lad was trouble, a bad egg through and through. This was a belief that had been held as an unquestionable truth between Deirdre and himself for that whole time.

Now she was defending Fortune?

Mr Pring's sense of wrongness was deepening at a rapid rate. There was something very odd going on here. What could possibly have made Deirdre change her tune enough to actually stick up for the boy? Mr Pring couldn't think of a single thing, but he knew he had to find out.

So Mrs Fisher wouldn't let him see the CCTV tapes; that was fine. He could work around that. After all, he'd been at Peregrine House longer than she had. Indeed he'd once been the caretaker here at the time she'd taken over the place from the previous owners over twenty years ago. He knew all the nooks and crannies of the place, all its secret corners, including the dusty cupboard on the second floor landing where Deirdre hid her master key.

She wasn't in her right mind, he told himself grimly. She'd thank him later for his initiative. With a calculating expression he headed off towards the carers' lounge, to gather his thoughts and plan how he was going to get into Deirdre's office undetected.

*

Sabrina Celestine stood open-mouthed as the ridiculous man with the fluffy beard came striding purposefully into the clearing inside the rhododendron bush. He beamed at her, placing his hands on his hips as he stopped in front of the remaining members of the G.O.C.

"Hello, girls!" the man boomed in a gratingly cheery voice. "I hope you don't mind me coming up here like this to your little wendy-house! I'm Colin, the activity organiser."

Sabrina raised a sardonic eyebrow at him. What did he want, a medal? "Yes?" she said in her best acid tone.

The man completely failed to notice it. "I'm looking for a young lady by the name of Sammi River," he said blithely, peering at their faces. "Would that be one of you, by any chance?"

Sammi put up a tentative hand. "That's me," she peeped. "Am I in trouble?"

The man laughed, throwing back his head in a stupidly dramatic fashion. Sabrina's lip began to curl. "No, you're not in trouble," Colin guffawed. "No, in fact I've come here to give you some good news!"

Sabrina was already growing tired of the man's irritatingly jaunty attitude. Sammi glanced over at her uncertainly. She returned the look with a threatening glare.

"Um…" Sammi said.

"Yes, it seems that due to a bit of a mix-up with our paperwork, there's an extra place available on our camping expedition – and we'd like you to come! How about that, eh?" The man pulled what he probably thought was a comically encouraging face.

For a second a hopeful expression crossed Sammi's face, then she looked at Sabrina again and her face fell. "I'm not sure…" she whispered.

"Don't worry about a thing," Colin insisted breezily. "It's all arranged, but you'd better hurry and pack, we leave in a couple of hours. Come on!" He held out his hand.

Sabrina found all this very suspicious. Why would anyone want Sammi the mouse on one of their stupid little trips? Sabrina had made it very clear to the G.O.C that they wouldn't be going on any of the outings this year. Let the unwashed boys and chattering younger girls have their juvenile fun, as long as it was a long way from her.

"Sammi," she said in a deceptively placid tone, "I didn't know you'd signed up for the camping trip."

Sammi looked terrified. "I didn't, Sabrina," she insisted in a tiny voice. "I promise."

"Never mind all that, young lady," Colin blustered, completely missing the threatening undertones. "I told you, it was our mistake, not yours. Now, are you coming? I have a lot to do, you know!"

Sabrina couldn't act overtly, not in front of this idiotic man. He may be a complete berk, but he was still an adult, and children at Peregrine House did not disrespect adults, at least not openly. She could see Sammi was torn by indecision, deliberately not looking at her leader for guidance. Sabrina seethed inside, unable to control the situation. If Sammi made the wrong choice –

Unexpectedly, stunningly, she did. "Okay," she said and quickly reached out to take the man's hand. Still not looking at Sabrina, she allowed herself to be led off, almost hiding behind the man, keeping him between her and Sabrina.

"Nice seeing you, girls!" Colin called back to the G.O.C as he departed. "Love the wendy-house! And remember, there'll be plenty more activities in the next few weeks, so keep your eyes on the notice board! First come, first served!"

Sabrina almost bit through her lip. She could sense the other girls moving carefully away from her. Sammi had just made the worst mistake of her life. When she got back from this stupid little holiday in the countryside, Sabrina vowed to make her regret ever being born!

Now the G.O.C. were down to three, at least for the next few days or so. That wasn't enough to even call a proper gang, or whatever the girlie equivalent was. "Dana, Lois," she hissed, eyes still locked on the gap in the hedge that Sammi and the man had just disappeared through, "let's go see Marshall."

*

Sammi and Tamsen hugged tearfully, as the boys stood around awkwardly, not looking at each other. Why were girls so gushy and touchy-feely?

Colin Herbert beamed down at them, as usual utterly misreading the situation. "That's right, folks, I can't wait to leave either, but it's nearly time to go and I've still got loads to do, so I'll just leave you to it, okay? See you at quarter to one in the entrance hall! Don't be late!" He breezed off whistling a merry tune.

"Thank you, Lucas," Tamsen sniffed, disengaging from Sammi. "Thank you."

Lucas felt his face burning. "'S' alright," he mumbled. "No problem." He gave Sammi an appraising look. "You okay?"

Sammi smiled shyly at him, nodding. Tears streaked her cheeks, her large brown eyes like jewels glistening in her pale face.

"You stay right next to me," Tamsen told her sternly. "Don't go back to the bower, or anywhere near Sabrina or the other girls, okay? We're all going to leave together."

Sammi nodded again. "I should pack some things," she quavered.

"Good idea," Lucas agreed. "Tamsen, maybe you could help her with that?"

"I was going to," Tamsen said archly. "I'm not leaving her side again."

"I'll go with them too," Timothy said suddenly. He looked around at their quizzical expressions. "It'll be faster," he clarified.

"Uh huh," Dion smirked.

So now there were six of them. Somehow, to Lucas, that felt right. He couldn't explain why, but he knew it was the right number.

For what, though, he'd have to wait some time to find out.

Chapter Eleven – Six Of One

There was one hour to go until the camping trip was due to set off. Colin Herbert and three of his student helpers had already loaded the children's bags onto the minibus, and now they stood out on the drive by the bus, poring over a map and arguing about the best route to take.

The twelve children who'd signed up for the expedition had been gathered together rather unexpectedly in the dining room for a final talking-to by Mrs Fisher before they left. This was unusual. She'd never bothered to send any of the children off personally in the past, normally delegating this job to a clearly annoyed and unfailingly glowering Mr Pring. Now she warned them sternly not to misbehave, and to uphold the high standards Peregrine House had set over the years. They were all becoming young adults, apparently, and as such had more responsibility to live up to than ever before. The children looked around at each other bemusedly. Fishy sounded almost wistful.

Mr Pring was nowhere to be seen. No explanation was given for this, but it mattered little to the children, whose excitement levels were reaching a fever pitch. Despite Fishy's firm warnings, they were fidgety and impatient, just itching to get out of the House and experience a small taste of freedom, even if it was only for a few days.

With just a hint of moisture in her eyes, Fishy dismissed them and hurried from the room. Lucas's friends grinned at him knowingly. It seemed his little talk with her had had some effect after all.

The other children on the trip were all familiar to Lucas, at least in passing. It was hard to live in a place like Peregrine House and not get to know almost everyone. There were three other boys, a group of dorm friends from the older boys' floor, and three giggling girls who knew Tamsen and Sammi. Lucas wondered why these three had not been a member of Sabrina Celestine's dumb 'Girls Only Club,' but he hadn't yet had the chance to ask. There would be plenty of opportunity to talk once they were under way, at least for the initial journey and the first night. He already had some other ideas on how to spend the rest of the time.

On that score, it would soon be time to start thinking about exactly what he was going to do once they were up on the moors. Unfortunately, this was where Lucas's plan began to get a bit hazy. For one thing, he knew the expedition was heading to Dartmoor, but not precisely where. It wouldn't have mattered if he had known anyway, as his knowledge of the moors was almost non-existent, having only been there once before on a previous outing two years ago. The place was big, empty and not always friendly; that was about all he could say with any certainty. To guide him he had only the vague urge to travel west, but he was growing increasingly worried that that urge wouldn't be enough.

The only thing he could do, the only course of action he could see open to him, was just to trust his instincts. He had to believe he would know what to do when the time came. He also had to trust that Rith would not lead him astray, whilst carefully ignoring the very real possibility that this whole thing could turn out to be an enormous, and not to mention highly dangerous, wild goose chase.

But what else could he do? There was nothing else to go on.

Time continued to tick away. The other residents disappeared off in various directions after the meeting, leaving Lucas and his friends to wait alone. They decided to go hang out in the garden until it was time to go, and this is where trouble found them.

Sammi River was alternating from moment to moment between radiant smiles and apprehensive glances over her shoulder. Lucas watched her covertly, knowing that what he was seeing in action was the legacy of Sabrina Celestine's cruelty and bullying. Tamsen sat close by her friend at the patio table, chatting animatedly with Aaron and Dion opposite, while

Timothy sat quietly on her other side, thinking his own inscrutable thoughts.

Dion was aware of something happening first. He stopped talking in mid-sentence, raising his head, a frown creasing his forehead. Conversation stopped, all eyes on him.

"What is it, D?" Aaron asked him, concerned.

"It's –" he began, but cut off with a cry of pain, hands flying to his temples.

As one, all of the other children cried out too, each clutching their heads in sudden pain; everyone, that is, except for Lucas, who felt only a slight pressure in his inner ear, like you get when you're in a car travelling down a long steep hill. He stared around at his friends, frightened. "What's the matter?" he cried, clutching at Aaron's arm next to him.

Aaron turned on him a gaze filled with tears of pain. "It…hurts!" he wailed.

"That's the general idea, pant-wetter!" a taunting voice cried out from behind Lucas. He jumped up and spun around.

Marshall Graves stood on the opposite side of the lawn, a triumphant smile on his face. Arrayed to either side of him in a loose line were his gang of followers, wearing various expressions of malice, spite and scorn: Billy Elsdon and Myles Lovell to his right, Sabrina Celestine, Dana Jackson and Lois Christie to his left.

A crashing silence seemed to fall over the garden, its vibrant colours draining away to a faded monotone. Wild thoughts raced through Lucas's head, strange concepts and suppositions. He was seeing everything as though in slow motion. Graves's expression changed to one of puzzlement as he saw Lucas standing there, apparently unaffected, and in a flash Lucas understood what was happening. This was Graves's doing! This must be his power!

And Lucas knew what to do.

"There's no pain," he suggested calmly to his friends, his voice reverberating oddly as though in a tunnel, and the world clicked back to normal, the cries of his friends trailing off. They all wore matching expressions of shock and confusion.

Graves was stunned. "What – how did you –" he breathed, his teeth bared like those of an animal. Around him the faces of his cronies registered similar confusion.

Lucas was aware of movement around him as he kept his gaze locked with that of Graves. He spared a quick glance to his sides, to see his friends climbing unsteadily but angrily to their feet, arranging themselves in a line to either side of him.

There was utter quiet in the garden as the two opposing groups faced off against each other, the air between them fairly crackling with undisguised fury and bitterness. Lucas felt something probing at his mind again, and he directed a cool look at Dana Jackson, whose eyes widened. "Feeling sleepy?" Lucas suggested, and she began to sway, eyes fluttering. The pressure on his mind cut off instantly.

He saw Sabrina glance angrily at Marshall, who was still standing there immobile, staring at Lucas. With a grunt of annoyance she took a step forward, placing her hands on her hips challengingly, surveying Lucas's group with a contemptuous sneer. "You bunch of lowlifes," she hissed in disgust. "Think you're better than us, do you?" She clicked her fingers imperiously. Lois Christie obediently trotted forward. "Hurt them," she commanded. The scarily vacant girl raised her hand with a dull smile to point at Lucas.

Things happened quickly then, almost too quickly to follow. Tamsen darted forward, directly in front of Lucas, while Timothy quite coolly began to walk towards the opposing gang, his skin rapidly becoming mottled and green. Within seconds he had vanished, his body taking on the aspect of the grassy lawn, completely camouflaged. Billy Elsdon and Myles Lovell stared at the spot where he had been in open-mouthed confusion.

Lois fired her shimmering blast of heat at Lucas's chest. It scorched across the lawn towards him, but Tamsen was there, grimacing in anticipation. The beam struck her –

– and passed straight through, emerging from her back at a different angle to sear past Lucas's head like a red hot arrow. He jerked away instinctively. Tamsen shuddered, turning to glance at Lucas briefly. "That was weird," she murmured with a half-smile, then faced back towards the others. With a determined stride she set off directly towards Lois.

Aaron and Sammi, meanwhile, stood frozen nearby. Mere seconds had passed, but to Lucas it already seemed like an eternity. Sammi was staring at Sabrina with a strange expression, and at that moment Sabrina locked eyes with her. The leader of the G.O.C. smiled nastily and gathered herself up. She began to come forward, obviously intent on having it out right now with her wayward former charge.

And finally, Sammi reacted. Her normally timid expression faded away, to be replaced by one much harder. "No," she said, not loudly, but nonetheless Lucas heard it quite clearly. She held up her hand, palm forward in the universal gesture for 'stop'.

Sabrina saw this and laughed sardonically, striding towards her. Lucas had the ghost of a premonition of what was coming. He just managed to squeeze his eyes shut in time. There was a silent white flash, some of it managing to penetrate his tightly closed eyelids in white and purple spikes, a faint hot wind washing across his skin. The air smelt of ozone. Tentatively, he opened his eyes a crack.

Sabrina was wobbling about a few metres away, clenched hands held tightly over her eyes, cursing incoherently. Lois Christie, who'd apparently been facing in Sammi's direction as well, was similarly afflicted, clutching her face with one hand, though she was still waving her dangerous shooting-finger gamely around in front of her. Tamsen simply strode up to her and shoved her roughly to the ground; she'd had her back to Sammi, so the flash hadn't affected her. Lois sprawled in a heap, curling up in a ball, sniffling pathetically. The fight had been knocked out of her.

Meanwhile, Myles Lovell gave a yelp and toppled over backwards, his fall broken by a thorny rosebush directly behind him. The thorns immediately tangled and caught in his clothing, some of them puncturing his skin, and he cried out in pain and anger. He was imprisoned. Billy Elsdon stared around him in wide-eyed panic, backing nervously away. Something poked him in the chest and he jumped as though stung, emitting a great girly shriek. He turned tail and ran off into the nearby woods without a backward glance.

All of this had taken no more than twenty seconds, and the whole time Marshall Graves hadn't moved, keeping his gaze locked fixedly on Lucas, expression unreadable. Whatever Sammi had done didn't appear to have affected him. He shook himself, glancing around to see his little troupe in disarray all around him. "You morons," he berated them. He turned back to Lucas, giving him an appraising look, then nodded slowly, unexpectedly. "We'll finish this later, you and me," he promised. He turned and stalked away, leaving his gang where they had fallen.

"Get up, Lois," Tamsen said tiredly. The little blonde girl rolled to her knees, eyes streaming. She stared up at Tamsen in incomprehension before lurching to her feet and stumbling away after Marshall. Tamsen turned away with a satisfied nod and headed over to where Sabrina stood silently alone in the middle of the lawn.

"It's finished now, Sabrina," Tamsen said to her former friend, not unkindly. "Now we all know, don't we? You hurt us, we hurt you. It's pointless, and stupid."

Sabrina looked at her through teary, streaming red eyes.

"Us and you?" she repeated dully. "That's how it is now?"

"It doesn't have to be, Sabbie. We used to be friends, not so long ago. We don't have to fight."

Sabrina glanced in Sammi's direction, and then faced Tamsen again. She drew herself up to her full, considerable height, giving her former compatriot a look of utter disgust that said to Tamsen, in very clear terms, that she'd lost her forever. There was no going back now, not for Sabrina, not for any of them. The lines had been drawn. Without another word Sabrina walked away from them, pausing only to collect a drowsy and bewildered Dana Jackson who was wandering aimlessly over by the flower beds. Myles Lovell tore himself free from the rosebush with a curse and lumbered off after them.

Silence descended again on the garden, leaving Lucas and his friends to numbly collect themselves together. Timothy reappeared, his skin returning to its normal dusky hue. He looked tired and upset, a feeling shared by them all. None of them were fighters, yet they had been forced to fight, and it didn't sit easily with them at all. Slowly they gathered back around the patio table and sat, unsure what to say or do next.

"Well done, Sammi," Timothy ventured after a long silent while. "Are you okay?"

Sammi smiled radiantly. "I am now," she said brightly, and somehow, in some way they couldn't identify, that was enough, and they all started smiling, then laughing. Just like that the mood was broken, and they were happy again, all in one piece and whole. Something strange and terrible had very nearly happened, but the children were able to draw strength and reassurance from each other, bolstering the whole group.

The six friends, finally, knew they belonged together.

*

The time to leave was upon them, accompanied by a rush of excitement that was almost enough to offset the sick feeling of dismay Lucas still felt over what had happened in the garden. He didn't know what would happen in the future, in fact he was unsure about a lot of things, but he had an inkling that the battle they had just been forced to fight would not be their last. It had been a learning experience for both of the opposing sides, a kind of feeling-out of each other's capabilities; and it seemed to Lucas that, on balance, Graves may well have the edge. He was meaner, his friends were equally unpleasant, and their abilities were of a pretty destructive nature. Okay, so Lucas and his friends had somehow managed to face them off this time, but if the two sides were to ever meet again, Lucas suspected sadly that things might turn out a whole lot differently.

How had it come to this? All Lucas had ever wanted from life, in the few brief years he had been on this Earth, was to live and be glad, to be free to enjoy himself and do whatever made him happy without harming anyone else. So he'd been known to cause the odd little bit of mischief here and there. He was just an ordinary boy, doing what ordinary boys did. He wasn't some gang-leader, some General leading his troops to war against the enemy! He bore no real ill will to anyone, not even to Marshall Graves or Deirdre Fisher for all the things they had done to him. It simply wasn't in him to think like that. He just wanted to be left alone. Was that so much to ask?

And then there were his friends, his close circle of companions who trusted and believed in him implicitly. Was he a fool to think he could offer them any solace? They'd been dragged into this mess and were now in danger because of him. Wasn't that the real truth? How could he forgive himself if anything happened to them?

Whatever the reason, (and there had to be one – right?), then the answer must lie with the voice from his dreams, the mysterious Rith, who lay in wait for him somewhere outside the encircling walls of the only place he'd ever called home. If it didn't, then everything he was trying to do was in vain.

He couldn't allow himself to believe that. He mustn't.

His face betrayed no trace of this self-doubting turmoil. Surrounded by the happy, laughing countenances of his friends and fellow trippers, he boarded the waiting Transit minibus gamely and took a seat on the back row. Dion squeezed in next to him, Aaron and Timothy filling the remaining space on the back seat, while Tamsen and Sammi sat just in front of them, all chattering excitedly to each other. With so much joy around him it was hard not to feel it too, and Lucas pushed his gloomy thoughts deliberately away, allowing himself a small but genuine smile. There would be time later to contemplate the future, (and that sentence made him smile even more).

"All aboard!" Colin Herbert sang, counting heads as the bus filled. Altogether there were to be sixteen of them on this trip, twelve children, three student helpers and old Herbie himself. What with all of their bags and camping equipment strapped to the roof, and sealed boxes of food supplies and other sundries stashed under seats and wherever there was space, the minibus was fairly groaning. "Not to worry," Colin reassured them even though no one asked, "these things are built to last. All set?"

There was a deafening chorus of cheers and whistles. One of the volunteers, a nervous looking girl by the name of Leanne, produced a register and began calling off names, her voice barely audible over the general din of twelve hysterically excited almost-teens.

The formalities finally done, the doors were secured, the tyres were kicked one last time and Colin hopped up into the driver's seat. "Okay ramblers, let's get rambling!" he cried, starting the engine, and they began to move, accompanied by yet more cheering. The tyres crunched deep grooves into the gravelled driveway, the bus rocking gently as Colin negotiated his way towards the front gates.

Lucas turned and gazed back at the house through the rear window. He had a strange feeling, like he might not see the house again, at least for a while. His eye roamed over the ivy-covered front wall, the four floors of windows reflecting back at him, the shiny black front door with the brass knocker, and the tidily manicured flowerbeds surrounding the driveway. Willows drooped their branches down to the gravel at the edge of the drive, while flights of swifts flitted in and out of their branches, trilling enthusiastically. All so mundane, so everyday, and yet it was everything he knew. He sighed and turned away, allowing himself no more melancholy. This was the start of a grand adventure!

As they turned out onto the main road outside, one of the student helpers started singing, falteringly. Soon the whole bus had taken it up, and Lucas joined in too, singing along heartily and happily.

The moors awaited.

Chapter Twelve – Leaving Home

The journey passed in a happy blur of songs, I-spy and companionable chatter. At Exeter they took the A30 and headed west towards Okehampton, the afternoon sun bright and hot as they sped along. At one point Colin was forced to pull over to allow one of the children, a boisterous curly-haired boy called Stephen Smith, to be copiously sick by the side of the road, much to the amusement of the avidly watching children. From then on the unfortunate child would be forever known, hilariously, as 'Sicko.'

After an hour or two they left the A30 and headed out into the moorland proper, the very sight of which was enough to quieten the children, at least temporarily. Great empty vistas rolled away in every direction, the cloudless sky like a vast blue dome on the world. It was a sight that made everyone feel small, especially those who were used to living in the cloistered environment of a children's home. The road snaked up the sides of steep, rounded hills, the minibus slowing to a crawl, then on down the other side like a rollercoaster ride. The hunched shapes of granite tors shouldering their way through the loam and bracken were dotted all around.

Twice they had to stop to allow wandering animals to cross the road in front of them. The first time it was for several placid sheep munching contentedly and unhurriedly at roadside grass, then later a herd of stocky Dartmoor ponies, skittering wildly over the tarmac in their haste to get away from these strange, noisy invaders in their domain. There were many 'ooo's' and 'aaah's' from the girls, while the boys laughed uproariously as one of the ponies relieved itself in plain sight all over the road.

The first signs of irritability and boredom were just beginning to set in when Colin announced, suddenly and loudly, "We're here!" Faces pressed eagerly against windows, a ragged cheer erupting. They had been driving through a great shallow valley forested with tall, spindly pine trees, a small river paralleling the road for most of the way. Now the river's course veered off into the trees, next to which stood a sign reading "Lox Valley Farm Camping." Colin slowed and steered the van down a well-maintained side road which wound through the trees. Somewhere in the distance there was a muted roaring sound, as of water tumbling over rocks.

The campsite was an ordered collection of neat, flat fields surrounding a shallow lake in the crux of the valley. Nearby was the farmhouse, an ancient stone structure with a steeply sloping roof; the house also had a more modern extension grafted gracelessly onto one end. Several caravans were spaced out in tidy rows around a modern-looking block-building in one of the fields, and in the field next to that a colourful row of tents jostled each other. Somewhere a radio was playing, the sun beaming down beatifically on the tranquil scene.

The bus pulled to a stop in a car park near the house and the children tumbled out joyfully, stretching and whooping. They were finally here! The student helpers gamely marshalled them into some sort of order whilst Colin walked stiff-legged and wincing into the reception office adjoining the farmhouse.

The children zeroed in on the lake right away. It was right in the centre of the campsite, a roughly circular and obviously artificial body of clear, cool water. Trees grew right up to its far bank, and on the nearside the river they'd seen earlier reappeared and emptied itself over a ledge of rock to tumble a metre or so into the lake. Several people, adults and children, were splashing about happily in the water, calling out and soaking each other. All the Peregrine House children developed a sudden overpowering urge to go for a swim at that point, but the student helpers vetoed that for now. There was too much to do first.

Several of the more uncomfortable looking children were led off to the toilet block, while the rest of them were told to wait in a nice line. In due course Colin emerged from the reception office accompanied by an older man, a sour-faced old fellow with prodigious mutton-chop sideburns and a vast belly which overhung his sagging trousers. "Children, this is Mr Milligan, the owner of the campsite," Colin introduced him. The children looked at him blankly, and he returned their gazes with a scowl before turning deliberately to Colin, dismissing them.

"Yer plots is numbers seven 'n eight, over t'wards the boundary of that field there," he grunted to Colin in a thick Devonshire accent, gesturing with a meaty hand. "No swimmin' after nine o'clock at night, cuz tha's when the staff goes home. Toilet blocks is there and there, an' the showers is token operated. Yuz' can buy tokens from the shop 'tween eight in mornin' an' six at night." He forced an insincere, yellow-toothed smile. "Enjoy yer stay." He spun about ponderously and trundled back into his office.

Colin watched him go with a raised eyebrow. "Charming fellow," he muttered, then addressed the children. "Alright, guys, here's what we're gonna do. We're all gonna help unload the bus and carry our gear over to the plots, then," he waved a finger in mock seriousness, "and only then, when the bus is empty, we might think about letting you have a quick dip in the lake." He was almost drowned out by a raucous cheer. "But," he emphasised, "only if everything is done. After that we can all help to pitch the tents and make camp. Okay?" There was a chorus of assent mixed in with a few groans, then work began.

It was a magical afternoon, the best that Lucas and his friends could remember. After the bus had been emptied and everything transported the hundred metres or so over to their designated plots, the children changed in to shorts and swimsuits and plunged joyfully into the lake, squealing at the stinging cold. They played under the waterfall and on it, slithering over the lip like crocodiles or leaping from the top yelling like Tarzan. Some of the boys found a rope swing hanging from a tree and commenced swinging out over the water, dive-bombing the girls with shouts of glee.

Soon enough it was time to get out, the helpers rounding them up and handing them fluffy towels to cover their shivering bodies. After drying-off and dressing they sat in a happy circle on the grass by the lakeside, eating packed lunches that had been prepared for them by the Peregrine House catering staff. Then it was time to set up the camp, a collection of four patched tents arranged two to a plot. Colin directed the tents to be assembled so that they all faced into the middle of the adjoining plots, where he had already piled a bunch of stones to make a banked fire for later. "Had to argue with Milligan a bit about that," Lucas overheard Colin commenting to one of the helpers as they worked. "I had to promise to keep the fire small, and to make sure it was completely extinguished before turning in. As though I don't know how to keep a campsite…hey, you, little girl, that's not how you peg a guy-rope! Careful with that hammer!"

The sun was lowering at the end of the valley when it was finally done, evening beginning to draw in. Red light threw long shadows across the campsite as the children lay on blankets in the centre of their camp, sipping hot chocolate that had been warmed on a gas stove. The helpers were still bustling about, making sure everything was secured and ready.

Lucas and his friends were exhausted but glowing with happiness as they sprawled together in companionable silence. None of them had yet mentioned the real reason they had come on this expedition. It had been enough just to enjoy the day for what it was, like normal children. Soon enough reality would intrude, but that could wait for now.

It grew dark slowly, stars appearing in the purpling sky as they gazed up in awe at this rare spectacle. Colin helpfully and incorrectly pointed out constellations and star clusters as they appeared, which made Dion laugh quietly; he was something of an astronomy buff himself, and it was pretty clear that Colin wasn't. The bloke could light a decent fire though, which he demonstrated to them by constructing a simple tepee of twigs, paper and dry mossy kindling which caught alight immediately at the touch of a spark produced by drawing a knife along a block of flint. Thankfully, he didn't go so far as to bring out his guitar, which was a small mercy as far as the now drowsy children were concerned.

That was how the day ended for the happy residents of Peregrine House Children's Home. It would forever remain in Lucas's memory as one of the most joyfully simple and wonderful days of his early life, a time of uncomplicated childish concerns and undemanding pleasures that the passage of time would never diminish or sully.

It would be a long time before he would ever again have the chance to be so happy.

*

Under a bright sliver of moon, Lucas stood on a dark hilltop overlooking the Lox Valley Farm Campsite, a sadness pressing in his chest. Around him his five friends stood in silence, gazing down at the camp below. They were all dressed in sturdy hiking gear, borrowed from Out & About's supply of equipment. In their own ways, they were all saying goodbye to their former lives.

It had been a simple matter for Lucas to keep the adults and other children asleep whilst his friends quietly disassembled their tent and distributed it amongst themselves for carrying. It had been easier still to introduce the thought into the minds of the slumbering campers that there had only ever been six children from Peregrine House.

No one would ever remember Lucas and his friends.

He turned away finally and met the gazes of his companions. Timothy nodded firmly at him, and the others' faces showed that they too were ready. With grim determination the six of them shouldered their packs and began their journey out into the heart of the wild moorland.

Part Two

Chapter Thirteen – Alone

All was still in the corridors of Peregrine House, Home for Children. Usually, after midnight, the only sounds to be heard were an occasional muted snore, or the creaking of ancient wooden beams as they settled, or sometimes the faint scratching and pitter-patter of tiny rodent paws as a hardy mouse ventured forth in search of crumbs and scraps.

On this night, however, a dark figure moved silently down the grand main staircase towards the entrance hall. Pale moonlight filtering through the high windows was all that illuminated the figure's passage, but that was all it needed. It knew this place better than anyone else, every loose floorboard and squeaky stair, every twist and turn imprinted indelibly on its mind from long familiarity.

Dressed all in black, as was his custom, Tarquin Pring considered himself to be the guardian of Peregrine House and all its occupants. Upholding its many rules and regulations, and seeing that everyone else did so too, was something of a sacred charge to him. He'd been doing this for more years than he cared to think about, even before the place had been called Peregrine House. He remembered when it had been known as the

Bellhaven Institute, and even further back, at a time when Mr Pring had been no more than a wayward child himself, when it was still Darkling Manor. It had been Lord Darkling himself who had first opened the doors of his ancestral seat to orphaned children and other such unfortunates, way back in the early part of the twentieth century, and the place had continued in that capacity, by and large, ever since.

Tonight Mr Pring had carried out his self-appointed nightly patrols as he did every night, prowling the halls on the lookout for rule-breaking and other mischief, even though many of the children were currently absent. If there was one thing he knew with absolute certainty, it was that where children were concerned, disobedience was inevitable. If people like Mr Pring didn't take it upon themselves to uphold the standards of decency set down by responsible adults, the result would be chaos.

Not on my watch, he thought grimly to himself.

This night was different, though. The ground floor was not ordinarily part of Mr Pring's patrol, containing as it did mainly offices, storage, classrooms and other areas out-of-bounds to children. After making a complete circuit of the upper three floors, where the various dormitories were all located, he would normally end his route outside his own tiny attic room. He would then rest for an hour or two, dozing fitfully, only to rouse himself and repeat the whole procedure again, often several times a night. To Mr Pring sleep was nothing more than a bothersome inconvenience.

The ancient grandfather clock ticked sonorously to itself in the darkness of the entrance hall, as it had done unfailingly since the days of the Darkling family. Next to it was the short side-corridor that led to Mrs Fisher's office. Feeling only slightly guilty at what he was about to do, Mr Pring took the borrowed master key from his pocket and used it to unlock the door.

He'd thought long and hard about what he was going to have to do, weighing up all the risks and possible dangers, but in the end there was really nothing else for it. He had to see those tapes, and if Mrs Fisher didn't trust him enough to give him access to them…ultimately, his responsibility was to the welfare of the children and the smooth running of the Home. Deirdre would understand that, once the truth came out.

He padded across the darkened office to the cabinet wherein lay the CCTV control station. It was a heavy metal box not unlike a safe, cunningly concealed within a shell of walnut veneer so that it blended in with the rest of the room's furnishings. Juvenile Services had paid for its installation some years previously, and technically only one of their authorised representatives could access it. It had only been opened twice before, both times by JS technicians carrying out maintenance or upgrades. Mr Pring had only a vague idea of how the system actually worked. His knowledge of technical matters was pretty rudimentary. He assumed that the system recorded everything and somehow stored those recordings in case they were needed. It was these recordings that he had to access and check through for the proof he needed.

He was not supposed to know that the JS people had left a spare key to the cabinet right here in the office, but Mrs Fisher had let that information slip one night after one too many glasses of Remy Martin. The key was for emergencies only (JS had been very emphatic about that, apparently), but wasn't this an emergency? No, probably not, Mr Pring had to concede, but it was still a matter of importance. A child had been up to something underhand, and no doubt thought they'd got away with it. What could be more important than that?

He turned aside and, using the master key, unlocked the bottom drawer of Deirdre's desk, where he knew she kept things to which no one else was allowed access. He was not sure what the CCTV key looked like, but it was a special security device that was apparently impossible to copy. Rooting around amongst papers and some other unidentifiable objects in the dark, his hand closed around a heavy, bulky shape with a short metal stem. This must be it! Triumphantly he withdrew it and squinted at the thing. It didn't look much like any key he'd ever seen, but nevertheless he knew this was it, a flattened black egg like a rounded off matchbox with a brassy stem protruding from one end. It reminded him somewhat of a car remote. Steeling himself one last time, he crossed to the cabinet and stared at it. He'd come this far – now it was time to finish it.

The cabinet opened easily with an anticlimactic clunk, the reinforced doors swinging open to reveal a bank of glowing lights within, a panel surrounding a small, blank TV monitor. Now all he had to do was figure out how it all worked...

It took a while, and much muffled swearing and head-scratching, but he eventually got it figured enough to be able to search through the recorded images. He learned how to zoom backwards and forwards through the recordings (which, it turned out, were not even on tapes, but stored on some kind of vast computer memory drive). Slowly he zeroed in on the afternoon of the previous day, narrowing down the time until...

There he was! The Fortune boy, strolling along the corridor like he owned the place! Double checking the date and time, Mr Pring confirmed that it had been the exact moment when he had been posting the lists of this year's summer activities. Fortune *must* have known that, the sneaky little rat!

Well, Mr Pring thought excitedly, *now we'll see exactly what you were up to!*

Clumsily navigating through the various different camera views, he tracked the boy's journey through the building all the way to the front entrance hall, where no unauthorised child had any business being. Mr Pring felt his pulse quicken; this could be it! He watched avidly as the boy paused outside this very office, head bowed in thought, then pushed open the door and disappeared inside.

Mr Pring sat back, confused. This is where the boy had been, with Deirdre, in her office? It didn't make sense, especially considering that Deirdre hadn't even mentioned it to Mr Pring. In fact, he'd gone straight back to the office just after posting the lists yesterday. That's when he'd spotted Fortune in the corridor. The boy must have left the office only moments before Mr Pring arrived! Why hadn't Deirdre said anything?

Mr Pring thought back over the conversation he'd had with Deirdre then. She'd seemed distracted, distant even, but there had definitely been no mention of Fortune. Perplexed, Mr Pring went back and watched the footage again to double-check. Fortune had definitely been in here!

What could this mean? Mr Pring couldn't think of a single reason why Deirdre would keep this a secret, especially from him. When it came to the running of this place, the enforcement of rules and discipline, and the pinpointing of potential troublemakers, the two of them had always been unanimous in both their views and their methods. Lucas Fortune was always at the top of their list.

Even stranger, there was the later conversation where Deirdre had actually *defended* Fortune. Why would she have done that? Could it be that Fortune had in some way threatened her, or was blackmailing her? Mr Pring snorted, dismissing that as preposterous. Fortune was just some arrogant boy, not a criminal mastermind!

The problem gnawed away at him. He was Deirdre's right-hand man, her most trusted lieutenant. Now it seemed clear that his instincts about the Fortune boy had been spot-on all along. To help Deirdre, there seemed no other choice but to find out what had been said to her. There was nothing else for it. Grimly he began searching through the recordings for footage taken from the hidden camera right here in the office. He had to help her, she would thank him later…

What he eventually found made no sense at all, yet it filled him with a peculiar sort of dread. Cursing the lack of sound on the recording, he watched as Fortune had some kind of strange discussion with Deirdre. The boy had his back to the camera, but from what Mr Pring could tell he seemed quite calm, not particularly threatening or agitated. Mr Pring watched as Deirdre stood up angrily only to sit down again, a look of confusion on her face. She was clearly not happy, but Mr Pring couldn't understand why she was even listening to the boy. The silent drama went on like this for a while longer, words shooting back and forth between the two protagonists until (and this made Mr Pring gasp at the sheer audacity of it) Fortune went and actually *leant over* Deirdre, causing her to recoil fearfully. The tears in her eyes were quite clear. It ended when Fortune left the room, leaving poor Deirdre to sit in motionless silence on her sofa. Mr Pring frowned, checking to see if the recording had stuck, but no, the timecode was advancing normally. It was Deirdre herself, sitting completely still, like some kind of mannequin.

What was this? The first thing he would have expected her to do would be to jump up angrily and perhaps call someone on the phone, but here she was frozen to the spot, doing nothing but blinking slowly. Whatever Fortune had said to her must have been terrible to shock her into such immobility!

Mr Pring had to fast-forward the recording almost five minutes before he saw any change. On the screen she abruptly began moving, calmly reaching for her tea-set as though nothing had happened. Moments later he saw himself enter the room, as he remembered doing, to sit painfully in his chair.

Sitting watching this now he felt faint, like the time he'd had his heart scare. His vision contracted, the room threatening to spin around him. His skin crawled. The sense of unreality was profound. Almost, he didn't want to believe what he had just seen, but the evidence was undeniably right there – at least the 'what', if not the 'how'...

The pragmatic part of his mind asserted control and brought him back down to earth with a jolt. What should he do with this information? His first instinct was to take it directly to Deirdre, confront her with it, but almost immediately he discounted that. She'd already demonstrated to him by her reticence in telling him before now that she wouldn't, or perhaps couldn't, discuss it. His approach to her would have to be more delicate than that. Who, then? Jacob Kwame? Again, he dismissed that out of hand. The last thing he wanted was for that over-ambitious busybody sniffing around Peregrine House. Deirdre might think the man was wonderful, but Mr Pring had always found the current proprietor of the Mill distinctly unpleasant.

That left the obvious: he would have to take the matter directly to Juvenile Services. With a heavy heart he noted the time references of the recordings in his little notebook and reset the CCTV system to continue recording from now. Was he betraying Deirdre Fisher, who'd been so good to him over the years? Okay, so she was a bit of a tyrant, short-tempered and slightly intolerant, but she had a heart of gold under that callous exterior, he was almost sure of it. If she was in trouble and couldn't speak out, then it was Mr Pring's moral duty to help her out. Wasn't it? She'd given an old man a home, a roof over his head and companionship on those long winter evenings, even if she did look down her nose at him sometimes. It was a clear cut decision.

He took one last look around the office, making sure everything was back as it should be. With shaking fingers he held up the business card he'd taken from Deirdre's desktop organiser. *Miss Danielle Fox*, it read, *Juvenile Services Client Advisor*, followed by a phone number. He hadn't particularly liked the JS woman when she'd been here a week or two ago, but it was the only number he had, the only course of action he could think of.

He would call Miss Fox in the morning.

*

It was a warm night, even high up on the hills of Dartmoor. This far from any human habitation, the clear sky was ablaze with starlight, only somewhat obscured by the icily bright crescent of moon hanging high overhead. Its light shone down on the ragged party of trudging figures moving slowly along below, threading their way carefully past stands of gorse and bracken, illuminating their way across the sometimes treacherous and boggy moorland.

Lucas was glad of the moonlight, and he knew Aaron in particular was even more thankful. Without its wan illumination progress would have been next to impossible. The children had never known isolation so profound, and it humbled them, keeping them quiet and subdued as they followed Lucas up hill and down valley in a generally westerly direction.

Lucas had deliberately not looked at his watch since leaving the campsite behind, but he knew they had been walking for several hours. Despite the sturdy boots he wore his feet ached, and he suspected his friends were doing little better. They never said it, never once complained, but this just served to make Lucas feel even worse.

Cresting a low rise topped by the bulky animalistic shape of a nameless tor, Lucas decided the time was right to stop. "Let's rest here," he suggested; the wave of relief that came from his friends was almost palpable. Moving over to a spot close to the base of the tor they gratefully unshouldered their packs, flopping to the cool earth with much sighing and groaning.

"Where are we?" Aaron moaned, stretching his tired shoulder muscles.

"Compared to what?" Timothy muttered darkly. "Does it matter?"

"Guess not. I was just sort of wondering –"

"Are we there yet?" Dion sing-songed. Aaron punched him on the arm.

Sammi, surprisingly, was showing the least tiredness of any of them. She had been bouncing along happily at the back of the line, gazing about her in the silvery light as though she'd never seen anything like this before. She probably hadn't, Lucas thought as he watched her now. She was contentedly tucking into some kind of energy bar Tamsen had pilfered from the camp supplies. Being out from under Sabrina Celestine's bossy shadow seemed to have done the tiny girl the world of good.

Timothy said: "Seriously, Lucas, can you tell us if we're close yet?" His dark eyes glittered in the moonlight, impossible to read.

What could Lucas tell them? He had no idea how close they were. The only thing he felt was a slight pull in a certain direction, which was the direction he had been leading them. Right now that pull didn't feel any weaker or stronger than it had back at Peregrine House. He only knew that they had to keep going, if they were really serious about finding the answers they craved.

"Yeah, we're getting there," he reassured his friends with barely a tremor in his voice. "Not far now, I reckon."

They nodded, satisfied, accepting his assurance. What else could they do? "We could probably set up the tent here, maybe try to get some sleep," he said. "What d'you reckon, guys?"

"Not really sleepy right now," Timothy answered, and the others nodded their agreement.

"Maybe we should just keep going, Lucas," Sammi suggested brightly. She looked around at the rest of them. "That is, if everyone agrees."

Lucas nodded. "Fine by me, I'm not too tired yet myself. We can just carry on as long as we can, stop later if we feel like it. Okay?"

There was general assent. Tamsen broke out some more of the energy bars (they tasted a bit like apple, but not much), and shared them around. Sammi had a second one. After a few sips of water to finish off, they reshouldered their packs and set off once again, falling back into line. Lucas strode out in front, a position he was not entirely comfortable with, followed a few paces behind by Aaron. Next came Dion and Timothy, the two of them reinforcing their already fast friendship. At the back came Tamsen and Sammi, the pair of them silent but attentive as though on guard. Against what, Lucas didn't know, but it was kind of reassuring all the same to have them back there.

They continued stoically on, not talking much, just ambling along in companionable silence. The course Lucas was following seemed, so far, to be reasonably safe, with none of the dangers Colin Herbert had enthusiastically warned them about on the journey out here. Once they'd passed near a bog, its earthy aroma obvious from a long way off, and another time they had to negotiate a fast flowing stream by means of a crude plank bridge covered in sheep droppings, but other than that it had been relatively easy going.

After a while Lucas realised he could see more clearly. He turned to see the eastern sky behind him lightening along the horizon. Dawn was coming, and it was an immensely cheering sight. Together they stopped to watch, marvelling at the spectacle. Light was returning to the world, and with its coming, the children's spirits received a healthy boost. When the sun was a ruddy ball just above the horizon, they turned away and continued their trek with lighter hearts.

The morning was well advanced when they finally decided to stop. Lucas figured they had been walking for about eight hours solid, putting a good distance between themselves and their former housemates. Exactly how much distance didn't seem important; what mattered was that Lucas and his friends were doing something positive about their situation. That was what drove them.

They pitched their tent beside a handy grove of hawthorn trees, standing alone and forlorn on a breezy hillside. The tent was not really intended for six people, but nonetheless they all crawled gratefully inside it, squashed together like a family of mice in a nest. A cool wind had picked up earlier, and now it flapped the tent material and whistled mournfully through the guy ropes. None of this prevented the children from falling almost immediately into exhausted sleep.

Chapter Fourteen – Do The Right Thing

Tarquin Pring was taking his morning walk in the grounds when the sound of tyres crunching on gravel caught his attention. He was in the side garden, near the old well, breathing in the cool morning air whilst having a crafty cigarette, well away from the prying eyes of any of the other residents. Despite doctors' orders, not to mention plain common sense, smoking was a habit he had never fully managed to eliminate from his life, though he was down to only one or two a day. It was one of the few guilty pleasures he still allowed himself these days.

He glanced at his watch, curious. 7:56 a.m. Too late for the milkman, too early for the postman. Who could be calling at this hour? Finishing off his cigarette, he tossed the butt down the well and went to investigate.

Rounding the corner of the house, he stopped as he saw a plain black car with darkened windows standing in the middle of the driveway. The driver's side door opened and a very tall man in dark glasses unfolded from within, straightening up until he seemed to dwarf the car. He looked familiar to Mr Pring. Where had he seen this man before?

As soon as the driver's door was closed again the man's hand dove into his jacket pocket, withdrawing something. There was a flash as he lit a cigarette, and Mr Pring remembered who it was. The man from Juvenile Services, what's-his-name…

The man went around and opened the passenger door. A blonde-haired woman emerged gracefully from within, her expression composed. "Thank you, Ptolemy," her voice came clearly. She produced a briefcase from within the car, and shut the door.

For the second time in the last twelve hours, Mr Pring found himself perplexed. The people from Juvenile Services were already here? Not only that, but the very representative whose card he still had in his pocket? The thing was, he hadn't even called them yet…

The tall man turned then and looked directly at Mr Pring. He smiled horribly, his teeth brown and glistening. He took a long pull on his cigarette, staring at Mr Pring. Miss Fox tidied herself up a little, straightening her suit and checking her hair in the car window. She looked up and spotted Mr Pring straight away. "Ah, you," she called by way of greeting. "Mr…"

"Pring, Tarquin Pring," he heard himself say. "Um, good morning."

"We'll see," Miss Fox said ominously. "Would you care to escort us into the building, Mr Pring? We have some issues to discuss." She swept up to the front door and waited.

Well, they're here now, Mr Pring reasoned as he hurried forward. So he hadn't actually called them in. Did it really matter? Their fortuitous arrival this morning had saved him the small bother of contacting Juvenile Services himself. They must be here on another matter, but it would be also be the perfect opportunity to unburden himself of last night's revelations.

He let the two of them in through the front door using the master key he still held in his pocket. The entrance hall was, of course, deserted and quiet, save for the eternal ticking of the Darkling's grandfather clock. Mr Pring put his hands together nervously. "Is there anything at all I can help you with, madam?" he said to fill the silence.

"It's Deirdre Fisher we're here to see," Miss Fox informed him brusquely. "Where is she?"

"Do you have an appointment? She doesn't see anyone without –"

"I don't need an appointment, Mr Pring." She rounded on him. "Juvenile Services have the right to inspect any care facilities without notice, especially when a severe breach of policy has occurred."

Severe breach? What could she be talking about? "I don't know what you mean," he said hotly. "There must be some kind of mistake. Mrs Fisher would never infringe the rules, I can assure you!"

"Your precious Mrs Fisher apparently doesn't tell you everything, sir! We wish to see her concerning a matter of security. I suggest you stay out of it if, as you claim, you have no knowledge of the matter."

Security? Mr Pring went cold. "Perhaps you would care to wait in Mrs Fisher's office, madam?" he said hollowly. "I'll let you in."

"Yes, that would be acceptable. Come along, Mr Withers."

Once they were all inside the office, Mr Pring closed the door carefully and locked it. Miss Fox stared at him. "What exactly are you doing, Mr Pring? We wish to speak to Deirdre Fisher, not some underling."

Mr Pring held his temper. "It's me you want to see," he said. "About the security systems, is it?"

Miss Fox gave him an appraising look. "Yes, as a matter of fact." She went and sat boldly behind Mrs Fisher' desk. "So it was you, was it?"

"I had my reasons. I was going to call you this morning, in fact."

"Of course you were," she purred. "Have a seat, Mr Pring."

He sat. Mr Withers lit another cigarette as he drew the curtains.

"How did you know?" Mr Pring's voice sounded old, uncertain.

Miss Fox smiled, her teeth beautifully white and even. Her red lipstick was immaculate. Not bad for eight in the morning, a part of Mr Pring's mind noted ruefully. "It's not common knowledge," she said, "but all of our facilities are linked into a master server at our head office. We don't continually monitor all of the goings-on in these places, of course, that would be far too impractical and expensive, but we are automatically alerted if any of the remote units are tampered with." She gave him a direct look. "As occurred here last night at approximately…" she consulted a pad produced from within her briefcase, "…12:16 hours. Care to shed any light on that, Mr Pring?"

He licked his lips, cursing himself for not having thought of that. Now it looked really bad for him, even though he had genuinely intended to inform Juvenile Services. How to convince this woman of that?

"I told you, I had my reasons," he said evenly. "I just want to say that Deirdre Fisher knew nothing about this, though."

"Perhaps not, but the fact remains that the emergency key that was used to open the cabinet is her sole responsibility. How did you come to have it, Mr Pring?"

"I took it," he admitted, "without her knowledge. I had reason to suspect that a… an incident had occurred, but I needed the CCTV footage to prove it. Deirdre, um, Mrs Fisher, refused me access."

"So you just went ahead and did it anyway, hmmm? Are you aware, Mr Pring, that it is a serious crime to access these images without the consent of a responsible agent? Why do you think we have such tight security measures in place?"

"I am aware of that, yes, madam, but I felt in this case that –"

"That's not your call to make," Miss Fox cut him off. "You should have reported your suspicions to a higher authority, which would then have made appropriate enquiries on your behalf."

He had no answer to that, though it galled him to admit it. In his day, there had been none of this modern-style lily-livered thinking so prevalent today. A clip round the ear or a sound thrashing was the solution to most problems back then.

Miss Fox must have taken his silence as an admission of defeat. She let up on him a little. "Just what was it that you felt was so important, hmmm?" She leaned back in Deirdre's seat, watching him.

Mr Pring sighed. "This may sound silly to you, Miss Fox, with all your fancy qualifications and training and such, but I've been taking care of children for longer than you've been alive. I can spot a situation from twenty paces, often before it's even started. I can tell the good eggs from the bad, and I know how to spot a troublemaker. It's an instinct."

Miss Fox looked amused. "Is that right?"

He ignored her. "I knew something was up on Sunday. I could just feel it. And let me tell you, Miss Fox, I'm very rarely wrong. Especially when it comes to that Fortune boy."

A peculiar change came over Miss Fox then. She exchanged a quick look with Mr Withers. "Lucas Fortune?" she said evenly. "Is that who this is about?"

Mr Pring frowned slightly. "Yes, that's right. Why, do you know something about him?"

She smiled. "No more than you, I'm sure. Why don't you carry on?"

He shrugged. "I suspected Fortune had been up to something whilst I was otherwise occupied with official business on Sunday afternoon. I caught the boy sneaking around the corridors later, looking suspicious, but I didn't have any solid evidence of mischief at that time so I let him go. I came back here to the office and spoke to Mrs Fisher." He recounted the conversation as best he could.

"Then what happened?"

This was the crux of the matter. "I noticed that Mrs Fisher seemed to be acting a bit…oddly," he said delicately.

"How so?"

"She was distracted, distant, like she had something on her mind. I couldn't put my finger on it at the time."

Miss Fox waited. "That's it?"

"No. I spoke to her again the next day, yesterday. That's when I asked about the CCTV thing. She said no to that."

"Good for her." Miss Fox sat forward again, steepling her fingers under her chin, her silence prompting him to go on.

He told her what had been said during that strange conversation. "She actually defended him," Mr Pring finished indignantly. "She accused *me* of having some sort of grudge against the boy!"

"Do you?" Miss Fox smiled sweetly.

"Of course not!"

"Good. So let me get this straight, Mr Pring. You didn't see Fortune actually doing anything wrong, and you think Mrs Fisher has been acting a bit odd lately. You're saying that these are your reasons for illegally tampering with government equipment?"

It sounded ridiculous when she said it like that, but he knew he was right. "See for yourself!" he said angrily, pointing at the CCTV cabinet. "See what I saw, then you'll understand! Look!" He produced the time references from the footage that he'd noted down. "Check it! I'm telling you, that Fortune boy did something to Mrs Fisher!"

Miss Fox grinned humourlessly. "Come now, Mr Pring, calm yourself. We intend to check the footage for ourselves, don't you worry about that. Why don't you have a nice cup of tea, hmmm? Ptolemy, if you would be so kind, I noticed a lovely expensive-looking tea set over there."

Mr Pring couldn't understand her reaction. Why was she being so calm? It was almost as if she wasn't surprised. He'd just told her that one of their charges had done something threatening to the head of this House, and she wanted him to drink tea? A hot cup was thrust unceremoniously into his shaking hands. He took a sip blindly.

"Calmer now?" Miss Fox asked him after a minute or two. He nodded speechlessly. "Good. Now we can take a look at this footage you seem so upset about."

Mr Withers pulled a chair up to the CCTV cabinet and opened its doors with his own key. Miss Fox handed him the page from Mr Pring's notebook with the time references and, much quicker than Mr Pring had managed it, zeroed in on the offending section of footage. "There," Mr Pring murmured as Fortune appeared on the screen, skulking around outside the office. Miss Fox ignored him. The three of them watched the strange scene unfold in silence.

"You see?" Mr Pring exclaimed when it was over. "It's just like I said, Fortune threatened her or something. You could see it! I told you!"

Miss Fox appeared not to have heard him. Her face was pale, devoid of expression, her gaze somewhere else. One red-painted nail tapped absently on her chin.

"Now you can see I was justified in taking the action I did, Miss Fox," Mr Pring defended himself eagerly. There was no response. "I say, Miss Fox?"

She shook herself. "Hmmm? Oh yes, quite right, Mr Pring," she said in a faint voice. "You did the right thing, indeed." She gave a significant look to her assistant, who was casually lighting another cigarette. He nodded almost imperceptibly.

"We'll have to ask you to keep this matter to yourself for the time being, Mr Pring," Miss Fox declared briskly, back in charge again. "Confidential, as it were. You understand."

Mr Pring wasn't sure that he did, but he nodded anyway. The relief flooding through his frail old body was so acute it made him feel weak. He'd done the right thing, and now matters would be taken to a higher level, vindicating his instincts. He breathed out a huge sigh.

Miss Fox continued, "We may need to take this up with you again at some point, but in the meantime we will take over from here. As I said, you are not to speak of this to anyone. Think of it as...privileged information."

He found his voice. "What about me?" he croaked. "Will I be in trouble?"

Miss Fox gave him an inscrutable look. "Not if you do as I ask, Mr Pring. If you play along we can make any possible charges against you just – go away. Are we clear?"

He nodded solemnly. Yes, it was very clear. Whatever he'd stumbled onto here, it seemed JS wished to keep a firm lid on it.

"You can go now," Miss Fox dismissed him with a wave of her hand. "And remember, Mr Pring – not a word."

He got up and stumbled from the office without a backward glance, obscurely thankful. He had been steamrollered by JS, it was true, but he comforted himself with the knowledge that he had been right all along.

He wondered how he would explain to Deirdre about the people in her office.

Miss Fox and Mr Withers exchanged triumphant glances as the door shut behind Mr Pring's retreating back. The evidence was far from conclusive, but it seemed to show quite clearly that they had been right all along to focus their investigations on this Fortune boy. He was the right age, for one thing, and had been mysteriously abandoned at roughly the same time that Agent Smith had vanished.

It had taken more than eleven long years to narrow the search down to this particular corner of the country which, taken by itself, was more than a little odd. With all the resources Echelon Nine could command, it seemed pretty unlikely that a straightforward manhunt (boyhunt?) could have lasted so long before finally yielding fruit. Miss Fox had noticed this and quietly wondered about it before. Seen from a different angle, it seemed almost as if someone had been deliberately stalling the operation from the inside…

But that was preposterous, of course. Her entire branch of Echelon Nine was dedicated to tracking down and capturing people like the Fortune boy. The only higher authority in the land was the government itself, and even they didn't know everything. No, it must simply have been a case of expert concealment. After all, Agent Smith had been an Echelon seeker herself for many years before hooking up with that enemy operative and having his child…

Miss Fox shuddered at the very thought.

She had Ptolemy replay the recorded scene again. "Look," she said excitedly, "he's clearly using some kind of mental coercion on her!"

"I agree," Mr Withers said in his fluting voice. "He's good, too. See how she tries to resist him there? And he's only twelve years old." He let that hang in the air along with the smoke from his cigarette.

Miss Fox waved her hand angrily in front of her face. "Your smoking problem is starting to become my problem, Ptolemy," she coughed. "Don't you know passive smoking kills?"

"We all die eventually," was his amused reply.

She snorted. "Very profound." She was pretty pleased, though. This recording, while not as high quality as she might have hoped, should be sufficient for Stanford to finally okay her requests to step-up and concentrate the search.

"You know," Mr Withers mused, "it occurs to me that there may be something else we can do to make this evidence even more compelling." He'd been thinking along similar lines, then.

"Oh yes, what's that?" she asked, interested.

He peered critically at the CCTV setup. "This model does not have audio playback," he said.

"Sound? No, it doesn't, but what…" she stopped, grasping what he was driving at. "But the terminals back at command do!" she finished. "There is sound here, only it's been recorded separately. We can listen to it at Headquarters!"

They grinned at each other. Ptolemy Withers might be a creepy psycho with the personal habits of a tramp, but he was as sharp as a tack, Miss Fox thought charitably. She turned to the monitor, where Lucas Fortune was running through his silent drama over and over again.

"We've finally got you, Fortune," she muttered delightedly. "Soon, there'll be nowhere on earth you can hide."

Chapter Fifteen – The Circle

Grumbling stomachs and full bladders woke the children sometime in the early evening. They crawled blearily from the tent, blinking. A mist had descended at some point during the day, surrounding them with a featureless grey wall. The temperature had dropped noticeably. Nearby a solitary sheep skittered away, startled. It stopped and gazed back at them reproachfully with its mad, slotted eyes before ambling off into the mist.

The boys and girls went their separate ways to take care of natures' calls, then they shared around more of the energy bars and some hardening sandwiches Timothy had thoughtfully retained from yesterday's packed lunch. It wasn't much, and more worryingly, they had only enough food left for perhaps a day of careful rationing. Concern was starting to show on the faces of Lucas's friends.

"Are you absolutely sure about this, Lucas?" Tamsen asked with doubt on her face, voicing all of their thoughts. Everyone looked at Lucas expectantly.

He wanted to be able to reassure them, but didn't know what to say. "How can I be sure?" he replied, trying not to let his own worries show. "We're doing this because of something I heard in a dream. Anyone would think we're crazy for coming out here like this, but I don't think there's any other choice." He looked around at their anxious faces. "You all put your trust in me. I can't give you any firm answers right now, I wish I could, but you're going to have to trust me just a little longer. Okay?"

They nodded gravely. "We're not questioning you, mate," Aaron said, glaring at Tamsen. She poked her tongue out at him. "We do trust you." He looked like he wanted to say more, but he held back.

"Okay," Lucas said gratefully. "I don't know what we're going to find, but the answers we need are real close now. Just a little further, I promise."

He hoped those words wouldn't come back to haunt him.

The tent was packed up and they moved off again, carefully threading their way down the hill. The mist seemed to cut off all sound too, leaving them with the creeping feeling they were the only people in the world. Lucas hoped it would clear off before nightfall. Navigating through this in the dark would be near impossible.

*

Byron Stanford watched the footage with no noticeable reaction. He, Miss Fox, Mr Withers and a technician named Randolph were standing around a monitor station that had been assembled in the dining room of the rented house in Exeter. This house had been completely taken over by Echelon Nine in the last few weeks, yet such was their level of professionalism that none of the neighbours even suspected a thing. As far as they were aware, a quiet family had moved in, rarely seen, keeping themselves to themselves. That was exactly how Echelon wanted it.

Stanford looked up as the footage ended. "Is that it?" he asked pointedly.

Miss Fox was dismayed at his reaction. "Sir, you can clearly see some kind of mental coercion technique being used here. I think this warrants further investigation, don't you?" She knew she was pushing her luck, but she didn't care. Couldn't the man see how important this was?

He raised an eyebrow slightly at her challenging tone, but didn't answer her directly. Instead he turned to the technician, who was squinting at the monitoring equipment, screwdriver in hand. "Randolph, how soon until you can give us sound?"

The man grinned nervously, mopping sweat from his upper lip, where a wispy moustache lurked like a stray caterpillar. "Any time now, Mr

Stanford," he said eagerly. "I just need to match up the time-frame references with the audio cues so I can synchronise –"

"Just let me know when it's done," Stanford interrupted. "I'll be in my office. Danielle, with me please." He strode from the room. Mr Withers gave her a small shrug and withdrew a cigarette from his jacket.

"Hey, you can't smoke that in here –" she heard the technician start to say before the closing door cut him off.

Fuming silently, Miss Fox followed Stanford up the stairs to the study he was using as an office. "Close the door," he said when they were inside. He sat in his chair and gave her an appraising look. "What's this about, Danielle?" he asked her evenly.

She spluttered. She couldn't help herself. "Sir, I can't believe you're not taking this seriously!"

He continued to stare at her. "I take my job, and Echelon's role in national security, very seriously, Danielle," he said softly. "I know you do too, but what exactly is it you expect me to do about this?"

"We need to upscale the entire operation!" she almost shouted. "This boy, this Lucas Fortune, is exactly the kind of person – of *thing* we've been looking for!"

"How do you know that, Danielle?" His voice was mild, but something in his expression spoke of danger just beneath the surface. She knew she was skating on thin ice here. With an effort, she forced herself to calm down.

"You haven't met him, sir," she said in a more even tone. "I have. There's something about him, I don't know what, I just…I have a feeling."

"A feeling," he repeated. "Danielle, you know I respect you and your abilities as a seeker, but without absolutely positive confirmation that this boy is the one we're looking for, I will not authorise any further action. That's the way it is, I'm afraid."

"Mr Stanford, we're on the same side here, aren't we? All I'm asking is that you allow me to do my job. To do that, I'm going to need access to Echelon resources. I need more…" she groped for the right word.

"Power? Is that it?" Stanford sat back, eyeing her.

Miss Fox was exasperated by his attitude. "Will you at least listen to the audio when Randolph has it ready?"

"Of course I will, Danielle. I will look at every aspect of this case, but unless that audio is very compelling I may have no choice but to shut down this operation and reassign you to another area. We've wasted enough time on this boy."

"Yes, sir," she said stiffly. "Will that be all?"

"Yes, for now, but stick around. I may need you later."

She turned and stalked out of the room with as much dignity as she could muster.

What an idiot, she fumed outside. Stanford wasn't even prepared to give her the benefit of the doubt! How was she supposed to carry out her function if her own superior didn't trust her? It was infuriating. *Wasted enough time on this boy?* They'd barely even begun!

She went out to the rear garden to calm herself, remembering back to when she'd first met Lucas Fortune a week or two ago. He'd seemed like any normal kid at first, nervous but cocky, a typical children's home brat. She'd seen hundreds like him during the course of her investigations. Her cover as a Juvenile Services agent allowed her almost unlimited access to these places. None of the other children she'd seen, though, had given her the strange, uneasy sensation she'd begun to feel in this boy's presence. She hadn't let on, of course, but he'd given her the creeps, especially when he'd faced down that idiotic Jacob Kwame. Then she'd looked Fortune directly in the eye, focusing her latent psychic ability, trying to read him, and had got – nothing. Not exactly a blank wall, but more like a veil, a concealing fog, betraying nothing. It had shaken her. There were plenty of people with the ability to block her powers, of course, but she'd never before met one so young. That kind of control normally only came after years of practice.

Why couldn't Stanford see it, damn him? She herself had been recruited into Echelon Nine all those years ago precisely because of her natural psychic abilities. It was what made her an ideal seeker. Why didn't the man trust her judgement now?

She chewed it over in her mind for a while until the door opened and Ptolemy called her. "We've got something," he told her, as usual betraying no emotion. She hurried gladly inside.

Stanford was already in the monitoring room when she got there. So was the technician, Randolph.

"I had to cross-link the cues from the backup track so that they…" the man caught Stanford's look and hurriedly brought up the footage on a large monitor. "Well, here it is."

Miss Fox watched and listened in mounting excitement as all her suspicions were confirmed. The Fortune boy was clearly controlling Fisher, grilling her for information about his parents. That in itself was interesting, something to be analysed in greater detail at a later date, but right now all she could focus on was the fact that she had been right! She turned to see how Stanford was taking it.

He didn't appear elated at all. In fact he had an odd expression on his face, somewhere between confusion and worry. He caught her looking and quickly blanked his face, but she'd seen it. Interesting. She filed it away for future consideration.

"It seems you were right, Danielle," he said stiffly, still staring at the screen. "I will need this analysed properly, of course, but in the meantime I will give serious consideration to your requests." He turned and looked at her directly. "Good job, Agent."

She smiled, a genuine one for once. "Thank you, Mr Stanford. Thank you indeed."

Stanford climbed hurriedly to his office and locked the door, annoyed with himself that Fox had seen his momentary lapse of control. He was better than that, far better, but he'd truly not expected what he'd heard in the recording. It had shocked him deeply. He sat down heavily and poured himself a large scotch from his secret stash.

He'd been so careful all this time, covering his tracks so well, only to have the boy go and blab everything in front of a CCTV camera! Now things would be a lot trickier, especially with the tenacious Danielle Fox sniffing around like an over-ambitious bloodhound. He'd tried stalling her, tried fudging the whole investigation, but with this new evidence it would be far harder to control the situation to his satisfaction.

So now Lucas was aware of the circumstances surrounding his abandonment at Peregrine House. That was unfortunate, but probably inevitable. It had been only a matter of time, really, before the corrupt Deirdre Fisher slipped up and let the truth out.

No matter. Byron Stanford was the head of Echelon Nine, a man with formidable resources at his disposal. The situation would be handled and contained, no matter what.

He wondered what Lucas Fortune was doing now.

*

It was growing dark on the moors, signified by a gradual reduction of visibility through the slowly drifting mist. Dew hung glistening on every shrub and low tree, settling on the children's clothing, not soaking through yet, but making them just damp enough to be cold and miserable. They'd been stumbling around for what could only have been a couple of hours since setting out again, but it felt far longer. Even Sammi River's spirits were beginning to flag.

Lucas led them grimly on, watching the ground ahead intently for any sign of hidden pitfalls or dangerous footing. Each of them had stumbled and fallen at least once so far, but luckily there had been no serious injuries. Aaron's ankle was slightly tender where he had twisted it, and Timothy had fallen heavily on his wrist a while ago, but still they pushed on, ignoring the discomfort.

For the past few minutes, Lucas had been aware of a slight increase in the mysterious pull he was feeling. It seemed to be guiding him more strongly now, urging him on with a silent, insistent call. Did that mean they were getting close? He didn't know, but ardently hoped that was the case. He wondered how much longer they could keep this up. How could six inexperienced children really expect to stand much of a chance against the wild moor? People died here all the time, he knew, adults and expert hikers alike. It was not a place for the ill-prepared.

They came at last to a shallow bowl-shaped depression resting in a space between two low, rolling hills. The light was fading rapidly, but there was still enough to see that in the depression was a flat circle, ringed by an evenly spaced group of standing stones. These stones loomed out of the mist, dark, twisted shapes, hunched and gnarled like ancient trolls, silently standing guard.

"Whoa," Dion murmured. "This is one of those ancient druid places, I reckon. They probably used to come here and do weird ceremonies and stuff. See, there's the altar stone."

In the centre of the circle, on a slight mound that lifted it about half a metre above the surrounding ground level, rested a low, flat shape like a long table. It was tilted up at one end and lay slightly twisted. A long crack crossed its width about halfway down, separating it into two neat sections. The children approached it cautiously, nervous and uneasy. The whole place reeked of dark secrets and ancient history.

Closer to, the centre-stone looked less like something man-made, more like a random pile of weathered rocks forming a convenient table-top shape. Maybe that's why the druids had built this circle here, Lucas thought. The stone was a curious red-brown colour, shot through with veins of twinkling quartz and darker rock. Coarse grass sprouted through cracks all around its sides and base.

The pulling sensation Lucas felt had changed into something else now, a weight settling on his shoulders like a cloak of some heavy material. He tried walking forward a few paces, then out to the edge of the circle, but he felt drawn back to the stone altar in the middle. "I think this is it," he said excitedly, the weariness starting to fall away from him.

The others looked at him quizzically. "What, this?" Tamsen said. She peered around her. "But, there's nothing here. What are we supposed to do now?"

"I – don't know," Lucas confessed. "All I knew was that I had to get…here, wherever this is. What happens next…" he shrugged lamely.

"Well, there must be something," Tamsen said, clearly annoyed. Of all his friends, she was always the most sceptical, the one most likely to voice her doubts out loud. She peered around again, even though the rapidly gathering darkness was making vision more difficult by the minute. "We should take a proper look around, I guess," she said. She and Sammi moved off to inspect the standing stones at the perimeter.

Lucas was at a loss. Tamsen was right: this place hardly seemed very promising. The rest of his friends stood round in awkward silence, not looking at him, concern written in their expressions. "We'll figure this out," he cajoled them. "Come on, guys, we were drawn here for a reason, we just have to figure out the next step. I reckon we should set up the tent, maybe get a fire going, have some grub, then we can think about what to do. Yeah?"

His friends nodded wearily, not convinced, but nevertheless they unshouldered their packs and began to assemble the pieces of the tent. Lucas was losing them, he knew, but what could he do or say? They looked to him for guidance, but all he could offer them was hollow-sounding reassurances and empty words. How much longer could he keep this up?

A chill wind began to blow, stirring the mist, thinning it, and by the time the tent was set up it had dispersed considerably, allowing the children a greater view of their surroundings. The low valley the children were in was topped on both sides by the mounded shapes of tors, the slopes around them littered with chunks of dark grey rock and stone. Stands of hawthorn and bracken thrust out of the damp earth here and there, and worn game trails, possibly rabbit, crisscrossed the slopes. Interestingly, none of these trails passed through the stone circle itself, though; instead they appeared to skirt carefully around the circle's edge a good three or four metres beyond the ring of standing stones.

A fire turned out to be more difficult to start than Lucas had thought. Twigs and sticks were in plentiful supply, but all proved too damp to catch light. The driest wood they managed to find just sat there inertly under the sparks Lucas inexpertly produced with the knife and flint he had 'borrowed' from Colin Herbert. *Why didn't I think to bring some matches?* he cursed himself silently, growing more annoyed by the second. *Some leader I am, can't even light a fire…*

"Hey, check this out!" Tamsen's voice called from somewhere in the dark. Glad of the distraction, the boys hurried over to her.

"This is weird," she told them excitedly as they drew near. She and Sammi were waiting next to one of the standing stones. It was about two metres high, a lumpy, twisted column that curved slightly up towards a flattened tip, where a wide oval rock balanced precariously on top. Dark patches of moss stained its surface like some kind of spreading disease.

Dion squinted at it. "It's a rock, Tamsen," he said.

She made a face and grabbed his hand, placing it wordlessly on the surface of the stone. His eyes widened. "Oh."

"Feels warm, doesn't it?" Tamsen exclaimed. "Pretty strange, huh?" She rubbed her hand along the stone.

The others reached out and touched it too. It *was* warm, not too hot to touch but far hotter than any rock had any right to be that spent its time constantly exposed to the harsh weather conditions of Dartmoor. "Maybe the sun, during the day…" Lucas hazarded.

"Oh, come on," Tamsen scoffed. "This stone is way too big to absorb enough heat energy from the sun to warm all the way through like this."

"What are you, some kind of geology expert?" Aaron put in fiercely. "Why don't you tell us what did it then, smarty-pants!"

She glared at him, but didn't answer right away. "Maybe…something underground," she said thoughtfully after a moment or two, "like a hot spring, or…magma, maybe. I don't know."

"Magma?" Aaron repeated incredulously. "What, like a volcano, or something? You're kidding, right?"

"Actually," Dion supplied, "this whole area was formed on top of a giant magma pocket, you know." He grinned.

Aaron groaned. "Not you as well, D."

Lucas left them arguing. It was an interesting discovery, but it didn't really help them much. Timothy came with him, Sammi River tagging along behind. They passed another one of the stones, a low hump leaning over crazily to one side, and just out of interest Lucas touched it; it was warm too. Probably this whole area was affected by the same phenomena, whatever it was.

Aaron was leaning against the first standing stone, still arguing with Tamsen; those two did that a lot, Lucas noted with amusement. Abruptly, Aaron gave a yelp and leaped away from the rock, tumbling to the grass. Lucas dashed back over to him.

"What is it?" he asked breathlessly.

Aaron pointed a shaky finger at the stone. "C – cold," he chattered, blowing on his other hand where it had been touching the rock. His fingers were blue, steaming slightly.

"What?" Tamsen exclaimed, leaning forward to touch the rock. "Ow! It's freezing!"

So it was; a sheen of ice was already beginning to form over its surface. "But that doesn't make any sense!" Tamsen cried.

"Does anything?" Aaron muttered, picking himself up gingerly. Lucas and Timothy grabbed his arms to steady him. They left Tamsen silently fuming at the stone as though it offended her. Probably it did, Lucas considered. She liked her world orderly and easily explained. *Good luck hanging around with us, then*, he thought.

"Haven't you got that fire going yet?" Aaron said miserably as they got back to the tent. "I'm cold."

"You do it, then," Lucas shot back, more sharply than he'd intended.

"Alright, I will!" Aaron scooped up the knife and flint and tried to make it spark, but only succeeded in clumsily dropping the knife into the pile of twigs. "Dammit," he said savagely, thrusting his hand into the pile.

There was a dull 'whoomph' as the twigs burst into flame, white smoke boiling out as though desperate to escape. The children danced back, yelling out in surprise, as Aaron yanked his hand hurriedly from the miniature inferno. "Fire!" he shouted redundantly. He sat back hard on his haunches and stared at his hand, which appeared completely unharmed. "Fire," he said again, wonderingly. He grinned at the rest of them, pointing at the now merrily burning twigs. "Look, fire!"

Not ones to ignore good fortune (no pun intended), the others crowded around Aaron and his fire, feeling the heat already warming their aching bodies for what seemed like the first time in ages. "How did you…" Dion began, but his expression changed in mid-sentence. "Your ability!"

It took Aaron a moment to cotton on. When he did, his expression was ecstatic. "Flame on!" he shouted joyfully.

"Took you long enough," Timothy taunted him.

Aaron waved his hand around, grinning manically. "I'll burn you up, dirtbag!" He wrestled the bigger boy to the ground, both of them laughing.

Lucas was glad for his friend. Up until now, he knew that Aaron had secretly been feeling a bit left out of the group, wondering what his role was and why he was here with them. As a side-effect, his discovery also served to lighten the mood considerably. Dion had joined in the scrap; he was currently in a headlock with Timothy, who was sitting on a struggling, cursing Aaron. Sammi watched bemusedly from nearby, a half-smile on her face as she warmed herself at the fire.

Tamsen wandered over eventually, face dark. She plumped on the ground next to Lucas, where they had laid out some blankets on the chill grass. "I can't figure it," she muttered, staring moodily at the flames.

"Does it really matter?" Lucas said. "I mean, it doesn't really affect us, does it? Just add it to the list of general weirdness."

She made a face. "I guess. Things like this just bug me, that's all."

"What, the hot stone going cold, or Aaron starting fires with his fingers?"

She gave him a strange look. "What did you say?"

"Which bit? Aaron starting the fire? It's his ability, we think, but why it took so long to come out –"

"He touched the stone," she whispered, half to herself. "It was hot before, then he touched it…" she trailed off, thinking hard.

Dion came over, pink-cheeked and messy-haired. He sank to the ground with a groan. "What are we talking about?"

"It's almost like he – took the heat from the stone…" Tamsen continued, ignoring him.

"…and channelled it into the fire," Dion finished. They looked at each other in surprise.

"How did you…" Tamsen began, perplexed.

"I don't know, I wasn't reading you. I just sort of – figured it out."

"You've been coming out with all kinds of stuff recently," Lucas recalled. "When did you get so smart?" He was bantering, but it was a serious question. He'd noticed that his friend had been volunteering lots of unusual information in the last few weeks. Dion was no dunce, but neither was he known as an educational genius. He was just a normal kid, like any other. At least, he had been…

"I don't know," Dion confessed. "Things have been just sort-of coming to me recently. Maybe I'm getting ideas from other people's thoughts, but it doesn't feel the same as that. When I 'read' people, it's like I can actually hear their minds working. With this, the knowledge just seems to pop into my head when I need it." He frowned. "I guess I'm just remembering stuff I learned in school." He didn't sound convinced.

Tamsen regarded him intently. "Interesting," she murmured.

The campfire did much to lift their spirits, giving them something to focus on while they chatted into the night, not to mention much needed heat and light. They carefully ate some more of their rations, but it was becoming harder to silence the pangs of hunger they all felt gnawing away in their bellies. They couldn't last much longer like this. If some significant progress wasn't made tomorrow, Lucas felt, then they might have no choice but to go back, empty-handed. *But we're so close*, he thought to himself, frustrated. *It's right here, I know it!*

The only problem was he had no idea what to do about it.

Chapter Sixteen – Follow The Leader

"School trip?" Miss Fox shouted. "Why wasn't I informed?"

Mrs Fisher looked surprised. "Miss Fox, this programme of summer events was organised by Juvenile Services." She didn't say it, but her implication was pretty clear: *try talking to your own people.*

Miss Fox calmed herself with a supreme effort. Fisher was right, of course. She should have checked for things like this before coming out here to Peregrine House again. It wouldn't do her cover much good if she allowed herself to get sloppy.

She forced a smile. "You're right. I apologise, Mrs Fisher."

Fisher harrumphed. "Yes, well, I imagine you have a difficult job to do," she conceded huffily. "On that note, I have to say that I'm not particularly happy about the way you came in here yesterday. Poor Mr Pring tells me you gave him the fright of his life."

Miss Fox gave the man in question a cool look, who was standing sheepishly behind Fisher's chair. "Did he?" she said evenly. "What else did he say?"

"He told me you turned up here unannounced before the working day had even started. It's a good thing he was able to deal with you on my behalf. I must say I don't appreciate these surprise inspections you've taken to springing on us recently. Is there something wrong?"

"Nothing for you to worry about, Mrs Fisher." She gave a warning glance to Mr Pring before continuing. "You run an exemplary facility here. No, the reason we have been showing such zeal recently is a policy change at Juvenile Services." She had prepared for such an eventuality as this. "We intend to introduce a new grading system for all juvenile care homes in the south-west, which means increased inspections and some disruption, I'm afraid. Peregrine House, because of its excellent record, has been chosen to be one of the first."

Fisher puffed up visibly at that. "Well, I just wish you would keep me informed," she complained, but she was clearly pleased at the news. "A grading system, you say? A bit like AA stars for hotels, perhaps?" She laughed at her own joke, a burbling sound that grated on Miss Fox's nerves.

"Something like that. You will receive a full briefing of our proposals in the next few weeks. In the meantime, we will continue with our business, which brings me to the reason for our visit today."

"Anything we can do to assist, Miss Fox," Fisher said eagerly.

Miss Fox smiled, but inside she was seething. Fortune had been almost within her grasp, only for him to wriggle out at the last moment. If Stanford had only allowed her to come back here earlier! She'd submitted all the proper requests, but it had taken Tarquin Pring's foolish meddling with the security system before any real action had finally been authorised. She was thankful for that at least, in a distantly resentful way, but she disliked such important matters being decided by factors outside of her control. "Excellent," she said out loud. "We will of course be reviewing all records and paperwork in due course, but for now we would like to begin by talking directly to some of the children themselves, at least the ones who are currently still here."

The faintest flicker of doubt crossed Fisher' face. "Oh? That's –"

"Policy," Miss Fox put in smoothly. It was a useful word. "But a forward-facing one, I'm sure you'll agree."

"Yes, of course. I'll have some of the children made ready for you."

Told what to say, you mean. "That won't be necessary. We have a list of children, randomly chosen from our own files, already prepared. We will take care of everything else."

Fisher looked slightly panicky. She exchanged a quick glance with Mr Pring. "As the owner and proprietor of Peregrine House, I would like to be involved in the interview process myself," she said shakily. "Out of concern for the children, of course."

Not likely. "Mrs Fisher, please understand me. Our presence here, whilst perhaps not entirely welcome by yourselves, is a vital part of our ongoing drive to improve Juvenile Services. To do that we are going to need honest evaluations and *unbiased* opinions. I hope I am being clear enough."

Fisher hid it well, but there was an undeniable current of hostility in her pose and expression now. "Perfectly," she said. "I'll have Mr Pring prepare a room for you. Unless you would prefer to do that yourself too."

Miss Fox smiled victoriously. "I'm sure Mr Pring's judgment will suffice. He appears to be a man who can read a situation and act accordingly." She was looking directly at him as she said this; he blanched and hurried from the room without a word.

"Don't worry, Mrs Fisher," she continued pleasantly, enjoying herself now. It was like watching a fish struggling on a hook. "I'm sure we won't uncover anything…untoward. In the meantime, while we're waiting, here's the list of residents we will be speaking to."

Fisher took the list with bad grace, peering at it sulkily. "As I told you just now, madam, a lot of the children are currently away on activity breaks, including the first name on your list here, Lucas Fortune. Many of these other children listed are with him too, I'm afraid. They won't be back for several more days." She said this last almost gloatingly, no doubt seeing it as some kind of small victory.

More delays. Well, there was nothing else for it. She had to go through with this charade. It wouldn't do for genuine Juvenile Services agents to start sniffing around now. Miss Fox's cover and credentials were virtually foolproof, all the correct records carefully put in place by covert Echelon operatives, but it was best to keep this operation as low-key as possible.

"Very well," she said grudgingly. "So tell me, which of the names on the list *are* actually still here?"

"Dear me, Miss Fox, you do seem to be a little – ill-informed," Fisher said silkily with a small smile. She made a show of looking down the list again. "Let's see now…"

Miss Fox didn't need her psychic ability to see exactly how Fisher's mind worked. The woman was quite obviously a small-minded, self-important little jobsworth with an over-inflated ego who thrived on making other people feel smaller than she was. If Miss Fox's own concerns hadn't been so pressing, she might have enjoyed taking the time to knock the woman down a peg or two…

Instead she smiled distantly, affecting unconcern.

"Ah, yes, here we are," Fisher said at length. "These children are still here, I believe. I will have to double-check with Mr Pring when he returns, but I'm certain they elected not to take part in the activities this year. In fact, this child here..." She broke off, a sly expression crossing her face.

"Yes?"

"I believe he is a good friend of Lucas Fortune, seeing as you seem so anxious to speak to that particular boy. I'm sure this child will be happy to talk to you."

Well, that was something, at least. "And who might that be?"

"His name is Graves. Marshall Graves."

*

Lucas woke with a start, his head aching. He'd not slept well, the six of them finally deciding to turn in sometime in the early hours of the morning. They'd been squashed together uncomfortably in the tent, such that Timothy had grumpily decided to go and sleep outside. That had left more room for the rest of them, and the others had fallen asleep quickly enough, but Lucas had lay there for a good while longer, doubt and concern running rampant through his addled brain.

Now he was alone in the tent. Wan light filtered in through the tent material. It felt like late morning. He blearily checked his watch, but the LCD display was blank. The battery must have gone. He shook himself and crawled wearily out.

Tamsen and Sammi were seated cross-legged on the altar-rock, the contents of their packs strewn all around them. "Morning," Tamsen greeted him. Sammi gave him a shy smile.

"Hi," he managed. His mouth was dry, voice croaky. "Where is everyone?"

"Tim is over by that big stone, still asleep. It's pretty warm if you get close enough." She held a sock up to the light critically. It had a hole in the heel. "Dion and the other one went off exploring about half an hour ago."

He sighed. "The other one? You mean Aaron?"

"I know what I mean," she said darkly. Sammi stifled a giggle.

"You don't like him much, do you?" He rubbed sleep from his eyes with the heels of his hands. It didn't help much.

"He's so bloody argumentative," she complained. "Why does he have to contradict everything I say all the time?"

This time Sammi looked straight at Lucas, eyes full of mirth. He kept his face straight. "Just the way he is, I guess." He felt a little mischievous. "He likes you, you know."

Tamsen pulled a shocked face. "Get. Off."

Lucas chuckled and went to find some water.

The day was overcast and blustery, grey clouds scudding low overhead as though in a great hurry to get somewhere. On one of the hills above the stone circle a small flock of sheep nibbled industriously at the tough grass, spray-painted red marks like smears of blood decorating their flanks. It was the only sign of colour in the otherwise dull and drab surroundings.

Lucas was thoughtfully eating half of one of the last food bars when Dion and Aaron returned. They were ruddy-cheeked and windblown, hair standing up untidily. "We went up to that tor," Dion said excitedly. "You can see for miles around. No idea where we are, though." He scooped up a bottle of water and took a hefty swig.

"It's pretty windy up high," Aaron said. "Dion reckons it's gonna get worse, too." He eyed the tent doubtfully. "I hope that'll be enough if it starts raining." He wandered off to find Timothy.

Dion turned out to be right. While he and Lucas were taking a good look around the circle, examining the standing stones in greater detail for any clues which might help them, the wind started to pick up considerably, gusting down between the two hills as though through a funnel. Timothy was awake now, hurriedly bundling his sleeping bag away into his pack. The other children looked up at the lowering sky apprehensively.

An especially strong blast of wind almost knocked them off their feet. It whistled around and through gaps in the standing stones, producing a mournful sound like wailing. The children shivered, instinctively gathering closer together for comfort. The tent flapped madly, rocking on its moorings. Lucas eyed it in concern. They really ought to think about taking it down; it probably wasn't too safe to leave it tethered like that…

Right on cue there was an ominous ripping sound. One of the guy ropes tore free, taking a ragged chunk of tent material with it. Wind poured into the hole, forcing it rapidly wider until, as the children watched dumbstruck, the tent suddenly ripped almost in half, collapsing in on itself.

"No!" Lucas shouted uselessly into the wind. There went their only shelter! The wind finished its work quickly, tearing free the remaining guy ropes and pegs, sending the ruined tent tumbling across the circle and off down the valley. Aaron and Dion made to run after it, but it was useless. Their only shelter was gone.

As if that wasn't enough, at that moment the first beads of rain began to fall. Big, warm droplets spattered noisily around them like miniature explosions. Tamsen and Sammi began feverishly cramming their belongings into their packs before the wind took them too.

They squeezed miserably together as the heavens opened. The rain soaked them through in seconds. It was warm, but that didn't stop them feeling instantly chilled as the howling wind snatched the heat greedily away from their bodies. They crowded around the red altar-stone, trying desperately to find some shelter. Maybe they could squeeze underneath…

The stone moved. As one the children jumped back, alarmed. It looked massively heavy. If it were to fall on them, it could cause a lot of harm. Somehow, the flat part that formed the table top had twisted slightly on the tightly packed rocks that made up its base. Under where it jutted out was now a small alcove, perhaps big enough to shelter one person. Lucas gave the top an experimental shove. It didn't budge. Maybe they could move it a little more, if they acted together! "Come on," Lucas shouted, demonstrating what he intended by leaning against the rock and pushing. The others saw what he was doing and quickly moved into place next to him, placing their hands on the rock.

Sammi was the last one to touch it. The moment she did so, the whole table-top gave a shudder and began to rotate from the middle with a hideous scraping, grinding sound, the two halves revolving away from each other as though hinged. Again the children leapt back fearfully, much farther this time, retreating almost to the edge of the circle. Wide-eyed, they watched from the relative safety of the standing stones as the altar-stone split apart, revealing a dark space within, until finally it came to a halt with a last grinding roar.

Soaked through and terrified, the children gingerly approached the now wide-open altar-stone. A gap extended back into the rock, angling down into dusty-smelling darkness at a steep angle. As Lucas looked closer he saw something that almost made his heart stop; carved into the very rock floor of the gap, worn and cracked but still clearly visible, a set of steps led away down into the gloom.

He looked up at his friends, realisation dawning. This had to be the secret they were meant to find!

There was no more time to think about it now, no time for doubts or second guesses. He could no longer allow himself that luxury. He had to show his friends that their faith in him had not been misplaced. With more confidence than he really felt, he turned and placed his foot on the top step, but a hand on his arm yanked him back.

"What are you doing, Lucas?" Aaron yelled over the wind, eyes wild and fearful. "There could be anything down there!"

"That's what we're here to find out!" he shouted back. "Don't you see? Rith led us here. This is the place!" He swallowed hard. "I'm going down! Come on!" He turned away, trying to ignore the hammering of his heart, and started down the steps into the cool darkness.

The others exchanged looks of fear and dismay, but there was really no other choice. One by one they followed Lucas in.

*

Miss Fox sourly regarded the boy sitting opposite her. He stared back at her challengingly, arms folded, a small smile playing about his lips.

Some people, she mused, you know just as soon as you meet them that you won't like them. The moment this tall ginger-haired boy had sauntered into the room she'd found herself having to quash an almost instant feeling of dislike. It was hard to say precisely why. So far he'd been reasonably polite and well-spoken, but there was a kind of disdainful arrogance about him that really put her back up, the kind of arrogance that only the really rich can breed into their children. He certainly came from a well-to-do family, according to the file open on the table in front of her; father in banking, mother a doctor, big house in Wiltshire, the works. What was he doing in a place like this?

"So, how do you find life here at Peregrine House, Marshall?" she asked him in a friendly tone.

He blinked slowly, like a recently fed tiger. "The service is adequate, I suppose," he said languidly. "Pity I can't say the same about the other…guests."

"Oh? You don't always get on with the other children?"

"Get on with them?" He regarded her narrowly. "Not exactly, no."

"But you have friends here, right? People you 'hang out' with, have fun with?"

There was that look again, disdain mixed with something like contempt. "I have some people who are…loyal to me, yes."

What an odd use of words, she thought. "Like a gang, or something?" she prompted.

He appeared to give that some thought. "Sort of," he replied, smiling humourlessly. "A group of like-minded individuals."

Who did this boy think he was? Miss Fox hid her unease. He'd answered every question she'd given him so far, sometimes cryptically, but she had the distinct feeling he was holding something back. There was a strangeness about this whole place, an atmosphere of disquiet that seemed to permeate the very walls. Was the boy hiding something? She pushed her thoughts out towards him, carefully, probing at his mind.

He looked straight at her then, a grin coming to his face. "Why, Miss Fox, how very sneaky of you," he chuckled.

She withdrew quickly, trying to hide her sudden panic. What she'd briefly seen – that horrible blackness, unspeakable emotions just beneath the surface…she exerted her training and tried to force herself back under control.

Marshall waggled a finger at her. "That's naughty. I wasn't expecting that, I must say. Do all Juvenile Services people come equipped with mental powers, hmmm?"

"I don't know what you mean," she grated unconvincingly. She felt she was losing control of the situation.

The boy sat back with a satisfied expression. "Okay. Whatever you say." He gave her a lingering look up and down. She shivered involuntarily. "Was there anything else you wanted to discuss, Miss Fox?"

Why was she feeling so disoriented? This boy, for all his arrogance and knowingness, was still just that – a boy. Danielle Fox was a highly trained and skilled hunter seeker for a covert government agency, with over fifteen years of experience under her belt. The things she'd seen in her time, the things she'd done…this smirking kid was nothing.

She returned his gaze levelly, clamping down hard on her feelings. "Just a few more things, Mr Graves."

His smile disappeared. "Go on then, fire away." He yawned, affecting unconcern. "I hope this won't take much longer."

"We'll see." She gathered her thoughts. "We were talking about your friends. Who would you say is your best friend?"

He rolled his eyes. "What do you think this is, playgroup? *'Best friend'?"*

"It's a simple question, Marshall. Whom amongst the other children do you consider to be closest to you?"

"Why is that important?"

She smiled. "We're just trying to build up a picture of life in this care facility, for a study we're doing, that's all. It's all about social interaction."

He pulled a face. "Sounds boring." He leaned forward again intently. "But why don't you write this down: I don't belong here, amongst all these homeless kids and common orphans. *I'm* here because my parents would rather spend the summer on their yacht than have me at home. Why should I be friends with any of these lowlifes? I don't care about them any more than I care about you." There was genuine bitterness in his voice.

She consulted the file, confirming his story. "I'm sorry you feel that way," she lied. It was difficult to feel any kind of sympathy for this brat of a child. "But I would have thought that, having been abandoned by your parents as you say, even temporarily, it would be even more important to make friends here."

"Would you?" he spat. "I told you, I have a group of companions who hear me if I wish to speak. What more is there to say?"

He certainly had a strange way of referring to his fellows, almost like he was their ruler and they his subjects. The monstrous ego of this kid…

"And who are they, specifically? I ask because I might like to speak to them too later, so I can get a more complete picture of life at Peregrine House."

He scowled but reeled off a short list of names in a bored voice. One name, in particular, was conspicuous by its absence.

"Is that it?" she said, looking up from the pad where she had written the names.

Marshall glared at her, his earlier poise now replaced with sullen anger. "I'm sorry, were you expecting the full cast of a west-end musical?"

"It's just, I was told you were particular friends with a certain boy. I must have been misinformed." She frowned in annoyance. *You idiot, Fisher.*

"Oh yeah? And who might that be?"

"Lucas Fortune," she said distractedly.

A curtain seemed to drop over Marshall's eyes then, a dark veil that completely masked his thoughts. "Fortune?" he repeated tonelessly.

"Yes, I expect you know of him, he's apparently one of Peregrine House's longest serving residents. Is he a friend of yours, then?"

His face was white. He didn't say anything for a long while.

"Goodness, are you alright, young man?" she asked him with concern in her voice, but secretly she was quite pleased at his reaction. Clearly this boy did know Fortune, had perhaps had dealings with him. Maybe Graves could be of some use after all.

"Yes, I know Fortune," he said as though from far away. "I know him quite well." He focused on Miss Fox suddenly, fixing her with his intense grey eyes. A knowing expression came over his face. "You're after him, aren't you? That's what all this rubbish is really about, isn't it?"

Miss Fox hadn't expected this, but she rallied quickly. "After him? Dear me, Mr Graves, you do have an active imagination! Really, what must you think of Juvenile Services? This isn't Victorian England, we don't take children away and put them in the workhouse!" She forced a laugh.

He was grinning now, not believing a word of it. "Pity," he said. "Because I want him too."

Miss Fox had a choice to make then. Should she carry on with the pretence, even though it was clear this child could see right through it, or let him in so she could use him? It seemed quite clear he had abilities of his own; in many ways, this situation reminded her of the way she herself had first been recruited into Echelon Nine…

The choice was obvious. She gave him a slow smile. "Very well. Let's talk."

Chapter Seventeen – The Net

The steps quickly descended into cool inky blackness, twisting around in a broad spiral until all light was gone. From behind them they could still hear the storm raging on the surface, but down here all they felt was a slight movement of the air. It soon became apparent that the going would be pretty difficult, and Lucas, despite his bravado, was beginning to have doubts. He wasn't at all sure about venturing blindly into this unknown place. Still he plodded gingerly on, feeling out each step before putting his weight on it.

Tamsen's voice echoed from somewhere behind him, making him jump. "This is ridiculous," she growled. "I can't see a thing! Sammi, d'you think you could…you know?"

Sammi sounded doubtful. "I'm not sure, Tamsen."

Lucas silently berated himself for not thinking of that sooner. "Good idea, Tamsen," he called back, his voice hollow in the confined space. "How about it, Sammi? Can you give us some light?"

"I don't know how I did it," she said miserably. "I haven't even tried since, you know, back at the house."

Timothy's soft voice joined in. "Well, when I do my thing, I just kind of think hard about what I want."

"Yeah, me too," Dion contributed. "It only seems to work if you concentrate quite hard. Why don't you try that, Sammi?"

"Okay," she said uncertainly. There was a brief pause. Nothing happened. "I'm rubbish at this," she said wretchedly.

"Maybe you're thinking of the wrong thing," Timothy suggested. "Back in the garden, you made a bright flash when you needed to, right?"

"Yeah…"

"Okay, well what we need now isn't a flash, but more like a, a –"

"Light bulb?" Aaron said impishly. There was a thump and a muffled curse as of someone having their arm punched.

"Put a sock in it, Osborn," Tamsen said sternly. "Can't you tell she's nervous?"

"I'm fine, Tamsen," Sammi said with some asperity. "Thank you." And with that she began to glow gently, a soft golden luminosity like sunlight radiating from her skin. It spread out in a slow wave, filling the passage. The others stepped back and shielded their dark-adapted eyes with murmurs of appreciation.

"Woah," Timothy said appreciatively. "That's cool."

Sammi turned a big smile on him.

The light made them all feel much better. Sammi's skin was hot to the touch, like she had been running, but it had no other effect on her except for very quickly drying out her clothes.

Now the passage could be clearly seen the going was much quicker, though still just as cautious. The walls of the passage were very smooth, like pebbles on a beach, and an even width apart. Lucas could touch both sides with his outstretched hands. Dion speculated about the smoothness as they descended, wondering if the passage had been underwater at some time in the past.

They kept going down, Sammi happily moving up to the front of the procession where her light would be most useful. The sound of their footsteps echoing back from further ahead began to change, until suddenly the passage ended. It came out into a wide oval-shaped chamber, the floor as polished and smooth as the walls of the passage had been. The colour of the rock was odd, a kind of dull yellowish hue like mustard, shot through with veins of something silvery that glittered in Sammi's light. The air was completely still, stale and unused, and slightly damp, with a faintly metallic taste. At the far end of the chamber was a dark opening; this appeared to be the only other way out.

The children gathered in a nervous huddle around Sammi. Aaron surreptitiously tried to warm his hands on her, but Tamsen gave him a hard look and he backed off hurriedly.

"This place is old," Lucas said into the silence. "It's been here for a long, long time."

"What is it?" Tamsen asked. "Is it – man made?"

Dion said, "It looks artificial to me. The geometry is too precise to be natural, I reckon."

"So it was built, then," Timothy said. "But who by?"

"It feels empty," Dion noted. "I don't think anyone's been down here for a while. And what was with that whole 'secret entrance' thing back there? Did we make it do that?"

Lucas had no answers, but there was one thing he was certain about: this was the place he'd been meant to find. He knew it in his bones, but there was something else; he had a peculiar feeling he'd been here before…

"Well, we're not gonna find out just standing about," he declared. "I'm going to take a look around. Anyone want to come along?"

Through the dark opening was another chamber, this one circular, a broad room with curving walls, about fifteen metres across. In its centre was a large empty dais, a knee-high platform of the same yellow stony material as the walls, approximately ten metres in diameter. Apart from this, the room was featureless. There were no other exits, the walls blank and smooth. The boys spread out to take a better look around.

Sammi sat down heavily on the edge of the dais, looking a little faint. "Phew," she muttered, "I'm really hungry." As she said it her glow began to fade slowly, the radiance from her skin growing gradually dimmer as each second passed.

Tamsen sat next to her, concerned. "You okay, Sammi?"

"Yeah, just a little tired," she said faintly. "I'll be fine…oh." She was staring at her hands. "The light – I can't seem to…"

"Don't worry about it," Tamsen calmed her as the last of the radiance disappeared. It seemed as though the darkness was again complete, but after only a few moments –

"Hey, I can see!" Aaron called out. "Look, there's light!" It was true; the walls were emitting a tiny glow, a feeble yellowish luminosity that nevertheless managed to softly light the whole room. It had been impossible to see it before in the overriding glow of Sammi's light ability. Criss-crossing the walls, the network of silvery veins now stood out like an arrangement of spider's webs in a way that was suddenly shockingly familiar to Lucas.

"This is the place from my dream!" he exclaimed. "I knew I recognised it!" He jumped up on the dais in celebration. The others joined him.

"That's great, Lucas," Aaron said warily, "but what do we do now? There's nothing else here."

Lucas was about to reply when the feel of the air abruptly changed. It was like someone had suddenly opened a freezer door. The temperature dropped several degrees. "What now…?" he murmured, gazing around.

The room was different. Dotted all around them were several covered shapes, exactly as Lucas remembered. "No, this is the place," he corrected himself. The walls glowed more strongly now, a sickly luminescence that, if the truth were told, was not very comforting. It gave a disconcerting impression of ill-health.

"This isn't the same room as before," Dion declared, peering around wonderingly. "We've moved, somehow. When we all got on that platform, it – it transported us here." He sounded more excited than worried. "How cool is that?"

Lucas jumped down to the floor, which was covered in little shallow ridges just like in his dream, only it wasn't concrete, or even stone; it was hard, yet seemed to give slightly under his weight.

He gazed around challengingly. "I'm here!" he cried, raising his arms. "Just like you said! Do you hear me? I'm here!"

I hear you. Welcome, Lucas Fortune.

*

"So let me get this straight," Marshall Graves said frostily. "You won't tell me who you are or who you work for, and you won't tell me why you're after Fortune, yet you want me to tell you everything I know about him. Does that sound about right?"

Miss Fox gave him a cool look. "Mr Graves, I have told you as much as I am permitted to at this time. To use a cliché, any further information relating to this case is strictly 'need to know.' For security reasons, you understand."

He shook his head irritably. "Security? What a load of rubbish. You asked me to help you, because you believe I have information you need. It doesn't take a genius to figure out you're not who you say you are. I bet you're not even from Juvenile Services, are you?"

"You don't need to concern yourself with that."

He crossed his arms. "Then we've got nothing more to talk about, Miss Fox."

She sighed. "I'm trying to be as nice as possible about this, young man, but there are other…*avenues* we could take, if that's what you wish."

"Ah, threats now? Finally we uncover the real you, eh?" He leaned forward, finally beginning to look interested. "That's more like it. It's so important that people are open and honest about their real intentions, don't you think? Saves confusion."

"Does that mean you'll cooperate, then?"

"Cooperate?" He appeared to give that some thought. "Here's what I'm going to do. I'll tell you something you want to know, if you tell me something in return."

She snorted. "Who do you think you are, Hannibal Lecter?" She was growing more annoyed with this arrogant young fool with each passing second. "Let me set you straight, Mr Graves. You seem to be operating under a serious misapprehension. You are not in any position to make demands. I can and will bring in other measures to ensure your cooperation, if I feel they are required. Do you understand *that?*"

He frowned. "Hannibal who? Look, Miss Fox – can I call you Danielle? – you don't know what you're dealing with here. You can bluster all you want, but I can assure you that you'll get nothing out of me that way."

That was enough. "Don't know what I'm dealing with?" she found herself yelling. "You little snot, I've been 'dealing with' things like this for more years than you've been alive!" She caught herself just in time, before she gave anything else away. How was this boy able to push her buttons so adeptly? He was grinning at her now, well aware of what had just happened.

"So what are you then, like the B.P.R.D. or something?" Amusement twinkled in his eyes.

"The what?" she said more calmly.

"Oh nothing, just something from a comic-book." He waved a hand dismissively. "You chase ghosts and goblins, do you?"

"What makes you say that?" She was wary of this boy now. Her inability to use her psychic skills on him put her at a distinct disadvantage. She had no sense of what he might come out with next. It was at times like this she realised that, just maybe, she relied on her gift a little too much.

"Well, Danielle, there's all kinds of weirdness going on here at Peregrine House, and I'm not just talking about that Fortune boy. Isn't that why you're here?" He was probing again.

"It's Miss Fox to you, and I've already told you why we're here. We're looking for information on Lucas Fortune. Either you assist us voluntarily or not. There's no middle ground." She gave him a direct look. "I believe you've met my assistant, Mr Withers?"

He looked slightly uncertain. "Tall chap, smokes like a train? What about him?"

"Well, I was just thinking, perhaps we should invite him to take part in this conversation. He'd be quite interested in your viewpoints, I'm sure." She looked concerned. "Thing is though, he's a little, how should I say…unpredictable. Prone to outbursts. Gets upset easily. Between you and me, Mr Graves, he's been in quite a bit of trouble with our bosses in the past over his somewhat heavy-handed approach."

Graves gazed at her levelly, but there was the merest flicker of doubt in his eyes. "I'm a minor, under the protection of Peregrine House and its staff," he said stiffly. "You can't touch me."

"Mr Graves, you have no idea what I'm capable of." She let that hang in the air.

He pursed his lips thoughtfully. "Interesting," he murmured. "You really want Fortune, don't you? Why, I wonder? Is it because of what he can do?"

This was better. For all his cheek and bravado, Graves was still only a dumb kid. They were all the same underneath. "Why don't you tell me, young man?"

"You want him because you know about his powers, don't you?"

"Powers? Care to explain what you mean by that?"

He looked frustrated. "Not giving anything away, are you?"

She favoured him with a small smile, confident that she had the upper hand now. "Just tell me what you know. It's a simple enough proposition, really."

Still he looked unsure. With a sigh she made a show of turning away to summon her assistant.

"He can make people do what he wants," Graves blurted with a scowl.

Finally. "Who can?"

"Who do you think? Fortune!"

"Really? How do you know this?"

He stared at her. "You're not surprised. You already knew, didn't you?"

She said nothing, just looked at him steadily with one eyebrow slightly raised.

He made an indelicate sound. "He attacked me, alright? Me and my friends, for no reason. Is that what you want to hear?"

"What I want to hear is the truth, Mr Graves. Fortune attacked you? How? Why?"

"You have to promise not to tell anyone about this, okay?" He was on the defensive now. "If anyone finds out…"

"Quite the big man on campus, aren't you?" She masked a triumphant smile. "But you don't need to worry, everything said in this room is in confidence." She could afford to be generous now she'd finally got him to change his tune.

He shook his head sorrowfully. "Okay. You want the truth? This is what happened. I was concerned about some of my friends who'd recently taken to hanging around with Fortune and his little gang. Now, as a rule, I don't normally concern myself with the affairs of others, especially Lucas Fortune; he can be…" he paused delicately, "…a bit scary. A nasty piece of work."

At least that tied up with what she'd heard about Fortune from the staff here. She hadn't thought much of him when they'd briefly met that one time, just an unassuming twelve year-old boy, sort of skinny and undernourished as boys tended to look at that age. You couldn't always tell the bad ones. She hadn't been able to read him, either, and she still hadn't figured out why. Was she losing her touch? Or was something else at work here? "Go on," she prodded.

"Well, Sabrina – that's Sabrina Celestine, another friend of mine – wanted to know if a couple of her little girly-pals were alright. See, she was worried about them, they'd been acting a bit strange, going off and hanging out with Fortune, for no obvious reason. Apparently they'd never even spoken to him before then." He was all earnest chattiness now, eager to help. Miss Fox didn't believe his pose for a second. He might be telling the truth about what had happened, but she had a sudden feeling she was being played again somehow. She waited for him to go on with a guarded expression.

"Sabrina asked if I would go speak to Fortune, maybe find out what was going on," he continued. "Of course I agreed. What are friends for, eh?"

Did he think she was stupid? Not ten minutes ago he'd been telling her he didn't have any friends, just a group of 'companions'. Just how much of anything he said could she believe?

"So I went to see Fortune," he went on. "I took along some of my friends, for moral support I suppose. Sabrina came too. I did not intend anything confrontational; I just wanted to see what was happening, for Sabrina's sake." He leaned forward conspiratorially. "I think she kind of likes me," he chuckled with a 'what-can-you-do' shrug.

Miss Fox had to try hard not to roll her eyes.

He settled back, apparently deep in thought. "That's when I first found out about Fortune's powers."

"What happened?" she said eagerly, despite herself. "Tell me everything." She would be able to verify all this later with the other children, anyway. Let him spin his little tale.

"I told you, he attacked us, me and my friends. It was a couple of days ago now, Tuesday I think. He set his little band of buddies on us as soon as he saw us coming. It was six against six, but as we soon discovered, it was pretty far from an even contest."

"Why was that?"

"Why? Because, as it turns out, Fortune's pals are just like him. They all have powers too!"

"What?" She felt faint. Had she discovered a whole nest of super-powered children here? This was even better than she'd dared hope. If Graves was actually telling the truth, this could be career-making stuff!

"It was touch and go for a while," he went on blithely. "We didn't stand a chance. I abhor violence, you see. I didn't want to fight him, didn't want to see my friends get hurt. I couldn't believe what I was seeing. Fortune's bunch were doing all kinds of crazy, impossible stuff, like going *invisible*, if you can believe that, and making poor Dana Jackson go mental. Fortune did that one himself, I saw him. And Lois and Myles got knocked to the ground before I could do anything to stop it."

"But *you* managed to get away, though," she said with a shaky voice. "You don't look hurt to me."

"That's because I got us out of there as quickly as I could! I didn't know what was happening, none of it made sense to me. I begged Fortune to stop, but he just laughed at me." He looked sheepish. "I'm not proud of it, Miss Fox, but that's what I did. That's why I didn't tell anyone about it. Anyway, who'd believe a crazy story like that?"

"Who indeed?" she murmured. "Okay, let's say I believe you. Will you be able to give me a list of all of Fortune's friends, and everything you saw them do?"

He sighed. "Yes, alright. I've gone this far with you people, I may as well finish it."

"That's the spirit. Oh, and just out of interest, do you happen to know if any of these other children are still here at Peregrine House? Fortune's friends, I mean?"

He grimaced. "No, as a matter of fact, they're not. They all left that same day with Fortune, on some camping trip to Dartmoor. Don't know when they'll be back." He leaned forward urgently. "Now do you see why I'm so anxious to catch up with him? He might need help."

That was pushing things just a little too far, but she kept her expression neutral. "Yes, of course." She tried to gather her scattered thoughts into some kind of order. Was it just coincidence that Fortune and all his friends had left together on the same day, just as Echelon's net was beginning to close around them? If Graves was to be believed, Fortune was growing more and more powerful and reckless every day, and he now had himself a little army too. This could well call for some serious intervention from Echelon. "I assume your friends can all verify this story?"

"Oh, yes," he replied with the ghost of a smile. "I can guarantee it." He paused. "Will you be going out to find Fortune?"

"That's not your concern."

"Only," he continued unheedingly, "I'd like to go with you when you do."

She frowned at him. What was he driving at now? "That won't be necessary, Mr Graves. We will be speaking to you again, rest assured. Your involvement in this affair is far from over."

"Oh, I know that, but I can help you further, you know I can." He was back to his super-confident manner of earlier. He seemed able to change between moods like flicking a switch. "You see, there's more I haven't told you."

"Is that so?" She considered him appraisingly. He'd volunteered some fascinating information, it was true, but only after threats had been made. That approach was too painstaking, not to mention tiring. She'd tried using the stick – maybe now it was time to use the carrot. "You want to come with us, do you?"

He nodded eagerly. "That's right."

"I'll think about it."

Chapter Eighteen – Sanctuary

The children stared around them in panicked confusion. "Where are you?" Lucas called into the freezing gloom. "I can't see you!"

Do not be alarmed. You are safe now. The voice seemed to come at them from every direction, not loud but insistent.

Lucas spun around, trying to locate the source. There was nothing to be seen. "You said that before, in the dream! Safe from who?"

Your questions will be answered soon enough, Lucas Fortune. For now, though, there are more pressing matters. You are hungry, thirsty and tired. You are wet through from the surface rain. This sanctuary will take care of your needs.

The friends looked at each other, bemused. "What is this place? Who does it belong to?" Lucas wondered.

It is yours now. Do not concern yourself with anything else for the moment. Soon I will have to leave, but I promise to return later, at which time I will endeavour to answer some of your questions. There was a pause, and an impression of weary accomplishment. **I am most pleased with your progress, all of you.**

"Are you Rith?" Tamsen said in a nervous voice.

I am. I have been watching your journey, when I have been able. You are a very resourceful bunch.

There was an embarrassed silence. Someone's stomach gurgled loudly. "Sorry." It was Aaron. "Kinda hungry."

Indeed. Please, make use of the facilities to revive yourselves.

"Okay," Aaron agreed readily. "Um – what facilities?"

First you will need to activate the energy cores. Once you have done this the sanctuary systems will come online and respond to your requests. The interface structure to your left will allow you to do this.

They looked. Where Rith had indicated was a hunched shape about a metre tall, something like a gnarled and withered tree stump, matt black and somewhat ominous. It had a ridged dome on top, but was otherwise featureless except for two small bulges about the size of footballs on the sides. Timothy went over and gingerly touched it. "Feels funny," he reported, running his hands over the surface. "Kind of like cold leather, or – skin." He drew his hand away. "Yuck."

"What do we do?" Dion said, mystified. "I don't see any buttons or switches…"

Aaron Osborn and Sammi River, it is you who must initiate the energy cores. Please approach the interface structure and engage the control surfaces.

Sammi looked terrified. She ducked behind Timothy.

"Us?" Aaron squeaked, going pale. "Why us?"

Your abilities, as you call them, are suited to this purpose.

"Oh. Right. Okay, then." He went over to the object and studied it. "Control surfaces," he muttered.

"I think it's those bulges on the sides," Dion called. "I can't see anything else."

You are correct, Dion Raven. Aaron, you and Sammi must place a hand on the control surfaces – the bulges. This will allow your energy siphoning adaptations to activate the start-up process. That is all that is required.

"Energy siphoning," Tamsen exclaimed. "Of course!" The others looked at her blankly. "I'll explain later," she said. "Sammi, go put your hand on that thing, and try to make some light." She sounded excited.

"I can't, I think I used it all up," Sammi said miserably.

"Doesn't matter, I reckon you only need a tiny bit."

"I think she's right," Dion joined in. "Kind of like a car battery, all you need is a surge to start the engine. Brilliant!"

Aaron touched one of the bulges with a nervous expression. Nothing happened. "Anyone got some jump-leads?" he quipped.

Sammi joined him. They looked at each other over the top of the object for a second with trepidation, then placed their hands on the bulges. Small sparks danced briefly around their fingers. "Tickles," Aaron said with surprise.

Something inside the object gave an audible clunk, and far away there was a distant boom as though in answer. It vibrated through the floor, shaking them momentarily. "Uh…" Aaron said nervously.

Do not fear. The energy cores are awakening. They will take a few minutes to cycle up. The process is automatic and self-sustaining from this point.

"You know about our abilities, then," Lucas said, confirming what he already knew. "Don't you?"

Of course. You have been adapted.

A chill went down Lucas's spine. That didn't sound good at all. "Adapted? What does that mean?"

I have no more time to speak now, Lucas. My window of communication is quite narrow. I will return later.

"You're not here, are you? I mean physically? Where are you?"

There was no answer. Rith was gone.

"Dammit."

The illumination emanating from the walls was growing, the sickly yellow glow brightening into something more comforting, like daylight. The children could now see the chamber properly. On the dais where they stood, there were several other objects like the interface structure they had just activated, though not exactly the same. They looked like they had been somehow grown in place, each assuming individual forms. The nearest of these objects began to glow now, small rivers of red and orange light crawling weirdly just beneath its outer skin. One by one the other objects followed suit.

The children gathered together nervously in the centre of the room. Spaced around the circular walls at regular intervals were a number of oval-shaped openings, leading outwards into ominous darkness. "What is this place?" Timothy muttered.

With a sudden hiss that made them all jump, the domed tops of the twisted objects around them on the dais slid back, retracting into segments that folded themselves up like the wings of an insect. Revealed within each were banks of rapidly changing lights and flowing bands of energy that leapt between several outstretched prongs. These prongs now extended with a busy-sounding hum to protrude above the top of the casings. The spaces between the prongs shimmered and flickered for a moment, then abruptly coalesced into moving images.

"Hey, that's the stone circle!" Timothy exclaimed, pointing at an image suspended in midair above one of the consoles. It showed the central altar stone that had parted to admit them, now closed up again. It must have automatically shut behind them. As they watched in amazement, the image changed to another view of the moors. It did this several times, cycling through different perspectives of the land above.

"It's a monitoring station," Dion breathed. He approached the console with a fascinated expression. "See, it's showing images of the surrounding area! That's the Tor me and Aaron were looking at earlier." He looked closer. "Still raining, I see."

"Are there cameras up there?" Lucas wondered. "How are they getting these pictures?"

"Didn't see any cameras," Aaron grunted. "Hey, what's that other one showing over there?"

They turned to look. This display was flicking through what looked like pictures of dark rooms and deserted corridors, though it was quite hard to tell. "I think," Tamsen said slowly, "it's showing pictures of this place. Other parts of it, I mean."

They watched for a while. "How big is this place?" Lucas murmured.

Other consoles were displaying different things. On one, the image was divided up into small subsections, each one filled with obscure pictures and symbols that flowed endlessly in all directions. The children stared but could make no sense of it. "It's almost like – writing," Dion murmured, intrigued. They left him there puzzling it out while they went to look at the other displays. The next one was blank, the prongs active and extended but showing no image. That left the last console, the one Aaron and Sammi had originally activated. On its floating screen were several large icons, strange unfamiliar pictures that had no obvious significance to the children. Around each icon the strange script scrolled upwards and downwards.

"No idea," Tamsen muttered savagely, even though no one had asked. This must be driving her nuts, Lucas thought.

Despite their awe and amazement, the initial novelty was already starting to wear off in the face of their growing hunger and discomfort. Rith had promised them food and relief, but had neglected to tell them how to get it. Also, Lucas's bladder was starting to send him urgent messages. He wondered if there were any bathrooms in this strange, abandoned place. "Maybe we should take a look around," he suggested uncomfortably. "Out there, I mean." He gestured towards the dark openings ringing the chamber.

Aaron eyed him. "Seriously?"

"Yeah, why not?" he blustered. "We're safe here, aren't we? At least, that's what Rith said." Though that was hardly a convincing argument...

"Oh, right." Aaron muttered. "Rith. That's alright, then."

"All I'm saying is Rith hasn't led us wrong so far. Whatever his reasons are for bringing us here, I don't think he'd let anything bad happen to us now."

"Are you sure about that, Lucas? 'Cos I'm not. I'm tired, hungry and fed up with all this cryptic mumbo-jumbo and weirdness. I don't know how you stay so calm."

Lucas didn't either. "Look, I'm going to have a nose around, just out there, down one of those side halls. You stay here if you want. I'll only be gone for a minute or two."

Aaron sighed heavily. "No, I'll come along too. Never know, might be *fun*."

Lucas pointed to one of the openings at random. "That one, then. Come on."

Beyond the opening was a well of chilly blackness stretching away from the small pool of light spilling from the chamber. "Maybe this wasn't such a good idea," Aaron murmured apprehensively, but Lucas put his foot firmly over the threshold onto the hard floor beyond. Instantly the walls glowed into life, starting right next to Lucas and flowing away down the corridor like a wave.

"Nice," Lucas said appreciatively. "I could get used to this."

Revealed, the corridor turned out to be long cylindrical tube about twice Lucas's height, stretching out before him for about a hundred metres before taking a slow bend to the right. Dotted down its length on both sides were several side-openings. Looking down at the floor, it appeared to be made of a similar material to the monitor consoles in the chamber, a dull black lustreless material that gave slightly to the touch. It was like nothing he'd ever seen before. The walls curving up overhead were composed of the same irregular panels as both of the chambers they had so far seen. The effect was like a glowing pattern of crazy-paving, but overlaid with a filigree pattern of silver strands that seemed to pulse and shimmer like mercury.

The two of them ventured gingerly along the corridor, pausing as they came to the first side entrance on the left-hand side. Beyond this was another dark, unknown space. Curious, Lucas put one foot over the lip of the opening…

…and it too lit up, just like the main corridor. The space turned out to be a small, featureless room, roughly square, empty and abandoned like the rest of this place. Only the ceiling here was covered with the light panels; the walls were non-reflective, featureless white, like stone. The room had no obvious function, so they left it and went on to the next opening down the corridor, the light panels within dimming back down to darkness as they went.

All the side rooms were the same, empty spaces with no apparent use. Lucas was growing quite uncomfortable now. What was he going to do? Aaron noticed his anxious expression. "You okay, mate?"

Lucas grimaced. They were standing in the last room before the corridor curved to the right. "Not really," he groaned. "I'm busting. Whoever built this place forgot to put in a bathroom."

There was a soft sliding noise from behind them. They spun around in alarm to see the rear wall of the room changing shape, extruding a ledge at about knee-height that had several small openings along the top. Peering closer, these openings appeared to lead straight down, dropping away into distant, unfathomable darkness.

Lucas and Aaron exchanged a look. "Alright," Aaron shrugged. "Instant toilet. Just add water."

Dion still stood by his console, deep in thought, when Lucas and Aaron came bursting back into the chamber. "Hey, you'll never guess what we found!" Aaron shouted happily.

"Actually, we would," Tamsen said with amusement, pointing to one of the displays. It showed the room just recently used by the two boys. "Don't worry though, we didn't look." Her eyes shone with mirth.

"Oi, that's not fair!" Aaron complained, mortified. Lucas peered back down the corridor. There was no sign of any camera or imaging device, and he hadn't noticed one in the impromptu bathroom either. Maybe they were tiny, like those miniature pin-hole cameras he'd once read about. "Where's Timothy?" he asked Tamsen, looking around for his friend.

"Oh, he went off down one of those other corridors. Oo look, you can see him on that screen thing there." She pointed. Timothy was happily wandering around a very similar corridor to the one Lucas and Aaron had just explored.

"I wonder what else this place can do," Lucas said.

"Hey guys," Dion called tentatively, not looking up from his screen. "Have a look at this. I think I've got something here." The others crowded around him. He pointed to a group of symbols in the top right-hand corner of the display. "See those? I noticed they kept recurring at regular intervals in several of these boxes, in a particular pattern. I don't how or why, but it kind of makes sense to me."

"You mean you can read it?" Tamsen said incredulously.

He made a face. "Not exactly, but parts of it seem to have meaning. I think each of these sections represent different functions that can be accessed from this terminal. For example, that one is something to do with environmental controls, that one is for some kind of internal transportation system – I haven't completely figured that part out yet – and this one," he pointed to the bottom left of the display with a flourish, "is the most interesting one."

"Well, what is it?" Tamsen said impatiently.

He grinned. "Let's see if I can get it to work." He touched the section of screen he'd indicated. Immediately that section expanded to fill the whole display, a collection of glowing orange symbols hanging impossibly in the air. "Alright, that one I think," he murmured, selecting the first symbol on the left.

There was a low humming sound from behind them. They wheeled around to see the fourth console, the one with the empty display, now active and showing an image of what could only be –

"Chips!?" Aaron cried. "How did you do that?" He rushed over to the console and gazed avidly at the image. It was so lifelike it looked like he could just reach out and touch it…

"Go ahead," Dion said impishly.

"You're kidding! Why are you torturing me like this, D? Haven't I always been good to you?"

Tamsen strode over to the console. "Out of the way, Osborn," she said brusquely, elbowing Aaron aside. She reached out to the image. "We'll see how funny this is when – OHMYGOD!"

Her hand came away clutching something which she promptly dropped all over the floor. The distinct fatty aroma of hot chips immediately wafted out towards them. Tamsen blew on her hand, eyes wide and incredulous. "I don't believe it!" she cried. Strewn all around her on the floor was a pile of steaming chips, still sizzling as though they'd come straight from the fryer.

"Oh yes," Aaron murmured, gazing at the machine with newfound adoration. "Coolest. Thing. Ever."

Lucas stared at Dion. "Chips?" he croaked. "It's a *chip* machine?"

"Not exactly. I think it must have somehow got that from my thoughts. Been thinking about chips quite a lot recently."

"Can it do other stuff, too?" Aaron asked. The gurgling of his stomach was audible even over the low humming of the consoles.

"Yeah, I think so," Dion replied. "I reckon the machine sort-of gets the idea from your mind and somehow – makes it. Anything you like."

A thought struck Lucas. "A bit like the toilet room," he said. "I was thinking about what I needed, and it just sort of appeared." He gazed around him with sudden appreciation. "This place is alright."

Dion shivered. "Even better, I've adjusted the temperature so it'll soon get nice and warm in here. Should dry us all out in no time."

Timothy came back in at that point, and once they'd excitedly explained to him what they'd discovered, the six of them spent the next hour or so dreaming up and creating ever more elaborate and ridiculous dishes, gorging themselves into a happy stupor until they thought they might burst. It was the ultimate gift, the very thing they needed the most, not only to take care of their immediate physical needs but their emotional ones as well. After all of their trials, it felt deliciously good just to be children again.

Finally, sprawled around amidst the quietly humming consoles like a pride of sated lions surrounded by the detritus of their creativity, they drifted off into contented sleep where they lay.

Chapter Nineteen – The Gift

Miss Fox carefully traced her finger along the map, plotting the route to the Lox Valley Farm Campsite. It was Friday morning, the day before the children on the camping expedition were due to return to Peregrine House, but there was no way she was prepared to wait that long. This was far too important a matter to leave idle for even one day.

She still inwardly cursed Byron Stanford's unbelievable reticence in fully committing to this operation. She'd presented all her evidence to him at the Exeter house last night, including the testimonies of Marshall Graves and his odd little party of friends, with full expectations of finally getting what she wanted, but still he had seemed unimpressed. Eventually he'd agreed to assign her two cars and two extra operatives, but he'd absolutely refused to scale up the operation any further. The man was clearly a spineless weakling, too concerned with budgets and other such nonsense to see the amazing opportunity that was staring them both in the face.

If that's the way you want it, Stanford, that's fine with me, she thought savagely. *You might be trying to strangle my operation at birth, but when I return with six super-gifted children in custody we'll see who ends up sitting in the big chair, won't we?*

What made it stranger still was that he'd seemed so committed to the whole exercise at the start, when she'd first joined his personal troop of seekers. He'd been the driving force behind the quest for all their goals, in particular the Agent Smith case. He'd seemed to take an almost personal interest in that one. Now, when they were so close to its resolution, he appeared to be losing his nerve. *Too bad, Stanford. Maybe it's time for you to step aside and let someone who isn't scared of results call the shots.*

Her assigned car was driven by an Echelon agent going by the name of Brown, a big lunk-headed man with no neck who said very little except when directly spoken to. That suited Miss Fox just fine. All she required was that he follow her orders. Behind them in the second car, Mr Withers was accompanied by their other assigned agent, a humourless, waspish woman called Jones. Why, Miss Fox had often wondered, couldn't the agency ever come up with better names than that? Unlike herself, most agents chose not to use their real names, preferring anonymity. Miss Fox had dedicated her whole life to Echelon Nine. She had no existence outside of it. Accordingly, she had no reason to hide behind pseudonyms.

Yesterday had been an interesting day, to say the least. After finishing her interview with the Graves boy, she had taken a few minutes to compose herself and check through the covert recording that had been made. She still couldn't fathom what the boy's real angle was, though it seemed pretty clear that he was not telling her the whole truth. However, enough of it tied in with her own observations and conclusions that she couldn't afford to disregard any part of what he'd said.

So she and Mr Withers had proceeded to interview a number of other children, including the five who had allegedly been involved in the altercation with Fortune and his gang. This had yielded something of a mixed bag of results. Most of the kids she'd talked to, it turned out, had no knowledge of any unusual happenings at Peregrine House, apart from the usual childhood concerns of who'd said what about that boy and who'd been seen kissing that girl behind the bushes. Fairly standard stuff, and all useless to her.

Then she'd come to the five children that constituted Marshall Graves's inner circle. She hadn't known what to expect, but the results had proven to be...interesting. First there had been the pair of boys, Lovell and Elsdon, who'd seemed so similar they could almost have been twins. She'd managed to get very little new or useful information from them. Their answers to her questions had been generally of the 'yes/no' variety, but they'd confirmed everything that Graves said had happened, parrot-fashion. They'd been primed, obviously, but for what purpose? She'd been able to sense their thoughts easily, but to little benefit. Their minds were clear and untroubled by much in the way of complicated thought.

The three girls, though, had proven to be far more useful, if in different ways. First had been Dana Jackson, a darkly pretty girl with a thick mass of curly brown hair. She had been polite and pleasant, if a bit reticent, but she had also confirmed Graves's story. Her mind was interesting, a bright and simplistic place full of sunshine and girlishness. Almost, it was as though it had been newly constructed. Miss Fox hid her reaction, because she had encountered people like this before; ones who'd deliberately erected a false front to shield their real thoughts. Another one, perhaps, to add to her list of people to be investigated at a later date.

Then there was Lois Christie, a very odd little girl who wore a constant half-smile and seemed to drift off into her own little world at random. She had been a difficult one to question, her replies sometimes irrelevant or incomplete and rambling. A simple reading of her thoughts had confirmed Miss Fox's suspicions that she was probably somewhat mentally deficient. Her mind was a confusing mishmash of sounds, flashes and empty spaces. Autism, perhaps, or something like it? This was not Miss Fox's field of expertise, but she suspected that this girl had retreated inside her head for some reason, perhaps as a result of some trauma or disturbing experience in her past. Strangely, Lois's records in the JS database had not mentioned any prior hint of this condition. Was this a recent thing? Could it in some way be connected to the Fortune case?

Lastly Miss Fox had interviewed Sabrina Celestine, a tall, severe-looking girl, pale-skinned and willowy, but with a diamond hard edge to her voice and demeanour. She had been clearly displeased at having to answer Miss Fox's questions, and had made no attempt to hide her disdain and contempt at the whole interview process. Her arrogance was almost on a par with that of Marshall Graves, though in Sabrina's case there was none of the false cheer and manipulation that Graves had employed. She answered the questions brusquely and frostily in a voice that could probably have cut glass. Miss Fox had been singularly unimpressed. By that point in the day she'd pretty much had her fill of snot-nosed kids with superiority complexes. Their dislike of each other was clearly palpable in the atmosphere of the interview room, but nevertheless Sabrina did condescend to backup Graves's story. There was nothing particularly special about her mind, though, in terms of unusual behaviour or veils of deceit. It seemed odd that Graves's would choose to associate with someone like her, given his own massive ego.

Miss Fox had finally returned to the Exeter base at the end of the day tired and irritable but nevertheless triumphant at what she'd managed to learn. Peregrine House, it seemed, was a veritable hotbed of bizarre and exotic activity, though the reason why this should be was far from clear. She'd been tremendously excited at the prospect of finding out what that reason might be, which had made Stanford's bull-headed attitude, even after hearing all the evidence, all the more hard to bear.

These were issues for a later date, though. Right now her mission priorities were clear and precise: find the Fortune boy and his friends, and bring them in to Echelon Nine as quickly and quietly as possible. There was also the small matter of Marshall Graves's request to accompany her on the capture. She hadn't really given it much thought after his interview had ended, what with one thing and another, but it seemed a harmless enough request. After all, there was very little an ignorant fourteen year-old boy could do to hamper the activities of well-trained and professional government agents, even if that boy did think rather a lot of himself. Let him come along, if it would ensure his future cooperation. Not even Stanford could object to that.

So now, en route to the Dartmoor campsite to which Fortune had fled, they sidetracked to Peregrine House in order to collect the Graves boy. Fortunately it was only a small deviation from their route. Agent Brown had merely nodded curtly when he'd been informed of the detour. Ptolemy Withers, as usual, had shown no visible reaction.

They pulled into the driveway of the children's home a little after nine a.m. and parked in front of the main entrance. Tarquin Pring was waiting for them, anxiously wringing his hands. "This is most irregular," he complained as he led them through the corridors inside. Brown and Jones remained outside with the vehicles.

"Irregular, Mr Pring?" Miss Fox said.

"Yes, that's what I said, madam. I don't see why these children have to be removed from Peregrine House in order for you to conduct your inquiries. We have perfectly adequate facilities right here, as you saw yesterday." He stopped and gave her a piercing look. "Is there something wrong that we should know about?"

"Not at all, Mr Pring," she said blithely. "We're just being thorough. There's really nothing for you to worry about."

His expression turned dark. "What about Fortune? What are you doing about him?"

"I thought I'd made myself perfectly clear on that matter, sir. We are dealing with the situation."

"But what about all these other children? Surely they can't all be involved?"

"Mr Pring, I'm warning you, if you don't…" She stopped, something nagging at her mind. "Children? What children?"

They arrived at the common room and opened the door. Marshall Graves sat there with a smug grin. Around him were his five friends.

"Hello, Danielle," he greeted her. "We're all ready."

She groaned. *Oh, no.*

*

Children.

Lucas opened his eyes. He was still lying on the floor where he had been all night. Next to him Aaron was sprawled, snoring noisily. What had happened…?

Awake, children. The voice sounded amused.

Lucas gazed around him blearily. They were still on the dais amid the humming monitor consoles. The temperature was appreciably warmer than it had been last night (was it last night? A quick check of his watch confirmed it was still not working – no help there), though still with a slight chilly moistness in the air.

"Rith?" he croaked.

Yes, Lucas. I see you have discovered some of the sanctuary's functions.

Lucas gave a guilty start. They'd made such a mess! Half eaten plates of food and glasses of congealing milkshake lay everywhere, as though some modern day Roman emperor had decided to have a party.

"Sorry about all this," he said lamely. "We'll – we'll clean it up."

Have no concern. I told you, this place is yours to do with as you will. It has no other purpose. There was a pause. **Not anymore**.

The others were stirring. "Whoozat?" Aaron mumbled thickly. He had crusted chocolate on his face. Tamsen raised her head and looked at him with a groggy expression. "Eeew," she muttered.

It is time for you to awaken, children. You have many questions for me, but I have only a limited time in which to answer them.

That got their attention. The six of them sheepishly attempted to tidy their mess away, but there was nowhere to put it. In the end it was piled in a messy heap over by the side wall, to be sorted out later. After using the newly created toilet room, they came back to the monitor chamber and waited expectantly.

"Are you there?" Aaron asked tentatively. It was somewhat unnerving having a conversation with thin air.

For the moment, the voice said. **I am very glad to see you are safe and well, though I wonder that a number of you are missing. I have not yet had the opportunity to find out what happened to the others.**

The children looked at one another, perplexed. "The others?" Lucas echoed. "I don't know what you mean. There's just the six of us."

Yes, indeed. The voice pondered silently for a moment. **It is a matter for another time, perhaps. For now, I can give you certain information and attempt to explain, in part, what has brought you here today. The archive contained within this sanctuary, though now sadly incomplete, is also at your disposal. Use it as best you can.**

Lucas articulated his burning question. "You said we had been 'adapted'", he reminded the voice. "I want to know what that means."

As is only proper. To help answer your concern, I will use an analogy. In your culture, for an individual to perform to the best of their abilities in a particular role, it is first necessary for that person to gain the appropriate skills and continue to practice them until they have been mastered. Correct?

The children were mystified. "I…guess," Lucas said lamely.

This is very much a universal law, not just for your people, but for many others also. As to how this applies to my case…I needed individuals with certain skills but, for many complicated reasons which I will not go into now, such people are no longer available to me. In order to rectify that shortfall, I was left with little option but to select another group of people and give them those skills.

This was all a bit much for the children, all except for Dion, who was frowning in deep thought. "So what you're saying," he said slowly, "is that this was done to us on purpose?"

"I don't get it," Aaron said, puzzled. "What was done on purpose? What's this guy talking about?"

Dion said, "It's us, isn't it Rith! We're the ones you chose, aren't we?"

Correct. You did not have the necessary skills I required, so I was forced to implant them in you. In order for your minds and bodies to accept the changes, you had to be adapted.

The children were stunned. Much of what was being said made little sense to them, but they could understand enough to finally begin to grasp the truth of what had happened to them. Of what had been done to them.

"But what does that mean?" Lucas cried furiously. "You still haven't answered the question! What have you done to us?"

Nothing harmful. You have been…improved. The changes I have initiated in you are to your benefit, and to mine.

"Why us, though?" Tamsen said. "Why did you choose us?"

My options were very limited. The adaptation procedure you underwent is not always successful, especially when applied to fully grown,

adult individuals. Young minds such as yours are best able to accept the changes.

Dion looked intrigued. "These skills – these adaptations: how are they useful to you? Are we supposed to do something with them?"

I will address that issue later, Dion. It is time for me to leave now. The more time I spend in open communication with you, the more likely it is my enemies may detect me. I hope to return soon. Use the archive; it has been damaged, but may still be of some interest to you.

Then the children were alone. "Convenient," Tamsen muttered. "He ducks out when the questions start getting too hard."

"But that doesn't tell us anything!" Lucas raged at the silent room.

Dion said, "I could try and find this archive thing he was going on about. Maybe that will be a bit more useful than Mister Nobody out there."

Lucas calmed himself down. There was little point in staying angry at an empty space. "Maybe," he sighed. "Good idea." He felt he'd been so close to the answer, yet it was still dangling just out of reach. The frustration and indignation he felt was starting to get to him. He needed a distraction. "I'm going to have another look around," he grunted. "Maybe find out what else this place has got."

"A swimming pool; that'd be wicked," Aaron suggested, gazing around him with a hopeful expression. Nothing happened. "Stupid weird bunker," he muttered. "I'll come with you, Lucas. Anyone else?"

Timothy, Tamsen and Sammi all elected to come along too. They were just as frustrated as Lucas, angry and annoyed that they were still pretty much in the dark about what was happening to them. The few morsels of information Rith had given them only served to create more questions in their minds, and with no obvious guarantees those questions would be answered. At least one thing was clear: Rith would not be hurried or cajoled into giving away his secrets.

There were five openings leading out from the central chamber, all, they discovered, connecting to long corridors exactly like the one Lucas had first explored the previous day. Each contained side rooms, though not all of these, to their surprise, turned out to be empty. Several held mysterious objects resembling boxes or crates made from some kind of cold, glittery metallic substance. They could not be moved, not even with them all trying. Whatever was inside them was immensely heavy. There were also several large, leathery egg-shaped objects in another room, but the children nervously steered clear of these. There was something quite sinister and unpleasant about them.

The only other thing they discovered, after rounding identical right-hand bends in each corridor, was that every one of the five passages ended in massive blockades, huge heavy structures of the same glittery metallic substance as the boxes they'd found. These structures completely filled the corridors and prevented any further exploration. Timothy speculated that they might be doors, but there were no obvious hinges, handles or locks. For all the children knew the corridors might just simply end right there. This whole place didn't really follow any apparent logic they could identify.

Having explored the limits of their domain, the five of them returned to the central chamber, wondering what they were going to do next. One of the most worrying aspects of what they'd found was that there was no obvious way to leave. They didn't know how they'd even got into this area in the first place. They were effectively trapped, at the mercy of a still unknown, faceless voice that seemed in no hurry to clue them in.

Dion looked flushed. "Wow. This is pretty amazing," he called out from his console. "Check this out." He manipulated the screen in front of him with confident hands. "Think I'm getting the hang of this." He pointed up. Above his head an image flickered into being, a greatly enlarged version of the display he was using.

"How are you doing all this, D?" Lucas wondered.

"Not sure," Dion admitted. "I'd thought my ability was just for seeing people's thoughts, but maybe I was wrong. It's like I can see inside this stuff too, these machines, and figure out how they work." He paused. "Actually, I'm not sure if they're machines at all. It's almost like they have some kind of, I don't know…living energy."

"You mean like – they're alive?" Tamsen asked.

Dion pulled a face. "Not exactly. It's hard to explain. This is not like seeing thoughts, like with people. With these things I just get a sort-of – sense of understanding." He looked up. "Anyway, I've found some stuff out. Have a look."

The image above changed to show some kind of plan or diagram, rotating slowly, glowing with a warm orange light. "I think that's here," Dion explained. "This place, I mean; and I'm telling you, it's *huge*."

At first what they were seeing didn't make much sense. The image showed a roughly cylindrical shape, with some sections attached to indecipherable floating symbols outside its boundary that changed constantly. Parts of the picture were just large empty spaces, while others were densely packed with intricate lines and boxes. "I'll try to clear it up," Dion muttered. His hands flew over the smaller duplicate image in front of him. The view changed, the perspective zooming in on a region near the top of the picture. The children could see a mass of tangled lines like spaghetti, twisted over and around themselves. "What is that?" Timothy frowned.

The view moved in even closer, until suddenly it became clearer. "Those look like corridors, or – roads!" Lucas exclaimed. He stared at the glowing image. "What is this place?"

"It's as big as a city!" Aaron breathed. "How can there be a whole city here? I mean," he looked around at the others for confirmation, "wouldn't someone have discovered it before now?"

"Apparently not," Dion said. "Look, here's where we are." The image contracted and focused on a tiny section right at the top, showing a small circular room with five passages radiating out from it like bicycle spokes. These appeared to go on for far longer than the actual corridors the children had explored earlier, twisting around in the image, joining with and splitting from other passages until eventually they merged with the greater tangle beneath. Lucas wondered what the huge doors they'd found were for. It was almost as if the corridors had been blocked off or barricaded at some point in the past. To keep something out?

Or something in?

"So is this the control room, or something?" Lucas wondered, fascinated. A whole hidden city, right here beneath Dartmoor? It was fantastic!

"No, I don't think so. I reckon it's more like an arrival point, like a train station, or...or an airport lounge. Remember how we got here? We stood on a platform like this one and got…moved. I'm not sure how yet." Dion thought some more. "The stone circle above, where we first came in... remember the standing stones? We wondered why they were warm."

Tamsen nodded. "Yeah. I couldn't figure that out."

"I think they're connected to the thing that brought us down here. Like – heat exchangers, or something. It worked before we even turned on the power."

Tamsen frowned, thinking about it. "Hmmm. Like long-life batteries. Or maybe solar panels. Sort of ticking over 'til someone switched the mains back on."

Dion nodded enthusiastically.

Aaron rolled his eyes. "What did Rith call this place?" he said. "A sanctuary, wasn't it? Doesn't that mean, like, a hiding place?"

"Yeah, or a place of safety," Timothy agreed. "Maybe that's why the whole place is underground. Whoever built it wanted to keep it a secret. I wonder why?"

"I'm still trying to locate the sanctuary archive," Dion said. "Maybe when I do we'll be able to find that out."

Lucas gazed around him again. Whatever Rith really intended for them, he'd already shown them wonders they could never have imagined: a transporter of some kind, a device that could seemingly create food at a thought from nothing, and now an entire hidden city to discover.

"I wonder if there's still anyone here?" he said.

"I can't tell from this," Dion answered, thinking the question was addressed to him. "But I don't reckon so."

"Abandoned?" Tamsen speculated.

"Could be. I can't think why anyone would just leave a whole city like this, though."

Lucas and Aaron exchanged a glance. "Rith said it was ours now, didn't he?" Aaron said.

"Yeah, he did. A whole city – just for us." Lucas grinned. "Awesome."

Chapter Twenty – Unity

Miss Fox had expected the journey from Peregrine House to the Lox Valley to be a noisy and testing one, but she was happily wrong. The three children sitting in the back of her car had hardly said a word since leaving the children's home, for which she was very glad. Marshall Graves sat in the centre of the rear seat, eyes closed as though asleep. Flanking him were the other two boys, Billy Elsdon and Myles Lovell; they simply stared into space with blank, disinterested expressions.

She pulled out her phone and dialled through to the other car.

"Yes," Mr Withers's voice answered shortly.

"Situation report. How are things back there, Ptolemy?"

"Fine. Very quiet. You?"

She eyed her passengers sourly in her visor mirror. "The same. Inform me of any changes." She hung up without waiting for a reply.

Bringing Graves's entire gang along had not been part of her original plan, but Danielle Fox was nothing if not adaptable. She'd been prepared to put up with Graves himself, in the hope it would make him more cooperative later, but finding him waiting with his buddies had been quite an unpleasant surprise. At first she'd flatly refused to take them all, but as they'd argued it back and forth, a sneaky thought had occurred to her: why not kill two birds with one stone? Her current mission was to capture a group of unusual children. Didn't these ones also fall under that heading? She'd planned all along to return at a later date and bring Graves's gang in as well. Certainly there were enough peculiarities about them to warrant further investigation.

Her current problem, though, was a lack of support from Echelon Nine, particularly from Byron Stanford. She couldn't risk the possibility that he would cancel the operation all together, before she'd had a chance to come back for the Graves gang. There'd seemed to be only one option.

She'd pretended annoyance and left the room to, as she put it, 'gather her thoughts.' Once outside she'd made a few calls, pulling in a favour or two. When everything was arranged, she'd returned to the common room and made a show of caving in to Graves's demands. The look of glee on his face had been a picture. *The hell with you, boy*, she'd thought with satisfaction, *your cooperation isn't worth that much. We'll get what we want from you back at headquarters, one way or another.*

Driving along the B-roads off the A30 now, she had to hide a triumphant smile. Imagine the look on Stanford's face when she turned up with twelve, count 'em, twelve potentials? And with only a bare minimum of official support? The name Danielle Fox would become a legend in Echelon!

In the second car, Ptolemy Withers sat in stoic silence next to his driver, Agent Jones. Jones's lack of conversational prowess was perfectly okay with him. He despised small talk. Why did people feel it necessary to fill their every waking moment with meaningless blather and pointless gabbling? This was one of the aspects of his current mission here that was hardest to bear. Sometimes he thought he might just crack and do something foolish, but that would be extremely unwise, not to mention dangerous. His masters were an awfully unforgiving bunch.

No, now was not the time get sloppy and let his cover slip. He'd spent a great deal of time worming his way into his present position within Echelon Nine, living with these people, thinking like them, becoming one of them. He was very good at what he did. He knew this as a simple fact, without a trace of pride. His only goal was to carry out his master's ambitions.

He pulled out his cigarettes, ignoring Agent Jones's disapproving frown. At least the three girls in the back seat were behaving. In fact, they'd barely said a word for the last hour or so. They were acting in a very subdued fashion, much more so than the other times he'd encountered them. They were not even interacting with each other. Strange. The only exception to this pattern had been once when he'd glanced in his visor mirror and caught one of the girls, the dark-skinned one called Jackson, looking at him with an odd expression. She'd immediately looked away, but he'd seen a quick flash of puzzlement in her eyes. Could it be she suspected him? Miss Fox believed this girl might possess some rudimentary mental abilities, and he tended to agree. He resolved to watch this one particularly carefully.

Soon they would have the enemy child in their grasp, the one they had been seeking for so long. Once Mr Withers's masters had mined the Fortune boy's brain for information, they would be able to step up their plans for the next phase of their operation.

Then things would change around here.

*

"I think yer infermation is wrong, missus," the man said with a frown of annoyance. "There's only one group 'ere from that Peregrine 'ouse, and there ain't twelve kids with 'em. I reckon I'd remember that."

Miss Fox stared at the oafish man in front of her. "Mr..."

"Milligan."

"Mr Milligan, I am from Juvenile Services. Here is my identification. On Monday of this week a group of twelve children and four adults set out from Peregrine House near Exeter with the intention of coming here to your site. This was prearranged by a company called Out & About. Are you telling me they never arrived?"

"No, missus, I ain't sayin' that at all. Yer busload o' kids arrived 'ere on Monday afternoon as they said they would, but there was only six kids, not twelve." He frowned. "Yeah. Definitely not twelve."

Miss Fox was alarmed. What was going on here? "Where is the party from Peregrine House now?"

He gestured sullenly. "Over there, by the lake. Noisy bunch, but pretty well-behaved. Bit rare in this day an' age, to see kids listenin' to their elders –"

"Thank you, sir. I'll be back. Ptolemy, wait here please." She stormed away angrily. She was starting to get a bad feeling about all this. It seemed that everywhere Fortune went, confusion followed. Such power, wasted on one so young! If someone like him was a part of the agency he would be a tremendous asset. If only he could be found! She felt she was always one step behind the boy, running to catch up. Just how smart was he? How much did he know?

She approached the indicated plot, a thunderous look on her face. Three tents were arranged in a rough triangle around an unlit fire pit. Several children were playing in the lake nearby, watched over by a couple of student types. A man dressed in shorts was bustling around the tents, humming happily to himself.

"Good morning, sir," she called out as she approached. "Would you be Colin Herbert?"

The man looked up sharply, surprised. "Uh, yes, that's me." He stared at her.

"Danielle Fox, Juvenile Services. I'd like a word, if I may."

He blanched. "Of – of course. Is there something wrong?"

"Wrong?" She stepped inside the ring of tents and stopped, glaring at the man. "Good question. Tell me, Mr Herbert, where are the children currently under your supervision?"

He looked perplexed. "Er, well, mostly down at the lake, as you can see. They're fully supervised! Two of my assistants are watching them!"

Miss Fox counted four heads in the water. "They're all yours?" A quick nod. "So where are the others?"

"Uh, one is up at the shower block I believe, and the last one went over to the campsite shop with another helper. They're all quite safe!" He looked stricken. "What's the matter?"

Miss Fox continued to stare at him. "Where are the rest of them?" Her voice came out as a hiss.

He blinked. "Rest of them? Rest of who?"

"Don't play games with me, Mr Herbert! That only accounts for half of the children! Where are the other six?"

His mouth flapped. "I don't…other six?"

She produced the list she'd had printed from Fisher's records. "Yes, other six! Are you telling me you don't know anything about these children?" She shoved the list under his nose.

He stared at it with a horrified expression. "These names…" he whispered. "I don't understand. They weren't here…were they?"

"Lucas Fortune?" she suggested. "Does that name ring any bells with you, Mr Herbert?"

"Lucas? Yes, I remember him back at Peregrine House, he wanted me to do him a favour, to get some girl he liked onto the list…" he trailed off, eyes unfocusing. "But he's not here now…I mean, I haven't seen him…"

Miss Fox recognised this behaviour. She'd seen it before, on the security recording back in Fisher's office. It finally confirmed her suspicions that Fortune had indeed been here, and apparently up to his favourite trick of fooling with people's minds. What was his purpose? What was he really after?

"So Fortune is not here?" she pressed. "Or his friends? Is that what you're saying, sir?"

"Fortune was never here," he said dully, as though reciting something he'd heard. "There are only six children from Peregrine House."

She nodded. There was little point in questioning this man any further. She'd already learned what she needed to know. "Very well, Mr Herbert." She removed the list from his unresisting grip. "My mistake. I must have been misinformed. I'm sorry to have bothered you."

His eyes snapped back into focus. "That's quite alright, Miss…Fox, did you say? I'm always available to Juvenile Services, of course, though I'm sorry you appear to have had a wasted trip all the way out here! You should have phoned first." He grinned disarmingly, his teeth shining through his scraggly beard. "Now that you're here, though, would you like a cup of tea with me? Or coffee?" He gave her an appraising look. "Glass of wine later, perhaps?"

She sighed inwardly. "That's a very kind offer sir, but I'm afraid I'll have to pass. Thanks for your time."

He produced a card with an obviously practiced flourish. "Well, here's my number," he said hopefully. "Perhaps we could get together sometime? I'd love to take you out for a drink, or something."

"I'll bear that in mind. Goodbye." She left him staring after her.

This Lucas Fortune is certainly a smart one, she thought ruefully. He'd used his influence to get what he wanted and then carefully covered his tracks, clouding people's minds to such an extent that they almost completely forgot about him. His ability was not completely foolproof, it seemed, but perhaps that was a result of his young age. It was possible he hadn't yet learned to use his powers to their fullest extent. Imagine the possibilities if Echelon could harness those abilities, use them for its own purposes! There would be no one on earth who could stop them!

Of course, all this would be just speculation if it turned out she was unable to even find the boy in the first place. Fortune must have planned this whole thing very well, getting all his friends onside, signing them up for this camping excursion and then disappearing off somewhere as soon as they were able. Clever. The question was, where would a group of twelve- and thirteen-year-old children go? Lox valley was in the middle of the wild moorland. There was nothing else for miles around.

Mr Withers gave her a quizzical look as she arrived back at the cars. She pulled him to one side, out of earshot of the others, and told him what she'd learned. He puffed on a cigarette inscrutably, betraying no reaction. "This could be a problem," was all he said.

"You think? We've no idea where Fortune might have gone, and there's no way to track him. 'Problem' barely even begins to cover it!"

"Excuse me, Danielle," a voice cut in from behind her. She spun around angrily.

"What are you doing out of the car, Graves?" she demanded. She really didn't need this boy's particular brand of supercilious charm right now.

He smiled coldly. "I told you before, I'm here to assist you. I couldn't help but overhear what you were saying just then, about Fortune getting away."

She stared at him. The cars were a good ten metres away. "How could you…?" she began.

He waved a hand dismissively. "Doesn't matter. The thing is, maybe I can help you with this one. Or, to be precise, maybe Dana Jackson can."

"Look, sonny, I haven't got time for this –"

"She knows where they went."

That stopped her. She considered him sourly. "How?"

"She used to be friends with Tamsen Nicoletta, one of the girls who's with Fortune now. Apparently Fortune used to go on about some place out on the moors, some place he wanted to try to get to."

"This had better be good, Graves."

"It will be." He looked smug. "Tamsen told Dana about this place, and Dana told me. She reckons she knows how to get there."

"What place? A house? A village?"

Graves looked deep in thought, almost as though he was listening to something. "Not sure," he said after a moment. "But it's not too far away." He looked west, up at the hills that reared up on either side of the valley. "That way."

This all sounded pretty suspicious to Miss Fox, but she was rapidly running out of options here. She still didn't trust Graves, but what choice did she have?

"Very well, but first I'll speak to Dana Jackson myself."

-Dana, remember what we said.-

-Yes, Marshall, I will.-

-Whatever happens, we must get to Fortune. I suggest you be convincing.-

-Yes, Marshall.-

"Is this true?" Miss Fox demanded of the girl. "Your friend Mr Graves here tells me you know where Lucas Fortune is."

"That's right," Dana answered brightly. "At least, I have an idea where he might be."

"Hmmm." Miss Fox stared hard at the girl, trying to peer through her layers of mental shielding. She got nothing but the same brittle static as before. "Are you sure about this?"

"Well, I can't think where else Lucas might have gone, Miss Fox. It makes sense for him to try to get to the place he told Tamsen about from here, you see. It's really not far from this campsite."

"How do you know exactly where this place is, Dana? How can you be sure? Have you seen a map, or something?"

"No, but Tamsen gave a pretty good description. I remember her saying it was near the Lox Valley."

"And you didn't think to mention any of this before?"

Dana looked upset. "I'm sorry. No one asked, and I didn't know it would be important until now."

"I see," Miss Fox said heavily. This whole thing stank, but she was committed now. If she went back to Stanford at the end of all this with her tail between her legs and no other results, he'd have her moved to a desk in the filing section of headquarters before the end of the week. Could things get any worse? "Can we get there by road, at least?"

"I don't think so. It's pretty much all cross-country."

Ah. Of course.

-Good. You did well, Dana.-

-Thank you, Marshall. Are you pleased with me?-

-Yes, I am. Remember to keep your guard up. This woman can read thoughts too, just like you. She must not discover the truth about us.-

-I'll try, but it's hard. It gives me a headache.-

-I don't care about that. Don't let her in, Dana, I'm warning you.-

-Yes, Marshall.-

-Soon it won't matter, anyway. Once we've found Fortune we won't need these idiots anymore, and you can tell them whatever you like. They won't be able to stop us.-

-Don't worry. I know what I have to do.-

-Glad to hear it. I want you to work harder on the mental link, too. Myles and Billy are still having a little trouble picking it up.-

-I'll try, Marshall, I promise.-

-I want all of us linked together properly by the time we find Fortune. He won't put one over on us a second time.-

-I'll do my best.-

*

Lucas and his friends were eating ice cream with hot fudge sauce when Rith manifested his presence again. Nothing changed in the chamber, but all the children instantly knew he was there.

"Where do you keep going?" Aaron said around a mouthful of food.

My body is…elsewhere, Aaron. I cannot physically come to you, the danger is too great, but I can project my thoughts to your location in short bursts. If I remain too long, I run the risk of being detected by my enemies.

"You keep talking about your enemies," Lucas said. "Who are they, exactly?"

There was a long pause before Rith answered. **They are representatives of a race of beings who once attempted to wipe out my people, Lucas. To all intents and purposes, they succeeded.** The disembodied voice sounded weary, heavy with sadness and remorse.

The children stopped eating, intrigued. What was this, a straight answer for once?

"Who are you, Rith?" Lucas asked. "What are you?"

I am a Tulir. We are – were – an order of beings that lived freely out amongst the stars. We were explorers, as well as the historians and archivists of the cosmos. Now, however – they're all gone. I am the last one.

"You're – you're an alien?" Tamsen whispered, incredulous.

To you, I suppose I am. I prefer to think of myself as a visitor to your planet. I have been here many times before, observing and recording Earth's bioforms for our archive. That was my purpose.

"Aliens, now," Aaron muttered. "Why am I not surprised?"

Despite the shock Lucas shared with his friends, things were actually starting to make sense to him at last. If he accepted the fact that Rith was telling the truth about his origins (which, on top of everything else that had happened recently in Lucas's life, was not really all that much of a stretch), then things began to assume a sort of order: the Dream, the spooky goings-on at Peregrine House, their abilities, this abandoned underground city, and all the rest of it. It gave Lucas little comfort knowing this, but at least it seemed to be a step in the right direction, in terms of getting closer to what he wanted most – the truth.

Dion, for his part, looked ecstatic. "I knew it!" he shouted. "Brilliant!"

Aaron gave him a scathing look. "Oh, you knew all along, did you, D? Just didn't feel like telling us?"

"No, I mean I knew that aliens were real! How cool is this?"

Tamsen didn't look happy at all. "I don't believe it! Aliens? Come off it! I don't know how Rith's done all this, but...but he's not an alien!"

Dion gave her a pitying look. "Why do you find that so hard to accept, Tamsen?"

"Why do you find it so easy? Do you believe everything you're told? People lie, Dion, they twist things to make you do what they want. Well I'm not falling for it!" She stormed off, tears in her eyes. Timothy and Sammi exchanged a look and went after her.

I am sorry that some of you are finding this difficult to deal with, Rith said. **I am aware that your species does not always adapt easily to new situations or concepts. I hope that Tamsen will come to accept the truth in due course.**

"I'm not sure how *I* feel at the moment," Lucas admitted, "but I'll listen to what you have to say."

Very good, Lucas. It is most important that you all to come to terms with the situation, in your own ways. We must achieve unity.

"So what happened to the other Tulirs?" Dion asked excitedly. Clearly he wouldn't need any time at all to accept what was going on.

There was a long pause. **Perhaps the sanctuary archive can better answer that question, Dion.** The voice was loaded with overtones of sorrow. **Have you located it yet?**

"I know where it is, but I'm not sure how to get to it. I can't seem to access it from these stations."

Then it is as I feared, Rith sighed. **The sanctuary was attacked, a long time ago. Many components and systems were damaged. It appears the link between the interface structures in this chamber and the archive assembly was also disrupted. In order to access the archive, it may be necessary to travel to the assembly itself.**

"But that's – down in the city," Dion frowned. "We're sort of…stuck in this room."

The sanctuary conveyer will be able to take you there, but only after deactivating the shielding that surrounds this chamber.

"Okay," Dion said doubtfully. "I'll give it a try."

"Hang on a tick," Aaron interrupted. "Why should we go down there? What's so important about this archive thing anyway?"

"And another thing," Lucas put in, "we've got no idea what's down there. For all we know it might be dangerous."

The sanctuary archive is a record of all the data gathered by the Tulirs over the course of a vast amount of time. Even damaged or incomplete, it contains a wealth of information and priceless knowledge. Moreover, it will be a valuable asset to your learning. There was a delicate pause. **As to any danger…that I cannot say. I can only tell so much from where I am.**

"Well, that's not very reassuring," Aaron said angrily. He folded his arms. "I'm not going anywhere."

It should only require one of you. That person can attempt to repair the disrupted datalink from the other end.

"That'll be me then," Dion sighed. He moved over to his console device. "I'd better get started."

"I'll go too," Lucas declared. The other two looked at him askance. "Once you get the shield down, that is." It was better than sitting around here, at least.

One last thing, Rith said then. **As you have already discovered, this part of the sanctuary will respond to your needs, to a certain degree. The small chambers leading from the inner axial corridors can be reconfigured to a more…comfortable state, if you require it.**

"How do you mean?" Aaron asked, puzzled.

Sleep chambers, Rith responded, **enough for each of you. I will leave now. I wish you good luck with your tasks.** Then he was gone again.

"Just like being back in school," Aaron complained. "He's even giving us homework now."

"I'll get started on the shield thing," Dion said, all innocence, slowly edging towards the nearest side passage, "soon as I get the best bedroom!" He raced off.

"Git!" Aaron shouted. He and Lucas exchanged looks, pushing aside their immediate concerns for the moment, and took off after him.

Chapter Twenty One – Getting Closer

Miss Fox watched impatiently as the big off-road vehicle rounded the bend in the road ahead and pulled up in the lay-by next to them. They'd left the campsite an hour or so ago, having learned all they could there. Now they waited a kilometre or so further down the valley for the arrival of the assistance she had requested.

A dark-haired man climbed out of the driver's side door, his face hard and serious. He spotted Miss Fox sat in her car and nodded stiffly at her. "Here it is, Sarah," he called out in a gruff voice.

She got out of the car angrily. "You took your time, Kent," she snapped. "I called you over an hour ago."

He glared at her. "You're lucky I came at all," he rumbled. "Do you know the trouble I could be in if the brass finds out about this?"

"Yes, Kent, probably almost as much trouble as if they found out about those secret bank accounts in the Caymans."

He scowled. "I thought we were done with that."

"We're done when I say we're done. How did you get this vehicle?"

"It's based at one of our facilities in Plymouth. I had it signed out for 'testing' and driven up here by a colleague of mine. I picked it up about ten kilometres south of here."

"Lucky you were in the area, eh?"

"Yeah," he muttered, "lucky old me."

"This colleague of yours, can he be trusted not to say anything?"

"I trust him, and that's all you need to know."

"Fair enough." She regarded him narrowly. "So, what were you doing up here, anyway?"

"What is this, twenty questions? Just take your damn car and go, Sarah. I'm finished here."

"Temper, temper," she said sweetly. "That's no way to treat an old friend."

He didn't deign to reply to that, just tossed her the keys with a grimace.

She had everyone swap vehicles. The off-roader was a big, powerful four-wheel drive monster with several rows of seats in the back, exactly as she had requested. Sometimes it paid to have dirt on people, she thought to herself, especially useful people within the other departments of Echelon. It tended to get results much quicker than going through official channels. It was even better when they didn't know your real name. Just occasionally that kind of subterfuge paid off.

When everyone was aboard and safely strapped in Agent Jones gunned the motor and they set off towards the end of the valley, where the trees began to thin out.

Thomas Kent watched them go sourly. He climbed into the front seat of Miss Fox's vacated car and pulled out his mobile phone. He hit speed dial and held the phone to his ear.

"Yes, sir, it's Agent Kent," he said tightly. "That's right, sir, the vehicle has been delivered." There was a pause. "No sir, there was a group of children with her, as well as the two agents. Yes, sir." Another pause. "She didn't say, sir. Sir, just to confirm, this means I'm off the hook now, right? I did as you asked…yes sir, thank you. I will." He hung up with a relieved smile. Flicking the radio on, he began to sing to himself as he drove away.

*

"I think I've figured out how we got here," Dion announced. "Into this room, I mean."

Lucas and Aaron crowded around him. Timothy, Tamsen and Sammi were off somewhere checking out the sleep chambers. "Oh, really?" Lucas said.

"Yeah..." Dion didn't sound too certain. "This machine seems to be some kind of device for moving objects from one place to another. I've no idea how it works, but I think it's possible to program it with different destinations."

Aaron looked sceptical. "D, isn't a device for moving things from one place to another called a car?"

"Ha. Ha. No, this thing can send you instantly between two points, as long as there is a correctly configured device at both ends. Even through solid walls."

Lucas whistled. "Sounds risky. How can someone go through solid walls?"

Dion made a face. "I don't know. This is advanced alien technology. I've only just figured out how to read a few symbols. There could be loads more I'm missing. I did discover something about the shield around this room, though."

"I don't see any shield," Aaron commented, gazing around.

"It's an energy barrier," Dion clarified. "Specifically arranged to stop the transporter device, the conveyor, from being able to move anything out of this chamber."

"That's stupid," Aaron said. "Why have a room you can get into, but not out again?" His expression changed. "Like...an animal trap."

"I can't tell from this, but I do know those big doors blocking the corridors down there are part of it. They're made of something that stops the conveyor beam from getting through, so the room is still physically sealed even if the power to the energy shield fails."

"Can you open the doors?" Lucas asked nervously. Someone had gone to a lot of trouble to shut this room off from the rest of the sanctuary. Maybe it wasn't such a good idea to go poking around.

"Let's see," Dion murmured. He selected a few icons and manipulated the display. There was a low hum from the food machine.

"What's that?" Aaron said, alarmed. On the display of the device where they had been creating their food a knobbly black object had appeared, rotating slowly. Dion went over and peered at it. "It's a key."

"Dion, I'm not sure about this," Lucas said. "I don't think we should we messing with this stuff. We don't really know anything about this place, but I reckon this room was deliberately sealed off."

The others looked at him, puzzled. "What makes you say that?" Dion asked.

"Think about it. An abandoned city. A heavily shielded room. Remember what Rith said? This place, this city, was attacked by someone. If you don't want someone getting in to your house, what do you do? You lock the door. That's what I reckon this shield is, like a door lock. The city people wanted to keep someone out."

"Okay, that sort of makes sense," Dion admitted, "but it still doesn't explain why the city was abandoned."

"That's what I mean, D, we don't know anything! Maybe whoever attacked the city found another way in. There could be anything down there."

Dion thought about that. "Hmmm."

"So what do we do, Lucas?" Aaron said, frustrated. "We might have everything we need in this room, but we're still trapped. We don't know what's going to happen to us. Rith could be telling us a whole bunch of lies for all we know."

Lucas was torn. The way he saw it, he owed his friends a lot; for all the trust they'd placed in him, for all the faith they'd shown in him since this whole thing started, and for all the discomfort they'd been through because of that. He still didn't know how or why, but he was certain his friends were involved in this because of him. On the one hand he desperately wanted to give them answers, to try and atone in some small part for what they'd been put through; but on the other hand, he really couldn't justify placing any of them in danger whilst in the pursuit of that knowledge.

Dion gave him a direct look. -It's okay, Lucas.- His lips hadn't moved.

Lucas jumped. -Dion? How…-

-I know what you're thinking. I'm not prying, I would never do that, but you're making it pretty obvious.-

-I am?-

-Yup. You've got to stop worrying about us, mate. Right, Aaron?-

-Yeah -, a new voice agreed. Aaron raised his eyebrows. -We're not idiots, you know.-

Lucas stared at the two of them. "You can share thoughts?" he said out loud.

-We all can,- Dion said in Lucas's mind. -I can form a sort of mental bridge between us. I've been working on it for a while. Took a bit of figuring out. I got Aaron to help me with it.-

-Sorry, mate,- Aaron said sheepishly, -we thought you had enough on your plate.-

"But that's cool!" Lucas said in amazement. He felt something hot blurring his vision. He hurriedly blinked back tears. The others pretended not to notice. They'd been worried about *him*?

"We're not babies, Lucas," Dion said aloud. "Do you think we haven't thought about this just as much as you? We're all in this together. It's not just your problem anymore."

"But I didn't…I mean, it's my fault…" he said lamely.

"Don't be a berk, mate. It's no one's fault." He considered. "Well, maybe Rith's fault, but not yours."

Lucas felt wretched. "You don't understand…"

"Stop going on about it, Lucas," Aaron cut him off. "We can take care of ourselves, you know." He and Dion exchanged a glance. -No one blames you.-

"Besides," Dion said with a huge grin, "I love all this stuff!"

Lucas sagged, feeling suddenly released. It felt like a weight had been lifted from his shoulders. He should have known, should have realised before that his friends were the exactly the right sort of people to have around him in times like these. Staring at them now in wordless gratitude, he realised just how lucky he was to have people like them in his life.

-Pull yourself together mate,- Aaron's voice echoed in his mind with gruff amusement, -the girls are coming back. Want them to see you like this?-

The six of them stood in front of the massive barrier Dion had chosen for the test. They looked at each other with trepidation.

-Dion, are you absolutely sure about this?- Tamsen's thought came through the shared mental connection. -Do you even know what's behind there?-

-There's nothing there,- he replied with confidence. -Relax, will you?-

This was a strange way to communicate, Lucas had found. It was almost like talking out loud, but distance didn't seem to matter, and thoughts would often arrive in his head accompanied by weird emotional harmonics and expressive nuances not present in verbal speech. Right now, despite his outward confidence, Dion was also sending out subtle undertones of uncertainty.

The rest of them, exactly in concert, drew back a step or two. Dion rolled his eyes. "We'll be fine, guys. Trust me!" He brandished the strange device he'd conjured from the console they'd christened 'the maker', which, as they'd found out after a little experimentation, could apparently bring into being a whole lot of other things besides food. They'd resolved to dig a little deeper into that whole area at a later date. "Let's see what this baby can do!" he said. He waved the device at the wall.

Nothing happened.

Aaron's eyes lit up mirthfully. "Have you checked…" he began.

"…the batteries!" Timothy finished for him, grinning.

"You took my line!" Aaron complained. "That's not fair, I do the jokes around here! Lucas, tell him."

Lucas spread his hands. "Nothing to do with me, mate. You should hide your thoughts better."

Aaron glared daggers at Timothy.

"Let me see that," Tamsen said sternly, her scientific curiosity temporarily overriding her nervousness. She plucked the thing from Dion's fingers and examined it frowningly. "Looks like an old potato," she grumped. "What are these lumps for?"

"I just told the system to provide access to the security shield matrix," Dion replied. "This is what it came up with."

"So, you don't actually know what to do with it, then?"

He mimicked her tone. "*No, I don't actually know what to do with it.* Give me a break, will you?"

She sucked air in through her teeth thoughtfully. "Maybe…like this?" She held up the device and pushed a couple of the nodules on its surface.

The metallic barrier seemed to waver for a second, then without warning it shrank away, folding itself up into an impossibly small cube that thumped to the ground with a thunderous clank that set their teeth rattling. A blast of foul-smelling, fetid air rushed forth and hit them full in the face, making them gag. They stumbled back with cries of alarm, falling over each other, choking and gasping.

The blast quickly dwindled to a breeze. The children sat up dazedly, staring in fear and apprehension at what had been revealed.

Beyond where the barrier had been the passage did indeed continue, but its nature changed drastically. It looked like a sewer tunnel, dismal and damp, the curved walls covered in stinking slime and encrustations of mould and fungus. Filthy water dripped from the ceiling and pooled in rank puddles along a floor which appeared to have been partially ripped up. It was like a bulldozer had been driven over it. The tunnel stretched straight on away from the children into inky blackness, farther than any of them could see. None of the illumination panels seemed to be operational.

Tamsen climbed stiffly to her feet, brushing herself off. She glared at Dion and Lucas. "Still think this was a good idea?"

Timothy and Sammi were hugging each other tightly. They saw the others looking and disengaged rapidly. "Surprised me," Timothy muttered. Sammi pretended to examine the ground.

"Alright, this seems okay," Dion said brightly. "Now the barrier's down, I should be able to focus the conveyor." The others could sense his real nervousness, but no one said anything out loud. That was the problem with this mental link business, Lucas thought: you couldn't have any secrets.

-You're not kidding,- Tamsen's thought came distantly. Aaron and Sammi nodded sagely.

"It's kind of like a sink full of water," Dion explained as they once again gathered around the monitor. "While the plug's in, no water can get out; take it out, the water escapes. Now we've opened the barrier, the conveyor signal should be able to get through. Let's see…" He twiddled the controls.

Lucas looked around at his friends. "Are you sure you want to do this?" he asked them again. "It's only Dion and me who should go, really."

Tamsen eyed him squarely. "Don't be silly, Lucas," she chided him. "We've been through this. We all want to find out about this place just as much as you do. Besides, why should you guys have all the 'fun'?"

"Okay," he conceded, holding up his hands. "Just checking."

-Worrier,- she admonished him, but gently. Aaron crossed his eyes at him.

"This should be it," Dion announced. "We all need to stand in the middle of the platform, like when we first came in. Everyone ready?"

Sammi grabbed Timothy's hand. He flushed but didn't let go. "Is this gonna hurt, D?" he asked nervously.

"Nah, we'll be fine," Dion blustered, almost managing to hide his own doubts. "Didn't hurt when we came through before, did it?"

"Yeah, I know, but that time it took us by surprise. We're all expecting it this time."

"Um, Tim…" Aaron said.

"Maybe we should, like, test it first, or something," Timothy continued. "Send something else through, see what happens."

"Tim…"

"'Cos I heard about this film once, where this guy built a teleport machine and there was this fly…"

-TIM!-

He flinched. "Blimey, Aaron, what's with the shouting?"

Aaron gestured impatiently around him. "Look, you pillock!"

Timothy looked. "Oh. Right."

They were no longer in the monitor room. The dais beneath their feet looked the same, only now it occupied the centre of a vast, echoing space wreathed in muted light and shadow. Above them a great ceiling of stalactites hung like the pointed teeth of a predator; from these emanated a milky white light, pale and ethereal, washing over them with a cold, ghostly glow. Next to the children on the dais itself was a single monitor station. At first it appeared inert, but within moments of their arrival it lit up and unfolded like the ones in the first chamber. Dion immediately crossed over to it and began manipulating the display with a happy little grunt.

"Handy to have around, isn't he?" Tamsen murmured.

"Uh huh," Lucas agreed. He peered into the gloom. "I guess this is it. The archive. I thought it would be like, you know, a library or something."

"Shelves of books and stuff?" Tamsen said. "Yeah, me too."

"It is a library," Dion called. He was staring raptly at his display. "There's tons of information here, but it's not in books."

"Woah, look at that," Aaron breathed. As their eyes adjusted to the pale light, they began to see more of the chamber. In the far distance towering walls appeared, encircling them, studded with walkways, ledges and balconies. All around the central dais, spaced at regular intervals, twisted columns like larger versions of the monitor stations thrust into the air, looming over them like limbless squared-off tree trunks rising to several times the children's head height. Many of the columns were broken or destroyed, their shattered remains strewn all across the floor.

"These columns are storage devices," Dion informed them. "Kind of like computer hard drives, only with no moving parts. The Tulirs would come here to upload their knowledge to these things, so that anyone could access it."

"It looks like someone had different ideas," Tamsen said pointedly. "Guess this is why you couldn't access any information from upstairs, eh?"

"Yeah. This place has been trashed. I can do it from here, though, I reckon. Just give me a minute. The more I see of this stuff, this technology, the easier I seem to understand it." He looked up suddenly. "Hey, guys, I've just had a thought. If I can understand all this, right, and if we can all link our minds together…"

"…then maybe we can all understand it too!" Tamsen finished. "Good thinking, Dion!"

He blushed. "Ah, call me D."

Something cold rushed into Lucas's mind, like a wave breaking over his consciousness. He gasped and shut his eyes, instinctively holding his breath. Around him he was aware of his friends doing the same. Then, as quickly as the sensation had come, it receded. He opened his eyes tentatively.

-How's that?- Dion's mental voice said.

-Feels weird-, Aaron complained. -What did you do?-

-I reinforced the link so the knowledge can flow more freely in all directions, instead of me having to send it.- He was met with blank looks. -Now when I see something, you should see it too,- he clarified. He stared deliberately at his display.

Through Dion's eyes, the children simultaneously saw the glowing orange display in front of him with its flowing symbols and graphics, overlaid on their own vision. It was very disorienting, like seeing wildly different images with each eye. Lucas's head started to ache almost immediately. Tamsen and Sammi screwed up their eyes in pain.

"Whoops," Dion muttered. The sensation faded away. "Sorry about that, guess I didn't think it through."

"Just get the damn library working," Aaron said irritably, rubbing his temples. "You can just *tell* us what it all means."

Dion looked hurt. "Only trying to help," he sniffed. "Okay, here goes." He selected a control and activated it.

Around them the remaining upright pillars began to unfold, a deep hum rising slowly up from beneath the floor. Each column extruded long, thin prongs like radio antennae; these swayed about like they were caught in a strong wind.

"They look like insect feelers," Tamsen observed distastefully, and Lucas found himself in agreement. There was something distinctly organic and insectoid about all the technology in this place.

"So, what do you want to know?" Dion asked his friends excitedly. "I'll have to filter through the data to find what we want."

Lucas stepped forward. "Why don't we start with the Tulirs?" he said grimly. "Let's find out who this Rith fella really is."

Chapter Twenty Two – Half A Dozen Of The Other

The sturdy off-road vehicle bounced along the narrow dirt track, swaying dangerously from side to side. Miss Fox hung on grimly to the sides of her passenger seat, trying not to let her nerves show. It wouldn't do to let any of her fellow passengers get the impression that she wasn't completely in control, not now with the end so very nearly in sight.

She wondered what she would find when they reached their destination. What sort of place would a twelve year-old boy and his gang choose to hide out in? Were there other people there, helping them? There must be. Maybe this whole thing had been prearranged. Maybe there was a whole nest of potentials up ahead, just waiting to be picked up and brought into the fold. She allowed herself a small smile. Director Danielle Fox. It had a nice ring to it.

She turned to check on the children. They sat facing each other on bench seats that lined the insides of the vehicle, Mr Withers on one side with the three boys and Agent Brown with the girls on the other. At least the adults were looking as uncomfortable as she felt. As for those kids…

They were quite the oddest bunch of children she had ever come across. They emanated an aura of serene, eerie calm, a kind of creepy self-possession that made Miss Fox feel distinctly uncomfortable. Despite repeated attempts during the course of the journey, she had been completely unable to penetrate that wall of stillness. Just what was going on behind those half-lidded, sleepy-looking eyes? Children didn't behave like this, not even the ones she tended to encounter in her line of work. Where was the selfishness, the whining, the impatience? They'd barely said a word since leaving the campsite several hours earlier, except for Dana Jackson's smiling prompts when asked for directions. Miss Fox had caught the children looking at each other intently once or twice, eyes darting, almost as though they had something to say, and wanted to speak out loud. What was stopping them? At first she'd been content with their serene behaviour. Now she wished one of them would just say something, anything. This wasn't doing her nerves any good at all.

"Are we close, Dana?" she asked, more to fill the silence than for any real reason. The girl had already assured her that this track would lead them in the right direction.

Dana turned her head slowly to regard her. Her smile switched on like car headlights. "Yes, Miss Fox, we're getting very close now," she beamed, looking almost exactly like a happy young girl without a care in the world. "Just a couple more kilometres, I'd say." She turned away again, the smile draining from her face.

Miss Fox shook herself. Creepy. "Thank you, Dana. Call out if you've anything else to say, won't you?"

Dana nodded without looking around.

At length the track reached a crossroads, or at least a place where another track intersected it. These must be tractor trails, Miss Fox thought; farmers out tending their sheep perhaps, or Dartmoor park rangers patrolling the hills. The sign back at the road had read Private Property, but such things were of little concern to Echelon. They had government sanction to roam just about anywhere they pleased.

"Go right," Dana advised without prompting. "Head towards that valley, the one with the two tors on the hills above it."

Miss Fox looked. About a kilometre away, amid a range of undulating hills shaped like giant ripples on a beach, two craggy grey outcrops overlooked the surrounding countryside, tumble-down piles of granite ringed by smaller heaps of rock and scrubby hawthorn bushes. They faced each other from opposing hills like sentinels guarding some hidden fortress. She felt excitement beginning to mount. *Stay right there Fortune. I've almost got you…*

The track petered out some distance from the valley, but that had little effect on their progress. Agent Jones simply steered their vehicle right onto the scrubby grass, guiding it across the uneven ground with a sure hand, concentrating ferociously. The children were thrown around in their safety restraints, heads lolling and banging against the sides of the vehicle, but not one of them so much as made a peep. Mr Withers wore a look of stoic fortitude, gripping onto his harness with white knuckles. Agent Brown had her eyes squeezed tightly shut, face white, lips puckered in a silent grimace of discomfort.

The car crested a steep grassy rise and dropped down the other side, the whole vehicle tilting forwards alarmingly like a rollercoaster ride. Miss Fox's stomach did a flip. With a sense of panic she felt her gorge rising in her throat. Not in front of the children…!

With a curse, Agent Jones slewed the car to a juddering stop at the bottom. "Sorry about that," he grunted. "But this is the end of the road." He gestured forwards.

They could indeed go no farther, at least in the vehicle. The way was blocked on all sides by scattered lumps of granite from the sentinel tors, some half-hidden dangerously in the grass, ideal for tripping unwary walkers or wrecking tyres. The ground was just too rough, even for the powerful off-roader. They would have to proceed the rest of the way on foot. "We're close enough," Miss Fox said weakly, swallowing hard. She was almost glad they had to leave the car behind, despite the lowering clouds and the increasingly strong wind that gusted around outside. It would be quite refreshing to take a little walk.

She opened her door and climbed gingerly to the ground. A few spatters of ice-cold rain immediately needled her skin, but it felt good after being cooped up in that car with those creepy kids. She took a deep breath, composing herself, then checked her hair in the outside mirror before climbing back inside. "Agent Brown, I want you to remain here with the children," she said, still feeling rather nauseous. She swallowed hard. "I'll take Agent Jones and Mr Withers and proceed to the location."

Marshall Graves stirred, turning to pierce her with a hollow stare. His pale blue eyes glittered. "We wish to come with you," he stated.

"Don't be silly. This is no place for children. You'll stay here where it's safe and dry."

He looked around slowly at his friends, who simply stared back at him mutely. After a moment or two he spoke again. "Whatever you say, Miss Fox." He didn't look at her. "We'll be no trouble to you."

"Good." There it was again, that disturbing sense of wrongness, the feeling of icy fingers running slowly down her spine. Not for the first time she wished she had more agents here. The children were behaving perfectly, exactly as she wanted them to, but still…

"Agent Brown, keep a two-way radio with you, call us if… well, if you need to. We'll be on channel two."

Brown nodded stiffly. "No problem, Agent Fox." If the agent was disappointed at being lumbered with babysitting duty instead of getting out in the thick of the action, she betrayed no sign of it. She turned to regard the children coolly, as though daring them to play her up.

In perfect concert, the six of them turned to stare back at her with steely eyes. She blinked, recoiling slightly. "Neat trick," she murmured, "but I was a supply teacher for four years. That stuff isn't going to work on me."

Graves grinned at her. "Don't worry about us, miss," he said, "we'll be perfect little angels. Won't we, guys?"

The others indicated their assent with solemn nods.

Miss Fox said, "See that you do." She dismissed them deliberately, jumping back down to the ground. After sitting in various cars with those kids for several hours, the prospect of facing Fortune and his cronies seemed almost pleasant by comparison. "Come on," she ordered Jones and Withers, and set off grimly towards the two tors.

It was rough going, especially as she was unused to such cross-country activity, but they made it to the edge of the shallow valley in only a relatively short space of time, and without incident. Puffing slightly, they rounded the bottom of the nearest hill and beheld what lay in the valley below.

An empty stream bed wound along the base of the valley, overgrown with hawthorn and juniper bushes. The two encompassing hills formed a shallow bowl, overlooked by the looming shapes of the tumble-down tors surmounting them. Directly ahead, in a wide clearing that didn't look natural, a ragged circle of stone pillars nestled forlornly amid the scrub-grass and stumpy trees. At the centre of this circle was a humped shape like a broken table, leaning carelessly to one side.

Miss Fox stopped where she was, taken aback. She had certainly not been expecting this! Where was the village or cottage where Fortune was supposed to be holed up? Where were the other people who were protecting him? There was clearly no-one here, and by the looks of it no-one had been here for a very long while. Anger exploded into her mind like a vengeful wave. Damn that Jackson girl! Had she led them all out here on a wild goose chase?

"What's that?" Jones exclaimed, pointing at a colourful mass pinned between a pair of trees halfway up one of the hills.

Mr Withers squinted against the stinging rain. "I believe it's a tent, or the remains of one." He took a pull from his cigarette. "It looks to be of a type similar to the ones employed by Mr Herbert's group back at the campsite. It appears to be quite badly damaged."

Miss Fox subsided a little. "Maybe they were here," she said. "But they're clearly not now. That damn girl led us out here for some reason, and when I find out why –" She turned away.

"Perhaps we should investigate this region first," Mr Withers suggested. He seemed strangely agitated. Miss Fox glanced at him. He was staring intently at the circle of stones up ahead. "This could be quite – useful," he said.

"How, Ptolemy? There's no-one here! No Fortune, no children, no potentials of any kind! How is this useful?"

He didn't appear to be listening. "I'm going to have a closer look," he declared, and set off with a loping stride towards the standing stones.

Miss Fox was annoyed. "Ptolemy?" she called after him. "Where the hell do you think you're going? Ptolemy!"

He ignored her. Agent Jones looked at her askance. "Any suggestions, Miss Fox?" he said carefully. "Should we assist?"

Miss Fox's jaw flapped for a moment. "What? Assist him with what?"

"With the search, Miss Fox. We came here looking for escaped potentials, yes? Perhaps we should begin by quartering the area. Shall I call Agent Brown for support?"

Her head began swimming, the monochrome world around her threatening to start spinning out of control at any moment. How could she have been so stupid as to listen to those brats and their crazy ideas? She should never have allowed herself to be duped into falling for their childish prattle, but she'd wanted so much to believe it! This was supposed to have been her ticket to success in Echelon Nine, the culmination of all her dreams and aspirations. And the thing that galled her the most? It looked like Byron Stanford may have been right all along. Damn him!

"Miss Fox?" Jones was saying. "Shall I radio for Agent Brown?"

"No, Agent Jones," she managed, blinking back hot tears. "She has to stay with the children. There's been enough damage today. Can't have one of them getting loose."

"Thanks for your concern, Danielle," a new voice interrupted. "But we can take care of ourselves."

She and Jones both wheeled around in surprise. Marshall Graves stood about ten metres away at the lip of the valley, hands on hips, grinning hugely, ginger hair flying rakishly in the wind. To either side of him loomed the bulky shapes of Billy Elsdon and Myles Lovell.

Miss Fox instantly snapped back into some semblance of control. This was something she could deal with, at least! "I told you all to stay in the car!" she shouted at them. "How dare you disobey me!"

"Now, now, Agent Fox," Graves chided her, cheekily wagging a finger. "Getting angry like that can take years off your life, you know."

"Where's Agent Brown?" she cried into the mounting wind, ignoring his goading. She took a few steps towards him. "How did you get past her?"

Graves tilted his head in mock concern. "Oh, I'm afraid Miss Brown won't be joining us," he said. "She saw the error of her ways, and let us go. Poor dear, it turned out her heart just wasn't in it."

Miss Fox went cold. "What did you do to her?"

"Me? Nothing." He smiled horribly. "A lifetime of stress and bad habits must have done her in. She's...resting now."

There was a frozen moment, the two sides staring at each other in silence. It was broken when Agent Jones's hand dived inside his jacket, pulling forth a Government issue sidearm with lightning speed. He pointed the weapon directly at Graves's head, backing off with slow steps as he did so. "Don't move," he ordered the boy in a steady voice. Miss Fox slowly began to creep sideways, away from the direct line of fire. The situation may be spiralling rapidly out of control, but she still had her basic training to fall back on.

Graves looked offended. "Guns, now? I'm quite disappointed in you, Agent Jones." He cocked his head quizzically. "Or should I call you Alan Wilson, born February 4th 1971, just outside Sunderland? Nice trick with that accent there, Al. No-one would ever know you're a macam."

Jones's mouth dropped open. "How the hell could you know that?" he spluttered, losing all composure. His gun arm dipped, wavering uncertainly.

"He's a reader," Miss Fox hissed, realisation dawning at last. She'd encountered other readers like herself before, but none quite like this child. He must be exceptionally gifted to be able to pick out complete thoughts buried in an agent's mind under layers of Echelon training and conditioning.

Graves tapped his nose infuriatingly. "Something like that, Danielle," he replied, amused. He took a few unhurried steps forward, still flanked by his unsmiling buddies. Instantly Agent Jones's arm came up again, pinpointing the boy in his sights. "I told you to stay still," he rumbled.

Graves stopped, shaking his head sadly. "Crisis management," he sighed. "Isn't that what you people call it? Highly trained to handle hostile situations and confrontations, drilled in combat and defence techniques, and all that?" He smiled. "Is this a hostile situation, Al? Really? I mean, we're just children."

Jones bared his teeth. "I don't what you are, sunshine, but if you've done anything to Agent Brown –"

"Her? I told you, I didn't touch her. She's just cooling her heels back in your MPV."

With his free hand Jones pulled out his radio, not taking his eyes from the children. "Echo three, this is Echo two. Respond, please."

There was nothing but static. He repeated his request, with the same results.

Graves shrugged elaborately, rolling his eyes. "What can I say? She looked pretty tired when I left her. Lifeless, you might say. Just let her rest, why don't you? She's had a busy day, the poor dear."

"You little snot!" Jones cried, surging forward. Miss Fox just stood apart and watched the scene unfold in grim silence. Part of her mind lamented the awful state this operation had got itself into, but at the same time the analytical, scientific part of her was coolly interested in just where this particular altercation might lead. As the commander of this mission, she could very easily call Jones back and defuse the whole situation with a few simple orders, but instead she kept quiet. What would Graves do now?

She soon found out, though it wasn't Graves who did anything at all, except throw a quick glance at each of his buddies. As one they both stepped forward, closing ranks to hide Graves behind their considerable combined bulk. With folded arms they stood fast, glaring at the fast-approaching agent.

"Out of my way!" Jones commanded, reaching out to shove them aside. He was a very big man, substantially larger than the two boys, but they made no attempt to move. Instead Billy Elsdon took another step forward, intercepting Jones's steam-rollering progress. The two of them collided with a sound like two slabs of meat slamming together.

Miss Fox watched with clinical detachment as Jones rebounded from the impact like he had run headlong into a stone wall, grunting as he tumbled heavily to the ground. The gun flew from his fingers and spun off into the undergrowth. Unmoved, Elsdon stared down at him with a horribly blank expression.

Jones rolled over and leapt athletically to his feet, adopting a fighting stance. "Don't make me hurt you, boy," he grunted, dismissing what had just happened as some sort of fluke. "I could cripple you with one finger. Stand aside."

Very calmly, Elsdon shook his head. He raised a hand and beckoned insolently.

With a snarl Jones surged forward again, murder in his eyes, but this time it was the other boy, Myles Lovell, who intercepted him. There was no impact. Instead Lovell merely touched the agent with one outstretched hand. There was an almighty crack, like the grounding of a giant static charge. Miss Fox flinched back involuntarily.

The effect on Agent Jones was entirely different, and much more dramatic. He literally flew backwards, catapulting through the air like a rag-doll, limbs flying as he twisted around to crash headfirst to the ground some four or five metres away. Bluish smoke drifted up from where he lay twitching, the front of his jacket completely melted away to reveal a massive sizzling burn on his chest. He made no sound at all. The smell of ozone and cooked meat wafted to Miss Fox where she stood in open-mouthed silence. After a moment or two Jones stopped twitching, and she knew what that meant.

"Well, Danielle," Graves called, stepping towards her over the tufted grass, all smiles. "Does that answer your question? The one you've been dying to ask?"

She looked at him squarely, determined not to show any fear. "What question is that, Marshall?" She carefully smoothed her hair back from her face.

"Don't play games, Agent. You know what I'm talking about. My secret." He looked delighted as he stepped right up to her, stopping only centimetres away, staring into her eyes with an intensity she found it hard it to endure. It was then she finally knew that Graves was crazy, completely insane, a horribly dangerous foe against which she could have little or no defence. What's more, he knew she knew it. He could read her like a book. He nodded solemnly. "So, now you know at least some of it, I have a question for you: can you keep my secret, Miss Fox?"

With no other option left to her, she forced down the part of her mind that screamed *'Run! Run!'*, pushing it away into the quiet depths of her consciousness. Slowly, gravely, she returned his nod. "I don't have much choice, do I?"

He clapped her on the shoulder, startling her. "That's the spirit, Danielle! Why, with the two of us working together, there's nothing we can't achieve!" He laughed mockingly before turning away, dismissing her completely. He moved off to confer with his cronies.

She took a few careful steps and bent to retrieve Agent Jones's gun, having made a careful note of where it had fallen. Its weight, as she quickly tucked it into the back of her trousers, completely failed to reassure her.

She'd never felt so alone in all her life.

Chapter Twenty Three - Dilemma

"I can't find much info on the Tulirs," Dion declared dejectedly after a while. He had been searching through what he could reconstruct of the archive storage system for over an hour, but so far had been unable to dredge up much of any use. Whoever had been the cause of all the damage to this place had managed to comprehensively scramble the remaining storage devices to such an extent that little practical information remained. What he had found made very little sense. It was immensely frustrating, especially as he'd been so sure that he'd be able to find the answers down here. He hated the thought of letting his friends down, especially Lucas.

The only one of them near enough to reply was Sammi River, the rest of the gang having elected to go off exploring around the archive chamber whilst they waited for Dion to do his stuff. None of them were in sight, but that didn't matter. With the mental link they were all just a thought away, no matter where they went.

Sammi was poking around one of the fallen storage pillars near the central dais. In the gloom of the vast chamber she was a clear beacon, her skin glowing gently like a comforting night-light. She looked up at Dion. "Keep trying," she encouraged him. "We know you can do it."

His frustration boiled over. "Do you?" he snapped before he could stop himself. "Are you sure? Because I'm not." He regretted his outburst instantly. The last person he wanted to have a go at was Sammi River, the most inoffensive, soft-hearted individual he knew.

Surprisingly, she smiled up at him, her glow increasing slightly. "Don't worry about me, Dion," she said. "Everyone thinks I'm some sort of delicate little flower that needs to be protected from the nasty world, but I'm stronger than they think." She climbed up onto the dais next to him and fixed him with a frank look. "I'm not that person any more, okay?"

He nodded uncertainly, respectfully not examining the open mental link between them too closely. The six of them had already developed a peculiar kind of etiquette between them; when you could pry deep into the mind of a person at any time, you had to have a special, conscious respect for one another's privacy. In order to maintain normal relationships, it was far easier to just ignore the link except by mutual consent. Even so, sometimes a stray thought like Sammi's concern for him still managed to make its way across, as had just happened. Everyone was still learning this brand new discipline. "Sure thing, Sammi. I – I didn't mean to offend." That sounded lame. He'd never been much good at talking to girls.

Shockingly, she leaned forward and planted a quick kiss on his cheek. Instinctively he recoiled, mortified. He was still at that peculiar stage of life when girls were starting to change from nothing more than an annoyance into something strangely intriguing…

She laughed and skipped away, obviously well aware of how she'd made him feel. He touched his burning cheek gingerly, staring after her. Girls! Who could ever predict what they were going to do next?

Still distracted, he absently fiddled with the controls of the interface station next to him, not really paying attention to what he was doing. The low humming pervading the room changed pitch, beginning to rise. New symbols appeared on the display, flowing too fast for him to decipher. He snapped his attention back into focus, staring at the display. "What did I do?"

Around him, on the floor of the chamber, the active pillars began to writhe, contorting and twisting as though alive. They grew taller, stretching upwards like flowers reaching for the sun. The slender tendrils they held forth snapped rigid, all pointing at a single spot high in midair.

-Um, guys?- Dion broadcast, peering upwards. Sammi came skittering over the dais back to his side. They exchanged a fearful look.

The focus point of the tendrils, a point in the air some ten metres above them, began to shimmer in a now familiar way. Vague shapes appeared, moving in ghostly fashion as though seen through frosted glass.

It was like a giant, super-sized version of the console displays, only this one was at least twenty metres across. The only problem was that it was not clear enough to see properly.

"See, I knew you could do it," Sammi said happily.

He avoided looking at her. "Thanks," he muttered. "Only, I'm not sure what I did." He frowned at the control panel in front of him. He couldn't exactly read the symbols directly, it didn't seem to work like that; rather some of them seemed to translate themselves in his mind into something he could comprehend. He had no idea how that happened, but he didn't question it. So far the ability had come in very useful. "Maybe if I adjust this group…" he said to himself, manipulating a set of symbols that seemed to have something to do with focus, or clarity. The giant image above wavered, becoming more distinct. Through its blurriness it looked somehow familiar…

-We see it, D,- the chorus of his friend's voices echoed in his head. -We're on our way back.-

"What is that?" Dion puzzled, eyes roaming over the vast image. He could make out several upright shapes, dark against a much lighter background, unmoving. Between them, a number of smaller shapes darted to and fro in eerie silence. He twiddled the controls a little more, almost like tuning in a radio when you have no idea of the proper frequency. The shapes resolved a little more…

"Oh, boy," he breathed, in time with Sammi's gasp. "That's not good."

*

"Well?" Graves snapped, standing near the centre of the stone circle, hands on hips. Miss Fox watched silently from the outside, unobtrusively half-hidden behind one of the standing stones. Curiously, as she leaned against it, it almost seemed warm. There was no sign of Mr Withers. Where could he have got to? It was not like him to just disappear when things got tense. He'd been at her side through more than a few unpleasant situations in the past.

Dana Jackson approached Graves cautiously, a puzzled expression on her face. "I – I don't understand," she confessed. "They were definitely here, the sound of their thoughts has left a pretty clear trace, but now…"

"You lost them?" Graves said dangerously.

Dana blanched. "No, no, I haven't lost them, Marshall," she protested, shrinking back. Miss Fox wondered what kind of a hold Graves had on his companions that could produce such fear. "They must be shielding, somehow. Maybe that Dion River has worked out how to do that, like I can."

Graves stared at her unsympathetically. "Break through it," he commanded. "Find out where they went!"

"Y – yes, Marshall," she stammered and hurried off, trembling.

"Must you be so hard on her, Marshall?" Sabrina Celestine said then, quite bravely under the circumstances. She looked pinched and withdrawn. There was not much trace left of the impatient, snooty girl Miss Fox had interviewed so recently at Peregrine House.

Graves transferred his intense stare onto her, but surprisingly after only a moment he softened slightly. "Maybe not," he admitted, "but I won't have Fortune slip through my fingers, not now when I'm so close."

Miss Fox noted how Graves rarely referred to his friends collectively when talking about what he was doing. It was almost as if he didn't really see them as real people at all, just tools to do his bidding, unimportant servants to be ordered around at his whim. It seemed pretty clear that he had some kind of power over them, for there was not one of them who didn't look slightly fearful of him, if not outright terrified. Well, except perhaps for Lois Christie, who appeared to be withdrawing into her own private world more and more. Right now the girl was crouching on top of the large, flat-topped stone that occupied the centre of the circle, grunting as she tried to force her fingers into a long crack that bisected it. Miss Fox almost felt pity for the girl. Clearly her mind was unravelling at an ever-increasing rate. What would Graves do with her when she started to become a hindrance? He'd already demonstrated his willingness to dispense with anyone who got in his way. Miss Fox feared the girl's future was pretty bleak, but there was little she could do about it.

"I get that, Marshall," Sabrina was saying, "but Dana's exhausted. Can't you see that? Her mind's been working on overdrive all day. I don't know how much longer she can go on."

"I can't worry about that now," he said dismissively. "She'll have plenty of opportunity to rest once I've got my hands on Fortune. Once he's told me all he knows about Rith, then we can all rest."

Miss Fox straightened, suddenly interested. Rith? Why did that sound familiar? She racked her brain trying to recall where she'd heard that particular word before, but for the moment nothing came. Was it something to do with an earlier Echelon case, something she'd read in a case-file once? She cursed her lack of support from Echelon. With full backup and operational approval she could have made a single call and had the answer in moments.

"Whatever you say, Marshall," Sabrina murmured, defeated. She turned away and trudged after her friend Dana.

"Billy, Myles, go look around outside the circle," Graves ordered his two constant companions, who looked more and more to Miss Fox like his personal guard. They nodded stiffly and hurried off. "Where are you, Fortune?" Graves hissed to himself.

Miss Fox fingered the grip of the weapon concealed behind her back. She detested guns, which was why she refused to carry one of her own, but right now it felt like the only real thing in a world that was rapidly spinning out of control.

*

"What are they doing here?" Tamsen said incredulously as they all stared at the image suspended above them, which showed the scene unfolding in the stone circle up on the surface. "How did they find us?"

Dion looked concerned. "It must be Dana Jackson," he said. "We all know that Graves and his buddies have some weird abilities, just like us; we saw that in the garden back at the House. Dana can pick up thoughts, kind of like I can. Maybe she was able to track us all the way here."

"But why?" Lucas wondered for all of them. "Graves hates us, and the rest of his gang don't like us much, either. Why would they follow us all the way out here?" His brain began to race ahead, new connections forming even as he thought. Through the mental link, the others began to pick up on it too.

They exchanged glances. -They're just like us,- the thought fizzed around their minds. Lucas didn't know who'd actually thought it, but it didn't seem to matter. Their minds were joining, merging, working as one.

-They want answers too.-

-Were they drawn here?-

-Who else knows they're here?-

-Should we help them?-

The thoughts came in a jumble, overlapping confusingly, and once again Lucas's head began to ache as it had earlier when Dion had tried to enhance the link, only this time it began to feed back on itself, looping around the connection between their minds in a tightening, contracting spiral. Grimly, Dion closed his eyes and deliberately broke the connection.

The six of them staggered back and fell heavily to the floor, gasping in pain. They stared at each other groggily as it began to subside. "I really need to work on that," Dion winced.

Dana Jackson's head jerked up, eyes widening. "They're here!" she said, grimacing in exhaustion. "I heard them!"

"Where?" Graves demanded, striding up to her and grabbing her arms.

She stared back at him uncomprehendingly. "W – what?"

"I said, where are they?" He shook her roughly. Her head lolled around.

"Under...underneath," she whispered, eyes starting to close. Miss Fox started forward, worried that the girl might be seriously ill, or at least fatigued almost beyond endurance.

Lois Christie began to jump up and down excitedly on top of the central slab, hooting like an animal. The other children stopped and stared at her.

"Somebody shut her up," Graves snarled, carelessly letting go of Dana. She flopped to the ground without a sound. Sabrina rushed to her friend's side, cradling the girl's head in her arms. The two boys Lovell and Elsdon looked at each other uncertainly, as though unsure what it was Graves wanted them to do.

With a growl Graves strode forward, raising a splayed hand to Lois. "Fine, I'll do it myself!"

Lois shot backwards as though hit by a train, so quickly she had no time to make any sound. There was a rending crack, the ground around the central slab buckling as though under some tremendous force. With a roar and a blast of dust the two halves of the slab rocked upwards, tilting and sliding away from each other.

Miss Fox stopped dead, stunned. She'd never guessed the Graves boy had so much power! It looked like some form of telekinesis, the ability to physically affect the world using only the mind. At least that explained why the others were so frightened of him. He didn't even need to get close to stop anyone in their tracks – or force them to do his will.

He was standing stock still, too, though for entirely different reasons. He gazed at a dark space under where the central slab had rested. He lowered his hand and took a step or two forward, peering excitedly at what looked like an alcove, or…

"A tunnel!" he crowed, clapping his hands gleefully. "Fantastic! Billy, Myles, come and look at this!" He was almost dancing with triumph. "Fortune went *underground!*"

Miss Fox risked coming a little closer, intrigue overriding her caution. A secret subterranean hiding place, right out here in the middle of the wild moors? She'd never heard of such a thing. Maybe it was some old, abandoned air-raid or bomb shelter left behind and forgotten after the last world war. She knew her history: Devon, in particular Exeter and

Plymouth, had suffered pretty heavy bombing by the Nazis back in the early part of the war. It wasn't inconceivable that someone had managed to hide some kind of bolt-hole all the way out here. The real question was, how had Fortune known about it?

Several metres beyond the newly revealed entrance, Lois Christie lay face down where she had fallen, next to one of the standing stones. At first Miss Fox feared that her earlier assessment of Lois's prospects had already come true, but after a moment or two the girl groaned and rolled over, clutching at her chest and belly. She opened her eyes and stared blankly at the grey sky, cold rain falling unheedingly into her eyes. At least Graves hadn't hit her hard enough to kill her, Miss Fox thought with relief, though she wondered what kind of damage he had done. Getting hit that hard could easily break a rib or two.

Graves had already completely forgotten about her, his mercurial attention now fully fixed upon Fortune's apparent hiding place. Miss Fox was coming to appreciate Graves's ruthless single-mindedness. He had an almost psychopathic ability to refocus his mind in an instant, totally dismissing the consequences of his actions if he felt they were unimportant or irrelevant. People like that were extremely tough to deal with, as one could never predict what their next move might be, or where they would fix their attention next. By the same token, however, sometimes they could be easily distracted…

She resolved to watch him carefully and wait for her chance. She had no intention of remaining under his power indefinitely.

Sabrina looked distraught, sitting in a forlorn huddle with Dana. Both of her friends had been callously incapacitated before her eyes. It was clear she was struggling, way out of her depth. Without a word Miss Fox approached and gently began to check Dana over, feeling for a pulse. There was one, but it was faint and irregular, a symptom typical of exhaustion. A little rest ought to see the girl right – at least physically.

Sabrina bridled slightly at first, glaring at Miss Fox in her customary manner, but she couldn't maintain it for long. She sagged and let Miss Fox take over. No words were spoken between them, but Miss Fox could see a faint flicker of something like gratitude in the girl's eyes. A little unsolicited comfort and support could go a long way towards mending bridges…and it didn't hurt to have allies, either.

"We're going in," Graves called, surveying the remains of his group. A faint flicker of annoyance crossed his face, as though he was just now noticing the sorry state they were in. "Billy, Myles, help the girls," he muttered. "We may need them, especially Dana Jackson, when we find Fortune."

Miss Fox and Sabrina stood back sullenly as Billy Elsdon manhandled poor Dana to her feet. Across the circle Myles Lovell was doing the same for Lois Christie. Sabrina shot an entreating look at Miss Fox; she shook her head quickly, no. Now was not the time to try anything.

Reluctantly, fearfully, they followed Marshall Graves into the mysterious opening.

And just where the devil was Ptolemy Withers?

A burbling, buzzing sound filled the archive chamber, bouncing and reflecting from the curving walls to produce confusing echoes.

"What is that?" Timothy cried over the din, covering his ears with a grimace.

"Some sort of intruder alarm, I think," Dion answered, rapidly scrolling through the display screen. The volume dropped to a more tolerable level. "When Gravy busted open the entrance it must have triggered this warning. Something's happening in the sanctuary systems, but I'm not sure what."

"Are they inside now?" Sammi asked worriedly. Tamsen put a solicitous arm around her shoulders.

"Well, they definitely got into the first chamber," Dion replied, "we saw that from those outside views, but I'm not sure how to track them internally. Yet." He did something else and the noise cut off.

"Did you see what happened?" Lucas questioned. "Dana Jackson somehow picked up our mental link! I reckon they must have one too."

Timothy nodded. "They seem to be very similar to us, in a lot of ways," he agreed. "Maybe they want the same thing as us, to find some answers. Maybe we should help them."

Aaron made a disbelieving noise. "You're joking, right? Help Gravy?"

Tamsen looked worried. "I can't believe I'm saying this, but Timothy may be right. Maybe we should try to help them. After all, we know a lot more than they do about what's going on. Imagine if we'd had someone helping us. Things would have been a whole lot simpler."

"We did have someone helping us," Aaron argued, "Rith. He guided us here safely, and told us how to get the answers for ourselves."

"But Graves didn't have that," Tamsen insisted. "He had to find his own way here. I don't know how he did it, but he's here now. If he and his friends are like us, what right do we have to deny them what we've learned?"

Lucas could see both sides. It was a difficult dilemma, with no immediate or obvious solution. Should he and his friends offer assistance to the very people who had so often gone out of their way to make everyone's lives miserable back at Peregrine House? Or should they just let Graves stumble about in the dark? If that was allowed to happen, then how did that make Lucas any better than Graves?

Through the mental link, which Dion was now carefully controlling, the whole group shared his predicament. There were no easy answers. Aaron, though, looked disgusted. "I can't believe you're even thinking about helping them!" he cried. For him, there was no dilemma at all: let Graves suffer, for all the things he'd done, for all the times he'd made them feel small and worthless.

Fortunately, or perhaps unfortunately, Lucas simply wasn't made that way. He sighed. "We have to make the effort, at least," he said. "We're not like Graves. We're better than him. If he throws it back in our faces, that's his decision, but at least we'll have tried."

"You're making a mistake, Lucas," Aaron warned, upset. "Don't you remember what Gravy tried to do back in the garden that time? He deliberately hurt us, and enjoyed it too. If you hadn't have stopped him, who knows how far he might have gone?"

"I know," Lucas said quietly. "I remember. I'll speak to him myself. The rest of you stay here."

"No way, Lucas," Timothy said, and Tamsen nodded her agreement. "We're in this together, remember? We're with you."

Lucas wasn't going to argue. "Okay, fine. We'll all go." He glanced at Aaron. "At least, those who want to."

Aaron looked away, silently fuming.

"Um, guys?" Dion called then, staring at his display. "We may have another problem."

The others crowded around him. "What is it now?" Lucas grumbled. Why couldn't things just be easy?

"That alarm thing," Dion said. "I don't think it was just an alarm. I think it's part of some sort of defensive system. When Gravy broke open the entrance, it seems to have sent the sanctuary into a sort of automatic defence mode."

"Right," Lucas replied. "So what does that mean?"

"If I'm reading this right, it means we're in trouble. The sanctuary reacts to an attack like a person reacts to disease. It goes after the invading forces internally and neutralises them. According to this display, the sanctuary is preparing to deploy its defences."

"Sounds good to me," Aaron said harshly. "Let the city deal with Graves itself. Problem solved, right?"

Dion looked scared. "Not exactly. You see, the sanctuary makes no distinction between types of intruders. When an immune system goes to work, it can't tell the difference between different kinds of foreign cells. It attacks them all."

There was a pause. The six of them exchanged looks of dawning realisation. "So…it'll attack us, too?" Aaron said slowly.

Dion nodded gravely.

"But we've been in here for ages!" Aaron protested. "Why didn't the city react before?"

Tamsen said, "Because we weren't attacking before. Now it thinks we are."

"So what can we do, D?" Lucas asked.

"I'm thinking. I've got a few ideas. But you should know, we don't have much time."

"How much?"

"Well, the sanctuary has to power up. It's been dormant for a very long time, and it's not in the best of shape."

"How long, D?"

"Maybe…an hour, at the most."

Lucas nodded. "Okay. That's means it's even more important I speak to Graves and his gang. I have to warn them of the danger."

Aaron made a face. "He won't listen."

"Still, I have to try. We can't just leave them. You see that, don't you mate?"

Aaron sighed. "I guess. You're such a do-gooder, Lucas. The only thing you're missing is a halo."

Lucas grinned tightly. "It's in the post." He turned to Dion. "D, is there any way to communicate from place to place within the city? If we can send a message from here, it'll be a lot quicker and easier than physically finding Graves's gang."

Dion looked strained. He didn't turn away from his display, where he was furiously manipulating icons. "There may be, but I haven't got time to look for it now, Lucas. Kinda busy over here."

Lucas thought for a second. "Okay, the mental link," he decided. "If Dana Jackson can hear us, then maybe we can talk back to her." He looked around at his friend's anxious faces. "I'll need your help, guys," he said. "I can't do this alone."

-We're with you, Lucas,- came the firm reply.

*

Far off in the depths of the city, down in the freezing lower levels where the air was unbreathable and toxic, faint movement began to stir in the stiflingly dark tunnels. Row upon row of red lights lit up balefully, casting a demonic glow over the racks of tightly packed repeller drones stored in their cradles. In response to the sanctuary's imperative they began to unfold, extricating themselves from their ancient slumber with jerky, spasmodic movements. Tendrils extended, questing blindly in the gloom. Hesitantly at first, the drones began to detach themselves, dropping to the squalid ground with muffled thumps. Many of them remained unmoving, too far gone with disuse to function, but an enormous amount still remained. Scuttling up the walls, chittering amongst themselves, the drones headed in a seething black wave for the entrances to the transport tubes set in the ceilings above like open mouths.

They spread out into the veins and capillaries of the city, heading directly upwards to the source of the invasion.

Chapter Twenty Four – A Meeting Of Minds

Marshall stood in silence at the base of the stone steps, staring round the oval, smooth-walled chamber. He shone the torch he'd taken from Miss Fox around the walls. Behind him Billy and Myles emerged from the tunnel, supporting the limp bodies of the two girls. They stopped too, impressed. "Not bad, eh?" Graves said to them. "Looks like Fortune's done alright for himself."

Despite his joyful triumph at their success so far, he was still annoyed that the mind-link operated by Dana Jackson was currently inactive. He cast a disgusted look in the girl's direction, draped as she was over Billy's arms like a deadweight. If he hadn't needed her skills, he'd have got rid of her long ago. The same went for the other girls too. Baggage, the lot of them. Even Billy and Myles got on his nerves sometimes.

Dana twitched then, her head coming up slowly as though she'd picked up on his thoughts. Maybe she had. Graves watched her coldly. "Nice nap?"

She stood upright, jerkily pushing away Billy's arm as he tried to support her. Her eyes blazed strangely as she gazed around the chamber. Sabrina and the agent woman came stumbling into the room then, almost colliding with Myles, who gave an annoyed grunt and glared at them threateningly. Sabrina spotted that her friend was conscious and rushed over to her. "Dana?"

Dana stared back at her blankly. "Yes?"

"Are – are you alright?"

"Yes." She peered around owlishly. "Ah, I'm here."

Graves frowned at that, but snorted impatiently. "You girlies can play 'catch-up' later. There're more important things to think about right now."

Dana's head swung around to fix him with a piercing stare. "Marshall?"

He strode up to her angrily, scowling. "Of course it's me," he snapped. "What's the matter with you?"

She smiled. "You should be nicer to me," she commented. "Everyone says so."

His expression froze. "Is that so?" he said. "And just who is 'everyone'?"

"People," she replied airily. "My friends, your friends, Lucas's friends..."

She broke off as Marshall grabbed her arms. "What did you say?"

She gave him a blank look. "Which bit?"

With a snarl he released her arms and pushed her away. She stumbled back against Sabrina, who supported her.

"You think this is a joke, Dana?" he hissed, raising his arm, ready to unleash his power.

"No, I don't actually, but you should hear me out, Marshall." Her voice was distant and unconcerned, almost as though she was not fully in control of what she was saying. Some part of this penetrated Marshall's righteous fury, staying his arm for the moment. Sabrina, for her part, was white with fear and disbelief at her friend's actions.

"Make it good," he advised, lowering his hand. "Now explain."

"I have a message from Lucas Fortune," Dana said calmly. "He's here, and he knows we're here too."

"A message?" He considered that for a moment or two. The casual mention of Fortune's name made him grind his teeth together. "And just how did you get a message from Fortune? Got a mobile phone I don't know about?"

"They have their own version of my mind-link. When I heard them in my mind earlier, they must have figured out a way to make it work in both directions."

Marshall forced himself to stay calm. "Is that right? And just what has Fortune got to say for himself?"

"He warns we're in danger. He says we should get out of here as quickly as we can. We don't have much time."

Marshall couldn't help himself. The laughter came bubbling up out of his mouth in an unstoppable torrent. "A…a warning!" he guffawed breathlessly. "That's priceless! Good old Lucas Fortune, coming through for his mates when they're in trouble! Hahaha!"

"He's serious, Marshall," Dana reproved him. "There's something going on here, in this place, which could threaten all of us, even Lucas and his friends themselves. He's trying to help us."

Marshall's laughter died away. He pressed his eyes with the balls of his hands, squeezing out the tears. "Of course he is," he said agreeably. "Because, as you know, me and Fortune go way back. What a guy!"

Sabrina said, "Maybe you should listen, Marshall." She sounded frightened. "I can feel it through the mind-link. I think Fortune's serious."

Silently cursing, he turned his thoughts inwards, searching for the tenuous threads of Dana's mind connection. He should have thought of that the moment the foolish girl regained consciousness. Frustratingly, though, the link proved difficult to grasp, slippery and ghost-like, not at all like it had been before. Why was it different? He couldn't tune into it properly.

"Why can't I find it, Dana?" he demanded out loud. "What are you doing?"

"This is not my link, Marshall," she replied. "It's Dion Raven's. I'm not even fully conscious. Lucas and his friends are supplying me with the energy to keep me awake." She smiled vaguely. "Feels funny."

With a snarl Marshall exerted his power and flung Dana to the ground, her head cracking against the dark floor. Instantly all the animation drained out of her. She lay there silently, unmoving except for the slow rhythm of her breathing. He went and stood over her, ready to crush the life out her. The very thought of Fortune and his cronies listening in on them through her mind drove him wild.

Sabrina grabbed his arm. "Please don't, Marshall!" she cried. "It's not her fault! She wasn't in control!"

He rounded on her. "And what about you, Sabrina? Were you in control? Or were you planning to betray me to Fortune? Is that why you picked up the link and I was excluded?"

"What? No, of course not! Dana and I have been friends for years, it was just easy for me to slip into her mind! As soon as I realised the link was actually coming from Fortune's lot I closed my thoughts off straight away!"

Marshall made a disgusted sound and turned away. "Whatever. Billy, Myles, bring them. We're going on."

She grabbed his arm again. "But, Marshall, what about the danger…?"

"Don't be stupid," he dismissed her, roughly shaking her off. "There's no danger. Don't you get it, Sabrina? Fortune just wants us out of his little den. That idiot foundling will say anything to protect his secrets. I'm not falling for it. We go on."

"That idiot!" Lucas fumed as the connection broke. For a moment back there he had seen through Dana Jackson's eyes, had heard Graves's ranting. If anything, Graves seemed even more unbalanced than ever before.

"Well, you tried, Lucas," Aaron said with only a faint hint of 'I-told-you-so'. "You can't make someone listen who doesn't want to. Besides, we don't even know what the danger really is, do we?"

Dion called out, "No, but I'm getting a pretty good idea."

"What is it?" Lucas asked. *Damn you, Graves, I only wanted to help!*

"I think this automated defence system thingy was activated once before, way back during the attack that caused this place to be abandoned in the first place. Look here." The giant image above, which had been cycling through random scenes from both inside and outside of the sanctuary, now changed to show the glowing diagram of the city schematic they had first seen in the upper chamber. It looked different from before, more active; the parts that had been blanked off now glowed with different colours. "This, as far as I can tell, is a recording of the sanctuary when it was fully active," Dion went on. "The glowing bits are the sections drawing power, probably the populated areas. Now watch this."

The image changed again, flares and spouts of light flashing on and off all over it. "This was during the attack," Dion explained. "Those flashes are energy discharges of some kind, maybe weapons. I'm not too sure about that." At the very base of the image, dark spots like ants began to appear, crawling rapidly upwards through myriad tunnels and ducts.

"What are those?" Aaron said breathlessly.

"The sanctuary defences. The archive calls them repeller drones. They're like automated machines that work together to neutralise any danger to the sanctuary."

"I guess they didn't work very well," Tamsen commented.

"Actually, I think they may have worked too well. I found some records that seem to indicate the attackers, whoever they may have been, were repelled in less than one day. But check this out." The image continued to show the dark dots swarming all over the city. "This is a speeded-up capture of what happened after the invaders left."

Lucas frowned. "But the drone things are still active. Wouldn't they stop once they'd done their job?"

"Yeah, they should, unless they found something else to attack." He paused ominously.

"What, you mean…"

"Yeah. The sanctuary's own inhabitants."

Lucas shivered. "The drones turned on their own people? But why?"

"I think the control mechanism that was supposed to switch them off was itself damaged in the attack. The drones just kept going until there was no-one left. Then they quietly scurried back to wherever it is they hang out and went back to sleep. In fact, I've got a strong feeling that most of the damage we've seen here may have actually been caused during that second fight with the inhabitants. All those dark patches we saw on the first city map are areas that are so badly damaged they're uninhabitable. The city pretty much destroyed itself."

"And now they're awake again," Aaron said shakily. "So, maybe we should, like, leave?" He stared imploringly at Lucas. "Right?"

"Unless D can shut those drones down, I don't see we've got much choice," Lucas said heavily. "How much time?"

Dion consulted his display. "No more than fifty minutes, Lucas, but I have to tell you, there's no way I can shut these things down, any more than you can stop your body fighting off a cold. The drones are built right into the fabric of the sanctuary."

"Fine, so just set the conveyor to get us back upstairs. From there we can get back to the surface, right?"

"Don't see why not. I'll just access the…" he trailed off, staring round-eyed at the console. "Oh, no."

"Let me guess," Tamsen said acidly. "The conveyor's busted, right?"

"Uh, not exactly. It's been automatically locked, probably when the alert first happened. Must be part of the defence system, to keep pockets of 'infection' localised." He looked up fearfully. "I can't get us out of here!"

"You what?" Aaron squeaked. "Are you saying we're trapped, Dion?"

Dion looked wretched. "I – I don't know…"

Lucas thought fast. "D, is there any other way out of this room? A physical exit of some kind?"

"Uh…I'm not sure…"

"Dion, get it together!" Tamsen snapped. "You're the only one who can find another way out of here! We don't have time to stand around chatting about it!"

Dion shook himself. "Right, right," he muttered, blinking. "Sorry." He bent to his task, rapidly scrolling through screens on his display. "Okay," he said after a moment. "There is a door, over there on the far side. It leads out into some sort of tunnel network. From there we should be able to find our way back up to the arrival chamber." He looked up worriedly. "Only problem is, we're quite a long way from there. It's gonna take us a while to get back."

"How long is a while?" Timothy enquired calmly. "Just so I know."

Dion shook his head. "Longer than we've got. I don't know if we can make it on foot."

The six of them looked at each other miserably. Lucas squared his shoulders. "We have to try," he decided. "We'll make a run for it. Get as far as we can." His words sounded hollow even to him. He tried to inject some confidence into his voice. "Come on, let's go!"

Everyone moved off, all except for Dion. "Lucas, what about the archive?" He clutched at the console. "We still haven't learned anything! We can't just leave it like this…"

"Dion, there's no time!" Lucas exclaimed. "We have to get going! I hate to leave it behind too, but unless you can figure out some way of taking the archive with you –"

There was a low whine, and the console in front of Dion began to close in on itself. He leapt back with a yelp. As the segments of the top dome slid back into place a square-ish black object about the size of a tennis ball emerged from within, rising up on a pedestal. Comprehension lit Dion's eyes. "Cool," he said. "Hard copy!" He grabbed the object and leapt down from the dais, stuffing the thing into his jacket pocket. "Clever machines!" he explained. "They know what you want! Come on then, why are you just standing there? Let's move!"

They raced across the uneven ground, dodging fallen columns and broken sections of floor. Through the mental link they all shared the same feelings of fright and anxiety, but somehow it didn't seem so bad. The six of them moved and thought as one, their very proximity to each other offering hope and comfort at the same time. Any one of them on their own might have given in to fear and panic, but the unified whole was much stronger than the sum of its parts. In rapid order they reached the far wall that Dion had indicated.

There was nothing there, just a blank curving edifice, featureless, stretching away from them above and to the sides. "I know there's a door here," Dion said, puzzled.. "I saw it on the map. It must be hidden somehow…"

Tamsen placed a hand on the wall. "Hmmm…" she said thoughtfully. She pressed harder – and her hand sank right in, the rest of her body following before anyone could stop her. She disappeared without a sound.

"Hey!" Aaron shouted, appalled. He pounded on the wall. *"Tamsen!"* His fist made a dull thumping sound as it hit the very solid surface.

-I'm okay,- Tamsen's voice came to them. She sounded amused. -I'm outside in the corridor. Can't see much, but I can do this…-

The wall suddenly dissolved, leaving a large oval-shaped gap through which Aaron, who had been leaning on the wall, now stumbled. He fell to his knees with a grunt of surprise. Tamsen was standing over him, grinning. "What are you doing down there?" she said sweetly. "Tired already?"

He jumped up, red-faced. "Neat trick," he said. "How did you know?"

"I didn't," she shrugged, "but I thought it might be worth a try. What use is a door with no handle? I used my ability to get through the wall, found this…," she pointed to a hemispherical lump protruding from the wall nearby, "…and gave it a push." She wore a satisfied smile. "And, Aaron – it's nice to know you care."

He snorted. "Can we go now?" he grumped. He stomped quickly off into the semi-darkness of the corridor. The others stepped through after him.

The corridor was a wide, curving avenue lit fitfully by flickering illumination panels. The damage here was extensive. Whole sections of wall and ceiling had collapsed in places, and a chilly breeze carried the smell of damp and decay. Lucas shivered. "Which way, D?"

Dion thought for a second. "That way." He pointed at a branching side entrance some way up the corridor. "I memorised the route," he explained after catching a few doubtful looks.

They set off quickly, the knowledge that there was now only about forty minutes to go lending them an extra, desperate urgency.

Dion led them through a twisting, circuitous route that tended generally upward. Everywhere they looked they saw evidence of the pitched battle that had been fought here. Some passages were completely blocked by debris, while others were passable only by wriggling through tiny gaps in the rubble.

Something had been bothering Lucas as they forged grimly on. Eventually he could hold it in no longer.

"Where are the bodies?" he wondered. The others stopped and looked at him quizzically for a moment. "Shouldn't there be, like, people's remains everywhere?"

"Don't know," Dion said. "Maybe the repeller drones cleaned up after they'd finished." He attempted a small laugh, but couldn't make it convincing. None of them were in the mood for jokes.

They pressed on, time ticking away in their heads. Despite their speed, and the growing weariness in their limbs, each of them deliberately tried not to think about what might happen when, and if, the drones caught up to them. At every junction they cast fearful glances down darkened side-passages, expecting at any moment to see a horde of terrifying monsters bearing down on them.

Eventually Timothy pulled up, breathless. His large frame wasn't built for prolonged bursts of speed. "Need...to rest...for a minute," he panted, bending double.

Concerned, the others gathered around him. "We can't stop, Tim," Dion said. "We've still got a long way to go."

Through his pain, Timothy smiled grimly. "Doesn't really matter, does it?" he wheezed. "We're never gonna outrun those things anyway."

Lucas wanted to argue, but there seemed little point. The facts were staring them in the face, had been all along. Their flight before the advancing horde was little more than a gesture to maintain their flagging spirits for as long as possible, and every one of them knew it.

That didn't stop some of them from trying, though. Sammi was crying. She pulled at Timothy's arm feebly. "Come on, Tim," she sobbed. "Don't give up!"

Gloomily, Lucas stared around him. Next to where they had stopped was a large opening, lit from within by a few flickering illumination panels. Several objects could be seen clustered on the floor in the space beyond, large flat shapes like trolleys or sleds, each perhaps four or five metres long. On the flat tops of each, several curving spurs like thin horns protruded upwards. The children had seen many objects like these as they'd been hurrying along, upturned or in scattered, broken pieces, but hadn't given them much thought. Now, Lucas's mind began to work. "Hey, Dion," he said. "See those things over there? What d'you reckon they are?"

Dion looked. He frowned too. "Dunno," he admitted, "but they look sort of like…sledges maybe, or…" His face lit up. "Oh, sweet!" He dashed over to the nearest one, checking it over quickly. He turned to beckon Lucas excitedly. "Come and see this!"

"Is it what I think it is?" Lucas asked as he joined his friend, growing excited too. If he was right...

"Yeah, I reckon so," Dion replied. "It's some sort of travelling machine, like a – a hovercraft, or something." He poked around it a little more. "No wheels," he confirmed. His face fell. "No power, either. Cobblers."

"We've got power, D," Lucas reminded him. "Remember what Rith said before? About how some of us can siphon energy? If we can work out how to use those abilities properly, we might be able to get one of these things working!"

Dion looked doubtful. "I don't know, Lucas. We don't know anything about how this stuff works."

Tamsen and Aaron joined them. "We picked that up," Tamsen said. "I like the sound of it. We may as well try, Dion. What have we got to lose?"

Aaron nodded grimly. "I'm up for it."

Dion shrugged. There was little other choice. "Okay, you're right. Let's give it a go."

At what was presumably the front end of the sled a bar or rail protruded upwards, curving over to form an arch at about the children's chest height. Upon this arch were a number of indentations and pits set into a flattened, angled panel. Dion reasoned that these were probably controls of some sort, but he could make no sense of them. Time ticked on as they struggled feverishly to figure the thing out, all of them growing ever more anxious and fearful. Nothing moved around them, and all was silent, but they could all sense something ominous in the atmosphere, an impending wave of doom approaching from out of the distant darkness. It didn't help their concentration one bit.

After what seemed like an age, but what was probably really only a few minutes, Dion threw up his hands in frustration. "Without power, I can't even link into whatever controls this thing," he complained bitterly. "It's like trying to read a book in a foreign language with the cover shut!"

Aaron and Sammi exchanged a glance. "Let us try," Aaron said to them. "After all, it was Sammi and me who first turned on the power systems when we got into this place. Maybe we can do the same with this thing." The two of them jumped up onto the platform and laid their hands on the panel at the front. The others stood back carefully.

The whole platform gave a sudden lurch, jolting sideways as though on ice. "Woah!" Aaron cried, alarmed. He let go of the panel and the sled instantly stopped where it was. Sammi grinned. "I think that worked," she said. "I could feel the power going through my fingers."

"It's a start," Dion said animatedly, jumping back up. "Now if we can just control it…"

"That's where I come in," Lucas said. His mind was whirring, new thoughts and ideas racing through his head like lightning. He didn't know where it was coming from, but the knowledge seemed to be right there in his brain. He knew what he had to do. "Everyone get on board," he said, wrapping his hand around a protruding spur.

The others jumped on with alacrity. "Aaron, you and Sammi put your hands on the panel, but don't do anything else yet," Lucas said. His friends could sense his assurance; no-one questioned him. "Dion, I need your help. Can you boost the mental link just between me and you?"

"I…suppose, but it didn't work too well last time."

"Do it anyway. I need –" He broke off as he heard a distant sound. The others heard it too.

"What's that?" Aaron said doubtfully. It sounded like whispering, or the far-off crashing of waves on a shingle beach.

"I don't know, but it can't be good. Dion, link me in!"

Lucas's perception expanded suddenly, the thoughts of his friends echoing around his mind like the clamouring cacophony of an out-of-tune orchestra. He gritted his teeth against the onslaught. After a second or two it subsided a little as Dion got control of it, damping it down until Lucas could think again, tuning out any irrelevant thoughts.

-I'm getting better at this,- Dion's thought came. -Now what do you want me to do?-

-Just keep the link going, no matter what.- Out loud he said, "Aaron, Sammi, power up the sled, but slowly, okay?"

"Lucas?" Tamsen said anxiously, peering into the gloom. "That noise – it's getting louder! Whatever you're gonna do, do it fast!"

The sled lurched and began to judder. Quickly Lucas reached out with Dion's power and plunged their joined minds into the workings of the machine's control unit. On his own he would have had no idea what to look for, but Dion had the knowledge he needed, culled from his recent experience of the sanctuary systems. This sled was based on the same technology; it was just a matter of adapting Lucas's own thinking to the simple commands the sled used. Now, with his own ability, he gently manipulated the sled's 'brain', feeling for the right movements…

"Everybody hold on!" Dion cried, understanding what Lucas was doing. Quickly the others grabbed hold of whatever handhold they could find and held on grimly. The sled bucked one more time then rose up smoothly to a height of half a metre or so above the floor. It slid forward noiselessly, rotating as it did so to face the entrance. "Not bad!" Aaron hooted from where he stood gripping the rail at the front-end. "Anti-gravity!"

"Something like that!" Dion said. "Just keep the power coming, we'll do the rest!"

Lucas carefully guided the sled out into the corridor. His senses felt preternaturally heightened, his vision piercing the semi-darkness like that of a nocturnal bird of prey. He overlaid the map from Dion's mind onto his vision like a head-up display, picking out the route. Behind him, from back down the corridor in the direction they'd come from, the rushing, whispering noise was growing louder with every second. Mixed in amongst it now was the faint sound of scrabbling, as of claws or pincers fumbling and scraping against walls and floors…

The sled moved off, away from the horrible sound, quickly gaining speed. The chilly air rushed past Lucas's face as the sled glided along the rubble-strewn corridor, but he ignored it, concentrating ferociously on maintaining control of the sled. He guided it around obstacles and over piles of debris, quickly getting a feel for how it responded and handled. Dimly he was aware of someone hooting with joy, but he had no time to spend on such distractions. The sound of their pursuit was the only other thing he allowed into his perception.

Worryingly, that sound didn't seem to be growing any quieter as they moved away.

*

Marshall Graves sat angrily on the edge of the dais, glaring around at the glowing walls as if they offended him. Miss Fox stayed carefully away from him, avoiding his attention as much as possible. She was still keeping her eye on Dana and Lois, who were not doing well at all. She didn't want to end up in the same condition as them. The two girls had been laid side by side on top of the dais, near its edge. Neither of them had moved for a good while. Miss Fox hoped they were only deeply asleep.

Despite poking into every corner of this room for the past half-hour or so, there were quite clearly no other exits. Graves's frustration was evident, and even Miss Fox herself shared it, at least in part. The analytical part of her mind clamoured to know where Lucas Fortune had got to, and if he had in fact come through this same room at some point. If so, then how had he gotten out?

Tiredness and hunger were also not improving anyone's mood. It had been several hours since any of them had eaten or had a drink. Spirits were flagging rapidly. Miss Fox wondered whether Graves had enough sense left in him to admit defeat, give up and return to the surface. She rather suspected not…

"Billy, Myles, check this platform again," Graves ordered his two henchmen harshly. "You *must* have missed something!" Unhesitatingly the boys jumped up and began feeling around the top of the dais again, searching for cracks or hidden hatches. Miss Fox sighed inwardly. This was the third time Graves had made them do this.

"Sabrina, you too," he commanded, beckoning her over. She had been lurking around the perimeter of the room much as Miss Fox was doing, trying to stay out of trouble. "Make yourself useful for a change."

The faintest flicker of loathing crossed Sabrina's face, almost too quick to see, but Miss Fox was watching alertly. Whatever the girl may have felt for Graves up until now, it seemed she was rapidly changing her opinion of him. "Yes, Marshall," she muttered tonelessly, and climbed up to join the rest of her companions. Miss Fox turned away for a second, trying to hide a smile.

"What are we looking for, Marshall?" Sabrina's voice came. "I don't…"

Silence fell like a hammer. Miss Fox looked up sharply. The children were gone. The dais was empty. "Jiminy Christmas," she breathed. "So that's how you did it, Fortune."

"Interesting technology, eh, Danielle?" a soft voice said behind her. She jumped and spun around.

"Ptolemy? Where the hell have you been?"

Mr Withers took a long pull on his ever-present cigarette, face expressionless as ever. "Here and there," he replied. "How're things?" He dropped the stub and ground it out on the floor.

"Are you *kidding?* Did you see what happened to me?"

"You weren't in any danger, Danielle. At least, not from them."

"What are you talking about?" She glared at her assistant. "Where were you when I needed your help? You could have got me out of this, called for backup, anything!"

"Oh, I called for backup alright. They'll be here very soon, don't worry about that."

"Well, good. I have to say, Ptolemy, I'm not very happy with your conduct. We're supposed to be partners! You don't just run off when I'm in trouble! What were you thinking?"

"I have my orders," he replied mysteriously. "Anyway, I'm here now. Do you know how the children activated this conveyor?"

Miss Fox frowned, suddenly suspicious. "What do you mean, 'conveyor'? Are you talking about this teleporter? Because that's what it is. I've seen them before."

"Call it what you like. I asked if you knew how the children activated it." He loomed over her threateningly. Up close his face looked strange, discoloured and lumpy, almost like he had been beaten.

She backed off uncertainly. "Are you alright, Ptolemy? You look like hell."

"Answer the question," he grated, his voice sounding strained and wheezy. He fumbled about his pockets, trying to find his cigarettes. "How does this technology work?"

She was starting to get a bad feeling about this. Was there anyone she could trust? She'd known Mr Withers for years, had worked with him on numerous cases for Echelon Nine though, now she thought about it, she realised she knew next to nothing about him. He had always been very evasive and close-mouthed when asked about his life outside of Echelon. "Who are you?" she said, backing off further. The entrance to the first antechamber at the foot of the stone steps was just to her right. She began to edge closer to it…

Mr Withers was wheezing badly now, face contorted in a grimace of pain. His badly-shaking hands were beginning to turn grey, veins standing out like blue cords. With a grunt of triumph he fumbled a pack of cigarettes from his pocket and lit one up. He took an incredibly long pull, visibly calming as he did so. Colour returned to his skin. He exhaled an acrid cloud with a huge sigh of relief. "That was close," he muttered, smiling slightly at Miss Fox.

"Those aren't just cigarettes, are they?" she realised. Things were beginning to fall into place now; the stinking cigarettes, the aversion to bright light, his creepy way of being able to move in almost total silence despite his great size…

"It doesn't matter, Danielle," he told her. "You were an important part of my masters' plans, but now you've served your purpose." He cocked his head. "The question is, what do we do with you now, hmmm?"

"Echelon will find out about you, Ptolemy," she said, not even scared any more. "They're very good at rooting out spies and turncoats."

He chuckled humourlessly. "Well, they've done a bang up job on me so far." He darted in front of her, blocking her slow sidle towards the exit. "I wouldn't worry about me or, for that matter, your precious Echelon Nine. The Taween know all about it."

Miss Fox gasped. She couldn't help herself. "The – the Taween?"

"My masters, yes. You are familiar with them, then?"

"I…yes, I am. I've heard of them." She had. The name was almost a byword in Echelon for the very thing it had been set up to defend against. "You're one of them?"

"Me?" He chuckled again. "No. I'm just a servant. I do their bidding. But in case you have any doubt they're real…" He grinned. "Let's just say you'll be seeing them very soon. And now I've finally found this last sanctuary, lost for so many years, there'll be nothing to stop them."

Chapter Twenty Five – Breaking Point

Marshall jumped up and gazed around him, astonished. A moment ago the empty, dusty room had had no exits; now he was surrounded by them. Several dark tunnels stretched away from the chamber, radiating out like spokes from a wheel hub. And that was not all…

Sabrina gave a little squeal. She was backing away from what looked like a blackened tree-stump that had somehow appeared on top of the dais with them. In fact there were five of these things, all surmounted with weird glowing images like floating TV screens. Billy and Myles looked scared. They leapt from the dais and scurried over to the outer wall like frightened sheep. A deep, throbbing hum reverberated through the floor.

"I know this place," he whispered in amazement. "I've seen it before." He crossed over to where Dana lay near the edge of the dais, apparently still unconscious. He nudged her callously with his foot, wishing the mind-link was still working. Maybe he had been pushing the girl too hard, he thought dispassionately. In the last few days he'd come to depend on the link more and more. It was so much more convenient than mere talking. "Sabrina," he called out, exasperated. "You remember this place, don't you? Myles, Billy, how about you, eh?"

Sabrina didn't look happy. Her face was pinched and drawn. She looked far older than her thirteen-or-so years. "I don't know what you're talking about," she said sullenly.

"Don't be like that, Sabrina. We've been here before, all of us. Haven't we?"

Myles raised his hand tentatively. "The – the dream?"

Marshall clapped his hands mockingly. "Well done, Myles! Have a gold star. Yeah, 'the dream', when this all started. Remember now, Sabrina? Or are you still trying to pretend it didn't happen?"

She didn't answer, just stared at the floor mutely. He dismissed her. Let her wallow in her delusions, what did he care? It didn't matter anymore. What mattered now was figuring out the connection between this place and Lucas Fortune. Whatever had happened to them all was clearly tied up with both this place and Fortune himself.

He began to take in the rest of the chamber. Piled near one wall were what looked like the remains of a hearty meal, beginning to smell bad. Clearly someone had been here very recently. Fortune? Then he spotted something else that clinched it for him: several brightly coloured backpacks, of the kind used by ramblers, hikers – or children on a camping expedition.

He allowed himself a small grin of triumph. "I've found your secret den, Fortune," he said to the room. "Now, where are you hiding?"

Dana Jackson began to stir then, half raising her head with a low moan. Sabrina was quickly at her side, an anxious expression on her face. "Dana!" she exclaimed. "You're awake!"

Dana looked confused. "What happened?" she said, her voice thick. "My head…it hurts…"

"About time you woke up," Marshall said, peering at her.

"Leave her alone!" Sabrina snapped back at him. "Haven't you done enough to her already?"

He raised his eyebrows, amused at this little show of rebellion. He found he was in an expansive mood, the triumph of discovering Fortune's hiding place mellowing his normally mercurial temper. "Now, now," he tutted.

Dana rolled unsteadily into a sitting position, clutching her head as though she thought it might spin off. Sabrina held her arm anxiously, peering into her eyes. Dana's normally pretty hair was matted and dishevelled, her face bearing the ravages of extreme fatigue. Dark rings circled her eyes, her coffee-coloured skin unnaturally pale and clammy. She stared back at Sabrina with unfocused eyes.

Sabrina's rage at Marshall was growing to epic proportions. She was finding it increasingly difficult to hide. Her outburst just now had slipped out before she could stop it. Her sense of self-preservation was enough that she knew she'd be in extreme danger if Marshall grew too displeased with her, but she didn't know how much longer she could go on bottling it up.

Dana climbed shakily to her feet, leaning hard on Sabrina's arm.

"You should rest some more," Sabrina said in a quiet voice. "You don't look well at all."

Dana blinked her vision clear. She took a slow look around the circular chamber, her gaze settling on the strange twisted objects growing out of the dais. She frowned, puzzled. "Those things…" she murmured. "I can…hear them, in my head."

Sabrina glanced around quickly, but Marshall had moved off to join his buddies over by one of the side passages. He was out of earshot. "What do you mean?" she hissed, fearing Dana might not be completely alright. After what Marshall had put her through, it was a wonder she was even conscious at all.

"I've seen them before, through someone else's eyes," Dana continued. "But that – that doesn't make sense." She gazed at Sabrina. "I don't remember how we got here, Sabbie," she moaned. "We were outside, in a stone circle…"

"You passed out," Sabrina told her. "We found some steps, leading underground. Billy Elsdon carried you down here." She paused. "You don't remember talking to me earlier, then? You talked to Marshall, too."

Dana stared blankly into the distance. "There were…voices, reassuring me, making me feel…better." She focused on Sabrina suddenly. "A message! A warning, from Lucas Fortune!"

Sabrina nodded. "Marshall didn't believe it. He made us go on, and somehow we ended up here, wherever 'here' is."

"But we have to get out!" She was growing more and more agitated, looking about her wildly. "The repellers are coming! They're on their way up here right now!" She jumped to her feet and stumbled over to one of the strange devices. She stared at it for a few seconds, then began manipulating the suspended image with shaking fingers. "There's no time!" she said, concentrating ferociously.

Marshall finally noticed the commotion and came striding over. "What the hell are you doing?" he thundered. "I didn't tell you to do that!"

She ignored him. Sabrina stepped in front of him, hoping to intercept his expected anger before he could lash out at Dana. "She knows something, Marshall," she said quickly. "She's trying to…" Trying to do what? She had no idea what her friend was up to. "…trying to find more information," she hedged. "That's why we're here, aren't we?"

"How does she know how to work these things?" Marshall fumed. Elsdon and Lovell drew up on either side of him threateningly.

"I – I don't know for sure, but I think it's something to do with the mind-link." Where had that come from?

-Don't let him stop me, Sabbie,- Dana's voice sounded in her head. Trying to hide her surprise, she blinked at Marshall, but he showed no reaction. Dana must still be excluding him from the link.

-I am, but I can't explain more now,- Dana's thought came. -I have to figure out a way to get us out of here. Let Graves stay if he wants.- She continued staring at the display.

"So the link's working again?" Marshall questioned alertly. He paused for a second, turning inward. "How come I can't find it, then?"

"I can't either, Marshall," Sabrina protested. "Honest! I don't know much more than you, but I really think you should let her do whatever she's doing! She sounded really worried!"

His eyes narrowed. "Ah," he said. "The warning from our little friend Fortune, eh? Is that it?"

"Yes, it is," she admitted. What else could she say? If only Marshall would listen, he might see sense. "Please let her be! I'm…I'm really scared, Marshall."

His face contorted unpleasantly. "Of course you are," he snarled. "You're always scared, aren't you? You hide it under that prissy hard-shelled exterior, but I've seen inside your mind! You're terrified of the world, terrified that people will see you for what you really are, a simpering, useless little brat who couldn't even make her own parents love her!"

She recoiled, stunned to the very core. Hot tears flashed to her cheeks. How could Marshall be so cruel? She'd admired him once, his calm self-assurance, his regal bearing and superior attitude. She'd even thought she loved him. Her fist began to clench, unbidden. Around the edges of her vision, blurred by tears, the world was turning red.

"Out of my way!" Marshall raged, shoving her aside. She fell to the floor.

"Dana, I'm warning you, step away from that…thing," he commanded in a voice like iron. She glanced up at him briefly, before bending back to her task without a word.

"Have it your way," he said. He began to raise his hand, summoning his power.

Sabrina leapt from the floor with a scream and cannoned into him, finally utilising the ability she had denied for so long. All the hurt and anger she'd suppressed was channelled into her lunge, producing a force that must have been roughly equivalent to that of a mortar shell. The two of them flew across the dais in a blur. Marshall just had time to emit a startled cry before they both crashed into one of the protruding console devices.

Graves got the worst of it. His head connected with the side of the console with a rending crack. Sabrina was slightly shielded from the impact by Graves's body, but she still fetched herself a mighty whack to the ribs. She felt something give inside her chest, and a pressure on her lungs, but there was no pain. She noted all of this in a remote, abstract kind of way. It was like she was watching things from the outside, like seeing a film played in slow motion. She had the fleeting pleasure of seeing Graves's face crumple up, his habitual expression of superiority replaced with a sort of base, animal fear, before the light went from his eyes.

All of this happened in mere seconds. Their forward motion interrupted by the unyielding material of the console, the two of them spun off and crashed heavily to the ground. Now the pain came, hammering through her chest like a knife through the ribs. She tasted blood in her mouth, but didn't care. She stared at Graves, sprawled unmoving nearby, one side of his face mashed and distorted unpleasantly as though it were made from clay. She wanted to yell triumphantly at him, but she couldn't seem to catch her breath.

-Sabrina, look out!- Dana's thought thundered into her mind. She managed to turn her head slightly, almost sobbing with the effort, to see the huge twin bulks of Billy Elsdon and Myles Lovell bearing down on her, murder in their usually dull, lifeless eyes. Unable to move, to escape, she squeezed her eyes shut so she didn't have to watch.

Stop!

A sudden silence descended on the room. Sabrina opened one eye tentatively. Lovell and Elsdon had skidded to a halt nearby, staring around them wildly. Who had spoken? From where Sabrina lay it looked like there was no-one else here, though her field of vision was limited. Pain coursed through her now in waves. Her vision seemed to be fading, contracting into a grey tunnel. She felt sick. She wondered, in some far-off corner of her brain, if she was going into shock.

Oh, my children! the sourceless voice said. **What has happened to you?**

The room faded and a wave of darkness swept up to claim her into its dark, smothering depths.

*

The effort of keeping the sled under control was monstrous, but Lucas grimly held on, tension knotting his muscles, sweat pouring from his skin. He no longer looked ahead of them as he had done at first. He'd sunk into a deeper level of awareness, a sort of enhanced instinct that guided his actions more surely than his conscious brain could ever manage. He could almost sense obstructions and obstacles before they even came close, using that knowledge to steer the sled down side-passages and across vast, crumbling chambers that logic would suggest led in entirely the wrong direction. Dion's memory map had turned out to be of little use, outdated by the destruction and crumbling decay all around, but somehow they were still making pretty good progress.

Through the mental link, he was dimly aware of the anxious thoughts of his friends as they clung on desperately to the back of the sled, but it was no more than a kind of background buzz in his mind, irrelevant and distracting. He tried to tune them out, but it was getting harder and harder to stay focused.

Tamsen sat at the rear of the sled, clinging grimly onto a couple of the knobbly, horn-like spurs. She didn't know if that was their true use, but they were certainly proving handy right now.

She stared up at Lucas with grudging admiration. She hadn't always been sure about the boy's leadership qualities, on occasion finding herself questioning his decision-making abilities. Sometimes he'd come across as wishy-washy and a little conservative. Now she was rapidly changing her opinion of him. He'd stepped up when they'd needed him most. He was right there giving his all, pushing himself to the very limit to keep them all one step ahead of their still unseen pursuers. She could see it in his rigid stance, in the knotted tension of his neck muscles. She wondered if, in a similar situation, she would have been capable of putting forth such effort.

Timothy crouched nearby, casting worried glances in Sammi's direction like some sort of solicitous guardian. Tamsen thought it was sweet, the way he doted on her. Sammi was obviously flattered by his attention. Right now Sammi was up at the front with Aaron Osborn, grinning hugely into the wind as they both continued to feed their power into the sled.

She was enjoying herself immensely, despite the prevalent danger they were in. Regardless, it was just nice to see her happy for a change. Other than Tamsen herself, Sammi had never really had anyone to look out for her; indeed, the whole experience with Sabrina Celestine and that ridiculous 'Girls-Only Club' had very nearly crushed all the spirit out of the girl. Ironically, however, it had really been the timely arrival of Lucas and his friends into their lives that had dragged both her and Tamsen out of that whole sorry situation. *Who'd have thought it? A bunch of adolescent boys turning out to be the best friends we could ever wish for…*

She was jolted out of this wistful line of thinking by a sudden shout of alarm. It was Timothy, who, in between checking up on Sammi, had taken it upon himself to also watch behind them as they travelled along, keeping an alert eye out for signs of pursuit. Now he pointed back the way they had come, wide-eyed and fearful.

"I saw something moving back there!" he shouted over the rushing wind.

Tamsen craned around to look. They were currently speeding down a wide, relatively clear passage that had probably, at one time, been a major thoroughfare. Darkened alcoves like looted shops yawned all along the sides, and many sleds similar to the one they were using lay scattered about, upturned and derelict. A continuous strip of illumination panels ran along the centre of the curved ceiling, which rose to a height of perhaps eight or ten metres over their heads, but every so often they would pass through long, shadowy sections where the panels were not working at all. It made distances difficult to judge.

"Where?" she called back, squinting. The passage stretched away behind them in a perfectly straight line, converging into a single point in the distance. Nothing appeared to be moving…

Then she saw something. "What is that?" she murmured, shifting herself around to get a better look. Far off, at the very limit of her vision, she could make out a faint flickering. It reminded her of the pattern of light seen when a lamp shines through a moving fan. She swallowed nervously.

"They're gaining," she called out, and Timothy nodded firmly.

"I can't tell how far away they are," he said, "but they're definitely getting closer. Dion?"

Dion spared them a glance, and Tamsen was shocked to see how tired he too looked. She hadn't realised quite how much effort he was also putting into their escape. "Yes?" he croaked.

Timothy's expression showed that he'd noticed his friend's condition too, but he gestured behind him wordlessly. Dion looked for a second and nodded slowly. "Maybe ten more minutes 'til we get back to the arrival chamber," he told them in a hoarse voice. "No worries." He attempted a smile, but it came out more like a rictus.

Tamsen squinted again at their pursuers. It was more than just a flickering now. There were disconcerting suggestions of thrashing limbs, accompanied by a distant fizzing like radio static. She shivered, silently willing the sled to squeeze just a little more speed from its ancient system.

*

The repeller drones were by no means intelligent, but between them they possessed a sort of shared rudimentary consciousness, like a hive-mind. It was what allowed them to function so effectively as a unified defensive force. Each individual was nothing more than an expendable cell, but the whole was something much more than that.

The lead drones had finally picked up a visual image of their quarry as they sped along a main artery on a reactivated machine-carrier. The carrier itself was giving out some unusual readings to the drones' sensory perceptions, but the hive-mind lacked both the imagination and inclination to speculate about what that might mean. Their function was simple: to neutralise any foreign invaders by any means necessary. Only if a direct, massed assault proved unsuccessful would other options come into play, and none of these required much in the way of hard thinking.

Swarming along every available surface of the artery passage the drones advanced like a scuttling, chittering tsunami, sweeping aside all obstacles before them. The part of the hive-mind that was aware of their exact location within the artery system spread the message that the invaders were very nearly at the top of the sanctuary, with nowhere else to run. The conveyor network was locked down. Even though the collective was incapable of feeling satisfaction, nevertheless a little ripple of something like anticipation swept through the charging horde of drones.

The swarm put on an extra burst of speed, beginning to close down the distance between them and their quarry.

Chapter Twenty Six – Flight From The Dark

Dana Jackson clung to the edge of the console pillar, fighting waves of dizziness and nausea. It was almost all she could do to keep herself from collapsing into a sobbing heap on the floor. Close by, both Sabrina and Marshall Graves lay injured and unconscious, and on the other side of the dais Lois Christie lay in a similar state. Strange thoughts and ideas fizzed through her head, further adding to her state of confusion, but from somewhere deep inside she'd found a faint upwelling of strength, like a volcanic vent deep under water. It was what was keeping her on her feet, but she didn't know how much longer she could keep it up.

I have made a mistake, the formless voice said. **I can see that now. Dana Jackson, you and your friends were never meant to end up like this.**

She gazed about her blearily, but the only others she could see in the room were Graves's moronic bodyguards Lovell and Elsdon, who were currently cowering by the wall of the chamber, mewling in fright. "Who – who are you?" she croaked. "I can't see you."

I am – the cause of all this, the voice said regretfully. **I was doing what I felt was right, but I…miscalculated the human ability to adapt.**

"Are you…Rith?" she wondered. "Marshall said you would have the answers…" she stopped, confused. "Or was it Lucas Fortune? I forget."

Your mind had been severely overstretched, Dana. I am unable to tell if the damage is repairable. I am sorry.

"I'll bet you are," she sighed, lacking the energy to even feel sad. "But I don't care about any of this, or about you. I just want to go home. I want all this to end."

You are free to go, Dana, always, Rith said. **I told you that once before, and it still holds true now. You have but to leave.**

Dana had no idea what the voice was talking about. She seemed to be having trouble focusing her thoughts. "How – how do I…"

Your adaptation allows you to interface with the sanctuary control systems. That is why you were given your 'ability', as you call it.

"Huh? What does that mean?"

You can control the conveyor that brought you here, reverse its direction. The correct sequences are easily accessible to your mind. Look within the interface structure before you.

Not knowing what else to do, she turned her attention to the console as Rith had suggested. She closed her eyes and immersed her tattered consciousness in the alien workings of the device, not really knowing what she was looking for. But the echo of Dion Raven's mind-link was still within her brain, and with it some of the knowledge he had gained from using these systems. She found she was able to navigate her way around this virtual world. It was almost beginning to feel familiar, when…

"The conveyor has been locked!" she reported breathlessly, resurfacing. "An automatic protocol has been invoked."

What? The voice sounded perplexed. **What kind of protocol?**

"Defensive. The sanctuary has released repeller drones to…counter an attack."

Rith's voice sounded horrified. **Repeller drones? How can this be?** There was a long pause. **Where are Lucas Fortune and his friends?**

"I haven't seen them," she admitted. "They weren't here when we arrived."

The archive! They must have been trapped in the lower levels when the protocol was activated! There was another pause. **Dana, I must ask for your help. I myself am unable to act, to influence the sanctuary systems in any way. I need you to operate the interfaces for me. Will you do that?**

She didn't reply straight away. She let her gaze slip slowly around the room, taking a long look at Sabrina where she lay still unconscious and bleeding. Marshall Graves sprawled next to her, his face a livid purple mass. Lois was hurt. She herself was functioning on the very last dregs of her willpower. All Rith had brought her and her friends was pain and horror. Now he wanted her help?

Then she thought about Lucas Fortune, about how *he* had tried to help her, to warn her. It had been Marshall who'd decided to ignore that warning. Tamsen and Sammi River were with Fortune too, somewhere down in the basement of this place, maybe struggling for their lives. Through the brief connection they had shared earlier, Fortune's good intentions had been quite clear. Now, perhaps, was her chance to return the favour.

"I'll do it – but not for you," she said coldly. "Tell me what to do."

*

The long corridor finally came to an end, opening out into a grand, dimly lit plaza that stretched off into the far distance. The scale of the place was astonishing – this cathedral-like space alone must have been more than ten kilometres long. Despite the situation, Dion was still able to notice such things. His attention was pretty evenly divided between observing their route and maintaining Lucas's connection to the sled's control system. He still didn't quite understand how Lucas was doing it, but he knew enough to know when to take a back seat. It was a distinctly strange sensation, the feeling of Lucas's power channelling through his mind. He likened it to a tumbling, fast-flowing river, full of hidden rocks and dangerous undercurrents. He knew this was own mind trying to rationalise what was happening. As for Lucas himself, the guy was standing rigidly in the centre of the sled, clinging on to one of the hand-holds, eyes screwed shut in intense concentration. Dion found himself quite in awe of his friend's manifest ability to maintain this level of effort for so long.

According to the mental map, they were now very close to their destination, only a few levels below the arrival chamber. However, two things were causing Dion increasing concern: would Lucas be able to keep this up much longer, and if they managed to actually make it back, what exactly would they do then? The drones were right behind them!

As if on cue, their pursuers exploded out of the tunnel exit behind them, swarming out across the buckled floor and up along the curving walls of the plaza like rampaging ants. The children finally got a good look at the things, and what they saw did very little to make them feel better.

The repeller drones looked something like over-large beetles or spiders, complete with armoured carapaces and segmented limbs, but the resemblance ended there. They appeared to have far too many legs, at least twenty apiece, and their central bodies were oddly proportioned, perhaps half a metre long, each shaped like an elongated, blunt triangle with the apex pointing forwards. At this front end, where a beetle would have had a head, these drones instead sported a cluster of twitching tendrils, each surmounted by glowing red 'eyes' that cast about independently of each other.

Repulsive though they were, though, the worst aspect of the things was the ghastly noise they made, a kind of seething hiss interlaced with clicking and buzzing sounds that sent dread chills down the children's spines. It was the primal fear that almost all humans felt towards scuttling insects and the like. Tamsen gave a little cry. Dion felt her distant wave of disgust and fear filter through the mental link despite the block he had placed on the other's thoughts.

The sled trembled. Dion tore his attention away from the horrifying sight behind them to see Lucas wavering, beginning to slump over to one side. His friend's skin was the colour of ash, glistening under a sickly sheen of sweat. "Lucas!" Dion yelled, clamping down hard on the mental link. He wasn't sure if it had been the slight leakage from the others that had caused Lucas's concentration to waver, or just the general exhaustion his friend must be feeling. Whatever it was, the sled straightened out and somehow, miraculously, put on an extra burst of speed, beginning to leave the clamouring horde behind. Dion offered a silent prayer to anyone, or anything, who might be listening: *just get us out of this…*

The sled began to describe a wide curve, banking to the right and aiming straight for a darkened tunnel entrance in the side wall. A quick consultation of the map confirmed that this passage lead to the final leg of the journey. It stretched on for perhaps a kilometre, curving and spiralling upwards, leading directly to the arrival chamber. *Come on…*

Then Dion spotted something that made his heart almost freeze in his chest. Inside the tunnel entrance they were heading for, back in the dim darkness of its depths, something was moving. "Oh, no," he moaned. As he stared ahead in numb dismay, a wave of repeller drones emerged from the passage, spreading up the walls and across the ravaged ground directly in the sled's path. In the part of Dion's brain that was still able to form abstract thoughts, he wondered idly how the drones had managed to get ahead of them, and how they'd known which passage to block. It seemed to imply a certain degree of intelligence on their part.

Lucas didn't hesitate. The sled's forward momentum didn't slow in the slightest. The drones began to link together across the gaping tunnel mouth, their spindly limbs intertwining to form a complex net. It looked a lot like a spiders' web. Dion found himself dispassionately admiring the drones' almost artistic construction, until a thin scream brought him back down to reality with a bump.

It was Tamsen. She was staring ahead with saucer eyes, an expression of almost terminal horror on her face. Dion himself was no particular fan of anything with more than four legs, but ordinarily he could tolerate such things, as long as they didn't bother him. But he knew it was much worse for Tamsen who, he knew through the link, was absolutely terrified of bugs, and of spiders in particular. This was her worst fear come true. He tried to send a soothing feeling of reassurance to her, but he simply didn't have the capacity to create a separate feed that wouldn't interfere with his link to Lucas. Regretfully, he turned his attention away from her. There was nothing he could do to help her.

The seething wall of drones was now only seconds away, and Dion finally realised what Lucas intended. He was going to try to punch straight through! In all the excitement Dion hadn't noticed it before, but now he realised that Lucas had used the flight across the wide open, relatively clear space in the plaza to boost the sled's speed. Somehow, Lucas must have known something like this was going to happen. Dion wished he could communicate with his friend, but he didn't dare disrupt the serpentine connection that was Lucas's power running through his mind. All he could do was hang on grimly, and shout a warning.

"Everybody hold on, and keep your heads down! We're going through!"

"*No, no, no,*" Tamsen moaned, but she nevertheless ducked down, covering her head. At the front of the sled Aaron and Sammi crouched behind the arching control bar. Timothy squirmed over to Tamsen and half-covered her with his own body, his face locked in a grimace comprising equal parts fear and excitement. There was just time for he and Dion to exchange sickly looks before the sled ploughed headlong into the chittering black wall. That was when Dion realised that Lucas was still standing bolt-upright in the centre of the sled…

"I see them!" Dana cried out as the image flipped up in front of her.

Rith said nothing, but she was aware of a strong sense of anxiety in the room. She ignored it, focusing her attention on the rapidly moving display. In the last few minutes she'd had a crash course in how to manipulate these control systems, though she knew she'd barely scratched the surface. Rith had told her just enough for her to be able to focus the internal imaging system where it was needed. She'd quickly managed to locate a huge disturbance in one of the lower chambers. She'd fooled around with the controls, moving the image around, until she was able to zoom in on what was apparently at the centre of the commotion: a flat-topped, trolley-like device zipping along at a rapid pace, on the back of which was what looked like a small group of people huddling together.

"But I don't know where they are!" she cried. "And what the hell are *those* things?"

The trolley was in the centre of a rapidly contracting black wave of some kind, a rolling, heaving mass of insectoid shapes that covered every available centimetre of space. In a matter of moments the things would overwhelm the small band of people.

They are repeller drones, Rith said hollowly, **a very effective and adaptable automated defence measure.** There was a long pause. **I fear for the children.**

Unbidden, another display sprang up next to the first, showing a detailed diagrammatic image of the network of passages underneath and surrounding the chamber where Dana was standing. Indecipherable data flashed between the two images, synchronising them until one particular part of the map stabilised. Dana peered at it. "But that's right here!" she exclaimed. "I mean, directly underneath this room! They must be trying to get back here!"

As she watched, the children on the sled ducked down. In complete silence the sled struck the side wall of the enormous chamber, scattering the black shapes of the massed repeller drones in all directions. Dana cried out, thinking the children had suicidally rammed the wall in a last ditch attempt to escape, but her mouth snapped shut when she saw the gaping mouth of a tunnel that had been hidden beneath the dull black bodies of the drones. Relief flooded through her, but it was short lived. The drones regrouped and poured down the passage in hot pursuit.

Frustrated at her inability to do anything to actively help the fleeing children, she thumped her hand on the console. "Dammit!" she raged. She rounded on Rith, or at least on an empty section of the room on which she could focus her anger. The only thing keeping her on her feet now was the adrenaline surging through her system, lending her thoughts a sort-of red-rimmed clarity. "Why don't you do something?" she shouted out. "This is your fault! Why don't you stop hiding and help my friends!"

I cannot, Rith replied. **Only my thoughts can enter the sanctuary. My physical body is a great distance away. At this very moment it is travelling to you as quickly as it is able, but I fear it will not arrive in time. In any case, I would be of little assistance even if I were physically there. My kind are not permitted to enter the sanctuary.**

"Well a fat lot of good you are!"

The voice sounded abashed. **That is one of the reasons I enlisted your help in the first place, to be my agents, to go to the places I cannot go and do the things I am unable to do.**

She was about to retort when she became aware of a distant sound, a kind of burbling hiss emanating from one of the side passages. With a sinking feeling she dashed back to her console. The tracking image showed both the trolley and the horde of drones driving rapidly down a long, narrow conduit that led…

…directly back to this chamber! The other four passages radiating from the room were all blocked just beyond the first bend, but this fifth one was wide open. Lucas and his friends must have known that, but what it meant in practical terms was this:

They were leading the drones straight here.

"Well that's just great," Dana muttered.

The sled barrelled along at a fantastic rate, tossing aside the compact bodies of any repeller drones that attempted to block its progress. The drones pressed in on all sides, but due to the sled's headlong speed they had so far proven unable to affect its progress. Cowering as low as he could, Dion wondered miserably how much longer that state of affairs could continue.

He risked glancing up. Lucas, by some mechanism he couldn't begin to understand, still stood perfectly motionless in the centre of the sled, apparently not bothered or affected by the horrendous armoured creatures crowding in from every direction. Indeed, the drones themselves seemed to be actively avoiding him. Several had managed to gain brief footholds on the sled on a couple of occasions, only to be knocked off again by a well-placed kick or another scrambling drone, but so far none had even gone near to Lucas. Timothy had noticed this too. He kept glancing up at Lucas with a perplexed expression. What was it about Lucas that was keeping him safe?

"Hey Dion!" Timothy shouted to him, his voice barely audible above the din. "Recognise this bit?"

Dion looked. The passage was dark and dismal, all the illumination panels here unlit or broken, but his eyes were dark-adapted enough to make out sections of wall and floor between the swarming bodies of the drones. The tunnel was festooned with slime and mould, the floor beneath them particularly badly damaged and wrecked. The floating sled passed over all this without hesitation; whatever mechanism it used to keep itself suspended above the ground was apparently unaffected by any vagaries in the terrain over which it passed. Recognition flickered.

"Yeah!" he called back. "This is the tunnel we opened earlier." He looked ahead. Was that a faint spot of light in the distance?

Something like panic began to rise up in his mind. There was just no way he could think of to stop these drones catching them. The goal had been to race back to the arrival chamber before the drones got to them, and somehow from there escape to the surface, but Dion didn't see how that was possible now. The drones were matching them every step of the way. There simply wouldn't be enough time to formulate the next stage of their escape. They might make it all the way back to the chamber, but the drones would be right there with them, and once the sled ran out of road...

The sled juddered again, and for a second Dion's heart lurched, thinking the end had already come, but something else was happening. They were going faster! The walls became a blur, and in only a few moments the horde of drones was left behind. Dion was astonished. How was this possible? He glanced up at Lucas, and was appalled at what he saw. His friend was still standing there, grimacing intensely hard, but blood was now dripping down his face, squeezing out from behind his tightly-closed eyelids like rivulets of red tears. What was Lucas doing to himself?

The light from in front grew rapidly. Dion could see the last bend in the corridor approaching at terrifying speed. Just around that corner lay the arrival chamber, but its supposed safety seemed almost as far out of their reach as it had been when they'd first set out from the archive. When he saw movement from up ahead, it was almost the last nail in the coffin for him. He was about to give up, to admit the hopelessness of the situation, when his overstretched mind finally alerted him to what he was seeing. A person stood there, a girl with long dark hair, waving her arms frantically.

The sled began to dip at the front, causing the back end to lift up crazily in the air. Tamsen and Timothy cried out, sliding forward. Dion felt the sled decelerating drastically. It was all he could do to keep holding on. With only metres to go to the sharp bend, the front right corner of the sled touched the ground and immediately dug in, flipping the whole thing over in an uncontrollable tumble. Screaming, the children were tossed forward like ragdolls, tumbling crazily through the air to land in an untidy sprawl against the curving bend in the corridor. The sled continued to roll until it turned fully on its end, where it jammed across the tunnel, dislodging huge chunks of sodden masonry as it slammed to a halt.

Dazedly, Dion raised his head, expecting the dread arrival of the repeller drones at any second. Instead he saw the same girl standing over him, staring back down the corridor the way they had come. "Quickly!" she cried. It was Dana Jackson! "Get to the controls! You have to reactivate the conveyor! I don't know how!"

He gasped as sharp pain shot through his right arm where he'd landed on it awkwardly. "It's no good," he grunted, not even questioning how Dana Jackson came to be talking to him now. "There's not enough time."

The roaring of the approaching drones was reaching a thunderous crescendo, amplified and condensed into a wall of sound by the cylindrical shape of the tunnel. Baleful glints of red light writhed and seethed in the darkness.

"I'm sorry," he murmured, but his voice was lost in the tumult. Mere seconds to go…he felt almost glad, in a way. He was so very tired.

Next to him Tamsen suddenly stirred. She rolled over and sat up, staring into the dark with an expression now devoid of fear. She produced something from her pocket and held it up. "No," she said simply. Dion stared at her.

There was a whine, and abruptly the passage was blocked by a glittering wall. Only a second later there was a rending crash as the first wave of drones caught up to them and smashed straight into the barrier, unable to check their headlong speed.

The new wall didn't even tremble.

All the air whooshed out of Dion's body. As the drones continued to furiously dash themselves against the unyielding barrier he thanked fate and providence that Tamsen still carried the device he'd created earlier to remove the barrier, and that she'd somehow figured out how to reverse it.

"Great timing," he managed before his overwrought brain finally shut down.

Chapter Twenty Seven – Close Encounters

Dana tried to ignore the strange looks she was getting from Lucas's friends as she helped them carry him along the short corridor back into the console room. They laid his unconscious form on the dais next to Sabrina and Marshall, who were also still out for the count. Aaron Osborn and the other boy supported Dion Raven's limp body.

What a sorry mess, she thought miserably as she surveyed the damage. Including Lois, fully half of her group were incapacitated in some way. Lucas's gang didn't look much better either. They all sported a variety of cuts, bruises and pained expressions as they wearily flopped down on to the dais. The big one – what was his name, Timothy something? – headed purposefully for one of the consoles, brushing past her as he did so without acknowledgment. She stepped back numbly, too tired to be offended or annoyed. The boy did something to the console and came away with a big tumbler of some clear, fizzy liquid that he commenced to gulp down noisily.

"Is that – lemonade?" she asked, amazed. She realised her throat was as dry as an old bone.

He finished his drink and nodded curtly. "We call it 'the maker'," he said. "Just think what you want and it'll make it for you." He turned away and drifted off to sit next to Sammi River. Neither of Dana's former girlfriends had yet attempted to speak to her, and she could hardly blame them. The last time they had seen each other was during a pitched battle in the grounds of Peregrine House. She shook her head sadly and went over to the unpleasant looking device.

After some experimentation she managed to conjure up a small glass of warm, flat cola which she proceeded to swallow down in only two giant gulps. It wasn't quite what she'd had in mind, but she was so thirsty she really didn't care. *It must take a bit of practice to use this thing*, she thought as she produced another glass.

The atmosphere in the room was one of numb melancholy. Everyone sat around looking shell-shocked, gazes far away. She wanted to ask them what had happened, but she had a strong suspicion they would not respond well to her enquiry. Despite Lucas Fortune's earlier attempt to warn her and her companions, something told her that it may not have been a unanimous decision.

She became aware of a peculiar echo in her head. She swung round to see Dion Raven sitting up, rubbing his head gingerly. Their eyes met for a second, and he nodded at her gravely. The echo stopped. Maybe it was the sound of their two separate mind-links interfering with each other. Still, she felt a little better at having finally been acknowledged. She cast about to see where Elsdon and Lovell had got to, but they were nowhere in sight. A quick pulse through her mind-link revealed they had run off and were currently skulking in a side-room leading from one of the other corridors, cowering behind some crates.

She sighed, feeling very alone. The adrenaline that had borne her through her recent experiences was beginning to ebb. She sat down on the far side if the dais, away from the others.

She wondered what would happen to her when this was all over.

*

Lucas swam lazily in a warm amber sea, letting the sluggish currents carry him where they may. His thoughts were fuzzy, like his brain had been wrapped in cotton wool, but he was not unduly bothered. It just felt so nice to relax, to just let himself drift…

Lucas, a soft voice called.

"Hmmm?" he murmured, rolling onto his back and gazing up at the green-tinted sky. Something about that didn't seem quite right, but he couldn't place what it was at the moment.

Your mind is detached, Lucas, the distant voice purred. **It is adrift, separated from your physical body.**

"Oh," he said. He paddled about for a bit. After a while, he thought he ought to say something else. "Where am I?"

In a realm between realms, where only thought may enter. Tulirs come here sometimes. There was a sad pause. **At least, they used to. Now it is empty and lifeless.**

Tulirs? Something stirred in the depths of his mind. He frowned. Where had he heard that term before? "Do I know you?" he said slowly. Small purple clouds were beginning to gather overhead.

Yes, Lucas. You know me, and I know you. I need your help. In fact, we can help each other.

"Rith," Lucas said, feeling his thoughts starting to sharpen. He stopped paddling and hung in the water, which was growing increasingly choppy. A breeze had sprung up, ruffling the tops of the waves into frothy little caps of foam. "Have you come to bring me back, then?"

You are still needed, Lucas, the voice said. **Your trials are not yet over. You must return with me.**

"Must I? I kinda like it here, you know."

You do not belong here. You cannot survive for long away from your body. If you do not return soon – you may not live.

That sobered him up. Bigger waves rolled around him now, pitching him up one side and down the other. Somewhere he could hear the sound of surf breaking roughly on some unseen shore. He began to feel afraid. "Okay," he said. "How do I get out of here, then?"

Just want it, the voice said, fading away.

"Could you be more specific?" he called, but the voice was gone. "Right." He was alone in this strange ocean. The booming of breaking rollers was louder now, though he still couldn't tell from where. The amber water churned around him, beginning to spin him slowly around. He struggled feebly against the flow but it carried him relentlessly on, the water starting to pile up into walls as its speed increased. Faster and faster it whirled, opening up like a pit beneath him. He cried out, thrashing desperately to keep his head up, but he was sucked down, the metallic-tasting water invading his mouth, forcing its way into his throat like a battering ram…

He cried out and sat up. He was sitting on some kind of hard surface, in a room with curving walls. Shapes bobbed in front of him, faces; he heard muffled voices, as though he was hearing them through a solid wall. He cringed back fearfully. What did they want from him?

Slowly, his mind started to piece itself together, synchronising with the input from his senses. The air smelled metallic, reminding him of the taste of that weird alien ocean, and he could feel a dull vibration through the surface on which he sat. His eyes were heavy and crusty, caked in some kind of thick, gluey substance. His mouth was sandpaper dry, lips cracked and sore, and on top of everything else there was a sound, being repeated over and over again…

"Lucas!" someone shouted. It was like a switch had been thrown. With the suddenness of a lead weight dropping, he was back in the arrival chamber. The faces of Aaron, Dion, Timothy and Tamsen hung in front of him, concern written plainly in their expressions. A little farther way Sammi gave him a hopeful grin. Then, surreally, he found himself staring at the face of Marshall Graves, or what was left of it. It looked like the boy had been arguing with a bus. Near to him lay his girlfriend, Sabrina, in much the same state. What on earth had happened here?

He winced at a sudden sharp pain in his head. "I'm back," he said, his voice emerging as a dried-up croak. He coughed, and someone handed him a cool glass of water. He took a few grateful sips. "What're Graves's lot doing here?"

"Never mind that, Lucas!" Aaron said breathlessly. "What happened, mate? You've been out for over an hour! We didn't know what to do! Dion's been looking through the sanctuary systems, but he couldn't find anything useful about medical stuff."

"I'm okay, I think" Lucas answered, trying to ignore the throbbing in his temples. "I don't know what happened, but I was…somewhere else for a while. I think being there helped me...get better."

"How did you get back here, then?" Tamsen said gruffly. She had a tough exterior, but Lucas was grateful for her obvious concern.

"I had help."

Dion said, "Who from?"

From me, Rith's voice joined in. **I am glad to see you are recovered, Lucas.** The children jumped up as though their teacher had just walked into the room.

"Not half as glad as I am," Lucas said truthfully.

Dion came forward. "I was wondering, Rith," he said nervously, "um, what happens now? I mean, we went to the archive like you said, but we didn't manage to repair the datalink before the repeller drones woke up. I'm afraid we didn't learn much."

The fault is mine, Dion. You were unprepared for the task I set you. I will not make that mistake again.

"Oh." Dion considered. "Okay. But the thing is, this whole place is swarming with those drones. I don't know why they can't seem to get in here, but they're still trying." Distantly, the muted thumps and crashes of the drones dashing themselves against the barrier could still be heard, unabated in intensity.

This chamber was the last stronghold of those that dwelt here when the drones originally malfunctioned, Rith explained. **Only a few survivors managed to make it here during that crisis, but the chamber is specially equipped with quarantine technology that is impervious to all forms of interference. It even blocks wave signals, as you know; that is why the barrier had to be disabled before the conveyor could function.**

"So some people managed to escape, then?" Aaron said alertly. "Not everyone was… killed?"

Some few did escape, yes, but many, many more were not so fortunate. It was a dark day indeed, though it was a very long time ago. I still remember it.

"You were here?" Lucas questioned. "Were you one of the ones that escaped?"

I was here, though not inside the sanctuary itself. Tulirs do not enter Sirella constructs.

The children looked at each other. This was more information than Rith had ever volunteered before. "Sirella?" Lucas repeated. "What's that?"

They are the builders. You will learn more about them later, when the time is appropriate. There was a long pause. **More pressing concerns must occupy your attention now. A crisis is developing.**

There was a collective groan. "Isn't there always?" Aaron muttered. "What is it now?"

You may now be safe from the repeller drones but a new threat is coming, from a more mundane, though no less dangerous source. Focus the external monitor on the outer entrance above.

Dion went quickly to the monitor station, cycling through different screens with a now-practiced ease. He was about to say something when a new voice cut in.

"And what about us, Rith? Huh?" It was Dana Jackson, rising from where she had been sat hunched on the other side of the dais. Lucas was startled; he hadn't even noticed her there. "What about my friends?" she continued. "We're hurt, all of us, and it's because of you! You talk about threats and crises, but you offer no help to us!"

The others said nothing, unwilling to interrupt. Dana had a point, and they wanted to see how it worked out.

Rith said nothing for a while. Lucas wondered if he might not answer at all. Then he said, **Dana Jackson. I am aware of your concerns. I do not mean to appear callous or unconcerned. I have already scanned your companions for injury, and while some are quite serious, none of them are outside the scope of the normal human healing process. Given enough time, there should be no long lasting damage.**

That answer didn't appear to satisfy her. "What about me?" she snapped. "You told me I might have permanent injury!"

No, I said I was unable to tell at that time if your injury would be permanent. I have since revised that opinion. You will be fine.

"I see," she said acidly. "And you were planning to tell me this *when*?"

When the opportunity arose, Dana. I am sorry that you feel aggrieved.

"Stuff you," she retorted. She went over to where her friend Sabrina Celestine lay recumbent on the dais. Lucas wondered what had happened here. Clearly there had been some kind of a fight, perhaps between the members of Graves's own gang. Lois Christie also appeared unconscious, and there was no sign of Graves's bully-boys, Lovell and Elsdon. It looked like Dana was the only one of them still around. They hadn't heeded his warning, it seemed.

"I don't want any part of your games, Rith!" Dana cried, tears rolling down her cheeks. She cradled Sabrina's bloodied head in her arms. "Just let us go home!"

I understand, Rith said softly. **Unfortunately, I am unable to accommodate your wishes at the present time.**

"Why?" she sobbed, her voice cracking. *"Why?"*

Dion answered for him. "Because we've got company! Looks like someone knows we're here!"

The oversized image above the dais blossomed into life. Everyone craned to see it.

It showed an image of the moorland surrounding the entrance circle from the perspective, by the looks of it, of the tors that overlooked the valley. There was a large, off-road vehicle of some kind parked on the other side of the hill, and farther away there was movement. Several more trucks were approaching, bouncing recklessly along the rutted track in convoy. Overhead, a black helicopter buzzed past, tracking backwards and forwards as if searching for something.

"Is that the army?" Lucas wondered. "Have they come to get us?"

They are from an earth agency I have had dealings with before, Rith said tersely. **They wish to capture you, and steal the technological secrets of this sanctuary.**

"They're called Echelon Nine," Dana Jackson said hollowly. "They know all about us. And you want to know something else?" She glared balefully around her. "I led them here."

"You what?" Aaron said. "*You* led them here?"

"I didn't have much choice," she replied, glancing at Marshall Graves's battered face. "I couldn't do anything about it. They came for us at Peregrine House. We went along with them. But Marshall had some plan of his own; he ended up using *them* as a means to get here." She switched her gaze to Lucas. "Actually, to get to you."

"Me?" Lucas repeated. "Why me?"

"Marshall blames you for what happened to him. To us. He thought that if he could find you, then you could somehow make it stop, or at least lead him to Rith." She sounded bitter. "Wasn't far wrong, was he?"

"So he knows about Rith," Tamsen mused. "But I wonder what else he knows?"

"Not much," Dana admitted. Lucas wondered if this was the first time the two girls had spoken to each other since they'd been reunited. There was obviously still some bad feeling between them.

"I think he's crazy," Dana continued. "He can't stand the thought that Lucas might be more important than him."

Tamsen nodded. "Ah, I think I see. That's what this is really about, isn't it? Why Marshall hates Lucas so much, why he dragged you all the way out here? He thinks he should be the one at the centre of all this, not Lucas."

Dana shrugged. "Pretty much." She cast an imploring look at her former friend. "Tammy, I…"

"Save it," Tamsen cut her off coolly. "You made your bed." She turned away, hiding her expression. Dana bowed her head.

Dion spoke up. "Hey, I don't want to worry anyone," he said, "but those army guys, or whatever they are, are getting pretty close. What are we going to do about it?"

"Do?" Dana repeated, turning an astonished look on him. "We let them in, of course! Don't you want all this to end?"

"Hell, no! Are you kidding? This is only the start! There's tons more to learn. This is the best thing that's ever happened to us!" He looked around at his friends. "Right, guys?"

Sammi and Aaron agreed enthusiastically. Tamsen looked more doubtful, but she gave a slow nod too, still not looking at Dana. Timothy wore a thoughtful expression. After a moment or two he gave a noncommittal shrug. All eyes turned to Lucas.

"Tell me, Rith," he said instead of answering, speaking carefully. "Just what will happen to us if we let those guys catch us?"

Echelon Nine are an Earth government agency dedicated to the discovery and capture of any beings or technology that is not earth-native. They have operated in secret on this world for a long time, and they know no limits when it comes to extracting information from captured 'hostiles', as they call them. If they conclude that you have been influenced by alien interference, then your future will be bleak indeed; you will be imprisoned, studied, examined and tested until they are satisfied they have squeezed every last drop of information out of you.

The other children looked uncomfortable, but Lucas had half-suspected as much. All it did was made his decision clear. "Alright," he said evenly. "I'm in. How do we get away from them?"

"Lucas, you can't listen to Rith!" Dana implored him. "Look what he's done to you! Look what he's done to all of us!"

"I don't claim to have all the answers, Dana," he said, "but I intend to find them. I need to. Right now, I reckon that means going along with Rith. I certainly don't intend to let those Echelon people get their hands on me." He gave her a direct look. "You could come with us, you know."

Tears glistened in her eyes. "I…I can't," she said. "I don't want any part of this! I'll take my chances with Echelon Nine. Miss Fox won't let anything bad happen to me!"

"Miss Fox? What, the lady from Juvenile Services?" He was surprised, yet at the same time it made a perverse sort of sense. The woman had seemed to show an undue interest in him, right from the start, and he'd picked up some strange vibes from her too when they'd first met. "Did you bring her, as well?"

"Yes, but I don't know where she got to. I think we left her in that room at the bottom of the stone steps. I was sort-of out of it at the time."

Tamsen cast a worried look at her former friend. "Dana, you can't seriously be thinking about letting those people get their hands on you. Didn't you hear what Rith said?"

"He's a liar!" Dana shot back. "I don't know where he's from, or what he really wants, but I'd rather trust my own people than some faceless voice! They won't hurt me!"

"He's not a liar!" Dion interjected, affronted. "He's never lied to us, not once! I believe him, and I for one am certainly not gonna let those Echelon guys put me on a lab bench!"

"Yeah," Aaron agreed. "No-one's probing me!"

Then your course seems clear, Dana Jackson, Rith contributed. **You must do what you feel is right. As for your friends...**

"You leave them alone!" Dana shouted. "You may have fooled Lucas and his mates, but I'm the only one who can speak for mine, and I say they stay right here, with me! Got that?"

As you wish.

Lucas was saddened, but there clearly would be no reasoning with her. All the things she said might well be true – but equally they might not. However, Dion was right when he said that Rith had never lied to them. The strange being had been evasive, even downright cryptic, but had never deliberately misled them. Lucas truly believed that. It was up to Dana what she did, and she'd made it very obvious what her opinion was. There was nothing anyone could do to dissuade her.

There is little time, Rith said, business-like now. **I cannot let the technology of this sanctuary fall into Echelon's hands. They must not enter here. Dion, you must initiate a power-down of the energy cores. It was your abilities that allowed the sanctuary to awaken, and once you have left here there will be no way for the humans to repeat that feat.**

Dion's hands flew across the controls. "Done," he announced after a moment or two. Then he frowned. "Hey, I've just had a thought: this chamber is shielded by quarantine technology, right? We had to remove that barrier to allow the conveyor signal to pass through. Doesn't that mean we're trapped in here, then? The repeller drones are still knocking around out there."

There is an escape hatch, Rith replied. **The surviving inhabitants who made it here during the original crisis used an override protocol to get to the surface. That is why the quarantine shielding was still in place when you first arrived; everyone had escaped, but had left the shield intact to stop the drones from spreading to the surface.**

"Oh, right," Dion said. He glanced about. "Um, where is it then?"

You cannot see it. It is a tiny gap, no wider than a proton, in the fabric of this chamber. Nothing physical may pass through it, but a conveyor beam is an energy wave, and as such has no mass. It will allow you to return to the upper chamber. That is the only place it leads.

"Wait a tick," Aaron pointed out, a confused expression on his face. "That doesn't sound like much of an escape to me! Those Echelon guys are almost right on top of us. They'll find the stone circle entrance above, and come piling right down the steps. Won't we be 'beaming' directly into their hands?"

The timing will be critical, Aaron. The sanctuary systems are cycling down now, but there will be enough power left for one extra conveyor jump. When you arrive in the upper chamber, you will have approximately twelve seconds before the conveyor resets and sends you to the secondary destination. It is the only way.

"What secondary destination?" Lucas said, growing excited. Everything was moving so fast, but he wasn't afraid. Not anymore.

A reserve site, some distance away from the stone circle on the surface. Echelon should not be able to see you, and you can make your escape while they are occupied at the main entrance.

"Cool!" Dion said.

"Escape to where, Rith?" Tamsen asked. "There's nowhere for us to go."

I will be there to help you, Tamsen. I am on my way.

"You're coming here?" Lucas said, surprised. "But I thought you said you couldn't come out of hiding? What about those enemies you spoke about? Won't they be watching for you?"

It is a calculated risk. Besides, once we are together, the need for concealment will be less important. Dion, you must set the conveyor interface exactly as I tell you. Echelon Nine are almost here.

*

Miss Fox sat quietly against the side wall of the dingy chamber, head bowed, feigning sleep. Ptolemy Withers had ordered her to remain there while he took a very close look around the room, apparently searching for some kind of control mechanism to access the teleport device, or 'conveyor' as he called it. So far he'd had no luck, and was growing increasingly frustrated. He growled to himself in some language she'd never heard before, smoking furiously. She wondered where he was getting his seemingly endless supply of cigarettes from. At first they'd seemed to calm him down, much as an oxygen mask helps to calm panic, but lately his agitation was winning out. She guessed that the cigarettes contained some kind of substance he needed in order to breathe properly. It was an ingenious disguise, she had to admit. All those times when she'd had to explain away his smoking habit, covering for him, he'd actually been concealing a very clever form of respirator.

A distant noise drifted from the direction of the adjoining room at the foot of the steps, a kind of grinding rumble like the sound of a powerful engine. She kept carefully still, ears straining. Could this be the 'backup' that Ptolemy claimed to have summoned?

He heard it too, but did not look pleased. She watched him surreptitiously through half-closed eyelids.

"You can stop pretending now, Danielle," he said gruffly. "Time's up. Stand."

She smiled ruefully and climbed stiffly to her feet. "No luck, then?"

He glared at her. "The Taween will find a way," he declared.

"Ah, but that doesn't look good for you, does it, Ptolemy?" she said shrewdly. "I mean, you're their 'man' on the spot, right? I bet they take a pretty dim view of failure, don't they?" She was goading him deliberately, hoping to provoke him into doing something rash. She fingered the grip of the sidearm she still carried concealed behind her back.

He just stood there, puffing on a cigarette, face expressionless.

There was a shout, and the sound of booted feet running down the stone steps. She realised right away who it must be. "Looks like Echelon got here first, Ptolemy. Sorry."

A tiny smile lifted the corners of his lips. "It doesn't matter. Your Echelon Nine is nothing to the Taween. When my masters get here…" he trailed off, staring about him curiously. "What's that?"

Miss Fox felt it too, a kind of shifting in the atmosphere. She glanced at the raised dais in the centre of the chamber –

And abruptly a group of children appeared there, staring about wildly. She recognised them straight away. "Dana!" she exclaimed. And nearby – "Lucas Fortune!" She was delighted. Right at the very end, when it looked like she'd lost everything, suddenly she was holding all the cards again! Echelon was almost here, and she would claim the capture!

Something was wrong, though. Lucas Fortune was grinning at her insolently. "Why, hello Miss Fox," he greeted her with a mocking bow. "Nice to see you again." Several of his friends jumped down from the dais, helping yet others who appeared to be semi-conscious and badly beaten-up. They laid them carefully on the ground and jumped back up again with intent expressions.

"Stop right there, Fortune!" she cried, drawing the gun at last. Her hand shook as she pointed it at the children on the dais. "You're coming with me!"

Fortune paled at the sight of the gun, but shook his head. "Sorry, Miss," he replied. "I'm a little busy right now." He flipped a jaunty little salute.

Mr Withers let out a growl of rage and leapt at the children. From a standing start he appeared to almost fly towards them. As he crossed the edge of the dais, there was another tiny change in air pressure. Before Miss Fox could so much as blink, the whole lot of them had vanished again, taking her turncoat former assistant with them.

"NOOO!" she screamed, dashing over to the dais. She jumped up onto it and began stamping her feet, ranting incoherently. It wasn't fair! She'd had them right in her hands, and they'd wriggled out yet again!

"Um, Miss Fox?" a frightened-sounding voice said. It was Dana Jackson.

"WHAT?" Miss Fox snapped, grinding her teeth in fury.

"Uh, there's…there's someone here to see you."

Fuming, she swung around to see what the girl was babbling about. Dana stood near the entrance, her two dim-witted friends Lovell and Elsdon cowering nearby. At her feet lay the apparently unconscious forms of Lois Christie, Sabrina Celestine and, yes, Marshall Graves himself. They all looked terribly battered and worse for wear.

She observed all this in a second, but it was what she saw behind the girl that really made her heart sink.

The anteroom beyond was filled with armed soldiers, all of them staring at her. At the front of the crowd was a face she immediately recognised.

"Really, Danielle," Byron Stanford said, regarding her like she'd suddenly sprouted horns. "Is that any way to behave in front of these children?"

She thought about arguing, but there seemed very little point. She let the gun fall from her fingers. "Probably not," she sighed. "Probably not."

Chapter Twenty Eight - Redemption

The room faded out, and suddenly the children were bombarded with excruciatingly bright light. They cried out, shielding their eyes. "Where are we?" someone shouted. It sounded like Aaron.

Tentatively, Lucas opened his eyes a crack. The ground felt soft underfoot. A cool, fragrant breeze brushed against his skin. "I think we're outside," he said, squinting around him.

Indeed they were. The conveyor appeared to have deposited them amid a stand of soft ferns somewhere out on the moorland. Nearby a small brook gurgled and tinkled merrily along its rocky bed. Shafts of sunlight were breaking through patchy cloud overhead. It smelled like it had rained recently.

The children took stock. They'd each brought along their backpacks, scooped up at the last minute, along with containers of water and juice provided by the sanctuary's maker. Timothy had also industriously stuffed his pack with bars of chocolate. "Good energy food," he'd commented.

"Hey, what happened to that big bloke?" Aaron asked. The last thing they had seen was the snarling face of Mr Withers just as the preprogrammed conveyor cycle had started up. He'd been leaping onto the dais, but now he was nowhere in sight.

"I guess he didn't make it," Lucas answered. "The conveyor wasn't expecting him, maybe. He must have been…" He waved his hands in the air vaguely, to indicate what he meant. He didn't want to say it out loud. The conveyor took objects apart to transport them, turning them into energy. If something didn't arrive at the other end… He shivered.

Tamsen looked around her. "This doesn't look like the place Rith said he would be," she commented. "I mean, I don't see anyone else about, do you?"

She was right. They were quite alone. Vision was good in almost every direction, except for a low hill close by to the south. Lucas pointed at it. "Let's get up there," he suggested. "We should be able to see better from the top. Maybe he's waiting somewhere nearby."

They shouldered their packs and started the trek towards the hill, revelling in the feel of the sun on their faces. They'd been underground for what felt like weeks. It was great to be out again.

In the distance they could hear the sound of powerful engines, and the occasional shout. There must be people nearby. The children hurried to the top of the hill, which was clad in thick gorse and spindly hawthorn trees. From the top they peered over into the next valley.

A kilometre or so away, a pair of familiar-looking hills reared out of the earth, each crowned by a weather-beaten tor. There was intense activity all around the hills. Green-clad soldiers moved carefully through the undergrowth, and at the head of the valley, next to a rutted track, a large cluster of vehicles had gathered around a hastily erected tent-structure.

"Wow," Aaron muttered. "They really want us, don't they?"

"And the sanctuary," Dion added. He looked sad. Lucas knew that his friend was lamenting the loss of Rith's gift to them. It had been intended that the children would stay in the sanctuary for as long as they'd needed, learning the things they needed to know, but no-one had reckoned on Marshall Graves's interference. It had actually been he, not Dana Jackson, who'd led Echelon Nine here, forcing Lucas and his friends to go on the run again. It had been Graves who'd caused the repeller drones to attack, when he'd busted his way in.

The aristocratic bully had a lot to answer for, and one day Lucas resolved to have a little talk with him.

Tamsen scowled. "How are we going to get out of this?" she said. "We're stuck out here in the middle of nowhere, there are 'men-in-black' everywhere, and we've lost our place of safety. There's nowhere left for us to go."

"Rith will come for us," Dion stated. "He said he would, so he'll be here."

"Fine," Tamsen retorted. "Just let me know when he shows up, okay? I hope he brings a bus or something. But I don't see how he's gonna sneak us away from those men. They're everywhere."

"I'm sure he's got something up his sleeve," Lucas said, with a confidence he didn't really feel.

*

Miss Fox was escorted to the command tent by a pair of stony-faced troopers touting big, threatening-looking machine guns. She strode along haughtily, trying to maintain her customary air of confidence and superiority despite the crushing humiliation she had suffered. Granted, she'd managed to capture a group of interesting potentials, but the real prize had got away again: Lucas Fortune. That boy was the real reason this whole operation had come into being. The child was unique. As far as she and Echelon were aware, there had never been another one like him. And she'd come so close to catching him she could almost taste it.

How had Stanford known about this place? He'd seemed unconcerned to the point of boredom when she'd gone to him with her plans for this mission. Damn him – he must have known all along! His pose of disinterest had been exactly that: a pose, a ruse to make her believe she was on her own. And he'd sent her out here with only two agents as protection! What was his game?

One way or another, she would find out. Danielle Fox was far from beaten yet.

"Miss Fox!" a voice called out from behind her. She stopped, glancing back over her shoulder.

"Wait," Dana Jackson said, hurrying to catch up. Her escort of soldiers kept pace. Farther back she could see Lovell and Elsdon scowling as they were marched along, and with them came the other three children, borne on stretchers by Echelon medics.

Miss Fox dredged up a smile. "Hello, Dana," she said. "And how are you feeling?"

Dana frowned as if the question meant nothing to her. "Uh, fine," she said vaguely as she drew alongside. She leaned in closer with a conspiratorial look. "Can we talk?" she whispered.

Miss Fox tried not to laugh. "Dana, talking is all we're going to be doing for the foreseeable future."

"I'm serious. I have to tell you something."

Miss Fox shrugged. "Go on then, but I have to ask: are you sure you're talking to the right person?"

"Yes, I'm sure. I've got some information for you, but you have to promise to help me first. Me and my friends."

Miss Fox was intrigued. "I'll...do what I can," she said evasively. Wasn't it obvious her hands were effectively tied? There were armed guards escorting her! When Stanford got through with her, she'd be lucky if she could get a job cleaning toilets. "What information do you have?"

Dana stared at her narrowly for a moment, as if deciding how much she could trust her. Then she shrugged. "I know the real reason you came here," she said. She held up a hand to forestall the expected protest. She tapped her head meaningfully. "I know a whole lot more than you think."

No more pretence then. "Go on."

"If you promise to help us, to treat us fairly, we'll cooperate fully with you. In exchange for leniency, I can give you what you really want."

Miss Fox held her breath, hardly daring to hope. "You mean..."

"Yes, Miss Fox. It's not too late. I can give you Lucas Fortune. Do I have your word?"

She suppressed a savage grin. "Absolutely! Oh, you wonderful girl!" She grabbed Dana in a spontaneous hug. The girl was like a rack of ribs, as stiff as a board against her. They disengaged hurriedly.

"I promise," Miss Fox said again, meaning it this time. "You just leave it with me!" She turned to the nearest soldier. "You!" she barked. "Radio Mr Stanford, have him meet me up here. I have vital information for him."

The soldier didn't bat an eyelid. "I'm sorry, ma'am," he said stiffly. "You are not to have any access to Echelon personnel. Those are my orders."

"Orders, eh? Tell me, *private*," she said the word sneeringly, "what will your commanding officer do when he finds out you deliberately ignored information critical to this mission? Hmmm? Think that'll look good on your evaluation?"

The soldier blanched, but didn't move. "Sorry, ma'am..." he began again.

"Look, son," she said in a more pleasant tone, changing her tack. "I'm not asking to speak to Mr Stanford myself. I just want you to pass a message up the chain of command. That's not disobeying your orders, is it?"

He considered that for a moment or two. "I suppose not," he said. He reached for his radio. "No funny business, alright?"

"Wouldn't dream of it."

She half-turned to see Dana looking at her with an odd expression. "You're good," the girl said very quietly.

"You have no idea," Miss Fox replied out of the corner of her mouth.

*

"Come on, Rith, where are you?" Aaron muttered. Lucas shared his friend's apprehension. How much longer could they go on skulking around at the top of this hill? Already the soldiers had begun to spread out into the surrounding moorland. It would only be a matter of time before they started coming in this direction.

Tamsen huffed noisily. "I've had enough of this," she declared. She tied up her backpack and slung it onto her back with a grunt. "I'm not just gonna sit here and wait for those guys to find us."

"What are you going to do?" Aaron asked her sullenly. "There's nowhere else to go."

"I'm making a run for it," she answered. "If we leave now, and keep this hill between us and them, we might be able to get far enough away that they don't see us." She looked around at their tired faces. "Anyone else?"

"I think we should stay together, Tamsen," Lucas said. "Rith said –"

"The hell with Rith!" she cut him off. "Don't you get it, Lucas? He's not coming back for us! We're on our own, like always!"

Dion held up a hand suddenly. He had been laying on his belly in the bracken, intently watching the activities of the distant soldiers below. "Something's happening down there," he said. Then his face froze, eyes going distant. "It's... it's Dana Jackson," he said, incredulously. "She's warning us to get away! The soldiers know we're here!" He jumped to his feet. "Look!"

In the fields below, the soldiers had ceased their ordered searching of the scrubby undergrowth. They were coming together, forming a fast-moving cluster that began to head directly toward the hill where the children lay concealed. Several of the off-road vehicles started up and peeled away from the tent, bouncing heedlessly over the bumpy terrain.

"That seals it," Tamsen said bleakly. "Guess we're all going, huh?" She turned and hurried away down the back of the hill.

"Come on," Lucas decided, pulling on his pack. "She's right. We still have to give Rith time to get to us. Let's go."

They scurried after Tamsen, catching up with her at the base of the hill. Grimly they set out across the moorland again, running as fast as they could, all the time expecting to hear the shouts of the pursuing soldiers.

On they ran, jumping over ditches, splashing through puddles and negotiating their way over low fences and drywalls.

There was a clatter overhead. Terrified, the children looked up to see a black helicopter swooping down on them, engine screaming. It buzzed so low they could feel the wind of its passage as it shot by overhead. It began to climb, circling around for another pass.

*

Miss Fox sat in the rear of the lead car, hanging on for dear life as it bounced along over the inhospitable terrain. Dana Jackson had been right! The message had just come through from the chopper: the children had been spotted only a few kilometres away! Her redemption was almost at hand!

Byron Stanford sat in front of her, not looking happy at all. Of course he'd been reluctant to listen to her at first, but she still knew how to get around men like him. She'd wheedled and promised and cajoled until he'd eventually caved in, agreeing to at least have a look at the hill Dana Jackson had indicated. Now, she couldn't decide if he was unhappy with the way she'd managed to redeem herself, or if he was just feeling car-sick.

She didn't really care.

Give it up, Fortune, she thought gleefully. *I'm coming for you.*

*

The helicopter circled overhead, marking the children's location. The first ground soldiers appeared, coming over the top of the hill where the children had so recently been hiding. As the children watched, a fast-moving 4x4 rounded the base of the hill and came bouncing towards them, rapidly followed by two more.

Lucas removed his pack and sat on it heavily. He could hardly believe it was going to end like this. After everything they'd been through, everything Rith had said and promised…it just wasn't right.

Sammi sobbed openly, leaning against Timothy for support. He patted her on the back, cooing words of support, though he himself looked shell-shocked. Aaron stared at the ground numbly, while Tamsen seemed angry enough to spit fire.

Dion was the worst affected, though. He was devastated. Silent tears rolled down his waxen cheeks. His fists were clenched so tightly they shook.

Oh, Rith, Lucas sighed, *what happened to you? We came so close…*

Lucas, a ghostly voice seemed to say. **Lucas...**

His head came up. What was that? He gazed about him blearily. The first soldiers were only about half a kilometre away now. He could hear them calling to each other, shouting orders. Had one of them just called his name?

Dion stood bolt upright, wearing a peculiar expression. Very slowly, his head tilted back and up. A disbelieving grin split his face.

The sun disappeared. A vast roaring shadow came over them, the grass and heather all around them whipping about as though caught in a hurricane. The children were knocked from their feet in a whistling, howling downdraft of hot air as an immense *something* descended to hang impossibly above them.

The approaching soldiers scattered and dove to the ground, raising their weapons defensively. The nearest car slewed to a halt, disgorging several people who started to sprint in the children's direction, shouting and waving their arms frantically.

"I knew he'd come for us," Dion exclaimed, and somehow his voice carried to all his friends. "I knew it."

"Rith?" Lucas croaked, astonished. He'd had no idea what to expect – but this? "You have a…a *ship?*"

"No, Lucas," Rith's voice boomed, and Lucas realised he was actually hearing it with his ears for the first time.

"I am the ship. Come aboard!"

Dion whooped joyfully as the bleak moorland faded from view around them.

*

Miss Fox stood open-mouthed as the children disappeared once again right before her eyes. The enormous bulk of the alien vessel blotted out the sun, casting a black shadow over the ranks of soldiers cowering below. She'd never seen anything like it before, not in any briefing or any of the orientation sessions she'd attended back at Echelon Nine headquarters.

The howling of the craft's propulsion system increased. It began to rise slowly, tilting back as it did so. Its shape was like that of a flattened egg tipped onto its side, mottled grey and brown in colour, covered in ribs and protruding spars that enveloped it like some kind of external skeleton. It was unsettlingly organic in appearance. It must have been at least two hundred metres long from nose to tail, and perhaps half that across.

As she watched, the vessel increased its height, rising rapidly now. It spun about until its rounded nose pointed upwards. With a boom it took off up into the heavens. In seconds it was gone.

"Interesting," Byron Stanford said dryly as he came to stand next to her. "You don't see that every day, eh, Danielle?"

She rounded on him, speechless. He smiled at her dumbfounded expression. "Don't worry, Agent Fox," he said. "You've done quite well, considering. I won't hold this against you. You couldn't have prevented it from happening. You're back on the team. And next time," he turned away, climbing back into the car, "be more careful who you trust." He waited for a second. "Well, are you coming or what?"

*

Ptolemy Withers stood in the centre of the dais, staring about him in utter triumph. He'd done it! Despite the human woman's taunting, he'd actually managed to penetrate the Sirella base! How his masters would reward him now! He'd calculated correctly. It had been very risky, throwing himself into the conveyor field like that, but it had most certainly paid off. The conveyor's controlling protocol had been unprepared for his presence, so had simply routed him backwards through the system to its origin point. He was pretty pleased with himself for that piece of quick thinking.

He gazed about him greedily, taking in the unpleasant organic-based technology the Sirella employed. Several console devices stood around him on the central dais, and a number of open passages lay invitingly all around the outskirts of the room. All for him – all for the taking!

Yet – was it growing dark in here? He frowned; were the energy systems not working properly? Maybe those human brats had somehow figured out how to power them down. No, that was preposterous. Wasn't it?

As the lights grew dim, he spotted something lying discarded on the dais near his feet. He bent to retrieve it with a grunt. It was a knobbly black device of some kind, shaped something like an earth potato. Several ridges and bumps protruded from its surface.

He examined it disgustedly. He'd never been comfortable with organic technology. Idly, he pressed a few of the lumpy buttons. There was a muffled thump from the direction of one of the side passages. He looked up, curious. What was that rushing, clicking sound?

As the last of the light faded, he caught the merest glimpse of a horde of black, insectoid creatures piling into the room.

He knew immediately he'd made a horrible mistake.

He dropped the device to the ground with a sigh, his personal triumph snatched away from him at the last moment. At least he'd been able to summon his masters. Once they arrived, nothing on this pathetic planet would matter anymore. He'd fulfilled his mission, had served his purpose as he was conditioned to do. He could take some brief solace in that.

He squeezed his eyes shut as the repeller drones descended upon him.

Epilogue

Marshall Graves lay quietly in his hospital bed, staring up at the ceiling with his one good eye. It was peaceful here, even restful. Strange thoughts wound their way through his head, twisting themselves around his memories like serpents. He remembered very little about what had brought him here, but there was one thing he did know, with a certainty that scorched through every fibre of his being: Fortune was to blame, and for that he would pay dearly. This was not even a promise to himself – just a cold hard fact.

The staff here treated him fairly, even courteously, and he lacked the energy to be rude or dismissive to them. He'd already ascertained that this room was under constant surveillance, with a pair of armed guards stationed permanently outside the door. Clearly he was of some importance to them, then. When he'd asked one the staff where his companions were, they'd been evasive, even slightly scared of him. That suited him just fine. He didn't need anyone anyway. He'd sort out his own problems, one way or another.

Marshall, a soft voice seemed to whisper. He tried to sit up, but he felt so very weak. His body was expending all its energy healing him from his terrible wounds. Instead he had to content himself with letting his eye rove around the room, as much as it was able.

Don't speak, Marshall, the silky voice said inside his head. **Don't show any sign you can hear me. They are watching you.**

He froze. -Who are you?- he thought fearfully. Was the mind-link was active again? -Dana?-

Not Dana, the voice said, amused.

Marshall's mind raced. The voice sounded almost familiar. He'd heard someone speak this way once before, maybe in a dream...

-Rith?- he said dangerously. -Have you come to taunt me?-

The voice darkened. **No, not Rith either, and I'll thank you not to confuse me with that pompous old fool.**

-Who, then? Don't play games with me, whoever you are!-

You are angry, Marshall, and with good reason. You have been dealt a grave injustice by Rith – you and all your friends.

-Yeah, so? What's it to you?-

We can help each other, you and I. We want the same thing.

-And what might that be?-

Why, revenge, of course. I too have been wronged by Rith. I have waited a very long time for an opportunity to...settle the score.

-Who are you?-

I am Karn. I am the last of the Tulirs.

That sparked something in Marshall's memory. -I thought…I mean, I remember something I heard…Rith is the last of his kind, isn't he?-

The voice made a disgusted noise. **He believes he is, but he is mistaken. *I* am the last one.** There was a hate-filled pause. **At least, I will be. If you help me, Marshall Graves.**

A slow, calculating smile spread across Marshall's battered face.

"Tell me more," he whispered out loud.

www.ingramcontent.com/pod-product-compliance
Ingram Content Group UK Ltd.
Pitfield, Milton Keynes, MK11 3LW, UK
UKHW041948190726
13854UKWH00004B/1862